The Other Side of the Fence

Pearl Allard

Copyright © 2021 Pearl Allard

All rights reserved.

ISBN: 9798510130997

Cover Photograph:
© mckaphoto/Adobe Stock

This book is a work of fiction. Names, characters, places and incidents are either a product of the author's imagination or are used fictitiously. Any resemblance to actual people living or dead, events or locales is entirely coincidental.

For my Husband.
I love you today,
I loved you yesterday,
I will love you tomorrow,
And I will love you always.

ACKNOWLEDGMENTS

My love and special thanks to:
My Husband, for his patience while I tapped away.
My Son, Tony, for editing and publishing this book.

To my lovely Great-Granddaughters. Watching you ride in a showjumping competition and hearing someone say, 'Those girls could be future Olympians.' stirred my imagination, as did the spirit of a horse and a surprise phone call.

Love to my Sister for listening, even though she would have preferred the story to be set on a spacecraft with aliens.

Finally, to family and friends. Your positive reaction and encouragement gave me the incentive to continue writing. My love and thanks to you all.

1

Rosa walked out of the equestrian shop into the warm May sunshine. As usual her sunglasses were pushed into her long black hair, loosely piled on top of her head. Born in 1976 she is now forty-two and still a very attractive woman. Rosa was wearing her usual clothes; an over large sweatshirt, with the shop's logo printed on the front, jeans and riding boots. She smiled to herself knowing, when she looked over to her right, that waiting at the paddock gates of her dad's farm, would be the two young colts she had helped deliver for her dad, Billy Maddox, a few weeks apart, months earlier.

"Hiya my lovely boys," she shouted, "I will be back soon to feed you and your mothers."

It had been a busy morning in the shop; Rosa and her friend, Gemma, had just finish kitting out a ten-year old youngster with a full riding outfit. They had decided that Rosa should take the first break. Looking around, Rosa saw some hay bales nearby.

"Just the job for a quick rest," she thought, "and I can still hear if anyone drives down the lane to the shop."

Closing her eyes for a few minutes, she thought, "I wonder what sort of riding future that young girl will have." It made her think back to when the years of trauma and heartbreak, she had suffered, started. She thought back to when it all began and the mental strain that no one, young or old, should have to go through.

All her life, she had lived in a small seaside town in Norfolk. Her family and extended family lived and worked on farms, way out in the countryside. From the time she was born, her life had always been spent around horses, dogs and most farmyard animals; in fact, she had been riding and competing in horse shows, since she was three years old. When she was young, Rosa's black hair was always pulled tight and tied back; she always wore trousers and a baseball cap. She was an only child and quite a tomboy, trying to be the boy her beloved daddy had always wanted. Because she lived and played out in the countryside, she was a match for any boy. Rosa spent every moment she could with the horses; the stables were her happy place, even helping to clean them out. If not at the stables, you could find her climbing trees, swimming in the river, or riding the horses through the woods.

Her first recollection of heartbreak was when she was nearly eleven years old. She had already become an accomplished horse rider and because Rosa showed she could do most of the jobs needed to look after a horse, her dad, Billy Maddox, thought it was time she had her own horse. He bought her a pony called Willow Lady.

"Rosa, Willow is your pony." he said, "You must look after her every weekend and an extra day during school holidays. If I don't think you're doing a good job, she will have to be sold."

The Other Side of the Fence

At first everything was OK; Rosa loved her pony, but it all started to get too much for her, it was a harder job than she thought, going to school, doing homework and looking after the pony. The water she needed, was near her in the stable, but was heavy to carry for a ten-year old.

After a few months looking after Willow, Rosa would always feed and water her, but started to neglect cleaning her and her stable. Rosa even had a warning from her father, he was not pleased with the state of Willow's stable. To make things easier for her, he had one of his stable workers get the water for her. Things got worse when the family dog gave birth to six puppies. She loved playing with them and they were so much more fun to look after than her pony. Rosa got her second warning during the school holiday, on the day she was supposed to work. Her dad came to the stable and saw the stable boy was cleaning Willow's stable.

"Where is she?" he asked.

The boy pointed to an empty stable further down. Her dad found her playing with the puppies.

"Rosa Maddox!" he said in a loud voice; it made her jump, "This is not a game! No more warnings, this is the last."

About six months later, arriving home from school, Rosa found Willow's stable empty.

"Where's my pony?" she asked one of the men who looked after the other horses.

"Your dad's sold her;" he said, "two men came and took her earlier."

"What!" she cried, a look of horror on her face, "He wouldn't do that."

"Well, he has. He came round early this morning and was disgusted with her stable; the one that you should have cleaned yesterday." he answered, brushing one of the other horses, not even bothering to look at her.

She sank to her knees and started to cry. "Not my lovely Willow." she sobbed, "How could he do that to me?" Her dad must've known how much it would hurt her.

Rosa ran as fast as she could up to the house calling for her mum. Her mum hugged Rosa and trying to comfort her said, "I'm so sorry my darling, I tried to stop it happening; but your daddy was very angry with how you were treating Willow."

"How could Daddy do this to me?" Rosa sobbed. Nothing her mum said, or did, helped. In her own mind all Rosa knew was, that if her daddy could do this, he didn't love her anymore. Willow was gone, and she had upset her dad; the one person in the world she loved the most. She ran to her bedroom and hid under the covers. She didn't want to face what had happened, or see anybody, especially her dad. At ten years old it was a hard lesson for Rosa to learn. When you're given a job to do, you're the one responsible; and if you don't do it properly, you must expect the consequences.

2

Rosa opened her eyes; she had heard Matt calling her name. He kissed her on the forehead and said, "Matt Johnson at your service Ma'am; Gemma's sent a nice mug of tea, for me and my lady. I told her I could stay for a while, so she has gone down to the office to order some more riding helmets, gloves and whips, from the equestrian warehouse.

As they both sat on the hay bales, drinking their tea, the timer on Rosa's watch started ringing, "Well, that was well timed, thanks." she said, as she handed her empty cup to Matt, "Must go; time to feed and water my hungry boys and their mums."

"I know this bit," Matt replied, "this is when you say, 'will you look after the shop for me.'"

"Please?" she said, laughing. As she ran off, Rosa looked back; Matt was smiling. He put his hand up for a slight wave. Working outside, he had a great tan and his dark hair was bleached by the sun; long, slightly curled and tussled. The rolled-up sleeves on his blue work shirt were tight on his upper arm muscles. The shirt was slightly open, showing off his tanned chest.

"I hope he gets a lot of women in the shop today." she thought, "They won't be able to resist buying something from him." She put her fingers to her mouth and blew him a kiss. He pretended to catch it and put it to his lips. She then shouted, "You're looking very handsome today, Mr. Johnson, be careful of all those women you're going to serve." Matt could hear her laughing as she went off happily to feed her 'boys', as she called them.

After Rosa had finished feeding the horses, she went to relieve Matt at the shop.

He heard her calling, "I'm back Matt."

"Oh! I'm so glad your back, Rosa." he said, cuddling her, pretending to shake, "I've been so busy, fending off all those women; they all wanted to take me home; I was so scared."

"Ha ha! Very funny." she said, smiling, "You do make me laugh. Seriously though, Matt, thanks." she said, "How about if we go out for dinner tonight; my treat?"

"Wow! That's a date." he said, "Let me know what time, later?"

"Ok, we have got a bit of sorting out to do in the shop first. Won't be too long though; I will phone you when I'm ready."

Rosa had forgotten that Gemma had gone to the office and then left for the day, so she was alone in the shop. As she started to arrange some of the new stock, she went to the private cubicle at the back of the shop. She was looking for a suitcase where she kept all the rosettes, she had won years ago. She thought they would look good, displayed next to all her trophies, which were already displayed. Customers could then see what a good horse rider she had been. When she found the case, she laid her mobile phone down on a nearby table, so she could open it. Inside she saw a large blue folder with the words, 'THE DREAM IS DEAD.' written across it. She started to open it, then closed it again immediately and put it back in the case. The blood had drained from her face and she had to sit down. She knew the folder contained her medical records from her time at the equestrian college. She had read them before, they also told why she was allowed to be at the college at fifteen, and the reason she left before the two-year course had finished.

Although it had happened many years ago, it was still raw to Rosa. She could remember every detail; she also had the scars to prove it.

"I'm too happy in my life right now to read through all that again." she said to herself. She took the rosettes out, closed the case and put it back in the cupboard. Rosa sat down again. Although it was getting dark, she could see the shine from all the trophies she had won years before. They were nicely displayed on a shelf. Just staring into space, Rosa thought back to how happy she had been, working in her dad's stables, after school and at weekends. She had proved to her dad that she had learnt to respect and look after horses; she was also becoming quite an expert rider. For her twelfth birthday, her dad had bought her another horse, a beautiful black stallion called Starlight Spirit; he would be trained for future top competitions. By the time Rosa was thirteen, she had her first sponsor, a well-known oil company, who paid for her to travel all over Great Britain, competing. By doing this, she and her horse Star, her name for him, progressed further into top junior horse riding and show jumping competitions. Rosa absolutely loved Star; and he, her. At fourteen and dressed in a top-class outfit, Rosa and Star had won the East

Anglia Championship. She was so happy; life was going to be good to her; or was it?

3

Rosa's phone suddenly vibrated, then started to ring; it brought her back from her thoughts. She looked at her watch, "My goodness, how ever long have I been sitting here?" she thought. She looked at the phone and saw it was Matt calling. Answering as cheerfully as she could, she said, "Hi Matt."

"Hi Hun." he replied, "I was just wondering if you'd forgotten me?"

"I'm so sorry, Matt, I didn't realise how late it'd got; I've been busy sorting things. Just give me fifteen minutes, while I pack these things away and I'll be ready." she said.

"Rosa, I was thinking; because you have been longer than we thought and it's got dark and a bit late; instead of you going home to get ready for us to go into town for that drink and a meal; what if I bring the dogs for a walk and meet you; then we could go to the river pub for our meal? Or, if you're too tired, just get a takeaway. What do you think?"

"Oh Matt, the pub's a great idea. It's such a lovely evening, we can sit outside; I'm sure the dogs will love the walk along the river. I will be quick." she said.

It was dark, she felt for the lights and put them on. She looked round to make sure everything was cleared away, picked up her coat, bag and keys; switched the lights off, and went outside to wait for Matt.

The pub-restaurant that they had arranged to go to was by the river, at the end of a long lane called River Walk Road, which ran past both Rosa's parents' and the Johnson's farms. The pub, which also had a children's play park, was very popular with families, walkers and boaters. The wide paths running along the river were also popular with people riding horses, dogwalkers and hikers; you would often see people running, or couples just strolling along, holding hands and taking in the lovely scenic views; and, of course, you could enjoy a nice, romantic meal at the restaurant. Rosa's parents owned a large farmhouse that stood on their own thousand-acre farm, called River Walk Farm. The driveway to the farmhouse was off the main village road and the farm itself continued on from behind the house to where the Maddox's stables and crop fields stretched way down River Walk Road. About two thirds of the way down the road, a short driveway led to the equestrian shop and riding school; this is where the Maddox's farm joined onto a smaller farm belonging to the Johnsons. The Johnson's farmhouse and driveway were off River Walk Road, further down towards the end of the road. Their farm ended before the end of the road and the pub, then ran parallel to the river. Opposite the two farms, on River Walk Road, were a number of smallholdings.

Rosa smiled, she could hear the two dogs barking as they got closer and closer. She locked the shop door and walked down the short driveway to meet him. She could see the light from his torch getting closer. They met on the road that led down to the river. The two dogs, one Alsatian called King and one black and white spaniel called Alvin, ran up to her and back to Matt, then back to Rosa again.

"Think they're excited." Matt said.

"So am I." replied Rosa, making a fuss of the two dogs, "I'm so hungry; this is just what I needed."

They enjoyed the walk to the river restaurant; they both had torches and laughed as the dogs played and chased their torch beams. As Matt was actually walking back the way he had just come, they passed the Johnson's farmhouse. Matt had to call the dogs back as they both thought they were going back to the house.

"Not yet!" Matt shouted, as the two dogs came bounding back from the driveway onto the lane's foot path. The dogs caught up with Matt and Rosa just as they reached the end of the lane; where they turned to the left and there was the restaurant. "The pub looks busy," Matt said, "better put the dog's leads on." They found a table outside and the dogs immediately lay down underneath it.

"You poor boys," Rosa said, laughing, "have we worn you out?"

They both looked at the menu and chose their meal and drinks. As Matt went to go inside to order, he turned to Rosa and asked, "You OK? I might be a while, seeing how busy they are tonight."

"I'm fine." she replied, then thought, "Love him, he always seems to do the right thing to please me."

Rosa sat looking over the river; it was calm, hardly moving. It was a clear night and she could see the bright moon reflecting on the water.

After the shock of seeing the medical contents of the blue folder again, Rosa sat there feeling reflective; she thought, "All these years later, I remember everything bad that happened to me at that time, as if it was yesterday." she thought, "It still upsets me to this day."

"I've ordered the meals; they are very busy, so they might be a while." said Matt, returning from the bar, "Oh, sorry Rosa, did I startle you? You looked miles away."

"Not miles away, more like years away." she said, "I was thinking back to when I was younger. Earlier, in the shop, when I was sorting things out, I found a folder full of old medical papers about me; and what happened to me all those years ago. I'm OK; I didn't read them; I know what they say. Just seeing them and knowing what the doctors said about me, shook me up a bit. So, this is nice, just the two of us sitting here."

"My poor baby," Matt said, moving next to her, "let me give you a special Matt Johnson cuddle." He put his strong arms round her, "How's that?" he asked, "Feeling better?"

"You always make things better, Matt." she said, as she snuggled into his chest.

Matt, kissing the top of her head, asked, "Do you remember how we met all those years ago?"

"I certainly do;" Rosa replied, "I had just had my twentieth birthday; the riding school was doing really well and papers were being drawn up for me and Gemma to become partners. It was my last lesson of the day; a young girl of seven, a very good rider, called Elsie. We were down at the old fence next to the start of your fields. Suddenly a really loud noise came from the other side of the eight, or even nine-foot, overgrown hedge that was all along one side of my training square; it startled Elsie's horse and nearly flipped her off; she was very good though, put into practice all she had been taught and managed to control him."

Matt was impressed that she was remembering the actual moment, exactly as he did.

Rosa continued, without hesitation, "I had to take Elsie back to her mum at the stables, then I came back to the fence to see what was going on. I stood looking at the bushes. Suddenly, this voice shouted, 'If anyone is near the bushes move away now! Danger! Move away now!' then I saw this big chainsaw cutting the top off the bushes. It went from one end to the other and then back again; it kept cutting more and more off the top. Then, I saw two heads looking over the fence and I just looked in amazement. 'Hello,' you said, 'this is my friend, Freddie, and my name is Matt Johnson; I'm your new neighbour. Well, not new, really, I've always lived here at some time or another. This is the first time we have actually met to say hello though; I know your name is Rosa and that you're Billy Maddox's daughter.' After you had cleared a space at the fence, we used to sit on it, or stand there, most days, just talking nonstop. I remember saying, 'If you have always lived there, how come I have never met you?' and you said." She laughed out loud and put her hands to her mouth, to stop herself laughing again, "And you said, 'Because I was always scared of you.'

Matt said "That's true, I was, when I was young. At first, I always thought you was a boy; you looked and dressed like a boy and you were always sitting high up in a tree or riding a horse. Once, you were walking your horse down the lane towards the river, when I was walking my dogs the same way. I was going to talk to you then, but you suddenly mounted the horse and rode straight past me. I just gave up trying to meet you after that." he said, pretending to be sad and sighing heavily.

"Oh, poor Matt." she said, laughing even more.

The Other Side of the Fence

They both sat up quickly, when Matt said, "I can see our meals are on the way."

"I'm so ready for this." he said, as the waitress placed their meals in front of them.

"Same here." said Rosa.

The meal and drinks went down well.

"That was delicious Rosa; thank you." Matt said, "Anytime you want me in the shop, just ask."

"Mmmm, I really enjoyed it too;" said Rosa, "and the long walk back will do us both good."

"You two ready?" Matt said, as he bent down to untie the dogs.

As they walked back Matt put his arm round Rosa's shoulder. Being a lot taller than her, he looked down at her and asked, "You OK?"

Rosa replied, caringly, "Yes, I'm fine. Matt, I just want to say that when you asked me, at the table, if I could remember how we first met; what I didn't mention was the terrible time that you were going through, at the time. About how you had just returned, after ten years, to help out because your dad had been taken ill and couldn't work the farm properly anymore. Then, shortly afterwards, your dad died and your mum left to live with your sister, leaving you the farm. On top of all that, because she hated farm life, your wife had left and took Paul with her; and, as it turned out, she had already met someone else and wanted a divorce. As you told me your story, over time, I did feel for you, especially about Paul. I'm so pleased you and Paul have stayed close."

Matt said, "Yes, it was a terrible time; it's amazing to think Paul's all grown up now; he's even got a serious girlfriend. I love it when he visits; he always wants to stay longer and help me with the farm."

Rosa replied, "I know, we were laughing so much at the pub; it didn't seem the right place to mention it."

Matt said, "I have got to say, you have passed the 'Do you remember when we first met test' with flying colours, while displaying the typical Rosa attitude of worrying about other people. We have been true friends for over twenty years; both have had rough times; and we have always been there for each other." He then gave her an extra squeeze.

As they reached the long drive, up to the Johnson's farmhouse; the two dogs raced up the drive and Matt grabbed Rosa and tried to tickle her neck. She pulled away, "I bet I beat you up to the front door." she said, as she ran off laughing. He chased after her.

They stood at the front door, both out of breath and laughing.

Matt said, "Rosa we are much too old to do this; I think we got carried away with talking about twenty years ago. It's been a lovely evening; I hope you enjoyed it and are feeling better now?"

"Yes, I am thanks; I enjoyed it very much. We both need to get a good night's sleep; got another busy day tomorrow." Then with a little flirting of her eyes, she said, "But first, a cup of hot chocolate to finish the evening off, would be appreciated."

Bowing, as he beckoned Rosa through the front door, Matt said, "Hot chocolate my lady? I'm at your service."

4

Rosa was getting ready for bed, she was sitting in front of her dressing table mirror, looking at herself; she smiled. "Think about it, Rosa, your life wasn't all doom and gloom." she said to herself, "You were happy sometimes. Think back to how happy you were, the months leading up to your fifteenth birthday and remember why you were going to be famous." she thought.

Rosa's riding had been going from strength to strength. Everyone wanted her and Star; they saw a potential Olympic rider to represent England. Her mother and father were proud when the Eastern Equestrian College said that as soon as Rosa was fifteen, they would make an exception and take her and Star as boarders and she could go home between terms. It was a wonderful opportunity for their daughter, so it was an easy decision for them to make. Smiling, she remembered the day of her fifteenth birthday. Talk about Happy Birthday Rosa; what a day that was. All the paperwork was done and signed and everything she and Star needed was packed. A posh horse

The Other Side of the Fence

box arrived to take them to college and an excited fifteen-year-old girl left home with Star to be a STAR!

Rosa was growing into quite a stunning young lady. With her long black hair, she also looked older than fifteen. Arriving at the college, she was introduced to the two girls she would be sharing a flat with.

"Hi, I'm Gemma with a G and this is Katie; hope we are going to have a great time and be the best of friends." said Gemma.

Katie asked Rosa, "Have you bought your own horse to ride?"

"Yes," replied Rosa, pointing, "he is the Black stallion over there, his name is Starlight Spirit; I call him Star; and I'm Rosa Maddox."

A man, of about forty, appeared. His black hair was plastered flat, he had a thin moustache you could hardly see and he was immaculately dressed in a full riding outfit, with the brightest orange cravat tucked into the neck of his shirt. He was carrying a whip, that he hit his hip with, in time with his walk. He introduced himself as Charles Davenport and that he would be their trainer for the two-year course.

"Right, you three young ladies," he said, "go and find your flat and unpack as fast as you can; someone will take your horses over to the stables. When you have unpacked, all three of you come and find me at the stables. I will show you round and explain what will be expected of you." Charles Davenport spoke softly but with authority.

As they left to find their flat, they all laughed when Gemma said, "Ok, yahh! You young ladies. Blimey he's posh!"

The Other Side of the Fence

They found the flat; it had a small kitchen, a lounge and a large bedroom, with three single beds in.

"Not bad is it?" said Gemma, "A bit small, but we'll manage." They talked while unpacking and found they all lived near each other.

Rosa liked Gemma straight away, "I just know we are going to be great friends." she thought.

During the next few months, the three of them had great fun and enjoyed going out and about together, even when they went back home. Rosa loved riding her horse every day and was getting quite professional at cross-country riding. She was expecting to get high marks in the big cross-country exams, coming up, the next day. The one thing she didn't like, was Charles Davenport; she thought he was creepy. Anytime he saw her, on her own, he made straight towards her; making any excuse to speak to her. He always put his arm round her, when he spoke, and left his hand very near her breast, making her feel very uneasy.

"Surely, if the other girls felt uncomfortable around him, they would have said something by now. It must be me, because I don't like him." she thought.

The night before the exam, Rosa thought Star didn't look as bright as he should. Before she went to bed, she said to Gemma and Katie who were already in bed, "I can't sleep, I've got to go and check that Star is OK and ready for tomorrow."

"Be careful," said Katie, "it's getting dark out there."

"It's OK, I've got a torch." replied Rosa.

Rosa was only dressed in a very large T shirt, with a pair of short pants underneath and her fluffy slippers. She put on her jacket, then went to the stables. Star was pleased to see her and looked fine.

The Other Side of the Fence

"Well, that's put my mind at rest; he's probably just as excited about tomorrow as I am." she thought. She gave him a friendly pat and kisses and turned to leave.

Katie was right it was getting dark and Rosa was glad she had a torch. She was startled when a voice said, "What are you doing in here?" She could see a figure staggering towards her. It was Charles Davenport; he was very drunk and still had a bottle in his hand.

"Mr. Davenport, you scared me." she said, "I came to check on Star." He came up so close to her, it made her step backwards. She could see he wasn't wearing anything from the waist up. "Please let me pass." she said, trying to pass him to the right; but he blocked her path; she then moved to the left, but he blocked her path again. He smelled of alcohol. "Mr. Davenport you're drunk! You're disgusting, get out of my way!" Suddenly, from nowhere, a fist hit her on the chin and she was knocked out.

5

It was still dark as Rosa slowly came round and for a few seconds she was confused and disorientated. Other than her T-shirt, which was up around her neck, she thought she must be naked, as she could feel the cold from the stone floor under her. She was then aware that she couldn't move; her arms were pinned above her head and there was a stabbing pain inside her. She opened her eyes and screamed, "Get off me!" as she realised that Charles Davenport was on top of her, forcing himself inside her again and again.

"Shut up;" he growled, "you know you have wanted this since you got here." He kissed her, forcing his tongue in her mouth; it made her gag.

Rosa struggled; she twisted and turned, but it was no good, he was too strong. She screamed again, "**GET OFF ME! GET OFF ME! PLEASE, SOMEBODY HELP ME!**"

The Other Side of the Fence

He suddenly let go of one of her arms to cover her mouth with his hand. With her now free hand and with her long fingernails, she scratched him on his naked chest making four, deep, long, bleeding scratches; this made him release her as he reeled backwards.

She was then able to push him off her; she jumped up, pushed past him and out of the horse's stall. As she ran, her torn pants fell round one of her ankles and nearly tripped her up. As she bent down to take them off, he caught up with her and spun her round; his eyes were wild, he was like a mad man.

"You bitch!" he said and punched her in the stomach; the force of it made her fall backwards. He leaned over her, inches from her face, and slurring his words, he whispered in her ear, "If you dare say anything about this, you will be sorry. I will deny it; who do you think they will believe, a respected teacher like me, or some little slut like you; parading out here with hardly any clothes on? It will be your horse that pays the price." He stood up and was gone as quickly as he came.

Rosa was trembling, she was in pain from his hard punch to her stomach and too traumatised to cry. It was after midnight when she found the courage to leave the stables. She could see the torch, still alight, under some straw at the back of the stable; she found her slippers and picked up her torn pants and finally made her way back to the flat.

The girls were still awake.

"Where have you been all this time, we were getting worried; is Star OK?" asked Gemma.

"He's fine. I'm sorry girls, I know it's late, but I really need to have a shower. I fell and hit my chin and landed in some horse manure." Rosa lied.

The Other Side of the Fence

Rosa shoved her dirty clothes into a large pocket in her holdall, turned the shower on, slid to the floor and let the water run all over her. She felt dirty; she kept pouring body wash over herself, washing it off and starting again. When Rosa finally got to bed, she was in a lot of pain and pulled the bed covers over her head, tears streaming down her face.

She thought, "If I can't tell anyone, how will I ever get through this? I hate him, I feel sick just thinking about what he did. He's ruined my life and I need revenge."

Rosa tossed and turned all night. In the morning, she was like a robot getting ready for the exam. The concerned girls asked, "Are you OK Rosa? That's a right old bruise on your chin."

Rosa was in a lot of pain; but replied, "I've got a headache, just had some painkillers." She didn't know how she got dressed, got to the stables or went inside. She kept looking round, expecting Davenport to turn up. When she saw Star, she gave him a hug; he seemed to know that she was upset.

The three girls joined their hands high up in the air and then pulled them down as they all released them.

"Right let's do this; good luck my lovely's." said Gemma.

Although she was in pain, Rosa was brilliant. Her and Star cleared sixteen fences. She had two fences left to jump for a faultless round and she would get top marks. She jumped one.

"Good boy." she said to Star, "One more to go."

As she approached the last and highest fence, she saw Davenport, all six foot two of him. He was smirking, holding two fingers like a gun and pointing it towards Star.

The Other Side of the Fence

Her heart started pounding; suddenly, she couldn't breathe, her hands were weak and she couldn't hold on to the reigns properly, as she felt her fingers going numb. Rosa wasn't concentrating, she was looking at Davenport. She didn't give Star instructions to jump the fence. He pulled up and she went flying over the fence. Star then tried to follow her and fell on top of her. She lost consciousness for a while.

People ran to her from all directions. Someone grabbed Star, who had got up on his own and looked fine. There was a lot of blood coming out from a long tear in the left leg of her jodhpurs; they could see it looked really bad and she was losing a lot of blood. An ambulance was called straight away. People could also see the damage to her right leg when the medics cut her jodhpurs and saw it was all twisted. They watched the paramedics put her right leg in a splint; Rosa was crying in unbearable pain. The paramedics checked that it was OK to give her a sedative, which calmed her. The ambulance blue lighted her to hospital. The next thing Rosa knew, was when she woke up in hospital. Her mum, dad and Gemma were at her bedside.

"How is Star?" Rosa asked.

"The vet has checked him over and he's fine." her dad replied, "Rosa, you're the one that's not. The doctors are on their way to see you now, to tell us what has happened to your legs."

Holding Rosa's hand tight, her worried mum said, "We love you; be brave my baby."

6

They sat in silence, waiting for the doctors. A nurse came and drew the curtains round Rosa's bed; her mum squeezed her hand. Finally, two doctors arrived; one, a man of about sixty, carried a large blue folder; he looked at Rosa over his black rimmed glasses and said, "Hello." Then, turning, he nodded, "Mr. and Mrs. Maddox, I am Doctor Nash and this," pointing to a rather smart middle-aged woman, "is my colleague, Doctor Rachel Taylor. We will be working together throughout your treatment at this hospital." Dr. Taylor sat down next to Rosa.

Looking at her parents, Doctor Nash continued, "We would like to see you, before you leave the hospital; Rosa is a minor, so we need you to sign some papers." He then moved his attention to Rosa, "Now, young lady, that's some accident you have just had; I hope we have made you as comfortable as you can be? Don't worry about the tubes attached to your hand, they are giving you something to relax you and to stop the pain. You might feel sleepy; if you can sleep, it will help you. If you can't stand the pain, the nurse has instructions to tell us and we will prescribe something stronger."

Rosa was holding her breath, her long nails digging into her palms, "Please, please, let everything be OK." she said to herself.

Holding X-ray plates up to the light and studying them one at a time, looking over his glasses again, Doctor Nash said, "These X-rays of your right leg show multiple fractures of your tibia and fibula; they are the two long bones from your knee to your ankle. You may also have hairline fractures in the ankle that haven't shown up yet." He looked directly at Rosa, "You will need at least three operations to get them sorted."

Rosa didn't like what she was hearing, she didn't want to hear any more and started slipping further and further down the bed.

"Are you comfortable?" Doctor Taylor asked, standing up, trying to get her back, sitting upright.

Doctor Nash stopped talking, looked up from his notes, walked over to Rosa, took a long thin torch from his pocket and looked into her eyes while he switched it on and off.

"Everything looks fine there." he said and continued talking as he walked back and forth at the end of the bed. "Tomorrow, we need you to have a CT scan. The scan is because, when you fell, you were knocked unconscious; it will show us if you did any damage to your skull. You also have large bruises everywhere; those in the lower rib area may indicate a broken rib or ribs, from when you fell off the horse. We also need to have a closer look at your other leg; any damage will show up clearer tomorrow. That's all we can tell you for now." Looking at Rosa's parents, he said, "We have lots to arrange and to do before tomorrow;

we need to make sure we are going in the right direction to proceed with this type of surgery. Mr. and Mrs. Maddox," he continued, "we know this is a lot for you and your daughter to take in and we will go into more detail about her injuries and the surgery involved, tomorrow." Then to Rosa, "Try and get a good night's sleep Rosa; Doctor Taylor and I will be back to see you quite early in the morning. We will be operating sometime during the day to check the damage done to your right leg." As they went to leave, Dr. Taylor gave Rosa's hand a reassuring squeeze and smiled to a pale, tired looking, Rosa.

Still clutching Rosa's hand, her mum said, "Weren't they nice?"

Rosa put the covers over her head, "Shush Mum, I am thinking." she said; then to herself "Now what did they say? Yes, everything works out OK."

"Whatever are you talking about Rosa?" her mum asked.

"Mum! The trials for the Olympics don't start till mid-September; that's about fourteen weeks away. That means a few weeks in plaster, a few weeks physiotherapy and by the end of September I will be ready to go." Looking at her dad she said, "Star is OK, isn't he?"

"Yes, he's fine." he answered.

"Well, no worries there then." said Rosa, relieved.

Her mum and dad looked at each other in amazement at what Rosa had just said. Winking at Rosa's mum, her dad said, "Don't let us forget, we have got to sign those forms for the doctor before we leave. We had better go Rosa; you know how busy the doctors get. Try and get some sleep."

"OK, don't worry, I've got lots to think about; I am so tired though, I will work it out later." Rosa closed her eyes and was sound asleep in a matter of minutes.

Her parents found Doctor Nash's office and told him and Doctor Taylor what their daughter had just said.

"Please sit down." Dr. Nash said pointing to two comfortable looking chairs.

'Oh dear, this doesn't sound good.' they both thought and as they sat down, they automatically held each-other's hand for support.

"Mr. and Mrs. Maddox; the college has already spoken to us and explained about your daughter's ambition for her and her horse, to be selected to represent England in a future Olympics. We have been told that, although she is young, Rosa had a good chance of being selected at the September trials and, if selected, it would be the start of a long process of selections. Apparently, it takes many years of training and preparations to be good enough, to trial and qualify for the English team. We didn't want to say anything in front of your daughter, about what we are going to tell you, because we don't know if she is strong enough, or how she would react when told. The horrendous accident, of her horse falling on her legs, has caused multiple leg injuries. I am so sorry to tell you that this Olympic trial is not going to happen for her now and might not happen, any time in the future." He continued, with a heavy heart, "With the surgery and the months of rehabilitation, that goes with these types of fractures, we will, literally, be doing a jig saw puzzle, to put the right pieces of bone back in the right place and fixing them so they stay where they are supposed to be. There is no way your daughter will be fit enough to do cross-country or show-jumping for that trial, or any competition, in the near future. Her right leg injuries are so bad she might still be in plaster when the trials start. The fractures she has, need plates and screws to keep them together. Each of the three operations needed, will take time to heal before we can do the next. We also think she may have numbness and weak muscles from that deep cut on her left leg. Basically, we are saying that even if she was ready, the injuries are so bad, Rosa would not have the strength in her legs to control a horse that's going to jump fences. It will take months of physiotherapy to build the muscles back up to full strength. However, we are optimistic that, at sometime in the future, she will be able to ride her horse again, for pleasure. It will be down to Rosa's determination and confidence on how far advanced she can get. For now, we have got to use all our skills to make sure Rosa doesn't have a limp after everything has healed. Doctor Taylor and I would like you to both be here tomorrow morning, when Doctor Taylor tells Rosa what the outcome from her injuries will entail. From what I have told you, have you any questions, or thoughts on how to tell your daughter, differently to what you have just heard?"

Rosa's parents looked at each other, both shook their heads. Her dad said, "We both understand everything you have just told us, it's definitely better it comes from you rather than us and we have every confidence in Doctor Taylor telling her." As they got up to leave, they shook the doctor's hand and left; two very sad and confused parents, worried how their daughter would react tomorrow, about what they had just been told and what her future would be.

7

The next morning, Rosa woke up very early; she was fearful of what the day would bring. She was gazing out of the window next to her bed; it was raining and she could see people darting about, trying to keep dry. Suddenly, there was a whooshing sound that startled her.

"Oh! sorry my lovely, I'm Brenda, your nurse; what's it raining again? I'm from Jamaica where the sun always shines." she said, laughing. She continued pulling the curtains all round Rosa's bed. "You will be seeing a lot of me while you're in here." she continued, "Sorry, there's no breakfast for you today, because you're going to have your operation soon. Sorry again, but you probably won't like this bit; we have got to work together, to give you a bed bath. I'm sure you will feel a lot better for it. The doctors will be doing their rounds soon, so best we get started."

Brenda was right, Rosa sat up in bed, feeling all fresh and clean. Her mum was already at the hospital, but she couldn't bring herself to come into the ward. She said that she would cry, when she heard the doctors telling her daughter that she was not going to the Olympic trials, and that it would upset Rosa more, seeing her mum cry.

Sitting in the chair next to her bed, her dad was holding her hand and said, "Don't worry Princess, I'm here and your mum will be here soon."

When the two doctors came in through the curtains; Rosa's heart started pounding so loudly, she thought everyone must hear it. Doctor Taylor sat down next to Rosa on the other side of the bed to her dad.

"Now Rosa, I want you to listen carefully." she said, as she opened the folder, she had brought with her. Rosa clutched her dad's hand hard. When the Doctor started talking it was like she was way down in a tunnel and her voice had an echo. "We have good and bad news for you. I know you don't want to hear this;" she said, as she leaned forward and patted Rosa's other hand, "I'm sorry to tell you, that with the injuries you have sustained there is no way we can get you ready for the Olympic trials in September." Rosa squeezed her dad's hand tighter and closed her eyes as she listened to her future being taken away from her.

Every sentence the doctor said, she gritted her teeth; in her mind, Rosa was thinking, "I hate that man so much; he did this to me. Davenport did this to me; I hate him, I hate him, I hate him." Then came the one and only sentence she wanted to hear.

The doctor said very clearly, "We are optimistic that sometime in the future, you will be able to ride again." That was good enough for Rosa to hear. She let go of her dad's hand and could feel all the tension in her body relax.

"You have been a very brave girl." Doctor Nash said. Rosa looked at him and smiled. "The pain relief we have given you, seems to be working very well. There is no indication of any trouble, so the CT scan can wait and be done tomorrow." He looked at Dr. Taylor, she nodded in agreement, "It's best we get things started. The sooner we do the first operation the sooner you will be able to go home for a while, till we are ready to do the next one. The nurse will be coming back in shortly to start the procedure for the operation. When you wake up you will be in a room on your own. Don't worry, it's just a precaution; it's to do with keeping you away from others, so there's no risk of infection. We won't see you before you have the anaesthetic, but one of us will be there when you wake up." The doctors parted the curtains and left.

Rosa could hear her mother's voice, as she came walking down the ward. She laughed at her mum, trying to find an opening in the curtains, to get through.

"Are you alright my darling?" her mother said, "Let me give you a big cuddle."

"Yes Mummy, I'm fine; everyone has been really lovely. Thank you, for making me laugh; I needed that."

Brenda came back in the room, with the anaesthetist, to prepare Rosa for the operation. Everything was moving fast!

"We must go now, Rosa; we love you. We will be here waiting for you." her mother said. As they left, they looked back through the curtains to see her; they smiled at each other as they could see the anaesthetics had already started to work. Rosa looked calm and relaxed. Much too calm and relaxed for Rosa Marie Maddox.

8

Ten days after the operation, still in her own room, Rosa woke to sunshine and the birds singing outside her window. Her operation in Doctor Nash's own words, was a great success. The CT scan had shown no skull damage and no broken ribs. The bruises they were worried about, only Rosa knew how she got those and there was no way she was going to tell anyone.

Nurse Brenda came in to take her blood pressure.

"Perfect as usual." she said, "I just saw your breakfast is on the way; eat it all, you need to build your strength up."

"Yes mother." Rosa replied, laughing.

"Now, my lovely, don't forget the doctors make their decisions today; they might say when you can go home."

Later that morning, Doctor Taylor did come to see Rosa, she told her that if everything continued to progress as it had, she would probably let her go home soon; but only for a short while, because, in a few weeks' time, they would be doing another operation on her leg. There were lots of conditions attached to her going home though; she would check with Rosa's mum and dad when they visited later that day, to check they could provide everything that was required. She would then confirm when Rosa could go home, once everything had been sorted. Rosa smiled, clapped and thanked Doctor Taylor, saying that that would be the best birthday present ever.

Although Rosa had already been told about her injuries; for the past few days, she had been visited daily, by a counsellor, Mrs. Bennett, mainly to help her deal mentally, with what had happened to her. Mrs. Bennett also explained why she would not make the trial. Rosa was told that when the cast finally came off her leg, if she wanted to ride again, there would be months of physiotherapy first. It was explained in great detail why there had to be three operations, why the right leg would be weak and would make it difficult for her to stay in control of a horse going to jump fences.

Today Doctor Taylor confirmed that the deep cut below her left knee, had damaged the nerves and muscles, so would be numb for many months. Doctor Taylor explained to Rosa's mum and dad, that when she went home there would be lots of different strengths of tablets Rosa would have to take; she advised to make sure they didn't get muddled and to keep them locked up. It would all be down to how Rosa was progressing and how much pain she was in, as to which strength tablet she would be given. Rosa's mum and dad agreed to take charge and said that they would be the ones to give her the tablets throughout the day. Rosa sat listening to the rest of her life being arranged, she felt helpless, also devastated; in one afternoon, all those years of hard work just wiped away.

When Dr. Taylor left, Rosa couldn't stop the tears.

"Princess," her dad said, as he cuddled her, "things sound bad, but let's see if we can find some positives?" He stood up, closed the door to her room and continued, "Now Rosa," he explained, "you have to think positive. Let's work out what positives there are. The main thing is, you will be able to ride again; you don't have to do show jumping, there's dressage and lots of other competitions you could do. If you don't want to do any of them, you could train to be a riding instructor, then you could start your own riding school; couldn't she mother?"

"What about that, Rosa? With your knowledge of horses and what you already know, it wouldn't take too long to pass the exam?" her mother said.

Her father continued, "If you're interested, while you're getting fit and well, we can start preparing everything. We can apply for a licence, I will let you have the bottom field; you know, the field next to the Johnson's farm. Me and your uncles would prepare it and make it suitable, so it passes the necessary requirements."

Rosa smiled; she was excited, for the first time in a long while. "Yes, Daddy yes, the riding school please; I love it, the whole idea!"

"That's that sorted then." he said. As they got up to leave, he bent over, kissed her and whispered, "See Princess, there was a positive."

"Bye dear, see you tomorrow; we love you." her mum said, as her dad opened the door for them to leave.

"Try and get a good night's sleep; see you tomorrow." added her dad.

Rosa called after them, "I love you both, more!"

Laying back in bed, Rosa thought, "Rosa Maddox riding school." then, said out loud, "WOW! What about that Davenport? You horrible, drunken, hateful man!"

9

Rosa was still in hospital, in her own room. Today was her sixteenth birthday, 24/05/1992. An excited Rosa was woken by Brenda and two others, singing Happy Birthday.

"Thank you so much." Rosa said.

"Here you are my lovely, lots of cards for you; the postman could hardly carry them all." said Brenda.

"Brenda, you're so funny. I'm sure he didn't have that much trouble carrying six cards!"

"If I am not busy later, I'll help you get ready for all the visitors you're expecting today."

Rosa absolutely loved Nurse Brenda looking after her. Brenda made her laugh with her wild stories. When Brenda was on night duty and Rosa couldn't sleep, if Brenda wasn't busy, she would come and see her and tell her stories, all about her life and family who still lived in Jamaica.

The Other Side of the Fence

Brenda finished helping Rosa get ready, then stood back and admired her work, saying, "There you are, my lovely, all spruced up ready for a party."

It was visiting time and the first person through the door was Gemma.

"Happy Birthday!" she said, excitedly, "Wait till you see what I've got for you." She pulled out her phone and played Rosa a video. There he was, her lovely Star, running up and down the field; then when Gemma called him, he came right up to the phone. On the video, in a silly voice, Gemma was saying, "Hello Mummy, Happy Birthday. Hope you will be home soon because I miss you so much. Lots of love, your lovely, adorable Star." They both roared with laughter!

"That is so funny, Gemma, I love it; thank you. Let me give you a big hug." They hugged and Gemma gave Rosa that little extra hug that meant, you will be OK.

"Katie will be here in a minute," said Gemma, "I left her getting drinks from the shop."

While they were waiting for Katie, Rosa told Gemma all her news.

Gemma grabbed Rosa's hand and said, "Well, I don't really know what to say; you go first and tell me how you really feel, then I will know what to say."

Just then Katie came through the door, "Guess who was buying you chocolates in the shop, when I was getting our drinks?" Turning back to the door, her arms in the air, she said, "Duh durh!" Then, in walked a smiling Charles Davenport.

Looking at Gemma, he said, "I can't stop long, just got Rosa some chocolates and came to see how our girl is doing. Thought she might be missing us." Rosa's mouth went dry and her nails dug into the top of her leg. "Oh dear, no smiles, Rosa, not even a cheery hello, for this poor hard-working trainer?" he said, smirking.

Just then Brenda came into the room, she took one look at a strange looking white-faced Rosa, whose big brown eyes were just staring at nothing.

"My goodness, what have you done to our girl?" she said, clicking her fingers, "Rosa, Rosa! Are you OK?" Rosa, who was lost for words, nodded. "You've gone as white as a sheet," Brenda continued, and looked at Gemma and Katie, "see what birthday excitement does to you?"

"I hope she's OK?" Davenport said, "I must dash, I only popped in to see how she was getting on, and to give her the chocolates." He bent down, kissed Rosa on the cheek, and whispered, "Don't worry, I'm looking after your horse. He's in safe hands with me." He then smiled at the two girls, "See you two later." he said and walked out.

"Brenda, quick!" Rosa shouted, "I'm going to be sick!"

"Are you feeling better now?" Brenda asked, fussing round the bed, making it neat again, "I know it's your Birthday, but too many sweets are not good for you. You look terrible, your friends are waiting outside; shall I tell them to go?"

Although Rosa wasn't over the shock of seeing Davenport, she replied, "I'm fine now Brenda. As you said, probably too much excitement and too many sweets." She then pointed at the chocolates Davenport had brought her and said, "Best you take those chocolates and share them amongst the others on the ward. Please let my friends come back in."

"OK, but I'm not far away; ring the bell if you feel bad again."

The Other Side of the Fence

Only Gemma came back in. "Katie's sorry, she's had to go; she has to pick her little sister up from nursery. Are you OK? What a worry that was."

"I'm fine," answered Rosa, "can you close the door; I want to ask you something."

"Wow! This is exciting," Gemma said as she closed the door, "what is it?"

"Now, you know I won't be going back to the college, so I want you to do me a big favour. Will you pack up all my things?"

"Oh Rosa, I just realized, you're not coming back!"

"I just told you what I will be doing instead." continued Rosa, "Please don't question what I'm asking you to do, because I am really upset and I can't cope with it all. I could break down at any time. I just need to get home and sort things."

Putting her bottom lip out, Gemma said, "But I'm going to miss you."

"Don't be daft, we will always be seeing each other; you only live half a mile away. I can wheel myself to yours in my wheelchair, any time you're there." They hugged each other, "That's enough," said Rosa, "or I'm going to cry."

Gemma sat on the side of the bed, "OK, seriously, I'm listening." she said.

"Now, Gemma, this is very important. In our bedroom at college, my black and gold backpack is under my bed; it's only got old clothes in it. Please take it and all the things in it to your house, dig a deep hole and bury it somewhere in your big garden. Don't tell me where; I never want to see it, or the clothes in it, again. Will you promise me, that you will do that for me?" Gemma nodded, then Rosa continued, "Make sure my mum, or dad, pick up all my other things and take them home."

Crossing her heart, Gemma said, "I promise. It feels like we have just done a murder and I am going to bury the body." she said, laughing, "I will put it in a plastic bag and someone will dig it up in years to come. They will think they have found some treasure, but it will just be your old clothes. How funny will that be?"

The door opened; it was Rosa's mum and dad.

"Is it alright to come in?" her dad asked; he had a big balloon with 'Happy Birthday' on it and her mum was carrying what looked like a birthday cake. Behind them was her auntie and two of her cousins. Rosa smiled.

"Happy Birthday Princess." her dad said. Suddenly another chorus of Happy Birthday started.

"Thank you all so much," Rosa said, "I needed that, it's made my day."

Making her way to the door, Gemma said, "I think it's time for me to leave." She looked at Rosa, made a cross on her heart and blew her a kiss. Rosa gave a thumbs up sign in return.

"Daddy," Rosa started, "will you make arrangements to get Star back from college? I am not going back there and I'm sure he can't understand where I am. Gemma's been riding him and says he's miserable. I know he would be happier at the farm and I could visit him when I get home."

"Of course, I will." replied her dad, "We were discussing it earlier. Now we know you won't be returning to college, consider it done; I will get it sorted first thing tomorrow."

The Other Side of the Fence

"Who wants birthday cake?" her mum asked.

10

A week later, everything had been arranged and was ready for Rosa to leave hospital.

At the farmhouse, to give her a bit of privacy, two rooms on the ground floor had been prepared, just to accommodate all that Rosa would need. One room they made into a bedroom, because it was connected to a downstairs toilet and shower room; the other room, her mum had put a table and chairs, TV and two comfortable armchairs, for when Rosa had company; this room was conveniently next to the kitchen, which made it all perfect.

A nurse would be in each day for a while and Rosa was told to expect to be back in hospital, in about three weeks' time.

At the hospital, Rosa had already practiced with her crutches and was told to only use them for a short time each day.

The Other Side of the Fence

Brenda pushed Rosa to the hospital exit door. As she was being helped into the ambulance to take her home, Brenda said, "I'm going to miss you, my lovely."

Rosa grabbed her hand and replied, "I'm so sorry Brenda, but I can't resist this;" then laughing and mimicking Arnold Schwarzenegger she said, "I'll be back!"

Rosa had been home for just two days and was coping very well. Her mum was in the kitchen, while Rosa was in her wheelchair in her mum's lounge; there was a knock on the door.

"Mum!" shouted Rosa, "Someone at the door."

"Tell them to come in," her mum called through from the kitchen, "I'm on my way."

"Come in!" Rosa called.

The door opened and in walked a grinning Charles Davenport; he said, "Why, hello there Rosa, how are you?"

Rosa started to shake. "Mum!" she shouted.

"Oh hello, Mr. Davenport." her mum said, drying her hands while walking into the lounge.

"Please call me Charles. I've just delivered Star to your husband, down at the stables and I thought I would call and see how this young lady is coping." he said. Then, looking at Rosa, "I bet she's lost for words being at home, aren't you Rosa?"

"Would you like to stay for a cup of tea Charles?" her mum asked. Rosa looked at her mum, scowling.

"No thanks, got to dash off. Perhaps next time I'm this way." he replied, "Anytime you need help with the horse, just give me a ring; this is my personal phone number and if I can help, I will; or," he continued, as he was going out

The Other Side of the Fence

the door, "if you need any help, taking Rosa anywhere, my car and I, are at your beck and call. Now, I must go, bye to you both. Take care Rosa." Then, he was gone.

Rosa's mum looked at her, "Whatever is the matter with you, you never said a word to Charles; and what was that look for? I only asked if he wanted a cup of tea." Then, waving her fingers in front of Rosa's face, "Rosa I'm talking to you."

Rosa blinked, "What?"

"I asked, what's wrong with you? I swear you were shaking the whole time Charles was here."

Rosa never answered, she just wheeled herself to her room and shut the door. She frowned and sneered, and thought, "The nerve of the man, how dare he ask my mum to call him Charles. I call him that disgusting pig!" She felt she couldn't breathe; she was gasping, trying to get air and didn't want her mum to see. After a while she calmed down and went back to the lounge to apologise to her mum.

"I know this is all too much." her mum said, "Come on, tell me what I could do for you, that would cheer you up. I know you would like to see your horse, but I'm not strong enough to push you to the stables."

"I know," Rosa said, "let's go visit your sisters and see everyone."

"What a good idea; I'm sure they will love to see us. I will phone and make sure they are in." Then she added, "We'll need our coats on. I will phone your dad and let him know where we are; then, I'll get you in the car and we will be on our way."

11

Gemma and Katie came to see Rosa the following weekend.

"How do you feel about going to see Star; then we push you to the village and visit Maize's cake shop?" an excited Gemma asked.

"That sounds like a perfect plan to me; we should always have a plan." answered Rosa, "Let me tell Mum where I'm going, or she will worry."

"Thanks girls;" her mum said, when Rosa told her, "that's a brilliant idea; she needed to go out. It will cheer her up no end. Her dad's been so busy, we haven't had time to take her to see her horse; and the fresh air will do her good."

"Bye Mrs. M. We will take good care of her." said Gemma, then laughing, "Hold on to your hat Rosa, it's going to be a bumpy ride."

The Other Side of the Fence

A more than happy Rosa replied, "It will be worth it."

Off they went, three happy girls, for their afternoon outing. When they reached the field where Star was, he had his back to them.

"Hello my gorgeous boy." Rosa called. Star stopped eating grass and looked up; Rosa could see he was thinking, 'I know that voice.' He turned to see Rosa and greeted her like a long-lost friend. Then he ran friskily round and round the field and came back and nuzzled up to her.

"Oh, how lovely; he's certainly pleased to see you." Katie said.

"I know." Rosa replied, with tears in her eyes. She kept rubbing his nose, patting him and kissing him. "I've missed you so much, my lovely, lovely boy. Gemma, will you ride him please, so he can get some exercise?"

"I certainly will." Gemma answered and went to get his saddle.

The other two girls waited patiently while she gave him a good run. Then before they left, they fed him some carrots and gave him lots of hugs. Suddenly, he ran off, when he saw the stable boy bringing him some hay.

They looked at each other and burst out laughing. Rosa smiled as she said, "Oh, OK, that's us finished with then, is it? Bye Star, glad you missed me."

They had a relaxing walk to the village, plus tea and delicious cakes, in the little café. Rosa enjoyed Gemma and Katie telling her all the gossip from the girls at college; who's got a boyfriend, who's split up with their boyfriend and who had run off with someone else's boyfriend.

The Other Side of the Fence

"This has been great fun," Rosa said, "I can't tell you how good it is to get out and have such a laugh with you girls." This was the most relaxed Rosa had been for days. At least while she was out of the house, she wasn't worried about who was knocking on their front door. She was having anxiety attacks and getting paranoid, every time there was a knock on the door. She didn't know how much longer she could keep up the pretence of everything being OK.

A few days later, Rosa received a letter from the hospital; it said that her next operation would be in the following week. She sat at the kitchen table, taking the green tops off of a load of carrots, ready to take to the horses. She could hear the phone ringing in the other room and her mum answering. When her mum finished talking, she came to the kitchen door and said, "That was Charles, he's coming this way and asked if we would like to go to Norwich for the afternoon? How good is that? I said yes, that would be lovely. Hope that was OK? I thought he could push you round the shops, so we could get what you need for the hospital." Without waiting for an answer, she left to go and get ready, shouting to Rosa, as she left, "I said give us half an hour, to get ready. I will come back and get you ready when I've changed."

Rosa started to panic; she had a flash back of a drunken Davenport on top of her.

"There's no way I'm going." she thought, "I will fall on the floor and pretend I've hurt myself."

There was a knock on the door. Rosa started to shake, and her heart started pounding.

"Oh no, he's here already!" she again thought, "I am not going!" and with one slice of the knife, she cut her left wrist. Although blood from the four-inch cut was going all over her, she didn't care, or about how much mess it was making. She never even felt any pain from what she had done. She then put the knife onto her right wrist to cut that as well. Although it was small, the cut was deep and it started to bleed quite a lot. She froze when she heard footsteps coming down the hall. "Mum!" she shouted.

With the knife still in her hand, ready to cut further, a voice came from the other room, "I knocked but there was no answer so I let myself in, hope that was OK?" It was the nurse. As she came into the kitchen, she cried, "Rosa! My word, what have you done?" Calmly she looked round, found a clean cloth and wrapped it round the cut on Rosa's left wrist, and raised her arm in the air. "Mrs. Maddox; come quick!" she called.

"Oh, hello nurse," said Mrs. Maddox, as she came into the kitchen.

"Mrs. Maddox if your husband is about; can you go and get him as quickly as possible? This is an emergency! If I can't stop this bleeding, we will have to take Rosa to hospital."

"Goodness me! What's happened? Whatever has she done? Where's all that blood coming from? Rosa, whatever have you done?"

"The knife slipped;" Rosa answered, "please go and get Daddy."

The nurse looked at Rosa suspiciously. "This young lady is much too calm and there are two cuts. There's more to this." she thought. Then, speaking to Rosa, "I'd better put something on this other cut."

Her worried dad came rushing into the kitchen.

"Daddy!" Rosa cried. He knelt down at the side of her and put his arms round her.

"Princess, what's the matter?" he asked.

"Daddy," she sobbed, "please make it all go away."

"Make what go away?" he said, looking at her.

"These pains in my head," she pleaded, "please, please make it all stop!"

"Stop crying and tell me what you want me to stop?"

"Stop my head hurting and help me to breathe. It happens every time that man comes here. Why does he keep coming Daddy? Tell him to leave us alone. I'm trying to be brave, but I get upset because he reminds me of the accident and why I am not going to the Olympic trials. I get upset because I'm not at college with Katie and Gemma."

Billy Maddox got up; he gave Rosa's hand an understanding squeeze. He looked at his wife, beckoning for them to go into another room.

"What's brought this on?" he asked.

"I don't really know," his wife answered, "I left her cutting the heads off the carrots, for the horses. Charles rang up and asked if we would like to go out for the afternoon, to Norwich. Actually, he should be arriving any minute. I told her that I'd said yes; I thought she would like to get out; and we could do some shopping. Oh yes; and she got a letter to say she will be having her second operation next week. Basically, that's it. She has seemed a bit low lately, one minute she's happy then she goes really low."

Just then, Charles Davenport pulled up outside the front door.

"I presume this is the chap she means?" Mr. Maddox asked; his wife nodded. "OK, I will sort this;" he said, "you go and make sure she's OK". He then went outside to meet him.

"Hello Mr. Davenport; I'm sorry you have come all this way, but Rosa's not very well. The nurse is with her at the moment. Sorry to say, they won't be coming to Norwich with you. I would also like to say thank you for your help with the horse and your concern over Rosa. Could I also ask you if you would mind not coming to the farm anymore? Rosa has got to have her second operation next week and it's making her anxious about everything; she doesn't even want to go out. I will ask Gemma to let you know how Rosa is getting on." As he turned to go back inside, he said, "I really must go to see how she is."

"Just a minute, before you go, Mr. Maddox, can I ask you to give Rosa a message? Tell her I said that I hope she will be up and about soon and that her horse stays well and healthy."

Rosa's dad turned back to him, then turned again to go inside, as he did, he said firmly, "Goodbye Mr. Davenport."

Davenport, with his usual smirk, got into his open top sports car, spun the wheels to made them screech, and drove off. Rosa's dad just thought to himself "What an idiot!"

12

By the time Rosa's dad came back indoors, his wife had changed Rosa's clothes and put the blood-stained ones to soak. The table and floor had been cleaned and everything seemed calm.

"Well, that was some episode," he said, "I have told Davenport not to come here again." Then, looking at Rosa, "How are you feeling, Princess?"

"Thank you so much, Daddy," replied a weak Rosa, "I feel a lot better, knowing he's not coming here again. I feel really tired; nurse said it's because I have lost a lot of blood and that I should go and lie down for a while; so that's what I'm going to do. I am so sorry everyone; it was such a stupid accident; I wasn't looking what I was doing and the knife just slipped. Thank you so much Nurse and Mummy, for all you have done."

Her dad said, "You go and lie down now, Princess; Mummy will help you through to the bedroom."

The Other Side of the Fence

As her mother wheeled Rosa through towards the bedroom, her mum said, "I will get her settled and come back as soon as I can."

As they were leaving the room, Rosa's dad followed them, saying, "I hope you do feel better now, Rosa; I will make sure he doesn't come here again. He's a strange chap; as he got in his car to leave, he asked me to tell you that he hopes you're up and about soon. He then grinned as he started to drive away and shouted to tell you that he hopes Star stays well and healthy. Strange thing to say; I don't know if I ever liked him."

The nurse sat at the table, filling in her report.

"Mr. Maddox, could you close Rosa's door and come and sit next to me while I fill in this form?" she asked. The nurse told him that Rosa was a lucky girl, "I'm so pleased I managed to stop Rosa's wrists from bleeding. She won't need to go to hospital to have stitches, as I have closed the wounds with steri-strips; they are like little thin plasters that hold the cuts together and, as you saw, I have bandaged both wrists."

Looking at the nurse, he said, "Thank you, for everything you have done, I can't tell you how pleased we are you were here to deal with all this."

"Mr. Maddox, I must tell you something important. By law, I have got to report this incident, because your daughter's a minor; secondly, because I need permission to come back and check there's no infection in the cuts and to redress them and thirdly, which is the main reason, there's more to this than anyone realizes. In my opinion I think this incident is a definite cry for help from your daughter. I don't want you to be alarmed but your daughter needs help. I will be asking her doctor for a home visit. The doctor will read my report, talk to Rosa and decide if she needs medication and a visit from a professional who deals with this sort of thing. This is serious; you heard the desperation in her plea, to make it all go away. Rosa has two cuts. To me, one cut could have been an accident, but two, one on each wrist, is a definite cry for help."

He stood up and gave a big sigh. "Why weren't we aware; we should have realized, she's only sixteen and been through so much. Too much for a youngster of that age to deal with. I've let her down; I will never forgive myself."

His wife came and sat down at the table.

"Phew! I'm beat." she said, "what's up Billy? Can you explain for me Nurse?" Billy sat down next to his wife and held her hand. His wife listened in silence, then said, "So, it wasn't an accident; Oh, my poor baby. Nurse, we are in your hands; please do what's right for her."

Billy, still in shock, said, "Yes please, just help her as soon as possible. We will do everything we can, or whatever we are told to do."

The nurse answered, "I'm so sorry for you all; I will get things started right away; just leave it with me." She packed all her things away, shook both their hands and left, leaving two bewildered people, just standing there, looking at each other in disbelief.

13

The next few months were a bit of a blur for Rosa, she had had the second operation, which was a success. Doctor Taylor told her it went better than they thought it would; and because the fractured bones were healing so well, a third operation was not necessary. That cheered Rosa up, as did seeing Brenda again, but that did not last long, as she was in and out of hospital in no time.

Before Rosa's second operation, her family doctor had been to see her and agreed with the nurse, that Rosa needed treatment for anxiety and depression. Rosa was prescribed a mild antidepressant and appointments were made for her to have counselling once again. After each meeting with the counsellor, Mrs. Bennett, she always told her mum and dad how things went and how she was learning what she had to do when she felt anxious or panicky. After her latest visit, she told them she was to have appointments, once a week for a while, with a psychologist, who she had already met and was really nice. The psychologist told her how pleased they were, on how well she was responding to her treatment. Rosa was not so

The Other Side of the Fence

sure; obviously, she had never told anyone about what Davenport had done to her. All she knew was the growing feeling of anxiety she was getting the nearer it got to the Olympic trial date. The more she tried to pull herself together and put the trial date out of her mind, the more she couldn't eat or sleep. The nearer the day got, the more she felt she was going backwards with her treatment.

The day before the trial, she was alone in the farmhouse, when there was a knock on the door. When she answered the door, she was handed a large bag of medicines. Normally her mum would take it and it would be put straight into a safe place. Rosa suddenly went into a numb state of mind; it was as if someone else had taken over her body. She took the bag into the kitchen and put it on the table; she then looked inside the bag, took out a large bottle of painkillers and put them in her pocket. She walked to her bedroom and put them under her pillow. Still in a daze she went back into the kitchen, resealed the bag, pushed it out the way and sat down.

"I can't believe what I have just done." she thought, "I feel so guilty." This is what Davenport had done to her. Having a change of mind, she got up to go back to the bedroom and return the tablets to the bag; but just then, her mum arrived back from the shops.

"You OK? I see your tablets have arrived; I will put them in the cupboard, out the way." Her mum picked up the bag of medicines and took them into the other room.

When her mum arrived back in the kitchen, Rosa was already up, making her a cup of tea.

"Thank you dear, that tea's just what I need." she said and started putting some of the shopping away. "I've bought some nice cakes; which one would you like?" she asked, putting them all on a plate. "Please eat one, and

The Other Side of the Fence

then I can relax knowing you have at least eaten something today."

Rosa drank her tea and ate a cake.

"Good girl." her mum said, "I've bought your favourite food for your tea, so I hope you will eat a bit more today."

"Sounds good Mum. Hope you don't mind, I'm a bit tired, so I'm going for a lie down before tea."

"Of course I don't mind, I've got loads to do. I will call you when tea's ready."

Rosa went to her room and took the bottle of tablets from under her pillow. Looking at them, she thought, "I wonder how many I need to take to get that pig of a man out of my head and make this awful, lost and I don't care, feeling go away. I don't think I can handle getting through tomorrow." Subconsciously, she started to undo the cap of the bottle. She sat, looking at the open bottle, then quickly did it up again, when there was a knock on her bedroom door.

"Rosa! Rosa! Hope you're not asleep yet, Gemma's here." her mum called through the closed door, "I'm getting her a glass of pop, do you want one?"

A startled Rosa jumped up, put the tablets back under the pillow, grabbed her crutches and shouted, "How lovely, yes please; I'm coming, I'm on my way."

"Hi ya," Gemma said, when Rosa entered the lounge, "I thought I'd better come and see my best friend and tell her I will be thinking of her tomorrow. I wondered if you wanted to go somewhere tomorrow to take your mind off things?"

"Yes please, Gemma, that will be great." answered Rosa.

The Other Side of the Fence

"Sorry I can't stay long, my dad's waiting for me in the car. I told him I must come to see you today, even if it's just a quick visit. Don't forget Rosa, we can go anywhere you want, for however long you want; just let me know and I will be ready. Thanks for the pop, Mrs. Maddox. I'd better go, Rosa, so big hugs Babe; I know you're going to be fine. Hurry up and get that plaster cast off, then you can concentrate on getting the Rosa Maddox Riding School ready." Then Gemma was gone.

"My goodness! Talk about a whirlwind." Rosa's mum said, "Wasn't that a lovely thought though?"

Fighting back tears, Rosa replied, "Yes, she's the best friend ever."

14

It was about two o' clock that night, Rosa was still awake, laying there, thinking about how painful it was going to be to get through the next day. She tossed and turned and finally decided to get up, to get a glass of water. She went to the kitchen, poured a glass of water and took it back to the bedroom. As she sat on the side of the bed, the tablet bottle rolled from under her pillow. She picked it up, walked through to her lounge and put it on the table; she must have looked at it for at least twenty minutes.

"What an horrendous few months I've had." she thought, shaking her head. She picked up the bottle, put it down, picked it up again, undid it, took the top off, started to tip some of the tablets out, picked them up, then put them back in the bottle and did it up again. She clasped the bottle tight with both hands and closed her eyes. She could hear her councillor's voice telling her what to do when she felt like this.

She slowly put the bottle to one side, placed her hands flat on the table and started to take deep breaths; as she did so, she said to herself, "Breathe; calm in, breathe; fear out, breathe; calm in, breathe; anger out." She repeated it several times. She stopped suddenly, picked the bottle up, walked to the bedroom and put it in her bedside drawer. She then returned to the lounge, sat down again at the table, clenched her fists and banged them on the table. A thousand thoughts were racing through her mind. She started to argue with herself, "What are you doing, you stupid girl?" she berated herself, out loud, "Why has all this got to be about you, you, you? It's not about you, it's about saving Star's life. Are you going to let that disgusting pig of a man win and let him take your life? What about all those wonderful people who have been helping you all these months? You're going to show that all their hard work has been for nothing! What was the point of the doctors doing hours and hours of surgery, putting you back together, if this is how you're going to repay them? What about all the people who love you, why do want to break their hearts? Don't forget, Star will be lonely and have to be sold. He would never forgive you!" She put her head in her hands and started to cry. "Shame on you." she said to herself, "You're a Maddox; and the Maddoxes are fighters. This is not you; I know you don't really want this?" she then sobbed out loud, "NO!" putting her head between her hands and bending down onto the table. She quietly sobbed; her head was in turmoil, thinking over and over, "Rosa is it worth all this hurt and pain?"

After a while, she sat upright, found a tissue to wipe her eyes, then stood up and went to the mirror. Looking at her tear-stained face, she said to her reflection, "Rosa Maddox has made a decision. No! It's not worth all this hurt inside her; she wants to be happy and wants to make other people happy. So, from now on, she's going to be happy." She went back into the bedroom and got into bed. "What a night." she thought, as she snuggled down beneath the duvet, "Tomorrow, I will try and get these tablets back into the cupboard, before anyone knows they're missing. From now on, everyone will see me as a happy, Miss Sensible. I don't even care about an Olympic ride anymore. It would have been years of hard work; then three rides and it would all be over. Probably wouldn't have won a medal anyway. No; tomorrow, when I get up, there will be a new me. I will have a relaxing day out with Gemma; then the next day, I will talk to my dad and he can get me all the right papers and requirements for what's needed for the riding school. And, from then on, I will make all the people who have believed in me and helped me, be proud of what I will achieve. I will work so hard to pass the exams, so I can have a riding school. Yes, it feels good, to feel good." Smiling and feeling happy and relaxed, Rosa closed her eyes and started planning the Rosa Maddox Riding School. Before she knew it, she was sound asleep.

Free at last, a happy Rosa Maddox.

15

The next morning, Rosa woke up nice and early. As she stretched out, she thought and laughed to herself, "Hmm, now I know how Scrooge must have felt on Christmas morning."

Through a small space in her curtains, she could see it was a sunny day. She looked round her room thinking, "Well, I never realized how pretty Mum had made this room for me; very girly, so right for my new image." she smiled, "Mrs. Bennett will be pleased when I tell her next week, about the tablets, what happened, and how well I coped with the situation." She got ready and went through to the kitchen, where her mum and dad were having breakfast. She walked up to her mum, bent down and kissed her, "Morning Mother." Then walked round to her dad, bent down and kissed him, "Morning Father. Well, I think this is a day for a full English breakfast." she said, "Shall I do it Mum?"

The Other Side of the Fence

"No, let me do it Rosa, it will be a pleasure to see you eat a full English breakfast, or anything else, really." answered her mum.

"This I've got to see, even if it makes me late." added her dad.

"Mum, I'm out all day, can I have all my tablets for the day please?" asked Rosa.

"Yes, I'll get them when I've cooked your breakfast." replied her mum. Then sounding agitated, continued "Oh, for goodness sake! Now, I will worry I might forget them. Rosa, here's the key, can you go and get the medicine bag please?"

What a great opportunity it was for Rosa to put the bottle of tablets, she had in her pocket, back in the bag.

"Sorted!" she thought and smiled, "What a relief, now I can relax and have a nice day out with Gemma."

During breakfast, Rosa said, "I just rang Gemma; she will be here soon. Her dad's taking us to the station in his van. We are going to Norwich to do a bit of shopping, then off to see a film. After that, we'll get a meal, then get a taxi back."

Her mum and dad looked at each other with an expression that said, 'What's going on?' Rosa ate all her breakfast; then, when Gemma arrived for their day out, Rosa kissed her mum and said, "See you later."

Her dad called Rosa back. "Here, take this," he said, as he gave her some money, "I hope it pays for a nice meal for you and Gemma."

"Wow! Daddy, thank you." she said, then gave him a big hug, saying, "Love you;" then smiling at her mum, "and you."

The Other Side of the Fence

Rosa and Gemma went out to the car with a bag full of all sorts of things that Rosa needed for the day. Her wheelchair and crutches were already being loaded into the car by Gemma's dad.

"I feel like we're going on holiday." Rosa said.

"So do I." laughed Gemma's dad, as he put the rest of Rosa's things in the boot.

"Cheeky!" said Gemma. She looked at Rosa who was laughing, "I love it when you laugh." she said, "Norwich here we come." Then helped Rosa into the car.

"Enjoy!" her mum called, as they got into the car. She closed the front door, then looking at her husband, she said, "Don't you just love them?"

16

The next few months passed quickly, and Rosa was getting stronger and stronger. They all planned to celebrate the day the plaster cast was to be cut off her leg and had booked a meal at the nearby restaurant.

When the plaster was removed, Rosa looked at her legs, then looked at her mum, "I don't think I will win any lovely legs competitions with these legs; I've got one fat one and one thin one." she said, puzzled.

The male nurse, who had just cut the plaster off, said, "That's because you've got to build all the muscles up again in your right leg. I'm sure if you do what the physiotherapists tell you, they will both be back to the same size in no time. We can't do anything about those scars though; hopefully, they will fade in time."

As she got up to sit back in her wheelchair, she thanked the nurse, and looked at her mum again saying, "It's a good job I wear trousers all the time, so no one can see them."

The Other Side of the Fence

Brenda came down to the plaster room to see Rosa. Rosa looked at her, shaking her head slightly and said as she held Brenda's hand, "As always, my lovely, caring, thoughtful Brenda. I was coming to find you." and filled up as she said, "I will never forget you Brenda. Thank you for all your help; you got me through a very traumatic time in my life. Your lovely happy face every morning and our night-time chats when you were on night duty. A big thank you for what everyone has done for me." Rosa took two cards from her bag, she had also written two thank you notes, one for Brenda and her colleagues; the other, for the surgical team that operated on her. She also handed her two big boxes of chocolate biscuits.

"Oh, bless you." Brenda said, "I will make sure these letters are read by the right people, and I know we will all enjoy the biscuits when we have our cups of tea." She wished Rosa all the best for the future, gave her a big hug and said, "Bye my lovely, I know you are going to be OK."

Two Christmases came and went. As New Year 1994 came in, it was the year of Rosa's eighteenth birthday. Over the last year, she had worked really hard on her fitness. Her legs were getting stronger; she had accepted that they would never be one hundred percent, but she was happy that she could walk OK; she only needed a walking stick when walking on uneven ground. She had already passed several of the preliminary riding instructor exams and had applied for information on what she had to do next. She felt confident that she was ready, so she applied for a BHS certificate. The date for her to go for the final exam came through a week before her birthday; what a great present that would be.

She needn't have worried; when the time came, she passed the test with flying colours and was now the proud owner of a framed BHS certificate. When Rosa and her mum arrived home from the test, she rushed indoors to show her dad that she had past the exam, but no one was there. She sat down at the kitchen table, and looked at her new, proud, possession.

"I'm so proud of you Rosa" her mum said, "You have come such a long way, in such a short time."

"Thanks Mum, that means a lot. You know Mum, I can't believe that even Gemma wasn't here, waiting outside, to see if I had passed."

There was a knock on the door, "Answer that please." her mum shouted from the next room.

Rosa opened the door, "Rosa Maddox?" a young girl asked.

"Yes." Rosa answered.

"Then, congratulations, these are for you." the girl said and handed Rosa a large bouquet of flowers.

"Oh, my goodness me! Thank you." a shocked Rosa said. As she closed the door, her mum stood there smiling. Rosa read the card,

'Congratulations Princess! We knew you could do it. All our love Mum and Dad. xx'

"Mum, that's the best surprise, they are absolutely beautiful." Rosa said.

"The look on your face was worth all the effort people have put in, to get them here for you. A lot of teamwork has gone on, since we knew you had passed the test. I texted your dad, who rang the florist, who was on standby to deliver them, for when you got home. So, they have done well to get them here so quick. I'm so pleased you liked them."

"Mum, I do, I love them, and love the idea you made me think no one cared if I passed. I will definitely need two vases, there are so many flowers. I am definitely a very happy girl." Rosa said hugging her mum.

17

Rosa took her flowers into the kitchen to get some vases. While there, she heard the phone ring and her mum answer. Then her mum called through, "Rosa, your dad's on the phone, asking if we've got time to go and see him?"

"Oh good, I can thank him for the flowers." called back Rosa, her head deep in a cupboard.

"Come on then, coats back on and get in the car; I know where he is."

Rosa's mum drove off their large forecourt, on to the road, then turned left onto the road leading to the river. She suddenly stopped the car halfway down the lane and said, "Right Rosa, put this blindfold on."

Rosa frowned. "You are joking, aren't you?" she asked.

"I know it sounds stupid, but your dad told me to do this." her mum said laughing.

"Ok, if it will please him." Rosa put the blindfold on and her mum started the car again. "I can't believe what we are doing. I hope no one I know sees me."

Slowing the car, a little further on, her mum said, "Almost there." and came to a stop, "Keep it on, here comes Daddy."

Rosa's father opened her door, "Out you come, Princess." he said, giving her a walking stick because the ground was uneven. He then led her a short distance and said, "OK, you can take it off now."

She opened her eyes; in front of her stood her two uncles, "Oh, hello!" she said, surprised; and with that her uncles parted, giving her a view of a large square of ground; all covered in sand, levelled and fenced off. Over to the right there were two stable blocks being built.

"When finished, they will stable four horses each." her dad explained, "I hope you're going to do well enough to rent out the stables you don't use. Now turn around this way." he said, pointing. She then saw a large building that had already been built and painted; over the door was a sign in big letters, 'ROSA MADDOX RIDING SCHOOL' and a phone number. On the door was the word, 'OFFICE', "Well Princess, what do you think?" asked her dad.

"Daddy, I'm speechless." she said, welling up, "I promise you won't be sorry, doing all this for me. I won't let you down."

"Oops, I forgot this bit; turn around." Rosa turned around and there was Gemma, wearing a purple T-shirt with 'Rosa Maddox Riding School' printed on the front. "Now, Rosa, this young lady is your weekend helper." he said laughing, "Gemma has agreed to help you every weekend and if ever you need her any other time, if she

The Other Side of the Fence

can help, she will. She has also agreed for her horse to be stabled here, to be used for teaching. She is going to sort out the proper papers and insurance. If you agree, Rosa, I have said that in the future, if the riding school is successful and needs to expand; with both your equestrian knowledge, and Gemma now doing an equine veterinarian course, perhaps a partnership might be in order?"

The two girls looked at each other and mouthed the word, "Wow!"

"Don't worry if you ever want a break or a holiday; my boys will look after the horses for you."

Rosa was amazed, as well as speechless. She shook her head, saying, "I hope I'm not dreaming Daddy, because this is better than anything I could ever have imagined. Daddy, I said I was speechless, but you're the best dad in the whole wide world. And you, Mummy; I love you both to the Moon and back." She went over to Gemma; they hugged and giggled, saying how they were going to be big businesswomen.

"Come on girls," said Rosa's dad, "there's lots to be done before we can open. Let's go back home, before we go to the restaurant, and plan what we are going to do. We need to write a good advert for the Rosa Maddox riding school."

When they arrived back at the farmhouse, her dad said, "Now Rosa, there is one other thing that needs to be done soon and that is for you and Gemma to get driving licences. I know you can both drive, but that's only on private land. You can't keep waiting around, asking people to take you here, there and everywhere in the town, when you want something. Rosa, I know you can only drive an automatic car, because of the weakness of your legs, but you can take the test in an automatic car to get your licence, although you won't be able to drive a manual car.

But I can't see that being a problem, can you?" Both girls, looking stunned at the speed of things, shook their heads. "If you two are going to be businesswomen, you both need to drive. If you get an instructor to finalise the things you need to know, and get it all booked as soon as possible, you won't have to do that big theory test that's coming in soon; they say you will have to pass that before you can even put in for your actual driving test."

"Good idea, Dad; I can't believe that we hadn't thought of it before. We will get ourselves booked in tomorrow. Is that OK with you Gemma?"

"Fine by me. I can't believe all this is happening. I feel privileged to be involved; thank you so much Mr. and Mrs. M. I can't believe we hadn't thought of getting driving licences before. Now, I can't wait to get one and get on the open road." said Gemma, smiling at Rosa.

18

A massive clap of thunder startled a forty-two-year-old Rosa; so much so, she dropped the book she had been reading.

"My goodness, whatever was that?" she said out loud, "Well Rosa, whatever it was," she thought, "it certainly brought you back to the present day." as she suddenly realized she had spent quite some time thinking about her past, just staring into the flames flickering behind the glass of the log burner. A chapter in the romantic novel made her think back to years ago, when something that had happened to the young girl in the book, had happened to her. She got up from the large armchair she was sitting in and walked over to the big bay window in the lounge. As she looked out over the fields, a flash of lightening lit up the sky, followed closely by another clap of thunder. Outside, the late autumn storm that they were expecting, was just starting. She could see the trees swaying in the wind. "Well, that's going to get really bad later;" she thought, "it's already getting dark and its only 4 o' clock."

The Other Side of the Fence

Earlier that day there had been a weather warning for Norfolk. Rosa knew that before the storm started, the horses needed to be inside. Rosa, Gemma and the stable girls, proceeded to round up all the horses, make sure they were all fed, watered and settled safely in their stables. Because of the weather, it had been a harder task than it normally would; it had been raining steadily for most of the day which had made the fields very soggy and made it hard for Rosa and the others to keep upright. They were slipping and sliding everywhere and the horses kept running away, thinking the girls were playing. Although they were all in hysterics at the horses' antics, there was a big sigh of relief from everyone when the horses were all safe and the job was done. The girls were all cold, wet, covered in mud and ready to go home.

When Rosa finally got home, she lit the log burner and hung some of her wet clothes round the room to dry; the rest she put ready to wash. Before she sat down, Rosa prepared everything for dinner; she had decided on stew and dumplings. She knew the others would arrive home later, cold and wet. She put the large saucepan of stew she had prepared on a medium heat, so it would cook slowly and be ready for the others when they got home. She checked the clock, she had a good two hours before it would be ready, but she still needed to make the dumplings.

"Better set the timer, just in case." she thought. She sighed with satisfaction and looked pleased with herself, as she said aloud, "They are so going to enjoy this dinner. I don't think I could have picked a better day to have made them my lovely stew and dumplings."

Rosa made herself a cup of tea, went back into the lounge and switched the lights on. Before drawing the curtains, she looked outside again, shivered and thought, "I wouldn't fancy going out in that now, it looks too dangerous." Putting two more logs in the log burner, she thought, "That will look nice and cosy when they walk in."

Snuggling down into the armchair, she picked up her book.

"Now, where was I?" she said out loud, as she opened the book, "This young girl had fallen in love with a boy she had just met on holiday. They were at the airport and she was crying because they were about to get on planes that would take them in different directions, back to their homes. They had each other's phone numbers, and through hugs, kisses and tears were exchanging addresses. Well, I can tell her, I could have written this book. I've been there, done all that and know it will end in more tears; won't it Eva Marie?" She looked over to the collage of photographs on the lounge wall. The photographs ranged from her daughter, Eva Marie, as a baby in 1997, through to her schooldays. The biggest photograph was Eva Marie, on her horse, Gemini Girl, jumping over one of the show fences at Olympia in a show jumping competition; finally, a photograph of Eva Marie celebrating her eighteenth birthday.

The phone rang, it was a wrong number. Talking to Eva Marie's photographs again, Rosa said, "I can tell you my lovely girl, a lot can happen from one phone call; it can change your whole life. It changed mine; that is how you came to be born. It happened because of a late-night phone call from auntie Gemma." She put her book down, pulled the blanket up over her shoulders and thought, "I'm so right there. If Gemma hadn't phoned me over twenty years ago."

Rosa smiled, recalling the phone call, and how an over excited Gemma's high-pitched voice came down the phone, "Rosa, I'm so excited, I just had to tell someone, I'm engaged! Jack has just asked me to marry him. I said yes. We both want a white wedding; I want lots of flowers. My mum's so excited; so is his. Oh yes, I've got to have bridesmaids; will you be my bridesmaid? And I will ask Katie, then there's Lyla and Mimi; her names Amelia but she only answers to Mimi. You don't know them, they're my two young nieces who live near Norwich; they are four and six. And my friend's daughter, Elsie, who you teach to ride. Won't they all look cute? They are so well behaved; I know you will love them. It will be wonderful, we can plan days out and all go shopping for our dresses; it's going to be in the middle of next year, we haven't set the exact date yet. Us girls have got to have a hen party; oh, I've just had an idea, just thought it could be on my birthday, the twentieth of April next year; WOW! What a date that is; better put that idea to Jack. Oh, my minds in a whirl, Rosa, Rosa, you're quiet, are you still there?"

"Yes, of course I am." Rosa answered, laughing, "I was waiting for you to take a breath."

Gemma burst out laughing, "What am I like? That's me all over; tell you what, when I see you tomorrow, I will be calmer by then."

"Gemma, listen," Rosa remembered saying to her, "first let me congratulate you, I'm so happy for you and Jack; you're a lovely couple. Tomorrow, come early before we start the booked riding lessons. Bring a large notebook and label it 'THE WEDDING' and we can sit and talk about the wedding and make a list etc."

"Love it, thanks Rosa." Rosa could hear Gemma still talking to herself on the other end of the phone.

"Right Gemma, take deep breaths and calm yourself. Rosa's in charge, because Rosa's motto is 'you always have to have a plan' and if we have a plan, everything will be fine."

"Bye, Rosa, see you tomorrow about nine o' clock. Love you Babe." Then, Gemma put the phone down.

Smiling as Rosa put her phone down, she thought, "Bet she won't sleep tonight."

Suddenly the timer went off. Rosa jumped up.

"My goodness, the time's just flown. I haven't got time for reminiscing just now." she said looking at Eva Marie's photos again, "Love you loads, my lovely, but I've got to hurry and get the dumplings on, or they will all be back before dinners ready."

"Well, I didn't get far into that did I?" she thought, as she put her book away.

19

Arriving home, wet and cold, everyone agreed that Rosa's stew and dumplings was a great success. The storm was still going strong by the time they went to bed.

Rosa couldn't sleep, the rain was hitting the bedroom window so hard, she thought it was going to break through the glass. The good news, especially for the horses, was that at least the thunder and lightning had stopped. As she lay in bed, she could hear the wind making weird howling noises through the trees. She kept turning one way, then the other. Another hour passed, still wide awake, she thought "I'm not getting up, it's too cold." She pulled the duvet up round her neck, "I need to go to sleep, I've got a busy day tomorrow, sorting out the horses."

She tried to think of all the different ways she had heard to fall asleep, "Whatever was the one that Gemma said she does?" she thought. She thought for a while longer and said quietly, making herself laugh in the process, "Probably talks herself to sleep. Gemma does make me laugh though; all these years she has stood by me, she's been the best friend and partner you could have. My life would have been so different had we not met at college and especially if she hadn't come round the next day after she got engaged." Rosa thought.

Rosa laid there and recalled how funny Gemma was that day; and what followed after that day's meeting was to be the start of the biggest decision and journey in Rosa's life.

At exactly 9am, the morning after Gemma's phone call, Rosa's phone rang, "Just checking you're up and ready for me?" Gemma had said.

"I certainly am, let's start the ball rolling." Rosa replied.

While Rosa was on the phone to Gemma, there was a knock on the front door. Rosa's mum shouted, "I'll get it!" She opened the door and shouted to Rosa, "It's Gemma!"

Rosa went to the front door, laughing, "Gemma you fool, you do make me laugh."

As they were going through to Rosa's lounge, her mum said, "I've just made a pot of tea, do either of you want one?"

"Yes please." they both said, in unison.

"I think that's tea for two then. I will bring it through. Congratulations Gemma, Rosa's already told me; I'm so pleased for you and Jack."

"Thanks Mrs. M." Gemma answered, "You will definitely be getting an invite."

"Oh, that's nice of you Gemma; that calls for me to bring you biscuits as well."

The Other Side of the Fence

The two girls, armed with pens and paper, sat down at the table.

Gemma said, "Before we start, Rosa, I need to ask you something because I know you will have to think long and hard about a yes or no answer."

"My goodness, you've got me worried, what is it?" Rosa asked.

"I know I'm excited about the wedding, but I am also a caring person. I care about my dearest friend and I don't want to leave her out of any plans; so, I want to involve you in what's going on." Gemma paused, looked at Rosa, reached out and held her hand, saying, "Would you like to come on the hen party to Ibiza with me, Katie and a few other girls we know from college? It will be a long weekend, Friday, Saturday, Sunday, coming back on Monday. It will be at the end of October, next month. I know the wedding's not 'til April, but we need to go then so we get decent weather. Don't forget that if it's a yes, you need a passport and they take time. Right, I will stop talking because I can see I have caused you a dilemma."

"No, Gemma, it's OK." Rosa stood up and hugged Gemma, "I'm touched by what you just said, and how you said it. Leave it with me, I will talk to mum and dad tonight and see what they think. Although I only go three times a year now, I'm still being counselled at the hospital, so it will be the councillor, Mrs. Bennett's, final decision."

Rosa's mum bought them the tea and biscuits and they had a nice couple of hours writing lists for the wedding. They decided on a Lilac, purple and pink theme. There would be four bridesmaids and the men would wear long dress coats, but no top hats.

"Better get down to the stables before the riders turn up." Rosa said, looking at her watch, "I really enjoyed that, Gemma; let's say same time next week?"

That evening, Rosa told her mum and dad about the hen party.

Her mum said, "I'm sure you can cope with a long weekend holiday, relaxing in the sunshine, swimming and nights out with the girls. Then, when you get back, it will be nonstop up to Christmas, then in the New Year, organizing for Gemma's wedding. You've just been for your four-monthly check-up and everything was OK; and your next one isn't until February. First thing tomorrow, I'd better ring Mrs. Bennett at the hospital and check if she thinks it's OK for you to go, and find out what, if anything, you have to do."

Rosa was pleased when the hospital and everyone agreed that if she felt confident enough to cope, they were happy for her to go. They would leave the final decision to her.

"I want to go. I am quite excited; I want to see what it's like to go abroad." she said to her mum, "All the other girls will be with me; Gemma said there will be eight of us if I go."

Rosa's dad added, "Don't forget, there's no worry with the horses, my boys will look after them while you're both away. That's what I said at the beginning when you started the riding school."

"OK, Daddy, then let's do it, I will get my photo done tomorrow and apply for my passport."

The next few weeks were hectic but enjoyable. She loved her friendship with Matt, she could tell him anything, except the one thing she couldn't tell anyone. When she told him about the holiday, he said, "Yes, go for it and enjoy. Don't worry about a thing; if you're happy, then I'm happy."

She stood on the tips of her toes and kissed him on the cheek.

"Thanks Matt, that means a lot." she smiled.

One day, soon after, she was giving a riding lesson to a young girl called Gracie. As she neared the fence, Gracie said to Rosa, "I like your new bench." Rosa hadn't noticed it before; Matt had built a bench; half was in his field and the other half was in hers.

Smiling, she thought, "That's because we normally stand there for hours just talking and my legs start to hurt. That's so lovely and caring of him; he's obviously telling me he enjoys our chats and has built the bench so we can both sit and chat without getting tired." Then, laughing, she said, "Next time you come for your lesson, Gracie, there will probably be a table."

20

The holiday was getting close and Gemma organised a shopping spree, with all the girls, to Norwich. They each bought a pink T-shirt and had 'Gemma's Hen Party' printed on them in purple; Gemma's had 'I'M GEMMA' printed on the front and 'THE BRIDE' printed on the back. They all bought a pink cowgirl hat and a lilac scarf, except Gemma, who bought a veil attached to a diamante crown.

"Us girls are going to have so much fun." said Gemma, trying on the veil.

Rosa had never been out of England before; she didn't even have a suitcase. Rosa enjoyed herself, buying loads of holiday clothes.

"Slow down Rosa, you'll never wear all the things you have already bought", said Gemma. We're only going for four days you know."

"I know," Rosa replied, "I have never bought girly clothes before; I've even bought myself some sandals in a bright pink; I've only ever had black or brown. You won't know who I am on holiday."

The Other Side of the Fence

The eight happy, but tired, girls ended their day out with drinks and a slap-up meal.

When Rosa got home, she showed her mum all the holiday things she had bought; she even paraded back and forth, wheeling her new purple suitcase behind her.

Her mum stood, looking at her daughter; she filled up and said, "Oh Rosa, I've waited such a long time to see my lovely daughter so happy; I do hope you all have a lovely time."

The day of the holiday arrived; their flight was at eleven o' clock in the morning. Rosa was packed and ready really early, she had already been to see the horses and told them she would be back soon. She was walking up to the window and back waiting for Gemma and her fiancé, Jack, who was taking them to Norwich airport.

Her mum said, "Rosa, you're going to wear that carpet out."

"Sorry, Mum," Rosa replied, "I'm just so excited; my stomachs going over and over."

Gemma finally arrived. There were lots of kisses, hugs, goodbyes and take cares, from her mum and dad.

"Make sure you enjoy yourself." called her dad, as they waved her off.

All the girls had arranged to meet at the airport; by the time Rosa and Gemma arrived, the other girls were already there. They stood in a circle, chatting away. Although it was a small airport it was still overwhelming for Rosa, she was wide eyed and quiet, not really knowing what to expect. Their flight was announced over the public announcement system.

"Come on Rosa, that's us. You need your passport and boarding pass." said Gemma. Rosa just followed what everyone else was doing. The time was going fast and she found herself following the girls up the steps of the plane. Her heart was pounding; if she ever needed her breathing exercises, it was now. They found their seats; Gemma was by the window, then Rosa, then an empty seat between Rosa and the aisle.

The Other Side of the Fence

"Strap yourself in, Rosa," said Gemma, "it won't be long before we take off; then, just over two hours and we will be there. I hope you are going to enjoy your first flight?"

"I feel like a child; I'm so in awe of everything." said Rosa.

Their conversation was halted by a voice saying, "Morning girls." A young man was putting his briefcase in the overhead locker, "I think this is my seat." he said, sitting down next to Rosa.

The other girls, sitting nearby, turned and looked at Rosa and Gemma mouthed the words, "Wow! he's gorgeous."

The cabin crew started their safety routine and the plane started to roll forward towards the runway. Then came the almighty roar of the engines as the plane started its take off. Rosa grabbed the man's hand. She held it so tight he looked towards her smiling, "Don't worry, you'll be okay, what's your name?"

"Rosa." she said, going further down into her seat.

"I presume this is your first flight?" he asked.

"Yes," she answered, "and I don't like it."

"My name's James, James Stirling; I'm from Ireland." he said trying to distract her from the take off, "I'm an accountant and my dad's one of Ireland's top lawyers; he's further down the plane with my brother, Michael. We're going to Ibiza on business for a few days; are you on holiday?"

"No, well sort of; it's Gemma's hen party," Rosa explained, pointing to Gemma. She suddenly realised that she was still holding his hand. "Oh! I'm sorry" she said, pulling her hand away.

"I'm not," he said, "I rather liked it."

Gemma laughed, "Look girls, our Rosa's blushing."

The Other Side of the Fence

The cabin crew started their drinks service. When James heard them asking the people behind, he turned to Gemma and Rosa and asked, "Can I get you two girls a drink?"

"It's a bit early for alcohol," Gemma said, "but a hot chocolate would be nice. Thank you."

"Mmm, that sounds nice," said Rosa, looking at James, "the same for me please."

James asked where they were staying; they told him where their two apartments were and he said he was staying in a hotel opposite.

"I've got a car; can I give you girls a lift?" James asked.

Gemma replied, "I doubt it, there's eight of us. It's not far, we're going to get taxis, but thanks for the offer."

They were soon landing; James held Rosa's hand until they were safely taxiing to the terminal.

As they left the plane, James said, "Bye girls, hope you all have a good holiday, and thanks, Rosa and Gemma, for being good company and making the trip pleasant. I'm sure we will bump into each other again; you should all come over to our hotel for drinks tonight?"

"We can't," Gemma said, "we are out on the town in our outfits."

"Come across to the swimming pool tomorrow afternoon then?" he said.

Looking at the other girls, who were all nodding, Gemma answered, "Now, that sounds like a good idea; we might take you up on that offer."

Looking at Rosa, he said "Please come, I will be disappointed if you don't."

They picked up their luggage and made their way to the taxi rank, James came up behind Rosa and put a note in her hand; she quickly put it in her pocket and got in the taxi.

The Other Side of the Fence

They arrived at their apartments and checked in; luckily both apartments were ready for them. They sorted out who would go in which apartment. Gemma suggested that they should meet up again in one hour, to go to a supermarket and stock up. They would then have a few hours to sort themselves out and be dressed in their outfits, ready to go out, at seven.

"Everyone happy, say aye?" Gemma said, as they went to their appointed apartments.

They all laughed and shouted, "Aye!"

"That's it, the last orders from me; you're all free to go and do as you wish after tonight."

"Aye!" they all shouted again.

"You horrible lot." Gemma laughed, as she shut the door of her apartment.

"This is lovely." Rosa said, as she stood out on the balcony, "We are overlooking the pool; and look at the mountains, they are beautiful. It's sort of like being in a luxury college, with all the girls here."

Rosa said to Katie and Sue, "I don't mind the sofa to sleep on, if you two girls want the bedroom."

"I will share the sofa with you then if that's OK" said Gemma."

"Sorted. It does pull out to a double." Rosa said. She took her jacket off and remembered the note; she opened it and read,

'ROSA, JUST INCASE, THIS IS MY PHONE NUMBER AND ROOM NUMBER AT THE HOTEL. I WILL BE IN THE BAR LOUNGE TOMORROW AT 7pm. HOPE YOU WILL COME. JAMES. X'

She showed it to Gemma, who said, "Oh my goodness, you'd better go, he was lovely. Go at seven, for a couple of hours, then meet up with us girls later."

"Let's get your hen night over first; I will decide tomorrow." said Rosa.

"I've already decided. If you don't go, I will." said a laughing Gemma.

21

At seven pm that night, the girls stood in a circle in the lounge bar of the apartment complex. They were all fully dressed in their outfits, with a glass of bubbly in their hands.

Katie blew into a whistle and said, "Attention! I would like to make a toast to our lovely friend, Gemma and her intended, Jack, who unfortunately couldn't be here with us this evening, because we wouldn't let him." They all laughed and shouted different rude comments about men. "Now now, girls, this is serious." Katie lifted her glass, "A toast." she said, "Congratulations to Jack and Gemma; may you have love and happiness always and lots of children, so we can all be their aunties and get told off for spoiling them." A round of cheers erupted from all the girls, as they chinked their glasses.

Gemma looked at them, tears in her eyes, "Thank you, that was lovely. You all look amazing, I love the purple tutus you've added; and thank you all so much for being here, you have made me so happy; don't forget to take lots of photos. We'd better get started, there's a lot of celebrating and drinking to be done."

They went along the sea front, going from bar to bar. They had drunk so many different drinks, they practically fell down the steps into a dingy looking night club. One look and they quickly did an about turn to make a quick exit; they were laughing so much, they fell over each other trying to get back up the steps. The evening was turning into a fun filled night; they looked so good in their outfits, several people stopped them and asked if they could have a photo taken with them. They finally ended up in a massive night club, with hundreds of people dancing to the loudest music Rosa had ever heard; you couldn't hear yourself speak. There were laser beams, flashing lights, balloons and bubbles flowing out of big tubes from the ceiling. The barman, called Antonio, who was serving them their drinks, was very friendly; he was already flirting with one of the girls, and her with him.

"If you come back tomorrow night, it will be foam and everything you can think of, coming out of those tubes." he told them, "It gets deep and covers everyone. It's a great night, full of fun; but don't wear anything you don't want to get messed up."

They all looked at each other, nodded and Gemma said, "We'll be here; see you tomorrow night, Antonio."

As the night went on, Rosa was realizing what a sheltered life she had led. Had she ever enjoyed herself, other than when she was with horses? Had she actually ever done anything that didn't involve horses?

"Well, I'm determined to change that right now." she thought, "I'm going to keep up with the other girls and enjoy every minute of the night and the atmosphere." For her, Rosa had had a lot to drink; she wasn't drunk, just pleasantly tipsy.

Gemma told Rosa, "If you start to feel giddy, change to bottled water. As long as you keep on your feet, you will be OK"

Rosa said, "I can't believe this place, I didn't know there was this many people on the island." Gemma grabbed Rosa's hand and pulled her out onto the dance floor.

"I can't dance." complained Rosa.

"Neither can half the people on the dance floor;" said Gemma, "just jig about."

They came off the dance floor doubled up laughing about Rosa's effort at dancing. When they finally found Antonio's bar, Katie looked worried.

"What's up?" Rosa asked.

"Will you come with me to find the toilets; I've already looked once, but this place is so big, I couldn't find one, and I nearly got lost. Do you know there's about seven different bars in here and they all look the same?"

"Of course I will, I could go as well. Anyone else want to accompany us?" The others that were there shook their heads, "No? Just the two of us then Katie."

They set off to find the toilets; they seemed to walk for ages, then saw a sign for toilets, pointing down a tunnel.

"At last!" Katie said, "But look at the queue Rosa; I need to wait" she said, as she joined the queue.

"OK," Rosa said, "I'm with you."

The Other Side of the Fence

When they came out of the tunnel, about twenty minutes later, they looked at each other and shrugged their shoulders.

"Which way is it to Antonio's bar?" asked Katie. They chose the way they thought they had come and started to walk.

Rosa suddenly stopped and said, "I think we are wrong Katie, I feel we are going the wrong way. Let's go back the way we just walked; I don't recognise anything. I think we came out of a different tunnel to the way we went in." In the end, they were well and truly lost.

They came across a 'way out' sign, "Are you thinking what I'm thinking?" Katie said.

"Yes." Rosa answered, "We might not find them, or they might even have left, thinking we have left and gone back to the apartments; we have been rather a long time. Right, let's get out of here; if they left, we might find them in a bar along the seafront. It's very late, they might even have gone home."

They started walking along the seafront, it was 3am and still very lively. Rosa stopped by a low wall and said to Katie, "I know we are near our apartments, Katie, but do you mind if we sit on this wall for a while; my legs ache, I'm not used to wearing heels. They might even come past."

They sat on the wall, actually enjoying watching everyone having a great time; they could also see quite a long way down the seafront road, so they wouldn't miss the others if they came past.

"Why hello there!" they heard a voice shouting from across the road, "Are you lost?" It was James Stirling, and, they presumed, the person with him was his brother.

"I know that Irish accent." Rosa said, "I can't say I recognise him; I was so scared of flying, I didn't make too much eye contact with him on the plane. Although he was lovely and helped me; I went all shy and daren't look at him. The girls were right, he is gorgeous, so is his brother." As James and his brother crossed the road, towards them, Rosa called back, "No, we're not lost, we got separated from the other girls. We are just sitting, waiting to see if they come past."

"Do you mind if we sit here with you then?" James asked, "There are a lot of drunks about and I don't want you girls to get upset if they start pestering you."

"Feel free." replied Rosa, shivering as she answered.

"Here." James took off his jacket and put it round her shoulders.

"Thank you, that's lovely and it's all warm. I think it's the breeze coming off the sea, while we have been sitting here, that's made me feel cold."

After a while Katie said, "Rosa, do you mind if I go back to the flat; they might be ages yet. We've had a long day and I'm quite tired and cold."

James looked at her and said, "It's Katie isn't it? Rosa, if you want to sit and wait, I will wait with you. Michael wants to go back to the hotel, so he can walk with Katie and make sure she gets back to the apartment safe."

Rosa looked at Katie, "Is that OK with you?" she asked.

"Yes, it sure is. I'm so cold and tired." she answered, "Come on Michael, best behaviour please; I don't want any funny business; I do karate and so does my boyfriend." she said smiling at Rosa.

The Other Side of the Fence

"Don't worry, he's quite harmless and he's got a girlfriend." said James, "The apartments only a few hundred yards away; you will both be fine."

"See you soon, Rosa." Katie said, hooking Michael's arm, as they began to walk away.

Michael turned and looked at James, "But am I safe James? She's very bossy." he grinned.

"You're Ok, you're Irish." James laughed. Then, looking at Rosa, asked, "You OK there, Rosa?"

"Yes;" she replied, "we have all had a brilliant night; it's a shame we got separated."

"Well, I must say you look delightful in your outfit; if you all look the same, I'm impressed."

"Thanks, we must have been stopped a hundred times for photos."

They sat talking for about twenty minutes, telling each other all about themselves and what they did for a living. Rosa loved the way James spoke; he had a slight Irish accent.

Suddenly, along the seafront they could hear a group of people coming towards them, singing and doing the conga.

"Oh dear, I think this sounds like the people I have been looking for." said Rosa and gave James his jacket back. As the girls, with about twenty other people attached on the back of them, reached Rosa and James, they all signalled for them to join on the back.

"I think that was more an order, than a polite gesture." Rosa said, as she joined on the end and James joined on the back of her.

The Other Side of the Fence

When they reached the apartments, there was a loud round of applause and everyone suddenly disappeared.

"That's nice;" Rosa said to James, "they've had so much to drink, they probably haven't noticed that me and Katie haven't been with them for the last hour. Didn't they look happy though? I'm glad we joined them for that last few yards at least."

James said, "Meeting you like that tonight has made my night; will you come to the hotel tomorrow at seven?"

"The other girls said they don't mind, so yes, just for a short while, because we are all going to the foam party; it sounds a lot of fun."

"OK, see you at seven tomorrow night." James made sure she got to the apartment entrance OK, then lent forward, kissed her on the cheek, said good night and left.

When she opened her apartment door, she looked in amazement, there were at least six girls fast asleep, still dressed, laying anywhere they could find space; some of them still had their hats on. She went to the other apartment, luckily the door was open. She went to the bedroom, there was one nice empty bed.

She got undressed, snuggled down and thought, "I can't believe what a great time I've had. I like James and I just love how he says my name. I can't wait till I see him again tomorrow night. What a lovely day and night everyone has had. Yes, definitely a day I will always remember." She then fell fast asleep.

22

The next morning, when Rosa woke up, she was pleased to find that she was none the worse after her night out. She looked at the now empty bed next to hers.

"I'm sure Katie was asleep in that bed last night." she thought, "So that's two of us who didn't sleep in their right beds."

She went next door to her apartment and was met with a chorus of moans and groans of 'never again' and 'I'm never going to touch alcohol again', from some of the other girls. They were all slowly waking, some wondering where they were, as they looked around, there were clothes, hats and shoes everywhere. They all agreed that the place was a mess, then laid back down.

"There you are." Rosa said, as she saw Katie at the cooker; she was making everyone coffee and toast.

"Who wants their coffee black?" Katie asked; several hands went up. "Who's going to the foam party tonight?"

The Other Side of the Fence

She looked around. "Oh dear, no one. Then it's just me." she said laughing, "I will ask you all again later."

Gemma was sitting on the balcony which overlooked the swimming pool. Rosa got herself a cup of coffee and some toast and joined her. Sitting down, she said, "Isn't this all lovely, Gemma? I'm so pleased I came. Well, how much did our bride enjoy her first hen night; was it good?"

Gemma replied, "Rosa, it was the best ever, better than I could ever have imagined; I felt like I was a celebrity, I loved everything about it."

"Even the conga?" Rosa laughed.

Gemma put her hands up to her face and said, "Oh my goodness, I forgot all about that. Yes, even that." Then, more seriously, Gemma asked, "Rosa, you are going to see James at six, aren't you? Those of us that are going to the foam party won't be going out till after nine, that's when Antonio said was the best time to go; so that will give you plenty of time to relax and enjoy your time with him. We will stay in and wait for you."

Rosa replied, "Yes, I am going; I thought I would wear that lavender blue dress I bought."

"Wow! you will knock him for six in that." Gemma said.

After some of the girls had eaten and had cold showers to wake them up; it was decided a lazy day by the pool was the plan for the day. As they laid on the pool sunbeds, the owner came round with leaflets advertising a pool party with a quiz, games and a BBQ on Sunday night, with fireworks on the beach at ten pm.

"What do you think girls?" Gemma asked, "Sounds like that's tomorrow night sorted." Those who were awake put their thumbs up. "Rosa, invite James and his brother; it sounds great fun and will be a good last night's celebration for us."

As six o' clock was approaching, Rosa and Gemma went into the bedroom, so that Gemma could help Rosa to get ready to meet James.

"I think just a pale pink lipstick and not too much make up, Rosa; you don't want to look like a tart." Gemma laughed,

"Gemma!" Rosa said, shocked, "Well, perhaps just a tiny bit." Rosa giggled. Rosa was tanned but the scars on her legs were still white; Gemma covered them brilliantly with a tan makeup, so Rosa could wear the short dress she had bought, which was a couple of inches above her knee; it had two thin straps, which was nice and cool for indoors. They left Rosa's hair curly and gripped it up at the back.

"Yes, I love it, very sexy." Gemma said as she pulled a few strands loose. They painted Rosa's nails with a very pale pink nail varnish. "And now the finishing touch, your open toed silver sandals with high heels." Gemma looked Rosa up and down and said, "Perfect."

They opened the bedroom door and suddenly there was a round of applause and wolf whistles.

Katie said, "Rosa, you actually look like a model, you look lovely."

As Rosa left the apartment with Gemma, there were cries from the girls for Rosa to enjoy every minute.

They got as far as the lift where Rosa stopped, "I can't do this, Gemma;" she said, "this is not me."

"For goodness sake, I know that." said Gemma, "The old you couldn't do it, but you're the new Rosa Maddox; and she can."

When the lift arrived, Gemma said, "Now, shoulders back and get in. I will come as far as the hotel with you, then you're on your own. And don't you dare let all my hard work go to waste. I will want a full report when you get back."

"Right." Rosa saluted, "You're so bossy."

Both laughing out loud, they got in the lift, ready for the new Rosa Maddox to go on her first date.

23

Gemma walked over to James' hotel with Rosa, she gave her a cuddle and said, "Off you go, make sure you enjoy yourself. See you later, Babe."

Rosa walked into the lounge bar; when James saw her, he jumped up from his chair, and went over to meet her.

"You look stunning." he said, "You quite took my breath away. Hope you haven't had dinner yet, my dad's invited us for dinner in the hotel restaurant."

"Thank you for the compliment, James," replied Rosa, "the other girls made me put on more makeup than I've ever put on; and no, I haven't eaten, I was going to get something later."

"Well, believe me, you look great. It's good that you haven't eaten yet; it's this way." said James, indicating the way to the restaurant.

The Other Side of the Fence

In the restaurant, James introduced Rosa to his dad, "This is my dad, Edward Stirling." He was tall, slim and quite handsome, with a full head of greying fair hair. Very well dressed, he looked every inch a well-to-do businessman. He held out his hand and Rosa shook it.

"Pleased to meet you." Edward said.

"Oh, um, erm, I'm pleased to meet you too." an embarrassed Rosa replied, which was a lie, because she wasn't. He looked powerful, which scared her; she just wanted to run away. James put his arm around her waist and guided her to their table. They all sat down and the waiter bought the menus. The meals and drinks were ordered and the usual small talk took place; where do you live? What do you do? What does your dad do? etc.

Edward seemed nice but Rosa was cautious; several times, she could see him look at her wrists, which made her feel uncomfortable; she was pleased when the meal was over and he left.

"Sorry about the third-degree, Rosa." James said, "My dad's a top-class lawyer and can't seem to switch off and relax. Would you like to go for a walk in the grounds?" he asked her, "They are really something, we can take our drinks with us, there are lots of places to stop and sit to take in the views."

They went outside and walked for a while.

"Are you cold? he asked.

"No, I'm fine." Rosa replied.

"Here we are, view one." James said, as he beckoned her to sit down. As they sat, James turned to Rosa and said, "Rosa, I like you; you fascinate me, I love your shyness, you're so different from other girls. I loved it when you blushed on the plane, I thought then, I've got to get to know this girl better. Now I've met you a few times I feel you have been badly hurt and you have built a wall of caution around yourself, which intrigues me. Oh dear, sorry, a bit of my dad coming through there. I would like to hold you in my arms, even kiss you, but I feel that if I touched you, you would run away."

Rosa laughed out loud, but deep down she knew he had sussed her out. "James," she said, "permission to hold me and kiss me, if that's what you want to do."

He looked at her, put his arms around her and kissed her. At first, he felt she was only kissing him because he had asked her permission, but when he kissed her again, he could feel her relaxing and responding quite passionately. He was getting near to going further, but he pulled back; he didn't want to take advantage of her vulnerability.

"Rosa, I'm sorry if I just took advantage of you."

"James, don't feel bad. You're right, I have been badly hurt; I wanted you to kiss me and kiss me passionately. I needed you to do what you did, as I wanted to see how it felt and it felt nice. I'm sorry, James, it's nothing to do with what just happened; I'm not running away, it's just that it's getting late and I must go; the other girls are waiting to go to the foam party at that big night club. But there's a big pool party at our apartments' tomorrow evening and fireworks, if you and Michael would like to come?"

"I will ask Michael; I will definitely be there. I also fancy the foam party, it sounds good fun, but I can't come tonight though, I've got a pile of work to do; Dad needs it by tomorrow morning. But tomorrow's a definite; thanks."

Rosa looked at him and said, "I'm afraid it's our last night tomorrow, but we will have a lovely evening, and perhaps we could go for a late-night walk along the beach,

I haven't been on the beach yet." She then stood up, saying, "Sorry, James, I must go."

"I will walk you over to the apartments." he said, getting up.

They arrived at the apartment entrance; he kissed her once more and said, "Good night, see you tomorrow."

As he started to walk back to his hotel, Rosa called after him, "James!" He turned round and gave her a puzzled look. "We forgot to look at the view." she said, laughing out loud.

He smiled and hit his forehead with the flat of his hand, "Tomorrow!" he called back.

When Rosa opened the apartment door, she was met with seven girls, sitting, waiting to hear how she got on.

"Well," Gemma said, "start talking."

Rosa answered all the questions without waiting for them to be asked, "Yes, I really like him. I love his Irish accent, but I definitely didn't like his dad. Yes, we did kiss, lots of times. Yes, I really enjoyed it and yes, he's coming to the pool party, hopefully with his brother, tomorrow night." she said, as she was taking her shoes and dress off and changing into shorts, T-shirt and trainers, "Oh, and yes, when he saw me, he said I look stunning and I took his breath away." The girls all clapped and cheered. "Right, I'm ready, are you all ready to go and get soaked?"

"Yes!" they shouted and out the door they all went, down the six flights of stairs to the ground floor, one behind the other, singing, "Hi ho, hi ho, it's off to get soaked we go…."

24

Walking along the seafront to the nightclub, Gemma linked arms with Rosa.

"How did it go really?" Gemma asked.

"I didn't like James' dad very much; he's one of Irelands top lawyers and every time he spoke to me, I felt I was being interrogated. James said that he's like that with everyone; still very scary though." she shuddered and held on to Gemma's arm tighter.

"Sorry, Babe, I don't like the sound of him already, hope the dad hasn't put you off James?" said Gemma.

"No way, he's really sweet and attentive." replied Rosa, "I really like him; and I mean, really, like him. Watch this space."

Gemma looked at her puzzled, "What are you up to?" she asked.

The Other Side of the Fence

Rosa answered by putting her index finger up to her lips, "Shhh, you will have to wait until tomorrow; because tonight is for us." she said, as she pulled Gemma forward to make them walk quicker.

When the girls got to the night club, several of them left to meet boys they had arranged to meet the night before; the others found Antonio's bar; he was telling one of the girls that he finished at twelve, if she wanted to meet him.

"There goes another one." smirked Katie, as they looked around.

The nightclub looked different, there was now a three-foot-high wall, built in large blocks, all round the massive dance floor; there were a few openings for access to the floor, each one had a couple of uniformed staff, standing next to piles of blocks, ready to fill the spaces when the show started. People were already in the circle sitting on the blocks, talking.

"Listen girls," said Antonio, "make sure you finish your drinks by eleven thirty, because sometime between then and midnight, everyone will be dancing in the circle, when suddenly the foam will start, and you won't find each other, let alone your drinks; it's very messy, but fun. Enjoy."

Just after eleven thirty, the girls that were left in the group, started dancing in the circle along with hundreds of others.

"I'm so excited." said Katie, "If we lose each other, meet at Antonio's bar." No sooner had she said those words, than the foam started, and did it ever come down. You couldn't leave because all the breaks in the circle had been quickly filled in and the foam was soon up above their knees. They tried to dance but they were laughing so

The Other Side of the Fence

much, because they were slipping and sliding all over the place. Suddenly, there was a drum roll; everyone stopped dancing and looked around, wondering what was going to happen. Then, from the speakers, a countdown started; everyone looked at each other.

"FIVE, FOUR, THREE, TWO," a long pause, then, "ONE." At least six more tubes appeared and foam came pouring in from every direction. Everyone was absolutely covered, from head to toe, in foam; you couldn't even recognise the person next to you. Coloured light beams of red, blue, yellow and green, were shone onto everyone, making them look like weird, coloured snowmen and to finish it off, coloured glitter confetti was being blown by massive fans onto everyone.

After a while, as quick as it had started, it all stopped. The foam was suddenly being sucked away through fine gratings. There were loads of odd shoes littered about the circle, plus a few bras, panties, and men's underpants; all you could hear was uncontrolled laughter and see people looking for whatever they'd lost.

The girls found their way back to the meeting point. Antonio was just going and a new barman arriving.

"Did you English girls enjoy yourselves, yes?" asked Antonio.

Gemma replied, "Well, Antonio, we must admit it was definitely something we have never seen before and quite spectacular. And, Antonio, it is an experience we will never forget."

All the girls nodded in agreement, then suddenly burst out laughing, as they looked at each other, pointing and laughing at how funny they all looked, with coloured confetti stuck all over them; some even had foam still stuck to their hair. In a strange way, although they were all soaking wet, they had had the most brilliant time ever and all agreed, that they really enjoyed it and couldn't stop laughing, trying to hold each other up on the dance floor.

"Where did all those pieces of underwear come from?" Gemma asked Antonio.

"The bosses throw them in to make people laugh. That make people think they lose them. A big joke you say, yes?"

"I see;" said Gemma, "Yes, a very funny joke and a great night. The trouble is, we are all soaking wet now and I need to go home and get changed. Anyone else?"

"Yes." said Katie.

"And I will." said Rosa; but the others all wanted to stay.

The three girls linked arms as they walked home, looking wet and bedraggled.

Laughing, Katie said, "Don't take this the wrong way, Rosa, but you look quite a mess to how you looked earlier this evening."

"Yes, you're right there, Katie." added Gemma, "I called her Cinderella earlier, well Rosa, you look like her now; you look like you left the ball and didn't get home before Midnight."

"Oh yes, ha ha, very funny." Rosa replied.

Nearly at the apartment, they suddenly stopped.

"Who's that, sitting on the wall Rosa?" asked Gemma.

"Oh no, whatever do we look like?" said Rosa, "Oh look at him though, he always looks smart; he reminds me of the blond, clean cut American boy you see in films.

The Other Side of the Fence

They are usually captain of the football team; the one all the girls like. Well, this girl really likes him. He's seen us, wave. Hi there!" Rosa called. Waving and going over to James, she said, "As you can see by our appearance, we have been to the foam party. It was great fun; the foam was deep, up to our waist; I haven't laughed so much in a long time. But it makes you wet and uncomfortable, so we are going back to the apartments."

James said, smiling, "Sounded good fun; you all look really wet though, so don't get cold; I am still at work with my dad, I just popped out for some fresh air. Nice to see you; what good timing was that? I'd better go back now, in case I'm needed. I'm looking forward to seeing you all at the BBQ tonight, goodnight Rosa." he said with a wink and a wry smile.

Giggling, Rosa went all shy and said goodnight back.

They continued walking and soon got back to the apartments. They showered and got ready for bed. Katie made them all big mugs of her famous hot chocolate and they sat on the balcony. Now all warm and cosy, all agreed what a great time they were having and were looking forward to the BBQ later; but all agreed that having so much fun and being this happy, was tiring. Cupping their hands round their hot chocolate mugs, they voted for a quick shopping expedition, followed by a nice quiet day relaxing by the pool; that would be the order of the day, for the three of them, tomorrow.

25

When Rosa woke the next morning, she laid there thinking, "I wonder what Matt and everyone would think of how they live here? It's so different to back home; I haven't even seen a horse while I've been here." she smiled to herself, "I've got so much to tell them when I get back. I've enjoyed being with all the girls; we have laughed so much. Then there's James, who ever thought I would meet someone like him."

Rosa's thoughts were disturbed by Katie shouting, "One hour to get ready, for all those going shopping for souvenirs. We are not waiting."

"That's me." Rosa said, as she quickly got out of bed and started to dress.

After two hours of shopping, eight worn out girls arrived back at the apartment.

Katie said, "That was hard work, whose idea was it to go out and buy souvenirs for everyone? Still, it was quite funny with the Spanish trying to speak to us in English and

The Other Side of the Fence

us to them in Spanish. I think an afternoon by the pool is in order; hurry up though, they are closing it early, to get ready for the BBQ."

When they left the pool, they decided to do as much packing as they could, after they realized how hectic it was going to be, in the morning, with everyone trying to get ready before the taxis arrived at six. Thankfully, it was only a short ride to the airport, to get their nine o' clock flight home.

Before going to the BBQ, they all sat on the balcony, drinking wine and making toasts to a great few days. Some of the girls were tearful and didn't want to go home; some, because they had met boys.

Rosa had to steady herself as she stood up; she tapped on her glass, and said, "A toast to you lot, I love you all. If one of you hurry's up and gets married, we can come back again for another great hen party; three cheers for hen parties!"

Gemma looked at her, surprised at her out of character attitude. Tugging on Rosa's skirt, Katie said, "Who's had a lot to drink then?"

"Shhh," Rosa whispered, "tell you why, later."

They all headed down to the BBQ; Rosa was wearing the second of her new outfits, a yellow crop top, that showed off her tanned midriff, and a black flared skirt, that had a large yellow daisy as a pretend pocket; her hair, she had left loose with a slide of small yellow daisies on one side.

"I can see James and his brother; they have a table for us." said Katie.

James and Michael stood up as the girls arrived, followed by introductions all round.

There were large jugs of sangria and beer on all the tables. James said, "This is all very nice; how much do we owe you?"

"Our treat," said Gemma, "we got a big discount because we are staying at the apartments."

"Thanks girls, cheers." he said, toasting the girls.

The BBQ food was excellent and the sangria was a big hit with the girls. The waiters chatted up the girls and refilled their jugs several times. After the food, everyone was put into teams to do the quiz and play the games, which were great fun. About an hour before the fireworks started, a group began to play, and everyone started dancing.

James was sitting next to Rosa. He looked at her and said quietly, "I know you told me you can't dance; how about we do that walk on the beach you wanted to do?"

"Oh yes." she said and grabbed his hand as they got up, "We won't be long." she said to the others at the table. As they walked through the gates that led to the beach, Rosa turned and smiled a cheeky grin at Gemma and Katie.

"It's a bit dark, are you OK with that?" James asked.

"Of course I am;" she replied, as she clung on to his arm, "you're here to protect me, you're my prince."

They walked along the sea wall for a while, the only light they had, was from the moon that was shining on the sea. They could see several places where people had made dugouts in the sand, so they could lay out of the wind during the day.

"James, can you see that dugout down there, near the sea?" Rosa asked, pointing.

The Other Side of the Fence

"Yes, looks nice and cosy; I bet it took a long time to find all those big pebbles to build the wall round it."

"Come on, James, let's go and lie in it and watch the fireworks." she said and jumped down onto the beach. Then James heard her say, "Oh no! My pretty slide has just fallen out onto the sand and I can't see it."

"OK, don't move, Rosa, your prince is on his way." James said, taking his shoes off and following her. James felt all round where Rosa was standing.

"I've found it," he said, "I'll put it in my zipped pocket for safe keeping." Rosa thanked him and they made their way to the dugout.

They laid in the dugout, looking at the stars, telling each other the dates of their birthdays and what birth signs they were, when James asked, "Are you comfy Rosa?"

"Yes, I am." she answered, "I just love it. I think it's so romantic."

"It doesn't take a lot to please you, does it, Rosa?" So he could look at her, he pushed himself up onto one elbow. He could see her lovely face by the light of the moon, her eyes were closed, "You look lovely and so relaxed Rosa." he said.

She didn't move, she just smiled. He put his finger to her forehead to get a strand of her hair away from her eye; then, lightly stroking the side of her face, he ran his fingers gently back and forth across her lips and down her neck to her midriff. He teased her with his fingers by lightly touching her bare skin, moving his fingers across her stomach and going up under her crop top, hardly touching her breasts; she didn't stop him.

They were both breathing heavy, "Are you OK with what I just did?" he said, kissing the middle of her hand.

"Yes" she replied. After what Davenport did to her, she always thought she would freeze if anyone ever touched her sexually again; tonight though, was different, James was being romantic and gentle; she was happy, she was relaxed and was enjoying being slowly seduced. Whatever James was doing to her, she liked; she put her arm up to the back of his neck, ran her fingers through his hair and pulled him down; she wanted him to kiss her again. He kissed her several times, each kiss, more passionate than the last. He could feel her whole body relaxing and he knew she was enjoying how he was touching and kissing her. He kissed her gently on the neck, then, hardly touching her face, brushed his lips against her cheek till he reached her mouth and he kissed her, this time it was longer, and with more passion; she felt all tingly. He moved his hand to the bottom of her skirt; she didn't stop him, even when his fingers went up her skirt to her thigh and on to the top of her panties; she was feeling such an excitement, she had never felt before.

"Rosa, do you want me to stop?"

"No, James, please don't stop." He was so gentle, she felt herself wanting more from his every tender touch. She even helped when he took her panties off.

"Rosa," he said, "you're so lovely, I never thought this was going to happen. I didn't plan it."

Rosa didn't hear him; she responded by pushing her body into his; she was lost in emotions and sexual feelings of excitement, she thought she would never have. In fact, she didn't want it to end.

James had made love to her; she was relaxed, content, and just happy to lie in his arms for a while.

"That was so lovely, James." she said, "Thank you."

The Other Side of the Fence

He looked at her puzzled, "Thank you?" he said, "Is this a dream?"

"No, not a dream, James, more like fate; let me explain. Without going into details, the traumatic time I went through a few years ago, you have just helped me breakthrough that wall, you said I had built round me. I was so afraid I could never respond sexually to anyone. I know I'm young, but I honestly thought I would never like anyone ever touching me sexually or let them make love to me. Then, you came along; you were so nice and caring. When you held my hand on the plane and you accidentally touched my leg several times, you stirred emotions in me that I thought I had lost forever. When we got off the plane and you gave me your phone number, saying that you wanted to see me again, I just knew if the moment was right it would be you I would let make love to me."

"Oh, Rosa, you poor thing, I'm so sorry; how could anyone ever hurt you." he said and he held her tight. They lay in each other's arms in their little beach dugout and watched the fireworks going off at the other end of the beach. It was very late as they walked back to the apartments; they ended the night when they kissed and said their goodbyes at the main door of the apartment block.

"Rosa," James said, "even if we never see each other again, I will never forget you, or this wonderful night; you were amazing. If you ever go to Ireland, look me up, you have my phone number. If I'm ever in Norwich, I sort of know where you live, I will find you, if that's OK?"

Rosa looked at him and held his two hands, saying, "Yes, of course it's OK; friendship only though, James, I don't want any commitment." Rosa looked into his blue eyes, smiled, and with tears streaming down her face she said, "I love Ibiza and I will never forget you, James

Stirling, you will never know how much you helped me tonight and even since the first day we met."

From a side pocket in his knee length shorts, James took a neatly folded hanky; and with it her slide, He gently wiped away her tears, and gave her the hanky. He kissed the top of her head.

"And I love Ibiza as well." he said, smiling, "The hankie's clean, you keep it, a reminder of me; and can I keep this daisy thing as a reminder of you?"

"Now, that's what I call lovely souvenirs of a most memorable night; especially for me." she laughed.

Both laughing, before going their separate ways, they kissed for the last time. As Rosa went through the open doors into the apartment block, James was walking away, but couldn't resist looking back for one last look at a remarkable young lady, called Rosa Marie Maddox. Would they ever meet again?

26

By the time Rosa got back to the apartment, it was quite late. It was all dark and quiet, she could just about see all the suitcases and bags lined up in the hallway, ready for their early start. Luckily, she could also see to get ready for bed without putting the light on. As she got undressed, something fell on the floor, it was the hanky that James had given her; she had forgotten that she had tucked it into her skirt. When she saw it had the initials JS embroidered on it, she smiled, and thought that actually, it was a bit of a posh souvenir for the most important night in her life.

Gemma stirred, as Rosa got into bed, "You OK?" she asked.

Rosa whispered, "Yes, go back to sleep; I will tell you everything in the morning."

Rosa got into bed holding James' hanky next to her cheek; she just laid there smiling, saying over and over to herself, "I've got emotions, I've got feelings, I've got that

The Other Side of the Fence

part of my life back." Finally, she fell asleep with a contented look, that never left her face.

"Come on sleepy head, time to get up." Rosa heard Gemma saying, "Hurry up if you want a shower and any breakfast before we leave."

"I'm up." Rosa yawned.

No sooner was she up and ready than the taxis arrived. They crept out of the apartments as quietly as they could and went down in the lifts, to the reception, to hand in their keys.

When Gemma handed her key in, the man at the reception said, "Can you tell the girl dressed in blue, with the long black hair, that I want to see her please?"

Gemma wanted to ask him what he wanted her for, but didn't; instead, she went over to Rosa and said, "The receptionist wants to see you."

Rosa frowned and looked puzzled; Gemma just shrugged her shoulders, as if to say, don't ask me; then said, "Just be quick, we will be getting in the taxis."

Rosa walked over to the reception desk.

"You wanted to see me?" she asked.

"Yes," he answered, "I see you kiss man outside apartments last night."

"That's right, I did." she answered, blushing.

"Well, he bring present in here for you late last night." As he said this, he put a pretty pink bag on the counter, "The man say to open it up on the plane if you get scared and think of him. You OK Miss? You pleased with what I say?"

The Other Side of the Fence

"Yes, I am very pleased." Rosa answered, taking the bag off the counter. As she hurried out to join the others, she thanked him and blew him a kiss.

All the way to the airport, no one said a word. Things ran smoothly and they were on the plane and in the air in no time. This time, they sat with Katie by the window, Gemma in the middle and Rosa in the aisle seat. They got three hot chocolates, sat back and relaxed.

"Now we are all relaxed," Gemma whispered to Rosa, "you can tell us why you haven't stopped smiling since you got up. And, for goodness' sake, open that present."

"I think she looks like someone who had sex last night." Katie whispered, giggling.

"Shush!" Rosa said, nodding yes, and mouthed the words, 'I did and it was wonderful.'

Rosa started to open the pink bag; then burst out laughing, because suddenly, she was surrounded by all the other girls. She pulled something wrapped in tissue from the bag; then, unwrapping the tissue, two teddies appeared, one blue and one pink, joined together holding a big red heart. Embroidered on the heart were the words 'WE LOVE IBIZA'.

"Oh, that's just adorable." Rosa said, holding them up to her cheek and kissing them. Looking at the confused girls, she winked and said, "You had to be there." Then, cuddled the bears again.

"Are you seeing him again?" Katie asked.

"No, I don't want to. I told him it was just the once; end of." said Rosa, "James is lovely, kind and caring, for someone else. I'm too young for any commitment."

The Other Side of the Fence

They all had had a great time and at Norwich airport, there was lots of cuddles and teary, emotional goodbyes, as they all parted and headed to their different cars. Gemma's Jack was waiting outside to pick her and Rosa up.

When they arrived at Rosa's mum and dad's house, everyone was pleased to see them. They both checked over the long list of things that needed to be sorted at the riding school, as well as a full book of riding appointments; things were going to be hectic.

"Well, we are back. OK with you for an early start tomorrow, Rosa?" asked Gemma, "Enjoy the rest of today." she said as she gave Rosa a big hug.

"That's fine with me, I'm already exhausted though." she laughed, "Thank you so much for the last four days; they have definitely changed my life for the better." she said quietly, as she hugged Gemma back.

The next six weeks or so were hectic; the riding school was getting more and more popular and Rosa was also helping Gemma with the wedding plans.

"I didn't know there was so much to organize when you got married;" Rosa said to Gemma, "I've never seen so many lists."

"I know and don't forget we have an appointment for dresses to try on in a couple of weeks." Gemma replied.

Rosa sat on the bench talking to Matt, "I know you have never been abroad before Matt; you must try and go one day, it's so different, you will love it. Mind you, it is tiring; I've been so tired since I got back from Ibiza."

"I will." Matt answered, "You coming with me?"

"Of course, I'm coming with you; someone's got to look after you." she grinned.

The Other Side of the Fence

"Cheeky!" he said.

Changing the subject, Rosa said, "I've never been so busy in all my life."

"Have you and Gemma thought about getting help? I know you can have equine students from the college; they have to do so many hours work experience, in holiday time and weekends."

"Matt, I could kiss you." she said, as she got up, "Of course, that's the answer. We are so busy, we need help; they could help us and we can certainly help them. I can't believe neither of us have thought of it."

"Where are you going?" he asked.

"Off to tell Gemma and find out how you get them." she answered.

"What about my kiss?" he said laughing.

"I owe you, take this as a down payment." she laughed as she blew him a kiss.

The girls contacted the college and the following Saturday at nine o clock sharp, two seventeen-year-old girls, studying Equine Management, drove into the riding school's drive.

Rosa looked at Gemma and said, "I'm impressed already!"

"Hello, I'm Jess." Said the girl who got out of the passenger seat.

"And I'm Sydney." Said the other girl, holding her hand out to shake Rosa's outstretched hand.

"I'm Rosa and this is Gemma." said Rosa, "We are so pleased to meet you both. We are very busy, so hope you like it here. If you both go with Gemma, she will show you where things are and what we would like you to do." Off they went and Rosa did the biggest sigh of relief; help at last.

27

Jess and Sydney were brilliant workers and the four of them made an excellent team; Rosa and Gemma often wondered how they had ever managed to do everything without the girls before.

Although both Rosa and Gemma had both passed their driving tests months ago, they still hadn't been able to afford the expense of a car; any extra money they were earning, they were putting back into the business, building it up. However, by the time Christmas came, they felt the business was doing well enough for Rosa and Gemma to pay themselves a Christmas bonus and buy themselves a second-hand car; something they and their business needed.

Matt's son, Paul, had come to stay with his dad for two weeks. Rosa's mum and dad had invited them both over for Christmas dinner; it had been so much fun, they ended up staying all day. Over Christmas, there seemed to be a

The Other Side of the Fence

Christmas party nearly every day, at one house or another. A happy, but busy Christmas was definitely had by all.

New Year's Eve was good; her parents had laid on a BBQ and invited family and friends, including Sydney, Jess and their parents. They all sat round a small bonfire and at twelve o clock it was kisses all round. Rosa kissed Matt and laughingly said, "That's the one I owe you." Then, all twenty of them crossed hands and walked round the fire singing Auld Lang Syne. After toasting 1997, they sat and watched the New Year Fireworks going off all over the village.

A few days later, it was back to work. As well as children, they were getting quite a few adults wanting to learn to ride. As children were still off school, the appointment book was full. Katie now had her horse stabled at the stables, so if her friends were extra busy, or one of them needed time off, she used her horse or stood in for them. Although he was getting old, everyone loved Star, but the one the children loved the most was Katie's horse, Davie Boy; he was so funny, the children named him Davie the Daydreamer. If Katie was standing next to him or holding him by the reigns, he was very good and did everything right, but if she let go or walked away to get something, even if he had a rider on him, he just stopped, looked into space as if he was daydreaming, but no-way would he move. If Katie called him from a distance, he just put his head down and looked sad. The children called Davie, pretending they had something for him, but he still wouldn't move. He stood like that until she came back, and as soon as she stood near him or held his reigns, off he went as if he hadn't done anything wrong. If there were several children waiting for their lesson, to make them laugh, Katie would pretend she had forgotten something, so Davie would do his party piece, as she called it.

As well as their own horses, there were four other horses being stabled. The girls liked it because it was easy money; the owners could come and ride their horse anytime they wanted but were responsible for looking after and cleaning out their own horses, or they could pay the girls extra to do it for them. The stables were becoming very popular; Rosa's dad had empty stables that were close-by and he was already letting the girls use them for their stabling. The girls were also in the process of having a smaller training square built for first time riders, as they didn't want them to feel intimidated by the more experienced riders having their lessons. A large new stable block was going to be their next priority.

By the end of January, it was time for bridesmaid dresses to be fitted.

"Only twelve weeks to go." said Gemma, "Time is going so fast."

Rosa was quite upset when she tried on her bridesmaid's dress, it was quite tight and would have to be returned for a larger size.

"Honest Gemma, I've been trying to lose weight but it's so hard." Rosa said.

"Don't worry about it, Babe, you're going to look gorgeous anyway." Replied Gemma.

They had left Sydney and Jess back at the stables, clearing out the horses and Rosa went to see how they were getting on. Jess came past her with a wheelbarrow full of horse manure; Rosa took one look, ran behind a tree and was violently sick.

Gemma ran up to her and asked, "Are you OK? Whatever bought that on? Come on, I will drive you home. We can manage, go and get a good rest, ready for tomorrow."

The Other Side of the Fence

"Thanks Gemma, I still feel a bit queasy. I don't know what happened, it was the smell that did it."

The next morning, Gemma drove up to the Maddox's house and pipped on the horn. Mrs. Maddox came out and said to Gemma through the car window, "She won't be long. She says she feels alright but I think she's still not well, she is always tired and feeling sick; not only from what upset her yesterday, I'm sure I heard her being sick again earlier."

With that, the door opened and out came Rosa.

"Bye, Mum." Rosa called, "I'm ready." she said to Gemma, as she got in the passenger seat.

Gemma drove out the drive onto the road but instead of turning left down the lane to go to their stables, she carried on.

"Where are you going?" Rosa asked.

"To the chemist on the High Street." Gemma replied.

"Are you ill?"

"No, it's for you."

"Gemma," Rosa said, "I'm OK now, I don't need anything; it's just a bug, and it will go away on its own."

"I don't think so, well definitely not for a few more months."

Rosa looked at her shocked, "Whatever are you on about?"

Gemma stopped the car in front of the chemist.

"Have you got any money on you?" Gemma asked Rosa. Rosa nodded. "Then go in and buy a pregnancy test kit."

The Other Side of the Fence

"You're pregnant? How wonderful." Rosa smiled.

"Rosa, are you stupid? No, not me, you!"

They looked at each other, Rosa's eyes were big and her mouth was wide open but no words were coming out.

"Rosa, just think about things. You're tired all the time, your dress was tight and now you're being sick several days in a row. Just go in and buy the test so we know"

"Don't talk daft Gemma." said Rosa shaking her head, "You're the one being stupid. I've only had sex that one time in Ibiza."

"Just do it to please me and we will go and have a cuppa at Maise's café. I've asked Katie to go in today and she will do the lessons until we get there."

"I will feel stupid; I'm going to tell them the test is for you. I will do it, but what a complete waste of money."

Rosa got out the car, as if she didn't care but was visibly shaking under her coat. She pushed the shop door open, stood on the mat and practically left the floor when the loudest bell ever, rang. The shop assistant came from the back of the shop.

"Sorry about that," she said, "it is very loud." Rosa managed to get the right words out, bought the test and left the shop.

28

Gemma drove to the café; fortunately, it was empty. They sat down with their drinks but Rosa took forever to drink hers.

"I know what you're doing, Rosa.", Gemma said, "You might as well drink up; this isn't going away, so let's get it over with." When Rosa had finished, Gemma looked around and said, "There's no one here; go to the toilet, read what it says; do it and come back; we will sit in the car and wait for the result."

"OK Miss Bossy Boots." Rosa said. As she got up, she pretended she didn't care, but she was still physically shaking. In the toilet, she locked the door, sat on the toilet, read the instructions and did exactly what it said. She then went back into the café, paid for their drinks and they went back to the car.

Rosa had wrapped the tester in a serviette.

"You look." she said, giving it to Gemma. "Hurry up, we look suspicious; no one will ever guess what I just passed to you."

Gemma looked at the tester; then she looked at Rosa, held her hand and said, "It says you're pregnant."

A shocked Rosa closed her eyes; her mind was all over the place. She leaned forward, putting her two hands on the dashboard and rested her head on her hands.

Putting her arm around Rosa's shoulders, a concerned Gemma said, "I'm here for you, Babe. I won't let you down; what do you want me to do?"

Rosa didn't answer, they just sat there in the car, neither one speaking. The silence seemed to go on forever.

Finally, Rosa lifted her head, she looked at Gemma and said, "I honestly don't know what to say Gemma, I think I need to be on my own for a while. I need to take in what's just happened and think about the consequences. Will you take me to the stables please? I would like to ride Star; take him down the lanes, while I think. I hope you can manage the appointments. I will meet up with you and Katie later."

A good five hours later, Rosa appeared back at the stables. She put Star in his stable and said to the girls, "As soon as you have all finished, can we have a meeting in the office? Gemma, can I see you as soon as, please?"

When Gemma got to the office, Rosa was sitting having a cup of tea.

"I've made a pot, if you want one?" Rosa said.

Gemma poured herself a tea, sat down and asked, "You OK?"

"Yes." Rosa answered, "I will tell you what's happened since I last saw you and what I intend to do. Well, basically it's all up to you and Katie."

"I'm listening." Gemma said

"Well, I was riding Star along the path by the river and met Matt walking his dogs; he was going the same way as me, so I got off and walked with him. You know him, he can read me like a book. Well, it all came tumbling out with floods of tears and what am I going to dos. Next thing I know, I'm booked in to see the nurse at the surgery at three o' clock. One of Matt's men came with his car, took Star and his dogs, then Matt drove me to the surgery; they were so lovely. I've got to make more appointments, but for now they have confirmed that I'm three months pregnant. I've decided that I want to keep the baby." Gemma squeezed her hand, as Rosa continued, "He or she will be born sometime in July. I will be OK to help at the stables for months, but then it will get harder as the due date gets near; this is where you and Katie come in. First, I would like you to become a partner; then, as I get near to the baby being born, I thought that with your agreement, instead of Katie just helping us occasionally and because we are so busy, and it's going to get even busier as the weather gets warmer; we could ask Katie to join us permanently, and if Sydney and Jess still do their work experience at holiday times, we could offer to pay them to work every weekend, to help us out. I'm sure we can manage; I know it will be more expense, but I'm willing to take a pay cut; and if we keep expanding as quick as we are, Matt said that if we get the funding for the new block of stables we need, he will help get them built. I think we could manage OK, with more livery horses its good easy money. What do you think?"

"Have you told your mum and dad yet?" Gemma asked.

The Other Side of the Fence

"No, because before I do anything else, I've got to know what you and the girls think, and if you're all OK with what I've just said."

With that, there was a knock on the door.

"Just a minute!" Rosa called, then looked at Gemma.

"I'm with you one hundred percent, Babe." Gemma said, "Let's go for it, and thank you."

A relieved Rosa stood up and hugged her, saying, "I won't let this take away the excitement of your wedding, I will just be the pregnant bridesmaid standing at the back on the photos."

They both laughed.

"Come in girls!" Rosa called.

The three girls stood in front of Rosa and Gemma, they all looked as if they thought they were going to get the sack.

"Come on my lovelies, give us a smile." said Gemma.

"Have we done something wrong?" Katie asked.

"Oh, bless your hearts, definitely not; this is to tell you all that Rosa's pregnant." Gemma said.

All three girls looked surprised. Then, looking at each other, broad smiles came across their faces; and, seeing a happy Rosa, they all went over to hug her and offered their congratulations.

"OK, OK, calm down, we want to put a proposition to you." Rosa said.

Everything was explained to them. All three girls agreed with the proposition and all three were excited with, as they called it, their new promotions.

"Thank you so much." Rosa said, "We will sort everything out tomorrow. For now, I've got to go and do the hard part and tell my mum and dad."

29

Rosa left the girls at the stables and hurried home. She opened the front door quietly and called, "Mum!"

"In the lounge dear." her mum called back. Rosa entered the cosy lounge where her mum and dad were sitting in front of a big log fire.

"Come and sit down and get yourself warm." her dad said.

"You're home early dear; everything OK?" her mum asked.

"I'm fine, I just need to talk to you both." she said, as she sat down, "But I don't want you to get upset or alarmed at what I'm going to say. I've sorted everything out and if you want me to leave when I tell you, I will understand."

"My goodness, Rosa, you're scaring me; what ever are you going to say?" her worried mum said.

Rosa took a deep breath and said, "I'm three months pregnant."

Her mum stood up and went to sit next to Rosa.

"We thought you might be." her mum said, as she put her arm around Rosa's shoulders.

Rosa looked at her mum and then at her dad, who just nodded and said, "Yes, Rosa, we have been thinking that you must be pregnant for a couple of weeks now, but we can't work out who the father is, unless it's Matt?"

"No, it's not Matt's, it is someone I met when I was on Gemma's hen party in Ibiza; he's an accountant, called James. I won't be telling him because he lives in Ireland and I will probably never see him again. It was just the once. I've already been to the doctors, Matt took me; the baby's due in July. Daddy, I haven't let you down, I've sorted the riding school out; Gemma and the girls were brilliant. I've asked Gemma to become a partner and they are going to run it. I'm going to work as long as I can and Matt said that if we get funding and your permission to use the field next to the riding school, he will help us build some more stables, that can earn us a lot more money." Rosa stopped talking and looked at her dad, "Daddy, say something. Are you ashamed of me? Do you want me to find somewhere else to live?"

"No, of course not." her dad replied, "In fact, we have already discussed how we would feel, and what to do, if you did tell us that you were pregnant. Now we know the situation, we can't say we are too pleased, but you know we will stand by you. Let's just have a quiet night; no more talking about things tonight. We just need to let it all sink in, think what's best for everyone and discuss it further tomorrow. All agreed?" They all nodded. "Then that's a yes then." he said, then he put his glasses on, picked up a newspaper and started to read it.

The Other Side of the Fence

That night, Rosa went to bed early; she laid there for ages, with everything going round and round in her mind. One thing she did know, was what a lucky girl she was; she had been blessed with the best parents and friends anyone could wish for. She couldn't stop herself from thinking back to the lovely time she'd had in Ibiza; meeting James Stirling, their holiday romance and saying to him that she didn't want any commitment.

"Well Rosa Maddox, now you're going to have his baby, so you have got commitment. If you never see James again, the baby will never know its father." she thought, "For goodness' sake Rosa, stop thinking; haven't you had enough to worry about for today? Just put that worry to the back of the queue for another day." she said to herself, "Consider it done!" she smiled to herself as she snuggled down into her warm bed, wondering if it would be a boy or a girl. Before she knew it, she had fallen fast asleep.

30

The next morning, Rosa woke up still smiling. As she lay on the bed, she stretched her whole body and said out loud, "Come on, up you get, Mummy." When she got up, she went and looked at herself in the mirror and thought, "No, can't tell yet, I hope I will look OK in my bridesmaid's dress for Gemma's wedding." She got dressed and went through to the kitchen.

Her dad looked at her. "Morning, Princess, did you sleep well?"

"Eventually, Daddy." she answered, "Mmm, that breakfast smells delicious, Mum." she said to her mum, who was preparing a full English breakfast.

"That's nice to hear, Rosa; instead of you walking in and running back to the bathroom. I've cooked plenty, if you would like some; but I will keep it warm because your dad wants to talk to you."

The Other Side of the Fence

As they all sat having a cup of tea, her dad said, "Now, Rosa, we have a lot to discuss today. First, good girl for sorting the school out, I'm sure it will run OK. Yes, to the field, I thought that would come up eventually anyway, so I was prepared. I would have lent you the money to build the stables but I need it, I will tell you why later. I will come with you and Gemma to the bank and stand as guarantor for you, so you can get a loan; then you will have the funding to build a block of eight stables, plus enough extra to lay on water and electric. You will also need an option to borrow more, because if what you are doing is successful, you will need a further loan to expand and build another block. How does all that sound?" he said to a dumbfounded Rosa. "Is Gemma calling for you today? Because it's about the name of the riding school; if she's to become a partner, we think it should be changed; you can't keep calling it Rosa Maddox, so we need to speak with her about all of this and see what name, if any, she thinks the school should be changed to."

Rosa's eyes and mouth were wide open, "Wow, Daddy; when you do something, you do it. I'm one hundred percent in agreement with everything you have said. It doesn't sound as if you and Mum have had any time for sleep."

As Rosa's mother got the breakfast on the table, they heard the hoot of a car horn.

"That's Gemma." Rosa said, as she got up, "I will go and tell her to come in."

"Hello, Mr. Maddox and Mrs. M." Gemma said, as she came into the kitchen.

Rosa said, "Can you sit down, Gemma; Daddy has something to tell you."

After hearing everything, Gemma just sat there.

The Other Side of the Fence

"Well, what an exciting year we have got ahead of us." she said, "Thank you for thinking of me and saying that about the name of the riding school. As it happens, I have a name I like, I read it in a book a while back. I'm fine if you don't like it though."

"Go on," Rosa said, "what is it?"

"The Four Horseshoes."

"Hmmm," Mr. Maddox said, "The Four Horseshoes Riding School." He looked at his wife; she nodded, "Rosa?"

"I love it Daddy." an excited Rosa said.

Looking at Gemma, Billy said, "I like it as well; so, The Four Horseshoes Riding School it is then. I will sort everything and get the new sign made. You two get your account books up to date and we will make an appointment at the bank as soon as possible. Don't forget you will need plans drawn up, so start a rough drawing of what you would like. Right, are we ever going to have this breakfast? Rosa, can you make some fresh tea? Gemma, help yourself to whatever you want, there's plenty."

They all sat eating a hearty breakfast. Rosa looked lovingly at her parents.

"I hope they know how much I love them." she thought, as she shook her head in disbelief, on what a lovely start to the day it had been.

31

The next few months flew by. Rosa was now seven months pregnant and was feeling quite well. The riding school was going from strength to strength; planning permission had been approved for the now much needed extra stables and the building work was well underway.

A month earlier, was Gemma's wedding and the whole day had gone smoothly. It felt quite warm, for an April wedding, with the sun shining for most of the day. The whole village seemed to have turned out to line the streets, as Gemma went to and from the church in a beautifully decorated horse and carriage. The whole wedding scene was colour coordinated, in lilac, purple, pink and white. The small bridesmaids, Elsie, Amelia and Lyla, all under five, were adorable, well behaved and a joy to watch. Both sets of parents looked stunning in their wedding outfits, with both mums wearing glamorous hats. Rosa hardly recognised Gemma's husband to be and his best man, who looked very smart in their suits, with the three-quarter length jackets. Then, there was the Bride, who looked breath-taking. When she arrived at the church and the wedding march started to play, everyone turned to see this beautiful bride walking down the aisle. Rosa's bridesmaid's dress was perfect; she looked a bit weighty, but passed the test of, was she, or wasn't she pregnant. Lovely slim Katie was her usual perfect blonde self and looked a picture in her bridesmaid's dress. As they left the church, a rapturous peal of bell ringing filled the streets.

The reception had the happiest of party atmospheres. At the given signal, everyone went outside and when the whistle blew, they all let go of a helium balloon, they had been given, to a chorus of 'Congratulations'. Just one special, happy wedding day.

A tanned Gemma, who had just arrived back from honeymoon, sat with all the girls in the office, excitedly looking through the wedding photos of, as Gemma kept saying, the best day ever, and the most perfect honeymoon. Then, looking sad, she said, "Now it's back to work tomorrow."

When Rosa arrived home from the stables later, her mum said, "There's a letter for you on the table, it looks important. A puzzled Rosa opened it. "What is it?" her mum asked, "You look all serious; what ever does it say?"

"It's from the hospital psychology department, to say I've missed my appointment by a month. They're not very happy and I must make an appointment immediately. I've been so busy with everything lately, I completely forgot. It's too late now, so I will ring them first thing in the morning."

On the day of her rescheduled appointment, her mum asked Rosa, "Do you want me to come with you? I can help explain how busy you have been."

"Yes please Mum, I am rather nervous; especially how things will be, when they see that I'm pregnant."

The Other Side of the Fence

At the hospital, Rosa and her mum sat in silence, waiting for her turn.

"Rosa Maddox?" a voice called.

Rosa jumped up and said to her mum, "I will go in first and ask for you to come in if I can't handle it." Rosa walked slowly into the councillor's room.

When Mrs. Bennett saw that Rosa was pregnant, a look of horror appeared on her face. Sitting at her desk, shaking her head, she said, "I'm not at all pleased, Rosa, I'm disappointed in you; you were doing so well. I'm afraid I will have to report this."

Rosa, looking puzzled, said, "I don't understand; can my mother come in please?"

When her mum came in, Mrs. Bennett started explaining to her why she would have to report Rosa's situation.

"This could set Rosa back a few years." she said.

"Why? Everything's fine, I feel so well." Rosa interrupted.

"Thank goodness it is and you do." replied Mrs. Bennett, "Don't you realize, Rosa, if anything had gone wrong and you weren't under supervision, there's no telling how or what your response would have been. A missed appointment on top of this; you have been playing a very dangerous game. So far, you have been lucky; now, I want you to make appointments every four weeks, and phone me immediately if there are any setbacks. OK Rosa, Mrs. Maddox?"

"Yes, definitely. We understand now; so sorry for any misunderstanding on our part." Rosa's mum said.

The Other Side of the Fence

After the shock at the seriousness of not informing the councillor about Rosa's situation, they were pleased over the next few weeks with Rosa's progress and health, and that all was well with the baby.

A couple of weeks later, Gemma was dropping Rosa off at home from the stables. As they drove up to the front door, Gemma stopped the car and said, "Wow! Rosa, whose silver Porsche is that?"

"I've no idea." Rosa answered, "Are you coming in to find out?"

"I sure am." Gemma replied.

They entered the house and heard voices coming from Rosa's parent's lounge. They looked at each other; Rosa shrugged her shoulders and shook her head.

"Is that you Rosa?" her mum called, "There's someone here to see you."

What a shock the two girls got as they entered the lounge.

"Hello Rosa, Gemma, lovely to see you both." In front of them stood a smiling James Stirling and his brother, Michael.

"James, what are you doing here; how did you find me?" a shocked Rosa asked.

"By accident actually." he said, "Michael and I are working in Norwich for a couple of days. We finished early, so I suggested we go for a drive. As we drove, we saw a signpost that named the village where I thought you lived, so we drove here. I knew you live on a farm near the river and as we drove past here, Michael saw River Walk Road. We drove down it and found this delightful pub and restaurant at the side of the river, so we had a drink and a

The Other Side of the Fence

meal. As we drove back, we were about to turn onto the main road back to Norwich, when I saw your mum pull up on the drive of the farmhouse. Michael got out the car and asked her if she knew you; talk about coincidences. We explained who we were and your mum kindly invited us in. And here we are." He looked at Rosa, smiled and said, "I think we need to talk, don't you?"

"Yes, definitely." Rosa said, "Excuse us everyone." She took James through to her lounge.

"I'm gobsmacked" he said, as she shut the door, "I just know it's my baby, isn't it?"

"Yes, of course it is. I've never been with anyone else."

"Wow, if we hadn't done this today, would I ever have found out that I was a father?" he asked.

"To be honest James, I am still getting used to it myself. I didn't' know what to do; thinking about how you would react, when someone you hardly knew rang you after a holiday one night stand and told you that you were about to become a father. I was waiting until the baby was born and knew everything was OK, to decide when to tell you."

James took both her hands and said, "I want to be involved with the baby. Promise me you will let me know as soon as the baby is born. Is there anything you need? What am I saying, of course there is, I'm sure you need lots of baby things. Before I go, I will write you a cheque; yes, that's the best. Do you mind, I need to sit down." He sat down at the table, still in shock. "Wow, I'm going to be a dad, I hope it's a girl; or a boy; I really don't mind which. Wait till I tell my mum and dad."

"James," Rosa said, "I still don't want any commitment between us two."

"I'm actually pleased you said that. You see, I have a girlfriend; well, let's say I might have a girlfriend; I don't know how she will take this news. I hope she will be OK because I really like her. I don't know if you have heard of her, Lily Louise Doyle, she's a well-known Irish model; she lives near me and we've been together five months."

Before he left, James wrote Rosa a cheque for five hundred pounds and gave her all his details.

"I will send you some more money next month and I will make arrangements, when the baby arrives, to pay you so much a month."

They agreed that James would be named as the father on the birth certificate and that he would always be involved with the baby. In all, he was proving to be a true gentleman. What could possibly go wrong?

32

A week later, celebrations were being prepared for Rosa's twenty-first birthday. As a surprise, her mum, dad, aunts, and uncles, had decorated the village hall and invited all Rosa's family and friends. They had got caterers in to do a buffet spread, had a twenty first birthday cake made and hired a DJ; all done without Rosa knowing.

On the morning of her birthday, her parents gave her their cards and all the cards that had come through the post.

"Happy Birthday, Princess." her dad said, "What have you got planned?"

"Nothing really, everyone's busy."

"You must be seeing Gemma or Matt today?" he said.

"No, well I might see Gemma, if she gets back in time. She had to go somewhere important with her husband; she said if they are not back too late, they will come round and we can go to the pub."

"What about Matt?"

"He's gone to see his boy; he forgot it was my birthday."

"Oh Rosa, I'm so sorry." her mum said, "At least you have got some lovely cards. What about if your dad rings the Riverside restaurant and books a meal for us three? And if Gemma gets back in time, we will already be at the pub. How's that sound?"

"OK, Mum, that sounds better than just sitting here all night." Rosa said.

"Let's do that then; Billy will you ring and book us a table for about six thirty tonight please?"

"Consider it done." Billy replied.

That evening, when it was time to go to the restaurant, Rosa said to her mum, "We all ready then? We'd better be going; where's dad?"

"I'm here." said a voice coming from the other room. Just as they reached the front door, the house phone rang; Rosa's dad went back to answer it.

Rosa could hear her dad saying, "I was just on my way out, so I will bring you my big torches; at least they will give you a bit of light later."

"What is it?" his wife asked, as he put the phone down.

"It's my brother, Henry, he's at the village hall. The choir will be arriving later tonight for practice and there's no electricity. It's too late to stop them coming now; he rung the electricians but there was only the answer machine, saying to leave your number and message and they will get back to you. He wants to borrow my big torches we use for night fishing, just in case, when they finish, it's too dark for him to see to lock up properly. It shouldn't take long, we can all go, then I will just hand the torches over and we will be on our way; it won't make us late. Is that OK?"

"Of course it is." Rosa replied.

When they arrived at the village hall, Rosa's dad got out the car, opened the boot and said, "Rosa can you give me a hand please? If you could be taking these two torches to Henry, I will bring the really big one."

Rosa got out the car; he gave her the torches and asked, "Can you go ahead and tell Henry we are here please?"

"OK, Daddy." she replied.

Rosa's mum suddenly got out the car and called Rosa, "Wait Rosa, be careful, it's very dark. I'd better come with you; I can say hello to Henry, I haven't seen him in a while." As they both walked up the path to the door, she said, "I was thinking, it's a good job they have a piano as well as the electric organ."

"Here, let me open the door for you Rosa." her dad said, coming up from behind the two of them.

The door swung open and a chorus of, 'SURPRISE!' and, 'HAPPY BIRTHDAY!' took a shocked looking Rosa completely by surprise; the hall was full of smiling family and friends in party hats, pulling poppers and blowing party blowers.

She put both hands up to her mouth; for a moment, no words came out. She looked round the hall at all the faces she knew; she saw Matt standing next to Gemma and her husband.

"Matt Johnson! I thought." Rosa gasped, "And you, Gemma. After what you both said," shaking her head and tutting, "I can't believe you two kept this from me."

Rosa continued looking round the hall; as she saw certain people she smiled and pointed at them shaking her head and mouthing the words, 'Can't believe you're so devious.'

Turning back to her mum and dad, she hugged them both and said, "Thank you so much. What a lot of work has gone into this; even to how you got me here tonight. I love it."

Looking at all those around her, she said, "I can't tell you how impressed I am by the organisation that's gone into all this; I feel truly blessed."

Rosa's dad then shouted, for the benefit of everyone else, "OK everyone, she's impressed and says thank you all for coming. Now start the music, open the buffet and let the party begin!"

With her family and friends, she felt truly loved; It was a wonderful Happy Birthday; a night she would never forget.

33

True to his word, four weeks later, James sent Rosa a further five hundred pounds; attached was a letter for Rosa, asking to let him know, as soon as possible, when the baby was born.

Rosa, Gemma and Rosa's mother had a fabulous day shopping in Norwich. They bought the baby lots of equipment, including a crib, a pram that doubled as a baby seat for the car, plus pram and crib covers and quite a few outfits for the baby. They had had a long but very enjoyable day; but they finally decided they all needed a rest, especially Rosa, at nearly nine months. What they didn't know, was that for the last few weeks, Rosa had been in a lot of pain with her back and legs. Being pregnant, she wasn't allowed her usual painkillers, so she was having to take the only mild painkiller she was allowed. If anyone asked if she was OK, Rosa would laugh it off as the aftereffects of too much dancing at her twenty-first birthday party. She was grateful when they stopped for afternoon tea and just sat talking.

The Other Side of the Fence

"I can't believe how much everything has cost." said Rosa.

Her mum replied, "Thank goodness James sent that money. He seems such a nice young man, Rosa, are you sure there is nothing between you two?"

"Mum, that's a definite no, anyway he's got a girlfriend. He said he wants to be involved with the baby and that's fine with me."

A week later, Rosa had one more counselling session with Mrs. Bennett before she gave birth. Her mum was driving her to the appointment at the hospital. As they sat waiting at traffic lights, a car pulled up beside them and several pips of the car horn made them look; It was Charles Davenport in his sports car. When the lights changed, he roared away, making his tyres screech.

"Stupid idiot!" Rosa said.

"Take no notice." her mum said.

They waited in reception for what seemed forever. Finally, a young girl showed Rosa into Mrs. Bennett's office and said, "Sorry, Mrs. Bennett's running a bit late but she shouldn't be too long."

Rosa's mum went to get a cup of tea while she waited for her daughter. Sitting alone in the office, waiting for Mrs. Bennett, Rosa's thoughts went wild; she suddenly felt vulnerable, she heard a noise, she looked behind her and then shuddered and thought, "What if Davenport threatens the baby when its born." Rosa started to shake, she clenched the arms of the chair and started to do the deep breathing she had been taught to do, but she couldn't get her breath.

Mrs. Bennett entered the room, she could see what was happening and rang for a nurse who came running in. She

The Other Side of the Fence

took Rosa's temperature and blood pressure, which was really high.

"I'm fine." Rosa tried to say, but it came out all jumbled.

"Better get her to maternity, a doctor needs to check her over." the nurse said, "I don't like that high blood pressure reading, it can be quite dangerous."

They called Rosa's Mum in to explain what they were going to do.

"Has she been ill before coming here today?" the nurse asked.

"No, we had a lovely day out in Norwich yesterday; perhaps she is over-tired?"

"No, something has upset her; this looks more like a panic attack."

Two hospital porters arrived with a wheelchair, to take Rosa up to maternity. As they left, Mrs. Bennett said to the nurse, "Make sure I get a full report of this situation."

By the time the doctor saw Rosa, she had calmed down and her blood pressure was reasonable. After a few hours rest the doctor gave permission for her to go home, on the condition that she rested and didn't do any work. Her Mum took full responsibility and they were able to leave the hospital.

When they got home her mum asked, "What ever brought that on Rosa? I was so frightened, I thought you were going to lose the baby."

"I'm so sorry," Rosa said, "it just came from nowhere. It scared me as well. I feel OK now."

The Other Side of the Fence

"You just sit and rest, I will make sure everything that needs to be done, will get done. From now on you must do everything the doctors say."

Over the next few weeks, Rosa didn't go far from the house, as it was nearly time for the baby to be born. Although Rosa didn't go out, Gemma called every evening to update her on what was happening with the riding school and the new stable buildings. Rosa was pleased it was all running smoothly, thanks to Gemma, Katie, Sydney and Jess.

"Do you know what, Gemma? I could get used to just sitting here and letting you four run everything." Rosa said.

"Oh no you don't." said Gemma, "As soon as the baby's born, you're off your backside and back to work; then, us four can all have a rest."

"Spoilsport." Rosa said, laughing.

Two days before her due date and feeling exhausted, Rosa went to bed early. Just after midnight, she woke up with a sharp pain in her stomach. She sat on the side of the bed and after a few minutes, there was another sharp pain.

"You need to get to the toilet quick." she said to herself. She got there, just as her waters broke. Talking to herself, she said, "Don't panic. Now think, is it too soon to wake mum and dad?" She got back to the bedroom and started to read the book about having a baby. She decided, "Yes, it's the baby, it's happening." She calmly started to get herself ready for the hospital. "I will ring the alarm, after two more contractions." No sooner had she thought that, than the first one happened, then she panicked and rang the alarm to call them.

Her mum came running into the bedroom.

"Is it the baby?" she asked.

The Other Side of the Fence

"Yes." Rosa said, "I think I need to go to the hospital, as soon as possible." She then screamed out loud, as a really strong contraction came.

"Two minutes to get our clothes on, then we are ready." her mum said, as she rushed out the door.

Once in the car, Rosa's dad said, "Don't worry, Princess, we will soon be at the hospital; the roads are practically empty at this time of night."

Rosa laid in the back of the car; besides the contractions, she felt quite calm. She had no idea whether she was having a boy or girl.

"I don't mind, as long as the baby's OK." she thought.

As the car pulled into the hospital grounds, her dad said, "We're here, are you OK, Rosa?"

"I will be soon, when it's all over and they hand me my little baby." she said.

They had phoned ahead, so by the time they arrived everything was ready. Rosa was whisked away and her mum sat in the waiting room, excitedly waiting for the arrival of their grandchild, while her dad paced up and down.

"This takes me back a few years Em." he said, making his wife smile.

Six hours later, they were called in to the ward to meet their beautiful blonde, blue eyed, seven-pound six-ounce granddaughter, Eva Marie Maddox. Everything had gone OK; mother and daughter were fine. Rosa and the baby were sound asleep, so her mum and dad, after lots of happy tears, left their daughter a note saying, she's so beautiful; can't wait to hold her. Love you both. See you tomorrow.

They left the hospital to go home. On the way, Billy said, "It's been a long day, but better ring and tell everyone about the baby first. Then we can get some much welcome sleep ourselves."

34

While she was in hospital, every time Rosa held her beautiful baby daughter, she couldn't help thinking that there was no way James Stirling could deny he was the father of Eva Marie. She had his blue eyes and blonde hair; Rosa could already see a few curls in it. Rosa smiled and thought, "She's even got a dimple in her chin, the same as his." Eva Marie was, in fact, his double. Rosa checked ten tiny fingers and ten toes, several times, even though the nurses had told her to relax, the baby was complete and doing fine.

Rosa was in a lot of pain, so because of the heavy medication she had been prescribed, she could not breast feed the baby. Giving birth and the weight she had gained over the last few months had taken its toll on her body; her back and legs were weak and painful and she was finding it hard to stand up for any length of time. She was only being allowed to go home the next day because her mum would be there to look after her and the baby. Rosa was beyond excited at the thought of going home.

Rosa was bottle feeding Eva Marie, when a head appeared round the door and said, "Hello there my lovely."

"Brenda!" Rosa said excitedly, giving her the biggest smile.

"Can't stay long, I'm back on duty in fifteen minutes; I just had to come and see this beautiful baby I was told about."

"How did you know I was here? I was going to ask someone before I got discharged, if it was possible to let you know I was here."

"You know me, I know everything that goes on in here." Brenda said, laughing, "No not really; one of my nurses was getting something from the maternity ward and saw you. They remembered how friendly we were, so they told me. They were right about the baby though, she is beautiful, a real cutie. They also said there was a wheelchair next to your bed, what's all that about?"

Rosa explained about her back and legs, and how much pain she was in. "The doctors said my legs will get stronger again. It may take a few months, but they will be OK."

Brenda gave Rosa a hug, then kissed her finger and touched the baby's forehead.

"I must go," she said, "keep me informed on yours and the baby's progress. Take this and buy her something from me." She put an envelope, containing money, in Rosa's hand.

"Oh Brenda, thank you so much. Give me your phone number, so we can keep in touch." They swapped phone numbers and Brenda left.

The Other Side of the Fence

The next day, Rosa left the hospital to go home. As well as her mum, she needed her dad to meet her, so he could push her in the wheelchair, from the hospital to the car.

When they Arrived at the farmhouse, her dad pushed her into their kitchen, he then went back and helped his wife carry the car seat the sleeping baby was in.

Rosa's mum had made sandwiches earlier that day and they decided that as Eva Marie was asleep, there was no rush for Rosa to go through to her rooms. Relaxing at the kitchen table, they sat talking, making lists of things to do and having tea and sandwiches.

Her mum said, "When you're settled, Rosa, you have all these cards and presents to open."

"Oh, how lovely." Rosa said. Looking round the room, she noticed several vases of flowers, "Are they all for me?" she asked, pointing over to the flowers.

"Yes." her Mum answered, "They came a couple of days ago. We didn't know how long you would be in hospital and I thought they needed water, so I took them out of the cellophane wrapping and arranged them in the vases. I've kept the cards from the senders." and gave Rosa two cards.

"Oh bless, one's from the girls at the stables and the other's from Matt; don't you just love him."

"They are the two big bouquets." her mum said.

"Who's the small one from then?" asked Rosa, looking around for a card.

"It's here in my pocket." her mum said, looking a bit sheepish, as she gave Rosa the card.

Rosa read the card.

'Congratulations, Rosa, you're a STAR. Hope BABY is keeping well. Charles Davenport x'

The writing on the card took Rosa's breath away. She went white and gasped for breath; she knew what he had written on the card had a double meaning. It meant that if she ever told anyone what he had done, he was now threatening her baby as well as her horse.

"Are you OK, Dear? you have gone quite pale." her mum said.

"I'm fine, Mum. It's him; he's creepy. I didn't like him in college and I don't want anything to do with him, or his flowers. Put them in the bin; it's just something about him I don't like." Then she thought, "If only they knew."

Just then, the baby stirred, which stopped Rosa saying anything more. With great difficulty, Rosa started to stand up; her mum and dad both jumped up, ready to help her, but leaning on the table, Rosa looked at them and said, "I'm OK, Eva's the most important thing in my life now, I need to get strong, so I can look after her properly. She's waking up, so I need to get her bottles ready." She looked at her mum, smiled and added, "Are you ready Mum? The hard work starts now. Dad, could you pass me the crutch they gave me at the hospital please? It's been a great help."

Later that night, Rosa was alone in her bedroom, feeding Eva Marie. Looking at her with tears in her eyes, she said, "Are you safe with me, my precious girl? What's that horrible man up to, why doesn't he stop hounding me and leave me alone?" When the feed was finished, she cuddled the baby for a while, then she leant forward and put the baby in her crib. She pulled the cord on a musical toy and as it played Brahms' lullaby, a tired Rosa laid back in the chair and closed her eyes. She smiled as she thought, "Day one completed; tick!"

The Other Side of the Fence

Rosa had been home for just over three weeks. They had informed James about the birth and he responded with excitement, saying that his mum, dad, girlfriend Lily and his brother would all be over to England for two days at the end of the week, and to let them know the best time to visit.

The baby was doing fine, putting on weight and was quite content. Although Rosa and her mum were coping OK, Rosa was still in a lot of pain with her legs, she had even taken to carrying the baby in a sling, while being pushed in the wheelchair, when they went shopping in the village. The doctor had said to give it a few more weeks before starting any strenuous exercise to make them stronger. All Rosa knew, was that thank goodness her mum and dad were there to help. As Rosa was tired a lot of the time, her mum would have the baby, while Rosa lay down and rested for a while; and to give her a break and a change of scenery, Matt had taken her out along the river a couple of times.

The time came for James' visit to meet the baby. Rosa had dressed her in a white frilly dress, with pink rose buds, and pretty, frilly, white socks. The doorbell rang, it was James with his mum and dad. They were carrying lots of presents and some flowers for Rosa and her mum.

"Please come in." Rosa's mum said, "How nice, thank you." she added, taking the flowers from James. She showed them into her lounge and went to make them a cup of tea. She could hear lots of 'ahs' and 'oh she's beautiful'. James cuddled his daughter, then his mum cuddled the baby; to the point of being tearful and absolutely falling in love with her granddaughter. Edward Stirling didn't speak, he just walked around stopping occasionally to look at things in the room.

The front door opened and Rosa's dad walked in; he had been in the fields all day and was quite dirty.

The Other Side of the Fence

"Hello," he said, "pleased to meet you all. I will just go to wash my hands and I will be back." he added, walking through to the kitchen. When he returned, he said, "Please excuse my appearance, sometimes being a farmer is hard, dirty work. Is everyone OK?" he asked, as he shook hands with them all, "I see you have met our lovely Eva Marie."

"Yes thanks, she's lovely." said James' mother.

Rosa's dad described life on his farm of over 1000 acres and explained that he was also a mechanical engineer, repairing and restoring farm equipment. A couple of hours later, with all the details from both sides exchanged and the baby sound asleep in her crib; it was decided that it was a good time for James and his parents to leave. As Rosa tried to get out the chair and hung on to the table, her mum gave her the crutch.

A concerned James asked, "Are you OK, Rosa?"

"Yes, I will be in a minute, thanks; it's just a temporary thing. Thank you so much for all the lovely things you bought for the baby."

As James was leaving, he kissed Rosa on the cheek and whispered, "Well done, she's lovely. Before we leave tomorrow afternoon, is it OK if we come again? Lily has asked me to ask, if it would be OK for her to come to see Eva Marie."

"Of course it is, I'm pleased she's asked. Just to say James, anytime any of you are in England, if you want to see her, phone me and I will make sure I'm here."

Just as they were leaving, James' dad took Rosa's dad to one side and asked, "Whose is that wheelchair in the hall?"

"It's Rosa's," he answered, "her legs are weak and she's in a lot of pain from the accident she had a few years back.

Her Mum helps a lot with the baby, so no worries there; everything is OK."

35

James arrived, with his Mum and girlfriend Lily, just after noon the next day.

"Sorry, Rosa," he said, "we won't be able to stay too long, we have to be at Stanstead airport by four o' clock, for our flight home."

Leaning forward and rubbing her hands together, James' mother was already walking over to the crib and looking lovingly at the baby. She spoke in a silly grandmotherly voice, "We have just called for a quick cuddle of my beautiful granddaughter." and seeing that Eva Marie was awake, she looked up at Rosa and asked, "Can I?"

Rosa nodded.

James's mother sat down in the armchair and Rosa handed her the baby.

The Other Side of the Fence

Rosa tried not to stare too hard at James' girlfriend; she was absolutely stunning, with green eyes and natural reddish blonde hair, pulled back into a ponytail; not secured with an elastic band like Rosa's, but with a pretty two-inch thick diamante slide, oozing class. She was immaculately dressed in a smart black suit and cream silk blouse which looked expensive; her shoes had the highest heels Rosa had ever seen.

Rosa's mum brought in tea and fresh cream cakes. Rosa was surprised when Lily tucked into hers; she looked lovely and slim, looking as if she only ate lettuce leaves.

Lily noticed Rosa looking at her and laughed, saying, "I do eat, honest; but I also have to do a lot of exercise and running afterwards."

"You look so immaculate." Rosa said, as she started to put the used tea things on a tray, to take through to the kitchen.

"But, Rosa, I haven't just had a baby a couple of weeks ago." Lily said, getting up from the table, "Please let me help you." she said, as she picked up some of the empty plates and walked with Rosa through to the kitchen.

They stood in the kitchen for a while looking out over the fields.

"Does all that land we can see belong to your dad?" Lily asked.

"Yes." Rosa answered and explained what her dad did for a living and how hard he worked in the fields; especially when all the different crops he grew, were ready for harvesting. Rosa told her about her accident and why she couldn't feed the baby because of the number of tablets she had to take each day. She also told her about how she and her friend ran the riding school and had stables in the fields at the end of the farm.

The Other Side of the Fence

"Rosa, how old are you?" Lily asked.

"I was twenty-one in May, two months before Eva Marie was born." Rosa answered, she then paused, puzzled, before asking, "Why?"

"I was just thinking; for how young you are, how well you have done." replied Lily, "With all your experience, I'm sure there's a little lady, just a couple of weeks old, who will grow up to be a champion horse rider, one day."

"Ah, thanks, that's such a lovely thing to say." Rosa said, "We still have big ambitions for the school's future."

"I know James has told you that I'm a top model, so dressed like this is seeing me at work. I call how I'm dressed 'my uniform'; I have to look like this when I'm out and about, in case I get recognised and photographed. Whenever they take my photo, they'll make up a caption to go with it. It's a dead cert' that I will be recognised and photographed at the airport, later today. The caption might read that I was off on holiday to the Caribbean. Sometimes, I don't even recognise it's me they are writing about. My bosses insist that I dress in their clothes when I'm going out, so if my photo gets taken, its good publicity for their outfits." she laughed, and added, "I'm like a walking advert. Believe me, Rosa, as soon as I get indoors, the makeup gets wiped off, the jewellery's off, the clothes are off and it's on with jeans, a big sloppy T-shirt and trainers; I love it. That's how James likes me the best." Lily said that she was twenty-three and told Rosa all about the fashion shows she worked on and how busy she is at the start of each fashion season, spending hours in studios being photographed, modelling the latest fashions to be advertised in magazines; she named some of the magazines Rosa would find her in. "It's been lovely to meet and talk to you Rosa, I hope we can be friends. James said that you were lovely and he's right. Although you have his baby, he says you and he are just friends, nothing more." Rosa

The Other Side of the Fence

nodded as Lily continued, "You know, James and I don't live together, we are at the stage where he sometimes stays at mine or I stay at his; we are very happy together. James is such a darling, a true gentleman and very caring." She bent close to Rosa and whispered, "He's not like his dad; he scares me, he's like a headmaster."

Rosa said, "I met him when I was in Spain; I don't like him either and I know he doesn't like me."

When they walked back into the lounge, the two mothers were talking and James was sitting in the armchair cuddling the baby.

A car-horn sounded outside.

"That's our cue to go." said James, "We came in a taxi and that's Dad in our hire car, to take us to the airport."

Rosa and her mum walked with James, Lily and his mum to the front door. His dad sat in the car, looking forward and never turned his head to look in Rosa's direction.

There were lots of kisses and hugs all round. As James kissed Rosa on the cheek, he said, "Me and Lily will be back again soon; I will phone you when."

They got in the car and as they drove away, they all waved goodbye, except Edward Stirling.

As Rosa closed the front door, she said, "Thanks, Mum, for all your help today and yesterday."

Her mum smiled. "That's OK, I rather enjoyed it; I think it all went well, don't you, Rosa? They all seem nice people."

"Yes, everyone was lovely; I even liked and got on well with Lily; I just don't like James' dad, he's so intimidating; he makes me feel inferior."

A couple of hours later, Rosa answered a knock on the front door.

A young man asked, "Rosa Maddox?"

"Yes." said Rosa.

"Then these are for you." He handed her a bouquet of pink roses, then about turned and left.

The card inside the envelope, in capitals, read,

'BEAUTIFUL FLOWERS, FOR MY BEAUTIFUL DAUGHTER EVA MARIE' and in brackets it said, 'and her mother'

"How lovely and thoughtful he is." said Rosa, "Eva Marie has definitely picked herself a good dad."

The Stirlings were well on the way to the airport, all talking about Rosa, how lovely the baby was and how Rosa's mum and dad had made them welcome.

"I liked her;" Lily said, "we had a nice talk. I know we will be friends."

James said, "Come on Dad, you haven't said anything; what did you think about your granddaughter?"

"I will let you all know what I think, tomorrow afternoon." he answered.

For the rest of the journey, the three people travelling with Edward never spoke, they were too confused and couldn't understand what he meant by his comment; but Edward Stirling remained silent on the matter.

36

After meeting Rosa Maddox and his granddaughter at the Maddox farm, unbeknown to his family, Edward Stirling had phoned his private investigator and ordered him to fly immediately to England. He didn't care what it cost, or how he did it, but he was to find out everything he could about Rosa's life; he wanted to know what was wrong with her legs, why she needed a wheelchair and was she capable of looking after James' baby.

-

As well as Edward's law firm, his wife, Angela and her sister-in-law run several successful designer dress shops and his two sons run a firm of accountants; they all do a lot of business across Europe.

The family live on the outskirts of a small village, near to Dublin's airport; most convenient for all the business trips they have to take abroad.

The Other Side of the Fence

They all live in a large mansion which the family bought after it had been converted into five luxury apartments. It was ideal accommodation for several members of the family, and each of them had bought their own luxury apartment. The Mansion stands in acres of grounds, part forest, part gardens; it even has its own roman style indoor swimming pool. The grounds also has a two bedroomed guest house and a small cottage, where a full time gardener and maintenance man lives. The front of the property is quite a way back from the main road, on a half-circle driveway that leads to the front door. If you drive out past the front entrance, to the right you would pass a building, purpose built by the Stirlings for offices, where the family members with businesses operate from.

Entering the front of the building through a carved wooden door, you are met with a large entrance hall; it is so big, that if you speak too loudly it would echo. It has a magnificent central staircase that splits as you reach the top.

To the left of the entrance hall, is Edward and Angela Stirling's 3 bedroomed apartment, it is so big you would think you were actually inside a large bungalow; it even has its own enclosed garden at the rear.

To the right, is Edward's parents' two bedroomed apartment, they also have a garden at the back, but a lot smaller.

On the left, at the top of the stairs, is James' two bedroomed apartment, it has a large balcony that overlooks the immaculate gardens at the rear of the property.

To the right, is James' brother, Michael's two bedroomed apartment, he shares it with his girlfriend Leah, she is a nurse and works at the nearby hospital; their apartment also has a balcony overlooking the rear gardens.

The Other Side of the Fence

Up another flight of stairs, is what they all call the penthouse; Edward's brother lives there with his wife and their fourteen-year-old daughter. Their balcony is at the front of the property, which although it stands quite a way back from the main road, they can still see families out with their children and dogs, in the large park opposite.

The park has a club house belonging to the golf course, that's situated further down the main road.

Although all the apartments have their own lounges; on the ground floor, behind the magnificent staircase, there are two large doors that lead into a large communal lounge come dining room. Most impressive is the long antique dining table that all the family can sit round. The whole room has been designed around this magnificent table. The large room has several glass doors that they open in the summer, to a BBQ area out in the garden. The families have had this large extension specially built; it's ideal for when they all get together for birthdays, anniversary parties and especially over Christmas. It's also used when one of their companies has a private meeting.

-

When Edward and Angela got back to Ireland and were settled in their apartment for the evening, Angela sat herself down opposite her husband and leaning forward she said, "Edward Look at me, I'm waiting for an explanation; what ever did you mean by that remark you made in the car, about your granddaughter?"

Edward looked about, before answering, "James is in his apartment with Lily, isn't he?"

"Yes," Angela answered, "they said they were tired and both have early starts for work tomorrow; so they won't be down."

"Angela, I want you to listen carefully to what I say before you say a word. What I'm about to tell you, I couldn't say in the car, because I didn't want Lily to know. I am having that Rosa Maddox girl investigated; I don't like where she lives on that farm, with all those smelly animals running around, and I think she's after James' money, so she can have a better life for herself. I need to know if she's capable of looking after our beautiful granddaughter properly. I don't know if you noticed, but it was her mother who did most of the work; that girl could hardly walk and never held the baby for very long, unless she was sitting down. Then there's that wheelchair, Angela, I can't stop thinking about it. What if the mother was out when the baby needed to be picked up and Rosa dropped her because she wasn't strong enough to hold her? I feel sick just thinking about it. What ever was James thinking of, going with her; and what a ridiculous situation he's got himself into now. I met her in Spain, I didn't like her then either. She looked like someone he had just picked up in the street. Now, if we were talking about Lily, she is perfect, and the right sort of girl for James. I'm expecting an Email tomorrow afternoon, to let me know what's been found out about Rosa Maddox." After a long silence from Angela, Edward said, "Well?"

Angela stood up, ready to leave the room, she looked disgusted by what she had just heard, and said, "Have you gone out of your mind? That poor girl has just had a baby. She had a really bad accident years ago with hours of painful surgery and carrying Eva Marie, for all those months, has put a strain on her legs. She has got to exercise now for months, to get the strength back into them. I like her and I know James likes her, but even when she found out about the baby, she still didn't want a relationship with James; so, she was never after his money. I can't even see she ever had any idea he had any money anyway; she didn't know very much about him. James says they only went together once, so Eva Marie wasn't planned. Rosa never told him she was pregnant; he didn't know until they met when Rosa was seven months, and then they only met by accident. So, my darling husband, you have that part of her life all wrong. So, try again!"

"Oh, I apologise then. But let's wait until tomorrow's full report before we make a decision on Eva Marie's future; agreed?"

"OK, yes, agreed!" she answered, angrily. She was quite upset and didn't even look at him as she left the room.

37

At exactly two-thirty the next day, while working in his office, the Email Edward Stirling was waiting for, from his team who were still in England, came through. It read as follows:

From: Stirling Investigations Team

Subject: Report On Rosa Marie Maddox

1. Lives with mother and father in her own private rooms.

2. Runs and owns the Four Horseshoes Riding School with her partner Gemma Adams.

3. Owns several horses for hire. Also rents out stables to horse owners

4. Has no serious boyfriend

5. Was an excellent champion horse rider

6. A serious accident at age fifteen ended her show jumping career when legs were crushed by a horse falling on her. Spent many weeks in hospital, in plaster.

7. Has a three-week-old baby named Eva Marie Maddox. Has no intention of having a relationship with the father.

8. James Stirling has acknowledged he is the father of Eva Marie Maddox.

We are finalising our medical investigation, it should be available to send at approx. 4 pm today.

Stirling Investigators In England

Edward printed the Email and took it over to their apartment to show his wife.

After reading it to her, he said, "To be honest, Angela, I am impressed; she has achieved a lot in such a short time, perhaps I'm wrong about her. The team are still putting together the medical report and I should receive it at four this afternoon, if this is anything to go by, it looks as if everything is going to be OK, and I've worried for nothing."

As he was leaving to go back to his office, he turned and asked, "Will you still be in later?" His wife nodded, so he added, "OK, I'll let you know as soon as I get the next one."

The Other Side of the Fence

Edward sat in his office, continually looking at the big clock he could see through the glass partition on the wall in the next office. His office door was open and it was so quiet he could hear every tick the clock made.

At last, the hands were pointing at four o' clock, but no Email had arrived. He got up out of his chair and started pacing. Suddenly, a notification ping from his computer made him rush back to his desk. When he looked at it, he saw it was not the one he was expecting.

"Typical!" he tutted. He started pacing again but did a quick U-turn as his computer pinged again. This time, he could see straight away that this was the Email he was waiting for. He opened it up and as he read it, he started to feel quite worried, even a sense of shock and upset.

He printed the Email and left his office; as he walked past his secretary, he told her that he wouldn't be coming back in the office for the rest of the day and that she could go home when she had finished what she was doing; he would tell the others to lock up.

He half walked, half ran back to the apartment, opened the door and called his wife, "Angela can you stop what you're doing please and come to the lounge?"

As she came into the lounge, she saw her husband laying back in one of the armchairs.

"What's the matter?" she asked, "Are you ill?"

"No, it's this." he answered, handing her the Email. As she was reading it, she slowly sat down in one of the other armchairs. She felt the blood drain from her face.

It read:

From: **Stirling Investigations Team**

The Other Side of the Fence

Subject: Medical Report On Rosa Marie Maddox

We have managed to find out the following regarding Miss Maddox's health.

1. Miss Maddox sustained serious leg injuries following a horse-riding accident, requiring months of operations and physiotherapy.

2. The weakness in her legs will slowly improve, but at the present time, a wheelchair is used for any distance.

3. At the age of sixteen, Miss Maddox attempted suicide by cutting both her wrists.

4. Miss Maddox was diagnosed with having suicidal tendencies, depression and prone to anxiety and panic attacks. She was put on medication under the supervision of a counsellor, Mrs. Bennet.

5. She was still under the care of the hospital and making good progress, until three months ago, when at seven months pregnant, she had a bad panic attack in Mrs. Bennet's office. A doctor was called and she spent some time in hospital, under observation.

6. At the present time, Miss Maddox is still under Mrs. Bennet's supervision and must attend regular hospital appointments.

7. Since the baby was born, Mrs. Bennet has visited Miss Maddox at her home.

Stirling Investigators In England

Angela and Edward Stirling just sat and looked at each other; in the end it was Angela who spoke first, "Edward, I apologise, you were right, what ever are we going to do about it?"

"I know what I want to do, I want to go and get our grandchild, but it's James' decision. Whatever it is, I will give him my full backing."

"Oh, my poor boy." Angela said.

Getting up from the chair, she went over to her husband, put her hand on his shoulder and said, "Yes, Edward; no matter how much it costs."

Edward put his hand on hers and squeezed it in agreement.

"Hopefully, when he comes home, Lily won't be with him. I will let him read this and hear what he has to say. If he's as shocked and upset as we are, I think I know what he'll want us to do." he said.

A tearful Angela nodded in agreement.

38

At six, that evening, a drained looking Edward Stirling stood at one of the three large bay windows in his lounge. James had been at a meeting and said he would be back at six, so he was hoping to catch him before he went upstairs to his apartment. As James' car turned into the driveway, Edward shouted, "Ang, he's here and he hasn't got Lily with him."

He hurried to his front door and met James coming through the big main doors.

James noticed immediately how strained his dad looked.

"Hi, Dad, what's up?" he said.

His dad beckoned James into the hall of his apartment, and asked, "Have you got a few minutes to come in, Son; we would like to talk to you?"

The Other Side of the Fence

As James walked down the hall and into the dining room, his mother came to meet him; giving her a hug and a kiss on the cheek, he said, "This is all very intriguing, Mum?"

Pointing to the dining room table, his dad said, "You had better sit-down, James, we have something to tell you."

They all sat at the table and his dad started to open a folder; as he did so, he looked at James and said, "We have found some disturbing news about Eva Marie's mother and we don't know what to do about it; or more to the point, what you think should be done about it."

He passed the two Emails to James.

"Take your time in reading them;" his mum said, "we will go and get you a drink and something to eat. We'll be back in a few minutes."

When they returned, James' head was in his hands.

Looking up, he said, "I don't know this girl; I can't believe this is the girl I met in Ibiza. I really liked her. The things I've just read about her, especially what she has done in the past, I am shocked. I was just thinking back then, to something she said to me when we were saying goodbye on her last night in Ibiza; I thought it was strange at the time, but now, reading this, what she said makes sense. After what happened only three months ago, she doesn't sound stable, even now. I feel I want to go to England and bring Eva Marie back here, where she will be safe." Looking up at his mum and dad he said, "What do you think we should do? Should I go for full custody?"

"Well, James, your mother and I are in agreement with you. We must realize though, that if we go for custody of Eva Marie, it will be a big step for all of us to take. It will change all our lives; we are talking about looking after a baby full time, while running the family businesses; I think we should hold a family meeting."

James' mum said, "Yes, I've been thinking that this will affect Michael as well, as it will have an effect on the accounting business, we should involve him and Leah. Working at the hospital, Leah may have an opinion on Rosa's medical report; if that's OK with you, James?"

"Anything;" he answered, "but we need to move fast; it's for the safety of my daughter, so it has to be done. Can you call him, Dad, please? He is in, I saw his car when I drove in."

Edward picked up the phone and dialled Michael's number, they heard him ask about Leah and then heard him say, "That's brilliant, Michael, you will? OK, the door is unlocked." He turned to them and said, "Michael's coming down now. Leah is on her way home from work; her friend, Karen's driving and will be dropping Leah off. Michael's sent her a message to come straight to this apartment."

When Michael arrived at the apartment, Edward explained to him what he had done and that James was quite upset with the outcome.

"We want to show Leah these Emails and ask her opinion." said Edward, handing Michael the Emails.

Michael read them, looked at James and said, "I am so sorry, James, this is hard to believe; she was such a nice girl."

Michael thought for a moment, then asked, "Is it OK to use the printer, Dad? I think we should print some more of these Emails, then when Leah gets here, it will be easier to look and discuss them together." As he returned with the extra copies, Leah walked into the dining room looking concerned.

She looked straight at Michael and asked, "What ever is the matter Michael?"

"It's OK, Leah; please sit down." replied Michael, "We have this family problem that we need to discuss." Michael handed Leah copies of the two Emails, "This is the problem; these are reports on James' daughter's mother."

The room went quiet while Leah read the Emails. After she had read them, she put them down on the table and asked, "Do you want custody of your daughter?" James nodded and Leah continued, "Well, with what I've just read, I think you should go for it."

James stood up and said, "If you are all in agreement and its OK with Mum and Dad; as this is such a serious issue and needs to be discussed at length, I would like to do it now, while we are all here. Are you all willing to stay and discuss the implications of the Emails and what I should do?"

There was a rounded chorus of a definite yes.

"That's brilliant." said a grateful James, "But first, it's important that I speak to Lily; she's important in all this. I will take the Emails round hers, to show her. Hopefully, when she reads them and I explain everything, she will come back here with me. She is expecting me, as we were going to stay round hers tonight and watch a movie; I'm supposed to pick up a bottle of wine and a Chinese takeaway. I won't be long. Mum, Dad, is it OK for us to be here, to work out what's best?"

"Of course it is, James. If everyone is staying, how about I buy us all a takeaway to eat, while we wait for James?" his dad asked.

"I should be back before it arrives; hopefully, with Lily; so, I will bring back a couple of bottles of wine and some beers for us all. Dad, to save time, can you order me and

Lily our usual Chinese meals please; I won't be long." James said, as he was heading out the door.

As James was closing the front door, he just managed to hear his dad shouting to him, "Will do Son. Good luck, I hope all goes well."

39

When James returned, he stood quietly in the doorway of the dining room; everyone was sitting around the dining table, talking and making notes. His Aunt had come down from her apartment and was talking with his dad; she was holding the Emails, so they had obviously explained everything to her.

"I see you have all been busy while I've been away." James said, "Thank you, I do appreciate it."

They turned and looked at him and then straight past him to the empty hallway. He looked back down the hallway and then back to them, smiled and said, "Yes, she is with me; She's changing into some flat shoes."

He walked into the dining room, carrying the drinks they had bought and put them on the table.

Just as he did that, a smiling Lily appeared, carrying two bottles of wine. James took them off her and put them on the table.

The Other Side of the Fence

"Hi, everyone;" said Lily, "sorry about that, its hard work wearing heels as high as mine have to be. I'm nice and comfy now, ready to help. James has explained what's happening about his daughter. We have had a long talk about the future, and I would like to tell you all, I'm with him all the way."

"Bless you." Edward Stirling said, as he walked over to her, and gave her a hug.

The takeaway meals had already been delivered and were being kept warm in the oven. Angela and Leah brought everything through to the dining table and they all chatted while they ate.

After they had finished, Edward Stirling said, "Now for the serious discussions to start."

For the next three hours, they talked and discussed the pros and cons of going for custody.

Finally, Edward stood up, "James, you have heard all the fors and againsts of going for custody, are you sure you still want to go ahead?"

James looked at his mum; he knew that he couldn't look after a baby without their help. His dad put his arm around his mum, Angela looked at her husband and smiled, then they both looked at James and nodded.

James mouthed the words, 'Thank you.' He then went over to Lily; he knew if his future was with her, she needed to agree. She held both his hands, looked into his eyes and said, "Yes, all the way."

He put his arms round her, held her tight and she snuggled into his chest.

He kissed her on the top of her head and said, "I love you so much, Babe."

James broke away, looked at his dad and said, "That's a definite yes from me. My daughter is my responsibility and it's up to me to protect her. Dad, tell me what I should do next?"

"OK, now let me see." Edward said, "First thing in the morning, I will get my legal team on the case. I will need a letter from you, James, to give to social services, telling them why you want custody of Eva Marie. That will be easy, because of the contents of the Emails. Also, tell them you can give her a life of love and stability. Second, I will draft a letter telling them that your mother and I fear for our granddaughter's safety and that we give you our full support. I will then take the letters and the Emails to social services; they will probably make an appointment to come and see us all and carry out an assessment. If they approve your claim, they will liaise with social services in England and carry out an investigation. They will interview Miss Maddox and her psychiatrists. I doubt you will hear anything for about two weeks, while they look into your claim. If you do get a letter to say they want to interview you, your mum and I; we will have everything ready to explain how, if you got custody, you will care for the baby."

"Thanks, Dad." said James. He then stood up and addressing everyone, said, "Just before you all leave, I want to say a special thank you, for all your help tonight. Most importantly, I want you to know that, although this has to be done, I am quite upset at what we are about to do to Rosa. She was this lovely girl I met on holiday in Ibiza; Lily knows all about her. It's true that dad didn't like her right from the start, but I did, so did Michael; right Michael?" Michael nodded and James continued, "Rosa is a proper farm girl from Norfolk, loves horses, was quiet and quite shy. At twenty-one, it was her first ever holiday anywhere and she didn't want any romance with me. I pursued her and her friends, insisting that she came on a date with me.

Rosa didn't want anything to do with me after the holiday; I only found out, by accident, that she was pregnant, when she was about six months. Basically, that's the story. Now, to my mind, something traumatic has happened to Rosa, sometime in her life; something she can't escape from or live with. It only seems to affect her every now and then; whatever it is, it's made her into this girl we are reading about in these Emails. I can't even go for shared custody, because Rosa's not stable, that was proved three months ago; who knows when or where it will upset her again. What we are about to do, will be devastating for her; but it has to be done for the sake of Eva Marie's safety." He filled up, sat down and put his head in his hands. Everyone looked at each other, they could see how upset he was and how hard it was going to be for him to go for custody of his daughter.

"I think it's time we all called it a day." said Michael.

40

Meanwhile, back in England, Rosa was totally unaware of the situation that was about to send her world into turmoil. Rosa would never admit to anyone, that even with her mother's help, she was finding it hard work looking after Eva Marie. She was always tired and in constant pain; she couldn't wait to start the exercises to make her back and legs strong again, so that she would have the strength to look after Eva herself.

Matt called most days to see how Rosa was and she knew he would always be there if she needed any help. Today, he came just at the right time; Eva Marie had been fed and was having her morning sleep. Rosa's mum suggested that if Matt had time, Rosa badly needed some fresh air, as she hadn't been outside for a few days. Matt looked at her.

"Always got time for my girl; so, I'm at your service; where would you like to go?"

"Matt," Rosa said, "what I would really like to do, is to go and see Star and the girls down at the stables, and if possible, go for a ride on him." she said, with a pleading, 'please, please, I need this.' look.

"Then your wish is my command, my lady." he said, "What do we need, Mrs. M?"

"Don't worry, I will sort everything you need; if you can be getting Rosa into the car?" she answered.

"Thanks Mum." said Rosa, pain etched all over her face, as she struggled to stand up.

"I hate this feeling of helplessness." Rosa said to Matt, as he helped her out of the chair.

"Cheer up," Matt said, "it's still early days yet, you will soon be able to start your exercises; then there will be no stopping you."

As she watched Matt gently steadying Rosa, as they went down the hall to the front door, Rosa's mum said, "I will phone the stables and let them know you are on your way. Have a good time."

When they got to the stables, Rosa got out the car and walked towards the stable doors, leaning on her one crutch. She didn't get very far before four excited girls came out to meet her. Although they had all been to the house to see her and the baby, this was the first time Rosa had managed to get to the stables.

"Hope you haven't come to get rid of me and get your job back?" Katie said.

"Katie, there's no way we are getting rid of you just yet; you're alright for a few more months and if we can afford it, probably years. I need all my strength, at the moment, just to stand up, let alone coming back and chasing horses around fields." Rosa said, smiling at Katie. "Right, where's my boy?" she asked, as Gemma and Katie took an arm each, to help her get along easier.

"I'd better follow you, just in case I'm needed." Matt said.

Sydney and Jess rushed on ahead to make sure Star was ready for Rosa, so she could ride him.

When Rosa arrived at Star's stable, an excited Star reacted immediately on seeing her.

"How's my lovely boy, have you missed me?" Rosa said, stroking his nose.

As Rosa stepped backwards to look at Star full length, Matt quickly put his arm around her to steady her.

"Wow, girls you have done a good job looking after him, he looks great; his coat looks in top class condition." said Rosa.

"That's what Mr Davenport said." Jess said.

Looking straight at her, a shocked, Rosa said, "What did you just say Jess?"

"I said, that's what Mr Davenport said."

"When?" Rosa exclaimed.

"The other day." Sydney said, "Jess and I were in different stables, getting the horses ready for the start of the day's riding school. He scared poor Jess; she was in Star's stable and when she turned round, he was right behind her; he really scared her. We don't like him, do we Jess? Tell Rosa what happened."

"He's always scared me, I still get upset thinking about him." said Jess, "He's so creepy."

"What was he doing here? What did he want?" asked Rosa.

Jess replied, "Well, when I turned round, I said, 'Mr. Davenport, you made me jump.' He just laughed. I said, 'Can I help you?' He said, 'Have you seen her and the baby?' I said, 'Who?' and he said 'Don't be a stupid girl, you know very well who I am talking about; your boss, Rosa Maddox and her baby; have you seen them? What's its name?' I said, 'No, I haven't seen Rosa or the baby; I don't even know her name.' 'Oh, it's a girl then, is it?' he said, 'Well, make sure you tell your boss, when you do see her, that I have been to see Star and was asking about her and the kid.' I was so scared, Rosa, I called Sydney, as I knew she was working in a stable further down the building near the doors that go out to the riding school's field. I just pushed past him and went as quickly as I could to find her. Sydney was already on her way to find me. She asked what I wanted. I pointed to Star's stable and said, 'Mr. Davenport's in there.' But when we got back to the stable, he was gone. We went to the office and told Gemma. She could see how upset I was and said I could go home if I wanted, but I said no, I would be OK. She went and made sure his car had gone, then locked the main doors to the stables."

"Oh, that's awful." said Rosa, "I'm so sorry girls. I can't ride Star today now, I'm too angry. I'm so sorry that happened to you Jess; I promise I will talk with Matt and Gemma tomorrow, to see what we can do to make us all feel safer. Gemma, can you come and see me tomorrow, any time after lunch, when you're not busy, and see if we can decide on what sort of security we need. In the meantime, can you try and work it so that there's two of you working together. If you need more help, I will ask my dad when I get back if he could let us have one of his boys for a few days. If he can, he will be down later today. How's that all sound?" she said, looking round at everyone; they either nodded or gave a thumbs up sign. She finished by saying, "There's no worry today girls, because Davenport should be at college."

Gemma said, "Leave it to me, Rosa, I will sort it; you just go back and concentrate on getting yourself strong, so you can get back to us as soon as possible; we miss you."

"OK thanks. Matt, I'd better get back." Rosa said.

There were goodbyes, kisses and hugs all round, then Matt helped Rosa into the car and they drove off. Matt turned right out of the big gates, ready to drive back up River Walk Road, to the farm, when he suddenly stopped the car, turned to Rosa and said, "My word, Rosa, you scared me when Sydney and Jess were telling us about that chap; I could literally feel you shaking and breathing so fast, I thought you were going to pass out. What was all that about?"

She reached for his hand, held it and said, "Matt you're such a good friend; Davenport is one of the top teachers at the college. He's always been weird like that, he creeps up behind you and then speaks, so you freak out; he used to do that to me and other girls, when I was at college; so, when Jess was describing what happened, I knew how she felt and how scared she must have been."

Matt gave her hand an understanding squeeze, then started the car and drove her home.

When they arrived back at the farm, Matt helped Rosa out of the car and her mum met them at the front door. Speaking to Matt, Rosa said, "When I've had a good rest, I will give some thought to what we can do. Can we talk about it tomorrow with Gemma, if that's OK? I've gone all tired now and I need to relieve Mum and see Eva."

"OK." Matt said, "I will do some research tonight. You ring me tomorrow when you and Gemma are ready and we can put our ideas together. Thinking about it, your dad will probably know what we can do; he must have security with all that farm machinery about, so don't forget to mention it to him. See you tomorrow, Rosa, bye, Mrs. M." He then got in his car and drove off.

Having heard what happened at the stables, Rosa was more stressed than ever. What if he gets even more intrusive? If she couldn't tell anyone about him and what he did to her, how was she supposed to protect her daughter?

"Everything OK?" her mum asked.

"Well, sort of, there's a bit of security needed at the stables. Other than that, the girls have done a brilliant job running them." Rosa answered.

Rosa knew what her priority was and went straight to her mum's lounge to Eva's crib; she was awake and kicking her legs in the air.

"Just going to wash my hands and then I will be back for a cuddle." Rosa said.

Hands washed, Rosa sat down and her mum passed her the baby.

Looking at Eva Marie, Rosa asked, "How's my gorgeous baby girl then? Who's got the bluest of eyes? Whose mummy just adores her baby daughter? And who loves Eva Marie the most in the whole wide world? I do." she cooed, as she pulled Eva Marie to her chest and snuggled into her neck. "Oh no! And whose nappy wants changing as soon as possible?" Rosa said, laughing out loud.

41

That night, Rosa spoke to her dad about the additional security she needed at the stables. She told him that Matt said he would help with any work she wanted done.

"What we want," she said, "is something to stop the public walking through the gates into the stables where the horses are. We have a sign saying all enquiries at the office, but people ignore it."

"You need CCTV and a sign saying private property, horse and riders only past this point, CCTV in operation." her dad replied, "If you ring Matt and ask him to come here tomorrow, before I start work, I will tell him what's needed and where to get all the equipment from. If he's OK to work at the weekend, I will help install it for you. It's expensive, but well worth it."

"No problem," Rosa said, "we still have money left from our loan." She kissed him on the top of his head and added, "Daddy, I love you so much, you're always there

The Other Side of the Fence

for me. What would I do without you and Matt? I will phone him straight away."

She soon returned. Smiling, she said, "All sorted, Daddy, Matt will be here at 7:30 sharp."

The next morning, Matt arrived right on time; he was given a list of what to buy and instructions for the work that was needed to be done before the CCTV could be installed.

Rosa was sitting with them at the kitchen table. Looking at Rosa, Matt asked, "Would you like to come with me to the warehouse tomorrow? We can take the wheelchair and then go into town to do a bit of shopping and even have lunch; you can have Eva in her baby sling."

"Yes please." she answered, "I would really like that; you're so thoughtful, Matt."

As he started to leave, he put his arms on her shoulders, gave them a friendly squeeze and joked, "Not really, Rosa, your dad said that you're paying."

She laughed as she stood up, got her walking stick and walked with him to the front door. As he drove off, she blew him a kiss and waved goodbye. Just as she went to close the door, she happened to look at the parking area of the row of houses across the road; she froze, there was a car parked nearly opposite; she was sure it was Davenport's and he was in it. She shut the front door so fast, she nearly caught her hand in it. She turned, leaning with her back on the front door, her body tensed and her breathing became rapid.

She thought, "What is he playing at? If it's to scare me, he is doing a good job." Tears of anger started to flow, "This shows how evil he is, through and through. I fear for my little Eva Marie, if only I dare tell someone what he's done to me, and how he's practically stalking me now; but I know I can't, I must keep Eva and Star safe."

The next day, Rosa's mum got Eva ready nice and early for her day out.

"Oh, Mum, she looks lovely." Rosa said, "I am so looking forward to today. I know we are going to have a nice time; Matt always puts me at ease and cheers me up."

Just as she spoke, a car horn sounded. Her mum looked at Rosa and said, "That's timing for you; I've put everything ready at the front door."

Matt knocked and opened the door. Picking up the wheelchair he said, "Hello, Mrs. M. tell Rosa her chauffeur's here."

"Cheeky!" shouted Rosa, from the next room.

Her mum took Eva, who was already settled in her car seat, out to Matt.

As he fitted the baby into the car, he saw her looking at him; he smiled at her and said, "Hello, Miss Blue Eyes, you're looking extra lovely today."

Rosa heard what he'd said, as she stood by the front door, waiting for Matt to help her into the car.

"I know I'm always saying this, Matt, but, again, thank you so much; you're the best friend ever." she said.

He helped her into the car, "Stop it, you make me blush; well, I would if I was a girl." he laughed.

That made Rosa laugh, "It's going to be a good day." she thought.

That weekend, the riding school was a hive of activity, as the CCTV was installed. When finished, they all crowded into the office to watch the TV screens, as Matt tried to enter the riding school and get past the cameras without being seen. They all applauded, when, whichever way he went, the cameras caught him every time. Rosa knew that the security lights, that had already been installed, where working. Luckily, Sydney was a keen artist and was in the process of finishing the 'Do Not Enter' signs. So, a happy Rosa was, for the time-being, feeling quite relieved and relaxed.

42

In Ireland, the Stirlings were surprised how quickly Social Services responded to their concern for James' daughter. Edward received an Email asking for a meeting, at his address, with him, his wife and son James, to discuss the Rosa Maddox matter. Edward Stirling agreed and a meeting was arranged for three days time.

At the appointed time, two social workers arrived, fully laden with notebooks and a tape recorder; the Stirlings all said their piece and stressed how concerned they were that Rosa Maddox was unfit to look after a child, let alone their precious child; in fact, James' mother got quite emotional when giving the reasons for her complaint. Everything they said was taped and noted. The social workers then requested to see around. An inspection of the two apartments involved and the garden was carried out; The Stirlings were also asked to explain how or who would care for James' daughter, should he be granted custody. James explained that as Eva Marie would be his responsibility, it would be mostly him. Edward said that he was willing to employ a part time nanny to help James and he also confirmed, once again, that he and his wife were fully committed.

The social workers told the Stirlings that they would write up their report, which would include statements from both of them, regarding their opinion of the Stirling family. It would then be passed on to their superiors, who would read it and if they thought the Stirlings had a case, it would be sent to the English Social Services, for their consideration. Finally, the social workers thanked the Stirlings for their cooperation and left.

As they walked down the drive to their car, the social workers discussed the situation; they both agreed that if Eva Marie ended up with the Stirlings, she would be one lucky girl.

Meanwhile, back in England, not knowing or realizing what was happening in Ireland; after her latest appointment at the doctors, Rosa was feeling positive that her back and legs would eventually get better. Rosa was trying not to take so many painkillers because they made her feel sleepy. With the help of her mother, she was living an invalid's lifestyle, trying to look after a baby. Rosa was a doting mother, but because of the pain and lack of mobility, she was finding it very difficult during the times she had to look after Eva on her own; it was the hardest thing she had done for a long time. Although her mum was doing Eva's night feeds, Rosa seemed to be lying awake, always worrying about something and she could feel her anxiety and stress levels building. She really wasn't sleeping at all well but there was no way she would take sleeping pills.

What was stopping her being anywhere near happy, was the feeling that she was a prisoner of her own anxieties, because of the actions of Davenport. She feared for the safety of Eva Marie and she was finding herself more and more in the lounge, hiding behind the curtains, looking out the window, always at the parking spaces opposite.

Sometimes, Davenport was there. The day before, she was shocked; he was there sitting on a fence reading a newspaper, as calm as he could be. Rosa was going through hell, knowing the college was now on summer holiday and that this was going to go on for weeks.

Whenever she went to the riding school, no matter what time she left, Davenport always seemed to be driving up or down River Walk Road. Whenever she was being driven out of the riding school gates, he never failed to sound his stupid horn to attract her attention.

When Gemma was driving with her, a few days earlier, Gemma, quite unconcerned, laughed saying, "I think he's stalking us, don't you, Rosa?"

This remark completely freaked Rosa out, to the point of a near panic attack. Rosa wanted to scream out loud 'YES GEMMA, IF ONLY YOU ALL KNEW!' She thought, "I don't think I will be able to rest until I know Davenport has gone to prison for what he did to me. I often wonder if there are any more girls out there, like me, that he has done the same thing to, and are too scared to tell anyone." Looking up to the heavens, she thought, "Revenge is needed; please Lord!"

A few days later, an excited Rosa came hobbling through the front door of the farmhouse.

"Mum!" she shouted, falling into a nearby chair.

As her mum came through from the kitchen, she said, "Calm down, Rosa, you nearly missed that chair; whatever is it?"

The Other Side of the Fence

"I'm so excited, Mum, I've had a lovely day; Matt took me to lunch at the riverside restaurant."

"Let me guess, he asked you to marry him?"

"Ha ha! Don't talk rubbish, Mum." Rosa laughed, "No, he had secretly taken Eva's pram, and put it in the boot of his car. After we finished lunch, he strapped Eva in the pram and said, 'Right, let's see how far you can push Eva?' Her pram has been there all this time but she has never been put in it. I got up, held the handles and started to walk with her; I got as far as those seats further along the path, about 350 metres away. Matt walked at my side, making sure I was OK. We then rested for a while on the bench. The sun was lovely and warm, I loved it and felt Eva loved it too; then, although with difficulty, I walked all the way back."

As she was saying, 'walked all the way back', Matt came in with Eva Marie in her car seat and said, "Yes, Mrs. M. she walked all of 700 metres."

"Matt! I will have you both know; those 700 metres were more like a marathon for me." Rosa remonstrated, with the biggest, widest, and so proud of herself, smile on her face.

After the success of Rosa being able to walk some distance pushing Eva's pram, her dad got the idea that Rosa might be able to walk with a walking frame that had wheels on it.

"It might steady you and help you move around the house easier" he said. No sooner was it thought about, than one was delivered.

A few days later, Rosa came into their kitchen pushing the frame.

"I just love it, it's the best thing ever." she said.

As Rosa sat down, her mum said, "That's lovely, Dear, but please don't overdo it."

Looking over at Eva in her carrycot, Rosa said, "I can't believe Eva's nearly five weeks already."

"I know, Dear; I'm sure she smiled at me when I bathed her this morning."

Rosa smiled, as she said, "Oh bless her, she loves her bath; she's sound asleep now."

43

"Post!" her dad shouted, as he came down the hall from the front door, "There's a couple for you Rosa." he said, putting them in front of her on the table.

"Probably bills; that's all I ever get." Rosa laughed, as she opened one.

"Same as mine then." her dad said looking at her, as she read the letter. "Rosa! what's the matter?" he asked, concerned. Bending down next to her; he could literally see the blood drain from her face.

"Em!" he called through to his wife, "Quick get her some water, I think she's going to faint."

He took the letter from Rosa, and started to fan her with it, but she stopped him and said, "Read it."

"What is it Billy?" his wife asked, as she gave Rosa the glass of water, dabbing some of it on Rosa's face.

"It's from social services;" he said, "they say that there have been serious complaints about Rosa, saying she is unfit to look after Eva Marie. They want Rosa to make an appointment as soon as possible; apparently, they want to hear Rosa's response to each of the complaints and interview her regarding her situation. They need to see where Eva Marie lives, and assess Rosa's health and mental state. Two social service officers will attend and they will be accompanied by Mrs. Bennett."

When Rosa had recovered from the shock of reading the letter, she got angry. Looking bewildered at her mum and dad, she asked, "Who would do such a terrible thing to me?"

Taking charge, her dad said, "Let's all stay calm. There's a phone number on the letter; I will ring it and see what they say."

When he returned, he said, "They won't give me any information on who's complained, but they have booked us in for the day after tomorrow, at eleven; we will be told more then."

Rosa sat at the table, dumfounded, and thought, "I bet it's that stupid Davenport."

Her mother bought them cups of tea and biscuits on a tray. Putting the tray down on the table, she said, "I've been thinking; it's got to be James Stirling, or his dad. His dad's a bit of a know it all." she said, putting her nose up in the air with her finger underneath, then mimicked him in a posh voice, "I'm a top-class lawyer in Ireland." then continued angrily, "More like an upper-class snob; I knew he didn't like us when they visited a couple of weeks ago. He couldn't wait to get out the door; it made me feel inferior. Yes, I bet its him."

The Other Side of the Fence

The next day dragged; Rosa went to the riding school after the days riding had finished and the horses were fed, watered and settled for the night. All the girls said their goodbyes to each other and as they left, Sydney asked "Do you want me to lock up tonight, Rosa?"

"Thanks Sydney, but I'm going to do a bit of work before I go, so I will do it. I will ring my dad for a lift." Rosa replied.

"OK; bye, see you tomorrow." and Sydney left.

Rosa locked the door and talking to herself, she said, "Right, there's a case in here somewhere, with a blue folder in it. After all these years, I feel strong enough to read what the psychologist said about me." After a few minutes searching, she said, "There you are." and pulled the case out from the bottom of a pile of boxes. She sat at the desk and opened it. "Aw, so many of my lovely rosettes. The girl was good. Come on Rosa, the girl was very, very good." She pushed them to one side and pulled out the blue folder. "Oh bless, Rosa." she said, when she saw that she had written, 'THE DREAM IS DEAD' in large letters across the folder.

Opening the folder, she took out the envelope that had, 'Rosa Maddox's suicide attempt' written on it and took out the letter, that read:

To whom it may concern,

For a young girl of sixteen to actually cut both wrists, in my opinion, was a genuine attempt at suicide. I have concluded from the one-on-one conversation we have had together, that it was a cry for help, from a deeply traumatised young lady. Rosa won't be released from her demons until she finds the courage to open up and tell what, or who, she is so terrified of. Until such a time, she must be classed as a high-risk patient. I can only hope the

The Other Side of the Fence

one-to-one talks, the stress control techniques she has been taught and the course of medication I have prescribed for her, will help Rosa come to terms with what brought her to such a low, she decided to take such drastic action. Because of her disturbing behaviour, this attempt must be taken seriously.

The next envelope had 'Three months later' written on it and the letter read:

I am pleased to report that the progress Rosa Maddox has made, has been quite remarkable. Rosa has responded to treatment to such an extent that I am willing to reduce her weekly sessions to monthly. Currently, due to her young age, I have not discharged her completely. I have explained to her that should she experience the slightest feeling of not being able to cope, she must ring me straight away. Rosa's mental attitude, over the weeks, has changed to such an extent that I am confident that Rosa is over the worst. Only Time will tell.

As Rosa folded the letters to put back in their envelopes, she thought, "Black, black bad days. The Psychologist was right when she said time will tell. I changed my life, so did my wonderful daughter, who now needs my protection." She put the envelopes into her pocket and put the case back into the cupboard. She let out one big sigh, as she did her deep breathing exercises and thought. "I will always be grateful to the NHS, for everything they did for me and taught me. I haven't got time to dwell on what the letters were all about, that was years ago, I'm a different, stronger person than that sixteen-year-old girl. Yes, done and dusted, as they say; I just needed to see what those letters said about me, because the social workers will have them. At least now I will be prepared."

The Other Side of the Fence

As she was about to lock up, there was a gentle knock on the door; it was Matt. Earlier, Rosa had asked him if he would get her a couple of things, the next time he went to the village.

"Hi, glad I caught you. Just bringing you your delivery Mam." he said, as he passed her the few things she had asked for, "Oh, and I hope this is OK; the woman in the shop said it was suitable for a baby." he added, as he handed her a pink teddy, "I couldn't resist it, I picked it up, it was all soft and cuddly, so I just had to get it for Eva."

Rosa took it and kissed him on the cheek. Smiling, she said, "She's going to love you when she grows up; so, start saving for when you hear, Uncle Matt can I have?"

On the way home, Rosa was pleased to see there was no sign of Davenport or his car.

That night she was restless, she kept waking up and laid for ages looking at Eva. For a split second, she thought, "Can I keep you safe, my precious girl, or would it be safer for you to go to Ireland with your dad, away from that wicked man? Stop it! Stop it!" she berated herself, "Don't think like that."

At last, the morning sun appeared and Rosa got up; she was full of dread, thinking about what the day would bring. She made herself a cup of tea and sat for a while. She reread the letters, then just stared into space, thinking.

At eight o' clock, Rosa could hear Eva stirring, so she got her bottle ready. While the bottle was cooling, she went round opening all the curtains; she ended up in the lounge and as she opened the curtains, the sun came shining into the room.

As Rosa's mum came down the stairs and into the lounge, she said to Rosa, "At least it's a lovely day today, Rosa; is Eva awake?"

Still looking out the window, Rosa answered, "Yes, I'm waiting for her bottle to cool." Her mum then heard Rosa tut.

"What's that for?" her mum asked.

"Oh nothing, just watching some idiot in his car." Rosa said. She had actually seen Davenport's car parked in one of the parking places opposite; he wasn't in it, but as she stood watching, she saw him come back to the car, carrying a newspaper. "He's been to the village post office to get a newspaper."

"Who has, Dear?" her mum asked.

"Oh, I didn't mean to say that out loud?" Rosa laughed, "That same idiot."

Just as she was about to move behind the curtain, Davenport looked over to the house, saw her, smiled and waved; he then got in the car and drove off, sounding his horn as he went.

"Right, that's the idiot gone, better get the baby fed." thought Rosa and picked up Eva's bottle. She put it in the little basket she had tied to the front of her walking frame and off she went. Eva was fed, bathed and dressed; then an emotional Rosa sat cuddling Eva in the bedroom.

Rosa spoke softly to Eva, "It's a very important day for us today, Eva; I honestly don't know what's going to happen today, but I promise you this, my beautiful daughter, I will do whatever it takes to keep you safe from people who want to harm you. No matter what happens today, or in the future, I will always be your mummy."

At eleven o' clock exactly, there was a knock on the front door.

The Other Side of the Fence

"Quick, you answer it Billy, it must be them." said his wife, panicking and quickly arranging things she had already straightened and arranged several times already.

Her husband opened the front door to see three people standing there; Mrs. Bennett, who they already knew, a very tall, thin man, wearing a trilby, and a woman looking very efficient in a smart navy suit and white blouse; they all carried briefcases.

"Mr. Maddox I presume?" asked the man in a voice that would scare the bravest of people.

"Yes, please come in." replied Billy, standing back behind the door, beckoning them to come inside.

44

The three of them walked through the hall into the lounge where Rosa was already sitting at the table. Rosa took one look at them, froze, and felt her nails starting to dig into her palms.

Her mother, who was standing behind her with her hands on Rosa's shoulders, felt Rosa stiffen up, so she gave her shoulders a gentle squeeze, to say, 'I'm here.'

As he followed them into the lounge, Billy said, "Please sit down. This is my wife and my daughter, Rosa; the baby, Eva Marie is asleep in the other room."

"Rosa, before we begin," said Mrs. Bennett, "this is Mr. Roberts and Mrs. Simms, they are social workers, working for the council, on your daughter's behalf. We all know why we are here; it's because there has been a complaint about your ability to look after your daughter, Eva Marie. Rosa, you will be asked a lot of questions relating to the complaints that have been made and we would like you to give your reasons why you think these complaints are unjustified. Do you understand?"

"Yes." said a terrified Rosa.

"Rosa, would you like your mum and dad to stay, while we go through the complaints against you?" asked Mrs. Sims.

"Yes please." she answered

All three of them opened their briefcases and took out different coloured files.

Mrs. Sims removed some sheets of paper from her folder, while saying, "We are going to give each of you a list of the questions we will be asking Rosa, regarding the complaints. We will wait a few minutes while you look through them, but we ask that only Rosa answers our questions."

Rosa became more and more terrified as she read through the complaints against her, because it was all true. But, because of Davenport's threats to Star and now to Eva Marie, she dare not explain why she had done any of the things listed.

Speaking in an authoritative voice, Mr. Roberts looked at Rosa and said, "Rosa, there are a few things we would like to know before you start responding to the complaints. Firstly, who does the night feeds for Eva Marie?"

Rosa's mum answered, "I do."

All three looked at their files, clicked their pens, and started to write in unison.

"And how far away is the child, when you have to go to feed her?" Mr. Roberts asked Rosa's Mother.

"She is in my daughter's bedroom, which is through there and my bedroom is upstairs." she said pointing to both bedrooms.

All three wrote again.

"And how do you know when the baby needs feeding?" Mrs. Simms asked Rosa's mum.

"We have a baby monitor in our room and Rosa has the other part in hers. When I hear Eva getting restless, or she cries, I go and get her bottle ready, feed her and change her nappy. Rosa is usually awake." replied her mum.

"I see, thank you." and all three wrote again.

Rosa could feel herself tensing up; her mum was thinking, "If this wasn't such a serious matter, you three would be hilarious."

Mr. Roberts asked the next question, "Could you tell us who baths the baby?"

"I do." her mum answered, or I should say we both do; the baby loves her baths; it's a happy time."

"Thank you." he said.

Rosa's dad, who had been sitting quietly, said, "Rosa will do it when she gets stronger. My wife only helps because Rosa is still very weak and in a lot of pain, as you know."

"Thank you, Mr. Maddox." Mr. Roberts said, not even looking up from what he was writing, to acknowledge him.

"Don't waste your breath Billy." Billy thought, "It's like talking to a brick wall."

The Other Side of the Fence

"OK, Rosa," Mr. Roberts said, "Now we will address the complaints, so please may I ask that only Rosa answers. If you have read and understood the complaints made, could you give us your response to complaint one please?"

Rosa didn't answer.

"Miss Maddox, we are only trying to help you and do what's best for Eva Marie. I realise that this may be difficult for you, but could you please give us your response?"

Rosa could feel herself starting to shake; she couldn't even hold the paper still. She knew everything on it was virtually true and that Mrs. Bennett knew it; she started to cry.

"I will say this to you, about how I feel about you people and the horrible person who is doing this to me." she sobbed, "I would never harm my beautiful daughter, she's my world. You're all wicked, especially you, Mrs. Bennett, you have let me down. You know I won't be able to answer any of these complaints; we have talked about them for years. Why won't you believe me when I say, 'I can't answer!'" she shouted and stood up. "I will show you what I'm going to do about this complaints list." she said, almost hysterical, then grabbed Mrs. Simms' pen and scribbled all over the list, ripped it in half and threw it on the floor. She then grabbed her walking frame and headed towards her own lounge. When she reached the doorway, she turned, sobbing, and said, "Haven't I suffered enough; why are people trying to hurt me? Why can't you all just leave me and Eva Marie alone?" She then went through the door and slammed it shut.

"Well, that wasn't very helpful." said Mr. Roberts. Then looking at Rosa's parents, he said, "I'm so sorry, Mr. and Mrs. Maddox, but as you can probably guess, this won't go down too well in our reports. If Rosa changes her mind and wants to answer the questions before we send in our reports, please give us a ring. Come along ladies, this interview is clearly over; best we leave."

Mrs. Simms said, "But I'm supposed to check the baby's accommodation."

"Rosa is clearly distressed by our presence and I hardly think that will matter in this case. If it's needed, we will come back another day; how does that sound?" replied Mr. Roberts.

Mrs. Simms nodded.

They all stood up, packed their briefcases, bid Rosa's parents a good morning and walked down the hall to the front door.

Rosa's dad followed closely behind them and heard Mrs. Bennett say, "I think this has just proved that my assessment of Miss Rosa Maddox was correct, don't you both agree?"

"Yes definitely;" said Mr. Roberts, "the Stirlings will be pleased to hear about that little outburst."

"I felt terribly sorry for her." said Mrs. Simms, "She's obviously a very troubled young lady."

"You can say that again." said Mr. Roberts.

45

Billy watched Mrs. Bennett and the two social workers drive out onto the main road. He stood at the open front door for quite a while; he knew the future of his granddaughter's life had just been decided and it didn't look good for his precious daughter. For the first time in his life Billy Maddox wasn't in charge.

"What do I do, where do we go from here?" he thought, "The next few days are going to be horrendous." He closed the front door, walked slowly back to the lounge where his wife was sitting, and as he sat down, he reached for his wife's hand.

"How do we help her, after that, Billy?" his wife asked.

Holding back tears, he said, "I'm not going to lie to you Em; after what just happened and if she won't answer the questions, it's not looking good. I can't see how they can let her keep Eva Marie. Shall we go into her?"

"No, let her calm herself down for a while; she's got Eva's bottles through there, so Eva's OK."

"Right," he said, as he got up from the table, "I'd better get to work. I will try and get back early." He leant over, kissed his wife and said, "Talk later." He then went down the hall and out the front door.

Rosa's mum made herself a cup of tea, then just sat in disbelief.

Rosa stayed in her room for a few hours; when she came out, she was wheeling Eva in her crib. Her mum could see she had been crying.

"I'm so sorry I lost my temper, Mum." she said, "I realize I've made it hard for me and Eva Marie. I just don't know why people don't understand that I can't give the reason I did those things; so, it's no good ringing Mr. Roberts or anyone else."

Her mum said sympathetically, "We can only wait and see what the outcome from today will be and what happens next. There's nothing we can do now, Rosa; if you can't answer, you can't. Come on, let's get ready; we'll go into town and treat ourselves."

The days following Rosa's interview seemed to stand still; the Maddoxes didn't know how they got through each day. Two weeks later, they all sat having breakfast, when they heard the postman pushing a letter through the letterbox. They all looked at each other; her dad pointed to himself and they nodded, so he went to get the post.

"This looks like it." he said, as he came back into the room.

"Read it first, Daddy;" Rosa said, "then tell us what it says."

The Other Side of the Fence

Rosa and her mum sat quietly, while Billy read the letter to himself. When he'd finished, he folded it up, looked up at his wife and then his daughter, shook his head and said, "It's not good news, Princess."

Rosa's blood drained from her face. "Are they going to take Eva Marie away from me?" Rosa asked tearfully.

"Well, cutting through all the official wording," he said, "it sounds like it had been decided two weeks ago, to let the Stirlings have her, when they left here. Basically, what it says, is this." He unfolded the letter again and started to read out relevant parts, "It says that because you were unable or unwilling to defend any of the complaints the Stirlings had made about your mental state and physical ability to look after Eva Marie; they feel that, at this time, they have no alternative but to award full custody of Eva Marie to James; but you will have the right to supervised visits; although, because of the distances involved, visits should be mutually agreed in advance. There is some hope though; it goes on to say that if, in the future, Mrs. Bennett or whoever your counsellor is at the time, discharges you as being mentally fit to look after Eva Marie again, you will be granted joint custody. It says that James has also been advised of their decision and that we should contact him to decide how and when we should hand Eva Marie over, and that it should be done in the presence of a social services representative. We should then advise social services of our decision, so that everything can be arranged. That's sort of it, apart from all the legal stuff."

The Silence was deafening and the tears wouldn't stop flowing long enough for anyone to speak. In the end Rosa got up, got her walking stick and walked to the front door. It was raining quite hard by now, but she needed to get outside to breathe.

Standing in the rain, she said out loud, "I knew it, knew it, knew it. There he is, Mr. Evil, as usual, sitting in his stupid car." This had been happening most days lately; Davenport parked up, goes to get a newspaper, then sits reading it in his car, opposite Rosa's house.

When he saw Rosa, he nodded to her and got out the car. She was so upset and angry, she started to walk towards him. He could see how angry she was, as she got closer to the end of the driveway, so he acted as if he was scared, and pretended to get on a horse and ride away, then he pretended he had a sleeping baby and was putting it in the car. She stopped, she was shaking with anger, she lifted her walking stick up to her eye, pointed it at him like a gun and pretended to shoot him. He just laughed, blew her a kiss, got in his car, waved and sounded his horn as he drove off.

The rain fell on her face as she looked up to the sky and said out loud through her tears, "My poor baby. Please, please, help me, she sobbed, and for the sake of my sanity, please make him go away."

Her mum came up behind her and said, "What ever are you doing out here, Rosa, you're soaking wet." She then looked around, "And who ever was you talking to?"

"To myself Mum." she answered, "I couldn't breathe in there; I just needed some air."

"When they got back inside, her dad was putting his coat on. He said, "I won't be long, I just rang my solicitor; he's going to look at the letter for me and see if there is anything we can do. He said if I go now, he can see me before lunch."

Rosa went and changed her clothes. She sat and fed Eva, then cuddled and kissed her. As she laid her down in her cot, Eva smiled at her. Rosa filled up, she sat down next to the cot, held Eva's fingers and just looked at her. Wiping away tears, she picked up her phone and dialled.

"Hiya Rosa," a cheerful voice said, "what can I do for you?"

"Matt." She paused and quickly covered her mouth, so he wouldn't hear her catch her breath with a sob.

Matt could hear the desperation in Rosa's voice and said, "I'm here."

"I need a cuddle!" she cried.

46

Matt went to the farm as fast as he could. Just as he was about to knock on the front door, Rosa's dad drove into the drive. Billy was surprised to see Matt at the front door; not only that, Matt looked upset; he was hunched over, his hands were deep in his pockets and he was stepping from side to side. As Billy got out of the car, he asked, "Are you OK, Matt? You look quite agitated."

Matt answered, "Rosa rang me to come round; she sounded really distraught, so I got here as quick as I could."

"Yes, she is upset, Matt; you'd better come in and let her tell you why."

Billy opened the front door and they walked down the hall to the lounge.

Billy called, "Em, it's me. I'm back, where's Rosa?"

"In her rooms." she answered, as she came through to meet him. When she saw Matt, she said, with a puzzled look, "Oh, hello, Matt."

Billy explained, "He's worried about Rosa, she rang him to come here; he says she sounded really upset, so he got here as quick as he could."

"She's probably waiting for you then, Matt; just knock on her door." said Emily.

Matt knocked on the door; when Rosa opened it and saw him, she sobbed, "Oh Matt." and flung her arms round him; she never even noticed her mum and dad standing there. Rosa, still hugging Matt, took him inside and closed the door.

Billy sat down at the table, but before he could say anything, his wife said, "Before you tell me how you got on, I'm just going to make a pot of tea; I need a cup, so I can concentrate."

Billy had been given a lot of leaflets to look through, so while he was waiting, he spread them out on the table and started to look through them.

Emily brought through a tray of tea and biscuits; she sat down and poured them both a cup of tea.

"Right Billy," she said pushing the leaflets Billy had put on the table to one side, "what did he say?"

"Well, first he read the letter and got annoyed that they would do such a thing. But when he read the list of complaints, I could see his attitude change; he just kept shaking his head. He said that he was really sorry, but it looked bad and he didn't think that it would be possible to reverse the decision. I said that there must be something that could be done, so that Rosa didn't lose Eva Marie. He thought, for what seemed forever, and I must admit Em, I started to fill up. Anyway, he finally said that if we wanted to take it to court, Rosa would have to cooperate and address the complaints. We would have to find a specialist lawyer, as this sort of case fell outside his field of expertise. Even then, even if we get a sympathetic judge, he could only see a fifteen to twenty percent chance of success. To be honest Em, I'm devastated; what do you think?"

Just as he said that, Rosa's door opened and out came Matt carrying Eva Marie. Rosa was following, using her walking frame; they sat down to join her mum and dad at the table.

Her mum smiled at Matt, and thought, "They just look so natural together, if Matt married Rosa, she would be able to keep Eva."

"Are you sure you're OK now, Rosa?" Matt asked, as he handed her Eva.

"Yes, I'm alright thanks. You had better get back, they are all probably wondering where you disappeared to." she said, smiling at him.

She caught his hand and squeezed it, holding Eva up to him, she said, "We love you and we thank you for coming."

Matt smiled and leaning over to kiss the top of Rosa's head, said, "I will phone you later." Then, looking at her parents, he nodded, said goodbye to everyone and left.

After Matt left, Rosa kissed Eva, jigged her about to make her laugh and said, "Isn't he wonderful, he's so good for me, he calms me. Not in a romantic way, but as a friend, so, don't start getting ideas, Mum. How did you get on at the solicitors, Dad?"

Billy explained to Rosa what the solicitor had told him.

"Obviously, the first thing the solicitor is going to do, is put the appeal in for us. If that fails, which he seems to think it will, he said that while they are going through the appeal, it will give us more time to find the right solicitor to prepare a case for us to take to court. I know a twenty percent chance isn't very good odds, but we have to do something; we can't just let them take Eva away. We have some money put by, which we were going to use to build a big extension to the house for you and Eva; we will have to use that. But there's one condition, Rosa." he said in a stern voice, "If we do this, you must play your part by cooperating and answering to those complaints."

"Yes, Daddy. Matt has explained about the appeal; he went through this with his ex-wife, to get shared custody of his son. He said if I want to keep Eva, I must explain, or she will be taken away. Its either explain or I'm going to have to run away with her. Daddy, I'm ready." she said, not looking at him, but looking down and arranging Eva's dress, "I can only give one explanation to all the complaints; it's because of how bad my accident was. I was, and still am, depressed; I'm also in pain twenty-four-seven. I was a brilliant horse rider and show jumper; the accident took that and my future career away. That's it." she said, shrugging her shoulders.

Her mum and dad looked at each other with a 'where did that come from.' look. They were suspicious of her explanation. Although the accident was bad, was it the reason she did all those things. They always felt that there was something more she wouldn't tell them. Still, it was a start and they were not going to question it.

"Right, let's do it then. I will ring the solicitor and ask him to start the appeal process. Meanwhile, I will read through these leaflets to find out how we go about taking it to court."

47

While waiting for a decision on the appeal, the next few weeks for Rosa was no time for relaxing. Rosa was going back to work at the riding school for a few hours, three days a week, while her mum had agreed to having Eva Marie. She would be teaching the beginners, with the help of Sydney. Rosa was looking forward to seeing the faces of the little ones when they first got on a horse. It had been decided that Rosa would be sitting, giving instructions, while Sydney would be with the pupil and horse on lead rein, walking them round. Rosa had also started her physiotherapy treatment and was already feeling the benefits after just two weeks.

The day before Rosa was due to start work, she was up and ready, nice and early. Gemma called to drop off Rosa's time schedule.

"I'm going into town later to post some parcels, is there anything you want?" asked Gemma.

The Other Side of the Fence

"Oh, that's brilliant." replied Rosa, "Yes, I need to get something to wear for tomorrow. Could you take me and Eva, so I don't have to ask Mum to look after her, because she has got her tomorrow. If I take her pram, could you have her for a while so I can try things on; I shouldn't be too long?"

"That's a definite yes from me, Babe," said Gemma, "I would love it. I will take her to that little park near the shops; I can show her the ducks and I can have a cuppa at the tea hut while I wait. You can meet us there and take over when you're ready, then I will go and post my parcels."

"Thanks, Gemma. Yes, the parks fine; it's not too far to walk with my stick."

"OK, I'll pick you up in an hour." said Gemma.

Gemma drove them to the shops and found a parking place nearly opposite. They unloaded the pram and put Eva in.

"Enjoy!" Gemma said, "See you at the park later." She then walked off, happily pushing the pram.

Rosa left the shop quite pleased with what she had bought. As she started to walk to the park, a car horn sounded. Looking round, Rosa saw Gemma sitting in the car with Eva already in her car seat. She walked over to the car and Gemma wound the window down.

"What are you doing in the car? I was looking forward to a cup of tea in the park." said Rosa.

"Just get in." Gemma said abruptly.

Rosa looked puzzled but got in; then Gemma quickly locked the doors.

The Other Side of the Fence

"Gemma, what are you doing? What's up; you're scaring me?" asked Rosa, concerned.

"You're scared? Rosa, I don't scare easily, but I'm petrified." Gemma answered, looking all around the outside of the car.

"Just tell me!" insisted Rosa, then quickly looked behind at Eva and cooed, smiling, "Hello, my gorgeous girl."

"Well, we got to the park and were sitting at an empty table, with a cup of tea, so Eva could see the ducks, when this voice asked, 'Mind if I sit here?' I just nodded and smiled because it was Mr. Davenport. Well, he suddenly changed and started talking in this strange, menacing voice that went on and on."

"Oh, Gemma, I know what you mean, he's been strange for years; what did he say?"

"He kept asking all these questions but never let me answer. Where's Rosa? Is that her baby? Do I look after her? Where did you say Rosa was? What day's do you come here? What's her name? How old is she? Will Rosa be here in a minute? Has she still got that horse? I just sat there thinking that he'd gone completely mad. He then stood up and held the pram handle with both hands; I swear, Rosa, I thought he was going to run off with her. I put my foot through the wheel spokes, in case the brake didn't hold if he tried to take her. He then bent over and kept talking to Eva; I was so scared; I have never drunk a cup of tea so fast in all my life; I'm sure I've burnt my mouth. I told him that I must be going, as I'd got things to do. He said that he would walk with me. I panicked and said that it was OK as I was meeting my husband who'd gone to get the car. He held Eva's hand and said, 'Bye, little one; what's her name again?' I didn't answer but he said that he would probably see you and the baby about

The Other Side of the Fence

soon. I practically had to wrench the pram out of his other hand. He's gone all weird and seems to have this obsession with you and Eva. By the way, I did wipe Eva's hands. I couldn't get us back to the car quickly enough; should we go to the police and report him?"

"I know he scared you Gemma, he has scared me for years, but you can't report someone for talking to a baby and thinking they are going to run away with it; they have only got two tables at the café, and he knows you, so it's obvious he would ask to sit with you."

"He really scared me though, Rosa, but I'm OK, now I've stopped shaking. Put your seat belt on because I'd better get these parcels posted."

"Poor Gemma, I feel for you. Are you OK to drive?" Rosa asked, "Or do you want me to drive? Let's post the parcels and go and get fresh cream cakes; I want to get one for my mum. We'll take them back to mine and I will make us all a nice cup of tea." Laughing, Rosa added, "I know, one not too hot for you."

The results of the appeal finally came through and sadly for Rosa, as expected, it failed.

Her dad said, "Well, it looks like there's nothing left, but to take it to court. I'll phone the new solicitor that I found, in a couple of days, to start proceedings."

Knowing that James' dad was a top lawyer and that the odds of winning the case weren't very good, Rosa was worried that her dad would lose all his savings; so, she said to her dad, "Perhaps it would be best if I just ran away with Eva."

Billy answered, "Don't be silly, Princess; I don't care about the money, and I must know that I've tried everything to keep my granddaughter."

The Other Side of the Fence

The next few weeks were quiet; every day was unbearable, while they waited for all parties involved to finalise a start date.

Everything was working well with her mother looking after Eva while Rosa went back to work at the riding school. Rosa was happy to be back at work; she had done away with the walking frame and now only used the walking stick to get about.

Rosa would often come home from the riding school and see Davenport sitting in his car opposite the house. If Gemma was dropping Rosa off and saw his car, she would always drop Rosa off at her front door, rather than the entrance to her drive.

Three weeks to the day of Rosa starting back at the riding school, Davenport's car was parked, as usual, opposite the farmhouse. The bonnet was up and Rosa looked as she got out of Sydney's car, but couldn't see him; she even looked down the road, but nothing. Opening the front door and walking down the hall, she called to her mum, to let her know she was home. Reaching the lounge, she suddenly stopped, a look of horror on her face; Davenport was sitting at the table, holding a cup of tea and talking to her mum, who was holding Eva.

Rosa tried to speak, but nothing would come out; she pointed to her mum then to Davenport.

"Oh, hello, Rosa, Mr Davenport's car has broken down. Luckily, it was outside our house, so he knocked, and asked to use our phone to ring a mechanic, as his mobile didn't work. While he's been waiting for the mechanic to arrive, he's been making the baby laugh; hasn't he, Sweetheart?" she said looking at Eva.

The Other Side of the Fence

Davenport looked at Rosa, "The mechanic said he would be here in thirty minutes, so he should be here any time now."

"In that case, Mr Davenport, you had better wait outside so you don't miss him. I will show you out." replied Rosa, mustering all the strength she had. She then turned and started to walk back down the hall.

"Oh, OK. Bye, Mrs. Maddox; bye little, oh, I still don't know her name."

"It's Mary!" Rosa shouted from the hall.

"Nice name." Davenport said, "Bye, little Mary, hope to see you and your mum again soon."

Davenport caught up with Rosa as she started to open the front door. He grabbed her round the waist, turned her round and tried to kiss her on the lips. Rosa slapped his face, kicked him hard on the leg and pushed him out the door. She watched him limp across the road, close the bonnet of his car and drive off. She was so angry, that when she slammed the door shut, she thought the house shook.

She ran up the hall, through the lounge and past a shocked looking mother. She just managed to get to the toilet before she was violently sick.

When she finally came back into the lounge, her mum said, "You OK dear? You look really flushed. What's all this about Eva being Mary."

"Because I'm angry, Mum. He annoys me; he's so nosey, don't ever let him in the house again." Rosa, trying to calm down, added, "Will you do me a favour please and give Eva her bottle; I need to go to my room and do some serious thinking."

48

Rosa settled Eva Marie down for the night. Then, carrying the baby monitor through to her parents' lounge, she felt that same calm determination she had in Ibiza when she met James.

Entering their lounge, she said, "Are you watching anything important on TV? I would like to talk to you both."

"Nothing very good;" her dad said," let me turn it off." He turned off the TV and said, "OK Rosa, you have our full attention; what is it?"

"Thank you, Daddy. What I've got to say is really important." she said, as she sat down on their sofa, "I need you both to understand that I'm in full control of my emotions, and please do not question my reasons, because there is no way I can tell you the full story of why I have made this decision."

"Rosa," her mum said, "you're worrying me; what is it?"

Looking directly at them, she said, "I have decided to let James have Eva."

"What!" her dad exclaimed.

"I have decided that Eva would be better off in Ireland, with James."

"Why? Rosa, are you crazy?" her mum said, "Why would you say a thing like that? Billy, talk to her."

"Because I now think that if she stays here, she'll be in danger." Rosa explained.

Her Dad got up and went to sit next to her on the sofa; he held her hand and said, "Talk to me, Princess, what's the matter?"

Looking at her dad, she said, "I did say that I can't tell you and I can't, I can't even go to the police because I have no proof that it's happening; but I can assure you both, it is. It's something that's been building against me for years, and it's now got to the point that it's starting to involve my precious baby girl. As I said, I can't go to the police, because I have no evidence at all. All these years, I've been hoping that one day it will stop, but it's still going on and it's getting worse. That's it. That's all I can tell you. It's got so that I'm scared every time I leave her with anyone."

"Is it because I let Mr. Davenport use our phone?" asked her mum.

"No, Mum. Now, stop worrying and stop looking for reasons; it won't help what's happening. I know it will break my heart to let her go, but I have thought long and hard about it; it's Eva's safety that's the priority, not my feelings. Daddy," Rosa said, now holding his hand with both hers and tears streaming down her face, "think about it, why would I say these things if they weren't true. With what I've just told you and with our own solicitor telling us we don't have much chance of succeeding against the Stirlings; and don't forget, James' dad is a top lawyer who must know lots of influential people. I'm telling you that your granddaughter will be safer in Ireland. Social services have already said that we can visit her anytime we want and that we can get joint custody as soon as I prove that I'm capable of looking after her. This way, I will have a chance. James is a lovely person and he will give her all the love we can. Tell me I'm right, Daddy? Please say that you will come with me to Ireland and if we don't like what we see, I promise we won't leave her?"

"Rosa, listen;" replied her dad, "what you have just told us has come as a big shock. There's so much I need to think about. Give me time to digest it all."

Wiping away her tears, Rosa stood up and said, "OK, I will leave you both to think about it. I'm not at work tomorrow, so we can talk then. Night, Mum." Her mum just sat there, her head in her hands; she hardly moved one hand in acknowledging Rosa saying goodnight. Rosa knew she was crying.

"OK, Rosa," her dad said. He stood up and gave Rosa a hug, "I think we all need to sleep on this; we'll talk tomorrow."

"OK. Night, Daddy."

The next morning, Rosa was still calm. If she had any doubts at all, she only had to think of Davenport and Gemma's panic-stricken face, saying that she honestly thought he was going to take Eva. And, of course, the day she came home to see Davenport sitting in her mum's lounge; then, with these images in her head, she would become as determined as ever to take Eva to Ireland.

She had just fed Eva and told her how much she loved her. She told her that what she was doing, was to keep her safe. She sat Eva in her rocker and walked through to her little kitchen to make herself breakfast, when she saw her mum standing in the doorway.

"Rosa," she said, "why are you giving my granddaughter away?"

"I'm not giving her away, Mum; social services are taking her away."

"She's right, Em." said her dad, as he came up behind her mum. Then, walking into the room, he asked, "Can you make us all a cup of tea please, Rosa." He then sat down at the table and beckoned his wife to join him.

"What ever do you mean by that?" his wife asked.

"I have been on the phone to my solicitor, and asked his honest opinion, on us cancelling the court case, because a couple of days ago, I got a letter from the solicitor who is preparing for it. I didn't tell you before, because I didn't want to worry you while I was deciding what to do. What Rosa told us last night has changed things. Decisions have to be made, and soon."

His wife and Rosa looked at each other in disbelief. Looking back at him, his wife said, a slow, curious, "Yes, and?"

"In the letter, he says that he has now reviewed both ours and the Stirlings' claims, plus he's read all the reports from the Irish and English social services. He wants to know if, before he started any proceedings, we realised how low the percentage of us winning was. He went on to say that in his professional opinion, our case is very weak and he wants to know, before he does any more work, if we want to continue?"

"Oh my goodness, Billy, what are we going to do now?" his wife exclaimed.

"That's why I phoned our solicitor this morning and read the letter to him. He said that it was pretty obvious that we didn't stand a chance, as the solicitor has practically told us that he would rather lose money than take our case on; and solicitors don't say those words easily. Plus, can we afford to lose a lot of money if we don't cancel. He thought it was decent of him to give us such a candid opinion. I also told him all about what Rosa told us last night. He said that it was quite disturbing and asked why we couldn't go to the police. When I explained, he said that he felt for you and was sorry. He wished us all the best, and said that if we needed him, he's just a phone call away. I thanked him, then phoned the other solicitor. I thanked him for his honest opinion and told him that we would like to withdraw our claim. He said that we had made the right decision and would only bill us for the work he has done to date." Billy let out a sigh, then continued, "So there you have it. I can do no more, only be here for you, Rosa." He leaned across the table to touch her hand, "You go and phone James; sort out dates and let me know when you want to go. We will go with you for support." he said, looking at his wife.

"I'm sorry, Rosa." her mum said, "I can't go with you. I know you're doing it for Eva's safety, but I can't bear the thought of walking out of James' house without her."

"I love you, Mum and understand. Don't worry, as long as Daddy is with me, I'll be OK. You're right; if you came, you might start me off. I will phone James and both social services to let them know what we have decided and find out what I have to do. It's going to be the hardest thing I will ever have to do but I know it's the best thing to do for Eva's safety. And, for my piece of mind, I need to take Eva to Ireland as soon as possible."

Going to his daughter and putting his arms around her, with tears in his eyes her dad said, "I'm so proud of you, Princess; you're one brave girl. As soon as we know what we have to do I will book our tickets to Ireland."

Her mum stood up and for a few moments the three of them stood in total silence with their arms around each other.

49

After phoning James, Rosa came back to her parents' lounge where her mum and dad were still sitting at the table. Looking at a piece of paper that she'd been writing on, she said, "I caught James just before he left for work; he really is one of the nicest men I've ever met. I've made a list of what he's told me."

Her dad coughed loudly,

"Daddy, I did say one of." she laughed.

"Don't forget Matt." her mum said.

"Yes, and of course there's our lovely Matt." Rosa answered. Then, reading from the piece of paper she said, "We'd better get the atlas out Daddy; he lives just outside of a place called Kildare, he said it's a 45-minute drive from Dublin airport. He said that I would enjoy the ride, as it passes by some world-famous equestrian centres. He apologised that it has come to this and realises that it's going to be difficult for us, as he knows how much we love Eva. He promises that she'll have the best of everything. He said that he'll sort things out over the weekend, so that he can take some time off work any time next week that suits us. It's about an hour's flight from England and he will meet us at Dublin airport. He said he will buy a car seat for Eva, so we won't need to take one with us. I could hear him telling his mum what was happening, then she asked to talk to me. We had a nice talk; she was quite concerned about how I was feeling. She asked me to bring photographs of us and promised to show them to Eva every day, and tell her that we love her; wasn't that a lovely thing for her to say? James then came back on the phone and said that we can go and see Eva anytime. If ever we want to stay over, they have a guest cottage that we can use for a few days. He told me not to worry; he will deal with social services and get back to me." Then, with a big sigh, Rosa sat down at the table and said, "That's it; I feel a lot calmer, now that's all sorted. But there is still a lot to do. Daddy, you pick the day that's best for you, and I'll let James know, so he can make arrangements with social services. Then, when it's confirmed, we can book a flight. I will go and see all the girls at the stables tomorrow, to work something out, so I can take next week off." With that, Rosa stood up and said, "I'm just going through to phone Matt to let him know what's happened; he's been through all this with his ex-wife and son, so he understands exactly how I'm feeling, and knows what to do."

Her mum and dad looked at each other with a look of hope that she would be this strong and calm next week.

Within minutes, Rosa was back.

"Love him to bits." she said, "He's going to take me and Eva into town on Saturday. He also said, that if we would like, he will take us to the airport and back. Knowing him, that's to make sure I'm OK. He's going to take the time waiting for us to come back from Ireland, to drive a bit further and see his son for a few hours."

"That's good; it will be really helpful." Then, laughing, Billy said, "Book him."

As promised, on Saturday, Matt picked up Rosa to go into town. Rosa decided not to take Eva; it was late September, and although everyone was back at the Equine college during the week, as it was the weekend, she didn't want to risk running into Davenport. Just before she left, Rosa pretended to joke, by saying to her mum, "And don't let anyone in the house while I'm out."

She was quite relieved when her dad said, "Don't worry, I'm not going out till late afternoon; you should be back by then."

When they reached town, Matt and Rosa decided to split up and meet at Maize's cafe when they had finished shopping. Rosa made her way to the jewellery shop, where she had previously seen a pretty music box in the window. Going inside, she asked to see it; it was a delicate pink with a picture of a baby on the lid. The assistant wound it up and passed it to Rosa to open. When she opened it, it played 'Brahm's Lullaby'.

"That's lovely;" Rosa said, "it's just what I wanted. I will have it, thank you. I sing this to my baby all the time; it's just perfect for what I want it for."

When she left the shop, she made her way to Maize's café. She sat at a window table, with a big grin on her face, thinking about the music box. It was for Eva to have in Ireland. In Rosa's mind, whenever Eva would hear it, she would know that her mum was near. Rosa had noticed that whenever she hummed that tune in the evenings, Eva seemed to like it. If she was tired, it soothed her and helped her fall asleep.

The Other Side of the Fence

Looking across to the post office, Rosa saw Matt come out carrying a newspaper; then, her heart sank when she saw Davenport follow Matt out. It looked like they said goodbye, then, Matt turned and walked towards the carpark, while Davenport headed towards the park. Rosa was shocked and went into a daze. She was sitting there, staring into space, wondering what to do, when the bell of the café door made her jump. It was Matt entering; he smiled when he saw her and sat down at the table.

"What ever was all that about?" Rosa asked.

"He's a strange one; your old teacher. I was in the queue at the post office when he came up behind me and started talking to me about you. He said that he saw you get out of my car. He thought that you are walking a lot better and asked how you were, in yourself. I said that you're fine, then he said 'How's Mary? Has Rosa got her at the park?' He said that he was going there to see if you were there. He then asked if I wanted to go to the park with him and get a cup of tea. I said that I couldn't, as I had to go because my carpark ticket had run out; that's why you saw me go to the car. You stay clear of him, Rosa; the girls at the stables are right; he is scary."

"He is, and a right pain." she said, "He's always asking questions. I told him Eva's name was Mary. I thought, what's it got to do with him."

Picking up the fresh cream cake menu, Matt said, "Come on, Rosa, let's forget about him. Let's see, what cream cakes do we want?"

While waiting for their tea and cakes to arrive, Rosa showed Matt the music box she had bought and told him why she chose it.

"Rosa, that's lovely." he said, "Very thoughtful with a loving meaning behind it."

The Other Side of the Fence

As she wrapped it up again, she asked, "Did you buy anything?"

"No, just the newspaper."

They chatted while they had their tea and delicious cakes; then they left and Matt drove Rosa home.

Arriving at Rosa's, Matt helped her out of the car, then turned to get back to the driver's door. Looking across the road, Matt asked, "Rosa, isn't that your old teacher sitting in his car?"

"Yes," replied Rosa, "he often sits there, in the sun, reading his newspaper."

Looking back at her, he said, "I don't know about you, Rosa, but I don't like it. I find his whole attitude worrying. Are you sure he's not pestering you?"

"Hello Daddy", she said, relieved at the distraction, as her dad came out the front door.

Billy said, "Hello, Princess. I've booked Tuesday flights, at nine a.m. out and eight-thirty p.m. return. I hope that's OK with you Matt?"

"Yes, that's fine Mr. Maddox. I'll pick you up at six on Tuesday." he answered and as he bent down to say goodbye to Rosa, he whispered, "If you ever need me, phone me, anytime." then kissed her on the cheek.

50

Rosa felt quite relaxed as she looked out the window of the plane. The scene below had just changed from sea to land.

Looking at her dad, she said, "Hasn't Eva been good? I must have the best-behaved baby ever." Rosa was holding Eva in front of her; she lifted her up so she could look at her and said, "Who's a proper little traveller then? And who's going to go travelling all over the world when she grows up? My lovely little Eva, that's who." She then snuggled into Eva's chest, making her giggle.

Her dad, seeing this tender moment between his daughter and granddaughter, said, "Rosa, what you are doing, are you sure this is what you want?"

"No, Daddy, it's not what I want; this is breaking my heart, but I must stay strong. You must trust me, it's the only way to protect Eva. I pray every night for it to go away. If there is any justice in this world, it will come right in the end."

The Other Side of the Fence

"OK, Princess, I promise that I won't question you again. I had a bad moment then, thinking about your mother breaking down as we left."

"Gemma said she would call in and check that Mum's OK, before she goes down to the stables."

Suddenly, the seat belt sign came on and the air steward announced that they would be landing in ten minutes.

"I can't believe how quick this journey has been." Billy said, "Sometimes if the traffic is bad, it takes me longer to get to Norwich. With this flight being this quick, any spare time we have at home, we can always pop over and see Eva."

"Yes, you're right, Daddy. Matt rang me last night when I was packing Eva's things. We had a nice long chat; he's so worried that I might have a panic attack when we have to leave her. I promised him I would be OK, because I know what I'm doing is what's best for Eva. He said that I should just pretend that I'm packing for her to go on holiday with her dad, so that's how I'm handling it. And now you saying that we can pop over anytime; it all sounds good to me." She looked out the window and said, "Everywhere looks nice out there, the fields are a lovely shade of green."

When the plane arrived at the terminal, Billy put Eva's big bag of bottles, nappies and wipes etc. over his shoulder and carried Eva down the plane steps. Rosa followed, with Eva's little pink suitcase and her own big shoulder bag.

"I think that's everything." she said to the steward, "How can someone so small need so much luggage?"

The Other Side of the Fence

They were pleased when Eva's pram came off the baggage carousel early and they settled her in it.

Rosa said, "I will push her, Daddy, because I don't want James to see me with a walking stick. I've brought a new fold up one which is in my bag; I will use it if I get desperate, but I want them to see how much better I am."

As they left the airport arrivals hall, they could see James waving from the pick-up area, across the road. Rosa thought to herself, "Yes, that's my daughter's father, immaculately dressed as always." Today, he was wearing a black polo shirt with the little alligator logo on the chest, light grey trousers and wearing black rimmed sunglasses. With his blonde wavy hair, she still thought he reminded her of a clean-cut American college boy; the one all the girls go after in films.

James gave Rosa a kiss and shook her dad's hand. Taking his sunglasses off, he bent down and looking at Eva, said, "My word Rosa, she really is lovely; a real cutie."

When Eva smiled back at him, Rosa, smiling, said, "Oh yes, Eva, I forgot to tell you that your dad is a real charmer."

He gave her a cheeky smile, then opening the boot to put the pram in, said, "I brought my dad's car; there's more room in the boot for the pram."

They were soon belted up and on their way; Billy sat in the front with James, and Rosa sat in the back with Eva; Eva fell asleep as soon as the car started moving. Looking out of the window, Rosa said, "Did you see that, Daddy? we just past an equestrian centre."

"We certainly did." James said, "Keep looking, Rosa."

"Look, there's a riding school over on the left, Daddy; it says that they do horse riding tours all through the woods." As they drove along, they passed several others and as Rosa's excitement grew, she said, "They all say they do the horse tours, how I would love to do that one day."

James said, "Keep your eyes open for the next equestrian centre coming up; its massive and really famous."

"Yes, I can see it. Everything is painted white and black; how smart does that look; it makes the whole place look clean. I like it, I'm going to get ours painted in white and black, when we get back."

"I Told you that you would like this road, didn't I."

"Yes, you did James, and I certainly do."

James then said to Billy, "You know what, Mr. Maddox? Before we met your family, the hundreds of times my family and I have driven along this road, we never really took much notice of the riding schools. Now, even my dad says that when Eva is older, we can take her for riding lessons; we have found one near where we live."

Rosa went cold, she filled up, and as she held Eva's hand, the reality of what was about to happen, hit her. She put her hand in her pocket and felt a piece of folded up paper; the panic and uncertainty receded. Reassured, she took her hand out and patted the pocket.

"Are you OK, Princess?" her dad asked, "You've gone all quiet."

"Yes, I'm fine. I was just thinking that in a few years' time, I can come over for holidays and do all those horse things with Eva; she might even become better than I was."

"Here we are.", James said, as he turned in and drove up the drive to the Stirlings house.

The Other Side of the Fence

"You are joking, James." Rosa laughed in disbelief, "Do you really live here? It looks more like Buckingham Palace."

"No, it's not Buckingham palace." he laughed, "It's all split into apartments. It's where all us Stirlings live.

Rosa got out the car and stood there in awe of what she was seeing. James got out the car and took Eva out of her car seat. He looked at Rosa to see if it was alright to give Eva to his mum, who had come out the house specially to meet them. Rosa nodded.

Looking at Rosa, she mouthed 'Thank you', took her and said to a sleepy Eva, "Hello, little one."

Rosa instantly liked how she held Eva, because she had straightened Eva's dress, so it wasn't all tucked up her back. Rosa thought, "Tick. Number one test passed."

James' mum then said, "Hello, Mr. Maddox and Rosa, please come inside; the social services representatives are already here."

Billy said, "Please, Mrs. Stirling, Billy is fine."

"Of course, Billy; and please call me Angela."

Rosa and her dad went inside and stood in the big hall.

Rosa whispered, "Wow! Daddy, this is magnificent."

"This way." Angela said, "This is my apartment; please make yourselves at home." She gave Eva to Rosa, who put her in her pram, while they were introduced to the very pleasant, social services representatives. They all signed the appropriate paperwork. The social services representatives then asked for any future queries to be directed to them immediately and wished everyone good luck for the future.

Angela saw the representatives out, then on her return, said, "My husband's offices are just round the corner and he will be back for lunch at two o' clock; I hope you will join us. But I'm sure you'll be really hungry by then, so I'll just go and make us all a drink and a snack for now."

51

During the tea and snacks, Rosa gave Angela the photos and a list of Eva's likes and dislikes; she explained that if Eva was restless, the music box would calm her. Rosa said that she hadn't bought all of Eva's cuddly toys, but the pink teddy was her favourite.

Angela, again promised that she would show Eva Rosa's photo every day, telling her that it's her mummy.

"Obviously, we are delighted that our granddaughter will be here with us, but should we need to know anything, I'm glad you're only a phone call away. I do feel for you, Rosa, I'm so sorry it's come to this. Mrs. Bennett has had a lot to do with the way things have turned out; she told social services that she has tried for years to get you to open up about your demons; it must be something horrific, if you don't feel that you can tell anyone."

Rosa nodded, "Thank you for understanding, Angela. It will break my heart when I walk out that door to go back home. I can assure you that I haven't done this lightly; it's because in England, a situation that's been haunting me for years, is getting worse. I just feel that Eva will be safer here. That's really all I can say."

Angela got up, went over to Rosa, gave her a big hug and asked, "Could Edward help you?"

"Perhaps, one day, when I get enough proof, I will take you up on that offer." Rosa replied, gratefully.

Billy and James had been listening quietly. To stop himself getting upset, James said, "Mum, you know they haven't got too long; they must leave here by six at the latest."

"OK, sorry." Angela said, "Right, come on Billy, I will show you round the place and introduce you to whoever is about. Is it OK if we take Eva in the pram, Rosa?" she asked.

"Mum, don't you mean you want to take Eva to show her off?" James joked.

James took Rosa to show her the two nurseries they had prepared. The one in his parents' apartment was decorated prettily in pink; it also had a single bed in it, which James explained was for the nanny, if they had to go away. James explained that the nanny, Karen, was a friend of James' brother's girlfriend. She was a nurse but also a registered nanny. Karen would visit before Rosa left, so she could meet her.

The nursery in James' apartment was really girly, he had made sure there was everything a baby would need, right down to a baby monitor.

"Tick. Test two, passed." Rosa thought, then said, "James, I am impressed; they are both lovely. You seem to have thought of everything."

The Other Side of the Fence

"Well, this is where she will spend most of the time. I intend to treat her like a princess."

"Tick. Daddy treats me like a princess. Test three passed." she thought.

"Come on," said James, "I will show you the rest of the place." He showed her the swimming pool and the gym, then they went out into the garden.

"Is that a gazebo over there?" Rosa asked, pointing.

"Yes, come on, let's go and sit in it; I need to tell you something before you leave." They went over to the gazebo and sat down. James held her two hands and looked into her eyes.

"Rosa," he said, "I know that what you're doing today, must be the hardest thing you will ever have to do, but I want you to know that whatever has been said about you, you will always be that lovely girl I met in Ibiza; the one who knocked me backwards in that blue dress when you walked into the hotel that night. I will never forget the few days we spent together, and to have our beautiful daughter from such a memorable time, makes it even more special. All I know, is that you must have had such a terrible experience in your life to have made you do the things you did, and that you are now paying a heavy price keeping it a secret, to protect our daughter. Even my dad has said that you must have been going through hell, knowing that if you didn't answer those complaints made against you, it would mean losing your daughter."

She smiled at him. "James, I love how you understand me. I pray every day, hoping that one day I can tell someone why, but until that day comes, this is what I have to do. From what I've seen, I am sure Eva will be happy here and you and your family will love her and keep her safe. You have the most wonderful place here; she is a lucky girl to have you as her father." She then gave a cheeky grin and said, "By the way, my dress was 'lavender blue' and I haven't worn it since."

They sat in silence for a while, enjoying the moment, then Rosa looked at James and said, "James, when it's time for us to leave, please don't come to the door to say goodbye. Will you take Eva out into the garden, so I can't see her; I just want to get in the car and go. Please explain to your mum and thank her; she's been wonderful."

James put his arm round Rosa and gave her a kiss on the cheek.

"Don't worry, Rosa, I fully understand, and I'm sure Mum will too. We all think you're being very brave. Come on, let's carry on with the tour." he said, with a smile.

It was a very amiable Edward Stirling that came home for lunch; he even gave Rosa a hug and whispered, "If you ever need a lawyer, ring me."

After a very pleasant dinner, Rosa met Michael's girlfriend and Karen. After talking to them both, she felt confident that Eva was going to be in safe hands.

Lily arrived just as they were about to leave for the airport. Rosa liked Lily and would have liked to spend some time with her, but the brief chat they had, boosted Rosa's confidence that Eva would be well cared for and loved.

"Don't worry about a thing," Lily had said, "you know how lovely James is; well actually I find the whole family loving and caring. I will keep you up to date with how Eva's doing and I'll send you photos. When you come to visit, I will try and get time off work; we can take her out and I can take you out to Kildare Village. It has a famous shopping centre; Angela and her sister-in-law have a boutique there."

The Other Side of the Fence

Rosa thanked her and said, "I feel happy knowing that. I will look forward to our trip when I come back." They then hugged goodbye.

"Rosa, are you ready?" Billy called, "We're ready to go; Edward is taking us."

Rosa called back, "Coming, Daddy; I just need to go to the toilet." She then turned to Lily and asked, "Is there a toilet near?"

"Yes, I'll show you." replied Lily and took Rosa to a toilet by the dining room.

Rosa locked the door, took out the piece of paper from her pocket, read it, took deep breaths, read it again and put it back in her pocket. Then, opening the door, she called, "I'm ready!" and walked straight out the front door and got into the car, without looking back. She sat there with her eyes closed. Edward started the car and Rosa clenched her piece of paper so tight, her nails were digging into her hand. She kept her eyes closed, as she didn't want to look out the window and see anyone waving goodbye; she didn't even want to look at the riding stables along the road; she just wanted to get on the plane and get home.

They reached the airport in no time. Getting out the car, Edward Stirling came round to say goodbye to her.

Looking at her, he said, "You're one brave girl, Rosa. Remember what I said. I meant it; anytime."

Getting off the plane in England, Rosa had to use her walking stick to get through the airport and out through to the outside as fast as she could. She then took several deep breaths of cool fresh air.

Her dad came up behind her and said, "Rosa, slow down; I could hardly keep up with you."

"Sorry, Daddy, I just needed to breathe that good old English air. Come on, there's Matt." she said and hurried towards him. The nearer she got, the more the tears flowed, "Oh, Matt, thank goodness you're here. Don't worry, I am fine, just hold me tight; I need one of your 'everything will be OK' hugs."

On the journey back to the farm, they chatted about their day, and before they knew it, they had arrived.

"Are you sure you will be OK, Rosa?" Matt asked.

She nodded and said, "Yes, thank you; I'll see you tomorrow." Then went inside.

Billy said, "I think she will be OK. She has been remarkable, though it's probably going to hit her now."

"Just ring if you need me." Matt said. Then got back in the car and drove off.

Although she couldn't wait to hear how they got on, Rosa's mum said, "You must be hungry; I've made sandwiches and a pot of tea, which we can have while you tell me everything."

Eating his sandwiches, Billy said, "Well Em, I definitely know one thing; our little Eva is the image of her father. They seemed a nice friendly family; Even Edward was friendly this time. You can see that they adore Eva and they have her best interests at heart. Em, I can't wait for you to see where they live, it's like a palace. Our solicitor was right; I can honestly say, that had we taken them to court over Eva, there was no way we would have won."

Looking at Rosa, her mum asked, "How are you, Rosa? You seem really calm."

"I know, it has all been down to this piece of paper." she said, taking it from her pocket, "Any time I was in doubt, I just read this and I knew I was doing the right thing. Anyway, I will be going to see her in a few weeks; right, Daddy?"

"Yes, you're right there, Princess. You coming, Em?" Then, remembering, he got a package out of his bag and giving it to Rosa, said, "Oh, Rosa, before he drove off, Matt gave me this parcel for you."

She opened it up; It was a pink teddy bear, the same as he bought for Eva; It made her gasp.

"Oh Matt." she said, as she clasped it to her chest. She walked over to her mum and dad and kissed them goodnight, saying "I'm so tired, I must go to bed. Now I've got something to cuddle, I will be fine."

She didn't get undressed but laid on the bed cuddling the teddy and holding the piece of paper. She looked at the empty cot and said to herself, "She's just gone on holiday with her dad. She's gone on holiday with her dad." Then a flood of tears started as she sobbed uncontrollably.

52

The storm had passed, although it was still raining by the time forty-two-year-old Rosa finally got to sleep, with all the memories of Eva still running round her head. It was still dark outside when Rosa felt someone shaking her awake and a gentle voice saying, "Love, love, Rosa, wake up."

She opened her eyes and said, "What is it, what's the matter?"

"Rosa my love, you were scaring me. You were really upset and crying in your sleep."

Sitting up in bed, she could feel her cheeks were wet and wiped them. Yawning, she said, "I'm sorry, Darling, I was having a bad dream about years ago." Then, looking at the clock, she added, "It's four o' clock; you go back to sleep. I'm OK; I'm awake now. I will go downstairs and get some hot milk."

She went downstairs and made a drink. Holding the mug of hot milk in both hands, she sat down in the big armchair and stared into the wood burner, where some of the ashes were still glowing red.

She thought to herself that the dream she had had of Eva and the day she took her to Ireland, all those years ago, was because she had been thinking about her during the big storm last night, when she had been looking at Eva's photos.

"So, it was your fault, Miss Eva Marie Maddox Stirling." she said quietly to herself, looking at Eva's photos again. "I wonder if I've still got the piece of paper that got me through that awful day?" She got up, opened a cupboard and took out a box covered in pink rosebud paper; written on the lid were the dates 1997/2007. "If I've still got it, it will be in my special memory box." she thought. She took the lid off and started to sort through the contents. "Here it is." she said to herself. She opened it up and read it, just as she had a hundred times on that day and the dark times afterwards.

Rosa had written down the exact words that Gemma had said that day in the park, when Gemma was afraid that Davenport was going to take Eva. It read:

'Rosa, I have never been so scared in all my life. Davenport grabbed the handle of the pram with both hands; I honestly thought he was going to take Eva away. He is dangerous; he's obsessed with you and Eva.'

That was the moment that Rosa had decided that enough was enough. The pain she went through on that day still haunted her all these years later. She thought that unless something like that had happened to someone, they could never explain the intense pain you go through, having to give your child away; the pain is there every day, churning away inside you.

She folded up the piece of paper neatly and put it to one side. She then looked through a few baby photos of Eva and of Gemma's two children. Next, she picked up a letter. Opening it, she remembered how happy she was the day she received it and the photographs inside; it was from Angela Stirling. she read the letter again, before putting it to one side:

Dear Rosa,

I'm writing this, as one mother to another. As you know, when James was awarded full custody of Eva Marie, the rule was, that until you were fully discharged by the hospital and joint custody was awarded; you could only see her under supervision, at a mutually agreed time.

Your visits to see Eva Marie over the last few months have been lovely and have worked well. I certainly feel your heartache and pain every time you have to leave her.

I must tell you that it was my husband Edward, and not James, who made the complaints against you. Although Edward is not sorry for what he did; now, having got to know you over the last few months, he finds you a brave and loving mother. He hopes, one day, you will be free of the pain you are suffering to protect Eva.

I have enclosed recent photos of Eva, taken by Lily; you can see what a real beauty Eva is turning into; her hair is very pretty and has started to go curly. Edward and I adore her. James is smitten and loves her dearly; he is a very good father.

With James' consent, I have thought of a way that you can see more of Eva. Next month, James and his father will be abroad on business for two weeks. My sister and I own a boutique in London, on Oxford Street, and we will be in London doing a stocktake for a few days, during the two weeks they are away. We also have an apartment at the Barbican Centre. My idea is that if we brought Eva and her nanny with us, it will be a good opportunity for you to come to London and spend some time with Eva Marie. Edward says we won't be breaking the rules as long as the visits are supervised. You could bring your mum or a friend and stay with us. Another thought I had, is for Eva Marie's first birthday in a couple of months; instead of you coming to Ireland, I thought we could bring Eva to Norwich for a couple of days, so your family and friends could see her. We can arrange a birthday cake and a small pre-birthday party for her at the hotel. You could invite your parents and friends and meet up with us there. I have put my phone number on the back of one of the photographs. I hope to hear from you soon, so we can make plans for you to come to London next month.

Yours Sincerely,

Angela Stirling.

Rosa smiled to herself and thought that she must have been very paranoid back then, as she had actually cut the Stirlings' address off the top of the letter, so no one would know where Eva was.

James and his mother were wonderful; they always made Rosa and her family feel welcome whenever they visited Eva in Ireland, or they brought Eva to London or Norwich. Even Edward Stirling, Eva's now devoted grandfather, pleased Rosa when she visited Ireland for Eva's third birthday. Edward had said that he often took Eva to the stables to see the horses, which she loved and never wanted to leave. He said that he was thinking of riding lessons for her and asked Rosa when she thought the time would be right? Rosa had smiled and said that she was three when she started, but she was brought up on a

The Other Side of the Fence

farm. She said that Eva could sit on them and be walked up and down, but to start lessons, she would guess that Eva would be nearer five. The instructors at the stables would let him know when she was ready.

Sadly, Rosa did miss several important times in Eva's life, like when her first tooth started to show, when she first sat up on her own, her first steps and her first word, which James was pleased to say was Dad, Dad, Dad. The best was when Eva Marie saw Rosa and she ran up to her saying Mummy, Mummy. Rosa always made sure she thanked Angela for keeping her promise.

Rosa wasn't tired, so continued looking through her memory box. There were loads of photos of happy times visiting Eva, Eva and her on horses, a few photos of Rosa on a boating holiday with Gemma, her husband Jack, and his friend Dave, who Rosa went out with for a few months. There were some great photos of Katie's hen night in Ireland; no Ibiza for her. Sydney and Jess had joined them and were excited to have been asked. Rosa had told them about all the high-class stables and the riding tours there, so they had deliberately booked a hotel on the road where all the stables were, so some of the days the girls could go on the horse riding tours through the woods, while on the other days when the girls went sightseeing, Rosa could see Eva. There were also photos of Katie's wedding, and photos of Eva on her birthdays. She sorted through loads of photos of James and Lily's rather grand wedding; her little Eva was one of five bridesmaids, dressed in very pale lemon dresses, carrying an assortment of bright yellow, pale lemon and white posies; there was one special photo of three-year-old Eva standing alone in her bridesmaid's dress, looking down at her posy; Lily had added small white flowers to Rosa's yellow sunflower clip, from Ibiza, and clipped it onto the side of Eva's hair. It was such a special photo; Rosa had had it enlarged and framed; it was hanging in her lounge. The last few photos were of a very smart looking Eva in her uniform, on her first day at school.

The saddest photos were of her beloved Star, who had sadly died of old age, a short while after Rosa's twenty fifth birthday. He was buried in one of the fields on her dad's farm. Rosa had bought a plaque with his name on, and the stable girls had bought and planted several rose bushes over him. The saddest times for Rosa, were when she had to walk past his empty stable and see his name, Starlight Spirit, on his stable door.

Rosa remembered saying, 'My beautiful Star, I am so sorry for thinking that now Star has died, I'm free of Davenports threats.' She also realized, that at the time, she had not seen Davenport out and about for weeks. The last time she had seen him, in person, he had stood behind her in the supermarket queue, and asked where Mary was, as he hadn't seen her with her lately. She remembered answering, quite confidently, that she was fine; that she'd left her at home.

Finally, she picked up a large brown envelope from the box, clutched it to her chest, smiled, and said out loud to herself, "I'm so happy; so very happy. Before I go back to bed, I'm going to relive and cherish, once again, every moment of what's in this envelope." She then opened the envelope, took out an old newspaper cutting, read the headlines, smiled again, then leaning back in the chair, she closed her eyes and thought back to one of the best days of her life.

53

Early July 2004, Rosa and Gemma went into town to book a trip to Ireland. This year, Gemma was going with Rosa and taking her four-year-old daughter with them. Edward Stirling had asked Rosa to come on Eva's seventh birthday, because he had a big surprise for Eva.

They had booked their flights and had gone to the post office to buy birthday cards. They chose their cards and queued up to pay. Rosa was about to pay when she felt her T-shirt being tugged enough to pull her out of the queue.

She turned round and said to Gemma, "Gemma, what are you doing?" Gemma looked at her and nodded towards the bottom shelf of the newspaper stand.

The national daily newspapers were on one shelf, and the local Norfolk weekly newspapers were on a lower shelf. Rosa read the large headlines on several of the local newspapers, which read:

'NORFOLK COLLEGE EQUESTRIAN COACH ARRESTED.'

They looked at each other; Gemma said, 'Maize's?'

Rosa nodded, bent down and picked up two of each of their local papers; they then paid and left the shop.

They walked over to Maize's, ordered their drinks and sat down at a table.

"Do you think it's him?" Rosa said quietly, "I'm too nervous; you look."

Gemma opened the paper, started reading and said, "Well, if his name is Charles Darwin Davenport, then it's definitely him."

"What's he done?" asked Rosa, excitedly.

"It says here that despite being warned about his drinking on several occasions, he was suspended for being drunk in charge of the students and their horses. Listen to this, Rosa; he has now been arrested for sexually assaulting some of the first-year college girls."

"Oh no, poor girls. He's an evil, dirty old man alright."

"The police are asking for any other victims to come forward; there's a dedicated police phone number to contact them. Are you alright Babe? You've gone all flushed."

"Yeah; I'm angry. I was thinking how young those poor girls are and how terrified they must have been, going to college, each day, knowing he was going to be there." Rosa had decided not to say anything to Gemma yet; her mind was racing and she needed time to think.

They finished their drinks, then Gemma said, "Ready to go, if you are."

The Other Side of the Fence

"Yes, I bet you are. I know you; you can't wait to go and tell the others." Rosa said, grinning as she got up from the table and divided the papers between them. She then said, "Can you drop me off at mine first please; there's something I need to do that's important. I won't be long; I will get my dad to drop me at the stables. I will be there before my first lesson after dinner."

When Rosa got home, she called for her mother; she was pleased when there was no answer. She sat down in one of the armchairs, banged her hands several times on the arms, lent forward and excitedly stamped her feet, while saying, in triumph, "Yes, yes, yes, got you. After nearly ten years of terrorising me, you're going to pay, big time!"

She thumbed through the newspaper, looking for the phone number. When she found it, shaking with excitement, she dialled it.

"Norfolk Police, Sergeant Wilson speaking, how can I help?" said the voice on the end of the phone.

After a slight pause Rosa finally said, "I'm phoning about the arrest of Charles Davenport; I want to report a rape at the Eastern Equestrian College."

The sergeant took Rosa's details, then asked if she would be available later that evening, as he would like the two officers dealing with the case to hear her story. If they thought it was important, they would ask her to make a statement.

Rosa said that she would be in all evening from five-thirty.

The sergeant thanked her and said that she could expect a Detective Thomas and Detective Sergeant Parker, at about six-thirty that evening.

The Other Side of the Fence

A relieved Rosa thanked the sergeant and took a deep breath as she put the phone down, thinking, "That will be the best phone call, I will ever make." She then picked up the phone again to phone her dad, to ask him if he could take her to the stables.

When Rosa got in her dad's car, she asked him to wait before he drove off, as she had something important to tell him. She then showed him the newspapers.

After reading the headlines, he asked, "Is it who I think it is?"

"Yes, Daddy it's Charles Davenport." She started to cry; then, from beginning to end, she told him the whole story.

"My poor Princess. All these years, what you must have been through, keeping that man's wicked secret. We had no idea. We knew you didn't like to see him, as you said he reminded you of your accident; and whenever your mum spoke to him, you said it was because he was nosey. You have been so brave; I'm lost for words about what he did to you and what you did to protect little Eva Marie. Everything makes sense to me now. All these years you have obviously been suffering from PTSD. I hope he's going to rot in prison for what he's done to you. You were so young when it all happened and I know how much you loved Star, so I can understand how frightened you must have been when he said that he would kill him if you told anyone what he had done to you. He's got to pay for what he did. Rosa, my poor baby; I'm so sorry for what you have been through. You say he's still terrorising you and has been for years; he's a beast, a very sick man. I should have been there to protect you. And now those other poor girls. I'm so pleased the police are now involved"

He leaned over and hugged her tightly; she could see how upset he was getting.

The Other Side of the Fence

"Daddy, before I get back from the stables, can you make sure mum reads the newspapers, and explain everything to her; I can't go through it all again. You know what she's like; things like this don't happen in her little world. I just rang the police; they are sending two detectives round at six thirty tonight to interview me."

"Will do, Princess. When the police arrive, we will go in your lounge, so you can talk to them in ours."

When Rosa finally got to work it was a hive of activity. The girls could only gossip as they passed each other between riding lessons. Rosa had decided not to tell anyone other than her parents until she had made her statement to the detectives. She couldn't wait till five-thirty; she just wanted to go home and see her mum and dad.

It was nearly six thirty; Rosa was ready and sitting in her parents' lounge. Glancing at herself in a mirror as she walked through to the lounge earlier, she laughed as she said to herself, "Look at you Rosa Maddox, nicely dressed, hair combed and makeup on. It's not a date you know."

At exactly six thirty, there was a loud knock on the front door. She got up; her heart was racing as she walked down the hall and opened the front door.

"Rosa Maddox?"

"Yes." said Rosa

"I'm Detective Shirley Thomas, and this is Detective Sergeant Vince Parker, she said introducing her partner.

"Please come in." said Rosa, opening the door fully.

Detective Thomas walked past Rosa, then Rosa went to walk behind her, but suddenly stopped to let the Detective Sergeant go first, but he had already stopped to let Rosa go first. He smiled at her and put his arm out for her to go first. She giggled shyly and walked in front of him.

54

Rosa and the detectives walked into the lounge where her mum and dad were still sitting; she introduced them.

DS Parker nodded at them in recognition, then looking at Rosa, he asked, "Do you want them to stay?"

"No, it's fine; I've told them everything. They will just be next door."

Detective Thomas said, "OK, Miss Maddox, please tell me everything you remember."

"Please, call me Rosa." she said, smiling at the two of them.

Although she felt embarrassed with the handsome Detective Sergeant sitting next to her, Rosa took a deep breath and begun, "Mr. Davenport was always over familiar; he would stand so close to me when he spoke, I often ended up taking a step back from him. My ordeal happened when I was fifteen; the night before a big show jumping exam. I was a very good horse rider and was the favourite to pass with top marks in my class. It was late evening; I went to the stables to check on my horse. I got to the stables." Rosa suddenly stopped.

DS Parker could see she was about to relive what happened to her. He reached over, touched her on the arm reassuringly and said, "No rush, Rosa, take your time. Continue when you are ready."

"Actually, I have written a lot of it down, so you can have it." she said, pointing to a folder full of papers on the table.

Picking them up, DS Parker said, "Thank you, that's very thoughtful; it all helps. As you can see, Detective Thomas is also taking notes; I'm afraid you will still need to come to the station to make an official statement though."

Rosa continued to tell the detectives her story. As she recalled the events, they could see the pain etched on her face as she was reliving every moment of the nine-year nightmare, she had been through.

She choked up again when she told them about Eva Marie.

"I have missed so many special moments in her life, as she's been growing up." she said, with tears in her eyes, "She is seven this month and I'm going to Ireland to see her on her birthday. Her dad and I have worked well together, with my visiting rights; so, I have seen her quite a bit. I'm glad that she is happy living in Ireland with her father and his parents; they all adore her. She lives a privileged life."

DS Parker stopped her, as she was getting upset.

"I think that's enough for now, Rosa; you have been very helpful. If it's convenient, we would like to come to the stables tomorrow, to interview the girls about the day Davenport scared them; we would especially like to interview Gemma, regarding her encounter with him in the park. Will you be there?" DS Parker asked.

"Yes, I've got lessons tomorrow, and I need to see the girls to explain what's going on and tell them why two police officers want to interview them. They don't know anything about what I've just told you; they only know what they have read in the papers about Davenport's arrest. No one knows my story, other than my mum and dad, who I only told today."

DS Parker then said, "Confidentially, you know, Rosa, even before we knew about you, Davenport was already in serious trouble; we don't know how he's got away with the things he's done all these years. You probably read in the papers about when his house was searched, hundreds of photographs of really young girls were found. Well, now that we've seen you, I can tell you that you are not alone, there were many like you. This hateful man is going to be locked up for a very long time."

"I could add a lot more words to your hateful, but you probably wouldn't write them down." said Rosa, smiling.

"Thank you, Rosa." Detective Thomas said, holding out her hand for Rosa to shake, "Considering what you have been through, you have done extremely well. Please stay there Rosa, we will see ourselves out. She started to walk down the hall, then looking back at DS Parker, she said, "I will be in the car, I just want to sort through these notes."

Shaking Rosa's hand, DS Parker said, "I hope you're OK; I know this must have been very difficult for you."

"Honestly, I'm fine. I am so relieved that after all these years, I can tell someone. I feel a giant weight has been

The Other Side of the Fence

lifted off my shoulders. I'm so going to enjoy seeing him squirm for a change. Revenge is going to be mine at last." she said, thumping the air. Then, seeing the look of surprise on his face at her outburst, she said, "Oh, I'm so sorry; I've waited such a long time for this moment, I got carried away."

"I understand." he said, giving her the loveliest smile, "Try and hold it together a bit longer though, Rosa; there is still a long way to go yet." Then, remembering, he asked, "Is eleven-thirty OK for tomorrow?"

"Yes, that's fine. I will make sure they are all ready." she answered, walking down the hall with him to the front door. As he left, she closed the door, thinking, "Goodnight my handsome knight, you have rescued me from this nightmare. I can't wait till tomorrow."

Rosa quickly went to the phone and called Gemma. She asked her if she could get to work tomorrow about twenty minutes earlier.

"No problem, Babe; see you then."

She then rang Katie, Sydney and Jess. They too were all OK with the earlier start.

Early the next morning, all four girls were sitting in the office, waiting for Rosa to finish making them all a hot drink. She had already told them that she wanted to talk to them before they started work.

Once they were all settled, Rosa begun, "OK, I've asked you here before we open, because I've got something important to tell you. I know you have all read the newspaper reports about Davenport."

"Yes." said Gemma, putting two fingers to her throat and pretending to be sick.

"Now that he's been arrested, I can tell you all something that I've been keeping to myself for nearly ten years. When I was fifteen, in my first year at the equestrian college, on the night before the main end of term show jumping exam; I went to see Star at the stables. Well, Davenport followed me there; he was drunk and attacked me, knocking me out. When I came to, he was raping me."

"Oh, Rosa!" Gemma exclaimed, standing up quickly, and in doing so, pushed her chair backwards making it topple over. She needed to put her arms around her friend as quickly as possible. "Babe, I remember. It was late when you got back; you were all muddy and said that you had fallen over."

Katie just sat there her head in her hands, visualising her friend's torment that night. Jess started to cry and Sydney felt the blood drain from her face in horror. For a few seconds, everyone was just looking one to the other, then to Rosa.

Why had she never said anything about it all this time, they all wanted to know? Why have you? Why did you? Why, why, why? The questions came thick and fast.

Rosa sat and told them the full story of her nine years of fear; first for Star, then for Eva Marie and Star. They all sat there in absolute shock and disgust.

"OK," Rosa said, "Anymore questions before we start work?" When no one answered, she added, "One more thing before you all disappear. At eleven-thirty this morning, two detectives will be coming to interview Jess and Gemma, about their encounters with Davenport. Just say exactly what happened and how you felt about him. One is a woman detective, the other, a detective sergeant; they are both very nice and caring; the detective sergeant is really handsome. Tell you who he reminds me of, that film star Jason Statham; you feel he's more suited to be in a TV series. I don't know how I got my story out with him sitting next to me; but I was so thrilled to finally be able to tell someone, it all came tumbling out. Yeah, that's him, Jason Statham; I think it's because he's got that shaved black hair, brown eyes and dark stubble.

55

Just before eleven-thirty, Rosa and Gemma were in the Four Horseshoes office. Gemma was standing, looking out the window, as a car pulled up outside. The two detectives got out and started walking towards the office.

Gemma said, "They're here, Rosa. Wow! You're right about him; he's one dishy detective. Good job I'm married."

"Are you scared?" asked Rosa.

"No way, Babe; especially if he's going to interview me." she answered. They both laughed, which lightened the mood.

Rosa opened the door to let them in. As they came into the office, Rosa said, "Welcome to my favourite place; it has been my saviour throughout all of this; as has my friend Gemma." she said, pointing towards Gemma. She invited the detectives to sit down and asked, "Would you like a drink?"

The Other Side of the Fence

Detective Thomas answered, "Yes please, coffee, two sugars for both of us, thank you."

"Is it OK if the other girls are interviewed between their riding lessons? We are quite busy today." Rosa asked, putting the two coffees and a plate of biscuits on the table.

"Thank you, Rosa, you spoil us. And that's fine. We'll fit in around you." DS parker answered, smiling at her.

Rosa blushed and said to herself, "Oh for goodness' sake, you're not twelve-years-old!"

DS Parker then turned to Gemma and asked, "Are you ready, Gemma? We would like you to tell us about what happened in the park."

"Yes I am." she replied and she didn't hold back. She told her story through gritted teeth. She hated Davenport and they could tell. She told them how scared she was of him and said that she honestly believed that he was going to take the pram with the baby in it. She filled up when she told them how she locked herself and Eva in the car, while waiting for Rosa to come back.

Then, she suddenly said, "I bet Rosa didn't tell you about the accident she had, the day after she was raped. Did she show you the horrendous scars from when she missed the last fence and the horse fell on top of her? Did she tell you that she was in hospital for months, having operations, physiotherapy and learning to walk again; all because of that wicked, evil, Davenport. He stood next to the last fence, and as she was about to jump it, he stepped out and that monster pretended to shoot her horse. She lost concentration and didn't give instructions for her horse to jump; she went over the fence and her lovely horse, not wanting to let her down, followed her and landed on top of her. How sick is that man?"

Both detectives looked at each other, shaking their heads in disbelief; why hadn't she told them? They looked at Rosa and waited for confirmation and an explanation.

"Sorry, Babe, it needed to be said." Gemma said.

Rosa looked at their puzzled faces.

"It's all true." she said, "I'm sorry, I thought you only wanted to know about him raping me."

"Thank you, Gemma." DS Parker said. He then looked at Detective Thomas, "Did you get all that?" he asked.

"Yes, I did." she answered, then to Rosa, she said, "Rosa, we will need an additional statement from you, regarding your accident. I can see you have jodhpurs on, but can I ask that you wear a skirt when you come to the station, so that we can see the scars and take photos. Gemma, we will want an official statement from you as well. If you both want to come to the station together that's fine."

Just then, the door opened and in walked Jess. As Gemma had finished her interview, she left, to let Jess tell her story. When Jess told her side of the story, she seemed nervous, as if she was worried that Davenport was about to turn up and scare her again. She did relax a bit, when she told them how, because Davenport had wandered into the private part of the stables, they had the expensive security system installed.

Katie and Sydney came in together. Their interviews didn't take long, because all they saw was Davenport coming out of the stable Jess was in, which confirmed Jess' story. They did add how they were all still scared, even after the security cameras were installed, because when they left off work, they would often see Davenport's car parked on the other side of the road, right opposite the stable gates. Sometimes, he was in it; sometimes, he wasn't.

They also told the detectives about how devastated they were to hear Rosa's story and that they wanted to say how brave they thought Rosa was, with all she had been through, all those years.

Hearing that, Rosa said, "Thank you, girls, I really appreciate it."

"Yes, that was a nice tribute to add, girls." said Detective Thomas"

"Rosa, before we go, can you show us the stables that Jess has just told us about?" DS Parker asked.

"I can do it, Rosa." said Sydney, "It's on the way to my next lesson. Gemma should have finished her lesson by now; she can show them the way back.

"Yes, thank you Sydney," said a tired looking Rosa, "That's very thoughtful. Is that OK, Detective Sergeant?"

"Yes of course." he said, then looked toward Katie, to see if she was going with them.

"No, not me;" said Katie, as she picked up her jacket and bag, "it's my turn for early lunch; bye all." she said, as she practically flew out the office door.

Rosa found herself alone in the office. Her mind was racing; everything was moving so fast.

"I need to slow down and relax somewhere quiet." she thought. She picked up the phone and dialled, "Hi, it's Rosa." she said, "Will you be in this evening? ..... You will; oh good.... Fancy some company?" she asked, "Yes, yes, that's lovely... Yes, you choose.... Yes, just one bottle; I need to stay sober.... Thank you so much, Matt, that's just what I need. I finish work about six; see you then."

She then rang her mum, "I won't be back for tea tonight, Mum, I'm going to Matt's for the evening; he's cooking us a meal, then we're going to watch a film he's just bought."

"That's lovely dear; you relax. If you have a drink, just ring Dad; he will pick you up."

"OK, that's great. Bye, Mum; love you." she said and hung up.

The office door opened and Gemma entered.

"The cops are going; they asked if there's anything else you want to say before they leave?"

"I can't think of anything." Rosa said, "We know that we've got to go and give statements."

Gemma shouted from the door, "She said no!" Then she waved and shut the door.

Thirty seconds later, it opened again; it was Detective Sergeant Parker.

"Sorry," he said, "I just thought; have you still got any of the letters or cards that Davenport sent you?"

"No, I destroyed them and threw the flowers away." Rosa answered.

"OK, that's a pity; they would have been useful. Bye, girls, nice to have met you all." he said and left.

Gemma went over to close the door behind him. Then looking out of the window, she said, "They are both sitting in the car talking. You know, I've just had a thought; do you think they would want the clothes I buried?"

"Oh yes, of course; are they still there?" Rosa asked, suddenly standing up and hurrying to the door.

"Yes, but they have started the car up. I will try and stop them." said Gemma as she ran after the car.

Gemma managed to stop the detectives leaving. DS Parker wound down his window and asked Gemma what she wanted.

"Rosa has remembered something." Gemma said.

When Rosa got to the car, she said, "I've still got the clothes I was wearing that night, will they be useful?"

"Did you just say you have the clothes you were raped in?" he said in amazement.

"Yes, she did; I buried them." said Gemma.

DS Parker got out the car.

"You two beauties, I could kiss you both." he said but quickly retracted it, "Not really, girls, it was just a figure of speech; it's definitely not allowed." he said smiling, "Seriously though, that's a big step. Do not, I repeat, do not touch the clothes. I will get a team together to retrieve them. I will phone you when we are ready, so you can take us to where you buried them. Gemma, thanks for your cooperation today. Enjoy your evening."

56

Rosa rang Matt and said, "I'm just locking up the office, then I will be walking to yours."

"The dogs need a short walk, so I will start walking to meet you." he answered.

When Matt reached the end of his drive, he could see Rosa walking up the road towards him. Both dogs saw her and pulled on their leads excitedly. Matt looked around and as no one was about, he let them loose; they ran up the road to meet her.

"Hello, you two." she said, making a fuss of them.

When she reached Matt, he said, "This is nice, Rosa, are you OK?"

"Yes, sort of. I need some TLC; I've just had the busiest mental twenty-four hours that anyone would ever want. I have loads to tell you later, but for now, I just need to sit quietly and relax for a bit." With that, as they walked,

Matt put his arm round her shoulder. Matt, being so tall, Rosa always snuggled nicely under his shoulder.

Anyone walking or driving up to Matt's house, would pass under a large sign; it went from one side of the drive to the other, painted white with black writing and pictures of various fruits and vegetables; It read, 'IVY COTTAGE, EAST ANGLIA'S TOP SUPLIER OF FRUIT AND VEGETABLES.'

As they walked up the drive, Matt said, "The sun's still on the patio at the back of the house; I thought it would be nice to have dinner outside, so I've put a table and chairs out there." And as they walked round to the back of the house, Rosa could see how Matt had made an effort, making the table look nice. "You sit down, Rosa; dinner will be about half an hour. I'll go and get us some wine, while we wait."

Rosa sat there and looked out over Matt's gardens. In front of her, there were immaculate rows of different vegetables, she stood up to see further down the garden, looking to the right, as far as she could see, were fruit trees and bushes. Over to the left side, you could see it was a busy working farm. Matt was a top producer of fruit, vegetables and hay, in East Anglia. She could see two large hay fields in the distance. There were two big, refrigerated lorries, a tractor and other farm equipment about. She could just about see the big barns and stables that were next to her Four Horseshoes riding school. Although Matt had stables, he only had a couple of horses.

When Matt returned with a bottle and glasses, Rosa said, "I've been admiring the farm, and all the hard work you have put into it. Your Dad would be so proud of what you have done with this place since he died; it's incredible."

"There is still a lot to do though. I'm lucky; it gives me a really good living, and I've got good staff who are not afraid of hard work." he said, pouring the wine.

"Matt," Rosa said, "I love this house; it's so big and spacious; but one thing I don't understand, is why is it still called Ivy cottage when there is no Ivy and it's no longer a cottage, as you've extended it and made it into a four-bedroom house; and very nice it is too."

"And there's still loads to do on the house yet." he said, smiling, "I know Ivy cottage sounds stupid; it's to do with the business. It's been called Ivy cottage since it was built many years ago. The Ivy comes from my great, great, great grandmother, who it was named after. Plus, that's what people round here and all the customers know it as. I might change it one day but not just yet." Then, handing her a piece of paper, he said, "Here is today's house menu, Miss Maddox. It read:

MATT'S RESTAURANT, MENU OF THE DAY.

Starter

Mixed salad, including Matt's home-grown vine tomatoes

Main

Selection of meats from the grill

Matt's home-grown new potatoes (in butter)

Matt's home-grown garden peas

Sweet

The Other Side of the Fence

Matt's home-grown, handpicked strawberries, with cream or ice cream

Tea or coffee, and mint chocolates.

Sitting down, she read it and she started to smile. She looked up at him, shaking her head and smiling, said, "You're so funny, Matt. This is the first time I've relaxed all day; you're just what I needed."

They both sat quietly, occasionally picking up their glasses and sipping their drinks at the same time, which made them smile.

Rosa was looking out over the gardens and thinking about when the best time to tell Matt about Davenport would be, when suddenly Matt got up from the table.

"I think everything is about ready, I hope you're hungry?" he said.

"Yes, Miss Maddox is definitely ready and hungry." she laughed.

They ate their meal while chatting, enjoying each other's company.

Putting her spoon down into her empty dish, Rosa said, "Matt, that was delicious, book me in for the same time next week."

"OK, Miss, I think we might have a table available." he laughed, "I will get the coffee and you can tell me what tonight has all been about."

"Shall I help with the washing up first?" she asked.

"That's OK, I will sort it later."

Matt took the dirty dishes through and returned with coffees and mint chocolates.

"Right, I've done my spectacular meal; now, you have my full attention." he said.

Through tears and sobs, it took Rosa over half an hour to tell a shocked and concerned Matt her story.

"Rosa, I want to hold you but I daren't; I might squeeze you too hard." he said, "I am devastated; all those years of pain you have been through, all on your own; never being able to tell anyone. I'm so upset about what you went through, having to give up Eva Marie. I could have been there for you; I should have been there for you. How did they find out what he had done?"

"The detectives didn't tell us, but Gemma spoke to a couple of mothers of girls who are at the college. Apparently, a teacher saw him lift a student rider off her horse and his hands went right up her top to her breasts. The teacher reported it and they started to watch him. The other thing he was doing, was when he helped the girls onto their horse; he held their leg, right at the top, near their privates. The teachers called all his students together and asked that if any of them felt that things weren't right, when Mr. Davenport helped them on or off their horses, would they let a teacher know before they left the college for the day. Apparently, six girls reported him, saying he had done other things; especially if he ever found them alone. They said he always smelled of alcohol and said that if they told anyone, he would kill their horse. He always picked on girls who owned their own horse, and, like me, they had kept it a secret. It was only that the teacher saw what he was doing and questioned the girls, that he was caught. I really feel for those girls and what they have been going through."

The Other Side of the Fence

"My lovely Rosa, you're such a lovely, caring person. The fear you had for Eva's safety and overwhelming love you have for her, to do what you did for her, and Star. All those years of pain and heartache you went through."

"Don't ever feel bad, Matt, you were always there for me; even if you didn't know why." she smiled.

Matt stood up, shaking his head in disgust at the things that Davenport had done.

"It's turned a bit chilly now the sun's gone down. Shall we go indoors?" he asked.

"Yes definitely; it's a good job I booked in for the whole evening." she said, then with a slight giggle in her voice, added, "Anyway, I haven't finished with all my problems yet."

She picked up her empty coffee cup and some of the chocolates, then went into the lounge. Matt closed the patio doors and said, "There, that's better." He then sat down next to her on the large leather sofa, with large maroon cushions on it.

He poured himself a glass of wine, and still holding the bottle, he looked at Rosa.

"Yes please." she said.

Handing her the glass of wine, he said, "OK, my lovely, tell me your other problem?"

"I have an appointment with Mrs. Bennett and social services tomorrow; so, my next dilemma is, what do I do about Eva Marie, if they say that I can now have joint custody." she said.

57

"Tomorrow;" Rosa said to Matt, "I will tell James everything that's happened here; then, at the end of next week, I'm going to Ireland for Eva's seventh birthday. Hopefully, by then, social services will have informed the Stirlings that I can now be awarded joint custody. What do I do? Do I take Eva away from the only life she knows and bring her to England?"

"Before you get yourself into a panic, let me tell you something. When my ex-wife took Paul to live with her and her boyfriend in Essex, I was awarded joint custody. I sat down and worked out a schedule; I sat for hours, trying to do what was best. Then it hit me; there are fifty-two weekends and around twelve weeks school holidays in a year. I decided to let him live with them, so he could have a stable life and education; then he could come to me any weekend he wanted and as many weeks as he wanted in the school holidays. We have him alternative Christmases. The clever bit is that when he wanted to come for a weekend, usually twice a month; I would go to Essex a couple of days before, so I could spend time with him after school, then bring him here Friday night and take him back Sunday. Don't forget, one or the other of the Stirlings are always travelling back and forth to England, so they can bring Eva with them. You can then meet up with them and have her for a while."

Rosa thought for a while, looked at him and said, "That's very clever, Matt; I see what you did. They had him when he was always at school, and you had him when he wasn't, so he was all yours; very clever."

"Well, what are you thinking?" he asked.

"I'm thinking that you're brilliant; my problem is solved. I'm ready to watch that movie now. And can I have another glass of wine please?"

A few days later, just as Rosa was leaving for work, the phone rang. Billy answered and called to Rosa, "It's DS Parker, for you."

Rosa went to the phone and said, "Hello, Detective, how may I help?"

"Hi, Rosa, we are ready to recover the bag of clothes Gemma buried. When will it be convenient for you both to accompany us? I know it will be emotional for you, but we need you to be there to identify and confirm that it's your bag and clothes."

"Well, the best time for us, would be during our lunch break; that's at twelve-thirty, or we could do any time after five, is that any good?"

"Twelve-thirty would be better for us." DS Parker said.

"When?"

"Tomorrow?"

The Other Side of the Fence

"Yes, that's fine. I will arrange everything today.... What? …. I hope no one will think we have been arrested…. Oh, OK; that's alright then." she giggled, "Yes, we will be ready. See you then; bye." she said, then put the phone down.

"Rosa!" her mum said, "You do know you were talking to a police officer and not your boyfriend, don't you?"

"What do you mean?"

"The smiling and swaying as you listened, the one leg bent in the air behind you and the silly giggle at the end." her mum mimicked.

"I Didn't realize; but if I was, it's because he is gorgeous; I can't help it. He's picking me and Gemma up at the stables tomorrow. His team are ready; they are going to dig up my sports bag, with my clothes in it."

"Are you OK being there while they do it?" her mum asked.

"Yes, I am if it helps to convict that pervert."

When Rosa got to work, before they started their different jobs, she read through the day's mail.

"Gemma, Katie." she said, "Read this; what do you think?"

They both read the letter; it was from the Equestrian College, asking if they could take two more girls on for work experience.

"I think we could, especially if they are as good as the last two they sent us." said Gemma,

"So do I; it will really help Jess and Sidney with their work. They will feel like the bosses." smiled Katie.

The Other Side of the Fence

"I agree. I will phone the college later and tell them yes. I will ask if the girls can start this weekend." said Rosa.

Rosa then told them about her earlier phone call from DS Parker and arranged for her and Gemma to have an early lunch break the next day.

"One last thing, Katie. When Gemma and I are in Ireland next weekend; I have arranged with my dad, for his head stablehand to be here each day. He will sort out any problems with the horses for you; any other problems, let my dad or Matt know."

Katie replied, "With Matt; your dad's stablehand and hopefully the two girls; we will be fine."

At twelve-thirty the next afternoon, DS Parker pulled up at the office in his black Sierra. Two excited, but nervous girls got in the back seat and waved to Katie, who was looking out the office window. DS Parker drove out to the road, where a waiting police van then followed them to the back of Gemma's parents' house. Three policemen, two in overalls with shovels etc. and one in a suit with a camera, got out the van; they all entered the garden, let in by Gemma's father.

Gemma went over to a wooded area, pointed, then stood back and waited with her dad, Rosa and DS Parker. Gemma whispered to Rosa, "Hold my hand if it gets too much for you."

The bag was soon recovered. One of the policemen had put on special overalls, a mask, and gloves. He put the bag on a sheet of plastic and unzipped it. When the policeman started to remove the contents, while another took photos; Rosa suddenly grabbed DS Parker's hand and Gemma held Rosa's other hand. When Rosa saw her torn panties, she let out a sob, turned and buried her head in DS Parker's chest.

DS Parker, seeing Rosa's distress, said, "OK, gents, stop. You've got enough photos; we can take any others at the station. I think we all just witnessed a positive identification. You know what to do now; see you all back at the station."

When Rosa had calmed down, DS Parker shook hands with Gemma's dad and thanked him. He told him that the men would tidy up and put the soil back before they left. Gemma said goodbye to her dad, then they got into DS Parker's car.

Before he drove off, DS Parker said, "Sorry to have to put you through that, Rosa, but you were very good, and as I said, a positive identification that they were your clothes, was what we were after. Now, do you want me to take you back to the riding school, or drop you off somewhere for your lunch?"

Rosa and Gemma looked at each other. Gemma checked the time and said, "I think we need to calm down before we go back. Can you take us down to the Riverside Restaurant please? We need a drink and something to eat before we go back, and we can easily get back from there."

"Of course I can. I'm off duty for a while now. I would have liked to come with you, but it's not allowed."

Rosa sat in the back of the car, with her eyes closed. Smiling, she thought, "I never realised revenge would feel so good."

When they arrived at the restaurant and got out the car, DS Parker got out with them.

He said, "It's been lovely to get to know you both, even if it has been through such a horrible case. Now, just to let you know, you won't hear anything from us for months, because we will be investigating Davenport further and following up on all the other accusations made against him. We will let you know when his trial is." He went to shake hands with Gemma and say goodbye, but she hugged him instead. He looked shocked but laughed. He then looked at Rosa and held his arms out for her to give him a hug, which she did gladly. He got into his car, gave them a wave and the loveliest smile; then, he was gone.

"One word; Corrr!" said Gemma, as he drove away.

"You can't have him, you're married; so, he's going to be mine. Yes, all mine." laughed Rosa.

58

Before entering, Rosa tapped gently on her parents' lounge door.

"Morning," she said, "just thought I'd tell you that I rang James last night and told him everything that's happened here. I'm now off to work. I can't wait till me and Gemma get on that plane to Ireland. This visit is going to be so special."

Her mum said, "Rosa, we were just talking about you and wondering what your plans for Eva are?"

"Nothing definite yet." Rosa answered, "I'm thinking that it might be best to leave her in Ireland with the Stirlings. When I'm there, I will speak to James and tell him what I would like to do. If he agrees, I can assure you, we will be seeing a lot more of her."

"That's good, Rosa. We are excited that our little girl will be coming to England and actually staying here with us again. We have missed her and so much of her growing up already. We realize life here is different to what she has been used to in Ireland, but we want to do our best for her when she visits. Have you got time before you go to work to hear what we have in mind?" her mum asked.

Rosa, looking intrigued, said, "OK."

Billy said, "Now Princess, there is no pressure; It's just because of what's happening now; we want to make the place more comfortable for you and Eva. We are also thinking more to the future; hopefully, you will be living here for quite a few years yet, or you might always live here. Then, in years to come, it might be Eva and her family, or you might have other children and they might want to stay."

"I don't think so!" exclaimed Rosa, "Eva's been more than enough trouble for me, thank you very much."

"Oh, bless her." he said, then started to unroll large sheets of paper out onto the table. "We had these plans drawn up a few years ago, but as you know, there was never a good time to do anything about them. We feel now is the right time." He spread the papers out and said pointing to the drawings, "These are plans for an extension to the house; well actually, the part you're in now. I know you have got to go to work, so I will just show you quickly. The plans show a driveway that comes in off River Road, up to your own front door. This big extension includes an extra bedroom and an extended lounge, with double doors that lead out to a small garden, walled off down one side for privacy from the road. There is space, when they block up the door you use to come through to ours, to extend the kitchen. Also, they will refit your bathroom."

"What do you think, Rosa?" her mum asked.

The Other Side of the Fence

"I can't believe it; I've got to sit down." answered Rosa, in amazement.

"Shall we go ahead with it then?" her dad asked.

"Yes, a thousand times yes. But can I change one thing?" she asked, standing up, ready to leave. Her Dad looked puzzled, as he looked at her. "Can the door I use to come through to see you both, stay, please?"

"Oh Rosa." her mum said, "That's lovely, I'm so pleased you said that."

"I don't need a bigger kitchen; I can't cook anyway." she laughed, "I only hope you understand that I might never want to leave now. It's so exciting but I must go now; we can talk later." she said, kissing her mum. Then, walking round to kiss her dad, she added, "You're both so good to me; you're the best parents in the world."

"That's that then." Billy said, then laughing, he asked, "Right Em, are you going to start cooking breakfast in our lovely big kitchen then?"

"Oh yes, very funny, Daddy! See you later; love you both." Rosa said as she went to the front door and left.

-

Rosa, Gemma and Gemma's daughter Sarah, left the airport arrivals hall.

Rosa started to wave frantically, saying, "There's James, he always seems to time his arrival just right."

They crossed the road to where James was parked at the pick-up point. James and Rosa hugged and kissed, then the usual pleasantries were exchanged. They were soon in the car and on the road to Kildare.

In no time, a very tired Sarah was fast asleep.

Gemma said, "It will do her good, she hardly slept last night; she was so excited about today."

James said, "Same with Eva, about you coming today. She has been up and dressed for hours. She also knows that when she goes to England next time, she will be able to stay with you on the farm. I think she takes after you in that department, Rosa. She did make us laugh the other day; we heard her telling Lily that she was going to stay with Nanny and Grandad England."

Rosa, sitting in the back of the car with Gemma and Sarah said, "James, I can't tell you how long I have waited for all this to happen." Gemma could see Rosa was about to get emotional, so she gave her hand a squeeze for support.

"I can imagine, Rosa; you're so brave. My dad says he's had cases similar to yours, and gives you credit for how strong you have been. He says you're a survivor and he admires that. He reckons that the things this bloke has done, are so bad; plus, because of the ages of you and the girls he assaulted, he's looking at a long prison sentence. With your case being the main one and with so many other underage cases and other prosecutions being added; he could get twelve, even fifteen years, because each sentence will run consecutively. He can't see him ever getting parole. He also said that when he gets out of prison, he will be put on the sex offenders register for the rest of his life. He will also have restraining orders, so will never be able to go anywhere near you again."

"That all makes me very happy; especially the last bit." Rosa said, laughing.

James pulled into a lay-by, just before the drive of the Stirlings' property.

He turned to Rosa and said, "Later, we will have a long talk about Eva's future, but for now, let me tell you something about today. Eva's friends will be arriving at four-thirty for her party. Before then, once you have settled and had something to eat and drink, Dad is taking you three and Eva to the riding stables." James turned in his seat to talk to Gemma, "That's if you want to go Gemma? It doesn't matter if you don't; they shouldn't be too long. Dad wants Rosa to look at a pony he wants to buy for Eva's birthday. To make sure that it's the right one, he wants Rosa to see Eva ride it and give her opinion. If you would rather not go, there are lots of games set out in the garden for Sarah to enjoy; we've even got two bouncy castles."

"I think we will take the garden option please, James." Gemma said, "Sarah likes horses, but knowing her, I think the two bouncy castles would win."

With that settled, James pulled out of the lay-by and continued to his house. As he drove up to the house, Rosa could see Eva and her grandad waiting outside for them. When Eva saw them, she jumped up and down waving both arms, shouting "Mummy, Mummy!"

"Oh Rosa, how lovely is that?" said Gemma.

"I know." said Rosa, fighting back tears; "I love her so much; she looks so grown up in her riding outfit."

"She certainly does." said James, "Mum and Dad bought it for her; we can't keep her away from the stables; she is growing up fast and is getting clever with it. She can make my dad do anything she wants; she runs him about something terrible, but he loves it. She has an answer for everything; the latest, is she wants to go to dancing lessons. Her school friends go twice a week, after school; it only runs during school terms, so I said, 'What about your riding lessons, shall I cancel them?' Eva said, 'No, Daddy, don't be silly; it won't affect my riding, because the dancing's on different days to when I go riding, so I can fit it in.' Good old Grandad's going to pay; he spoils her and she knows it. Lily is going to take her, when it starts again, next term. I think she only wants to do it so she can be in the stage shows they do twice a year; especially the one at Christmas."

"That's girls for you, James." Rosa said, laughing.

59

Eva ran up to Rosa and into her arms.

"I've got lots to tell you, Mummy. I've got loads of presents and cards." she said, as they cuddled.

"Happy Birthday, Darling; you look very grown up, now you're seven." Eva smiled and cuddled harder. "Eva," Rosa said, "this is my friend, Gemma and her daughter, Sarah. Sarah is four and she's looking forward to your party; especially the bouncy castles."

Eva smiled at Sarah and said, "Hello Sarah, the bouncy castles are brilliant; me and Daddy have already been on them. I've got to go to the stables before my party, Grandee wants to show Mummy something, then I will be back for my party. I've got lots of friends coming; I will see you when I get back, or you can come with us to the stables if you want?"

Sarah went all shy and shook her head.

The Other Side of the Fence

"She's going to stay here with her mum." Rosa said.

Eva went up to Sarah and whispered, "We are going to have a clown magician, after tea."

"Who told you that?" James asked.

"Grandee did; he said it was a secret." Eva answered.

"Do you know what a secret is, Eva?" Rosa asked.

"No, is it bad?"

"No, Darling, it just means that Grandad told you a secret, but he didn't want you to tell anyone else. Some secrets are good, like the one grandad told you; but sometimes, secrets are really bad. If the bad secret is hurting you or your family, those secrets are best told to someone, if you possibly can."

"Oh, OK." said Eva, "That sounds stupid to me. Come on Sarah, I will show you the bouncy castles." and off they both went, chatting away as if they had known each other for ages.

They all arrived at the stables, including Sarah and Gemma, because Sarah and Eva had suddenly become inseparable, much to everyone's amusement.

A groom brought a delightful black and white pony for them to see; he said that his name was Archibald the Protector, or Archie, for short, and that he was very gentle. Rosa checked him over, even his teeth and ears. She then asked the groom to run with him. All looked well, so the groom took Archie back to fit a saddle, so Eva could ride him.

Rosa was leaning back on the fence while they waited, when she felt something nuzzling into her neck; she turned round.

"Hello there." she said to a large black horse that had come from the other side of the field to see her. She patted him and rubbed his nose.

A groom came over and said, "He likes you, Miss. He's normally very quiet; a bit of a loner, who doesn't like people. But that moment with you has made my day. I must tell the other grooms. His name is Penric the Second; his dad won the Irish Grand National a few years back. He is for sale, if you're interested?"

"I wish." said Rosa, "He reminds me of my old horse; he died of old age, a few years back. I run a riding school and stables, but I never got round to getting myself another horse." Giving Penric a kiss and a pat, she said, "Sorry Penric, as much as I would like to; not today." Then seeing Archie being led up to them, saddled up, she said, "Eva, here comes Archie."

Eva eagerly got on Archie.

"Are you comfortable?" the groom asked her. "I've got to hold the reigns for a while to make sure everything is OK, but I will let go soon."

After talking to the groom, Rosa had a word with Edward Stirling.

"I found out that he is an all-rounder. He can jump, so after her initial training, Eva can enter show jumping competitions. He's a cutie and a perfect size for her, for the next three to four years; then she will be ready for a larger horse."

"OK, thanks, Rosa, I will go and see the owner." replied Edward. Then, because Rosa was holding Sarah on the fence while they watched Eva ride, Edward asked, "Rosa, do you mind if Gemma comes with me to look over the paperwork?"

"Of course not; we're fine." she answered, getting a smile from Sarah.

When Edward and Gemma returned, lots of photos were taken of Archie and Eva, then with Archie and everyone else. Rosa managed to get her photo taken with Archie and Eva, with Penric in the background.

Edward was left alone with Eva while the others waited in the car. They saw Eva jump up and hug her grandad; they could lip read her saying I love him, then she reached over to pat Archie.

"He's obviously just told Eva that Archie is her pony; she will have so much fun with him." said Rosa.

Before long, they were all back at the Stirlings' and the party was in full swing. James, his mum and dad and Lily, had gone to a lot of trouble to make everything perfect for Eva's birthday. Rosa, watching her daughter playing happily with all of her friends, including her new friend, Sarah, knew that she had made the right decision to leave Eva in Ireland.

When the party was over and everything was quiet, James and Rosa went to his apartment and discussed Rosa's plan for joint custody.

"I'm more than happy with your suggestion." James said, "Can we go to Mum and Dad's, so I can tell them your plan; they have been worried sick that you would want to take Eva to England."

When James told his parents, there were smiles and hugs all round.

Edward gave one of his 'from the heart' speeches, "Rosa, you know we didn't get on when we first met and our lives clashed, but you have proved to be one of the bravest, most reasonable women, I have ever met. I am glad that you two met and you had our beautiful granddaughter, who brightens up our day, every day. I know Angela feels the same, when I say that we are all willing to help you with Eva's visits to see you. One of us Stirlings visit England most weeks on business, so we can always bring Eva with us and you can pick her up at the airport, or we can bring her to you and pick her up again later, or you can come to Ireland and Stay in the guest house for a few days, before you take her to England. I'm sure we can work to whatever arrangements suit you best, Rosa. How does that all sound to you two? Are you happy with that James?"

"Yes, more than happy, Dad. I always told you how lovely Rosa was, I think we are all happy." he said, looking at Rosa, who smiled and nodded, holding back the tears.

"Is it OK for me to come in?" Gemma asked, tapping on the lounge door.

"Of course it is." said Angela, "How are the two best friends; are they still in the same bed?"

"Yes, they are sound asleep; they looked so comfortable, I left them. I hope that's OK?"

"Of course it is; it's so lovely. I think they are going to be great friends."

"Eva gave Sarah one of her cuddly toys to hold, to go to sleep. She said that Sarah could keep it, because now she's seven, she's too old for it."

"Sounds like her; seven going on sixteen." James said, laughing.

Gemma said, "Eva's excited that they are staying the night at yours, Angela. She told Sarah that Nan makes the best breakfast."

The Other Side of the Fence

"That's our girl for you." Edward laughed, "Now the youngsters are asleep, let's have a birthday drink to a special little girl and a toast to her future happiness."

They all chinked glasses and said, "To Eva and happiness." They then had a nice evening, chatting quite happily, while drinking and finishing off the party food.

"Ang, I will sleep well tonight." Edward Stirling said.

60

When Rosa got back to England, she told her parents all about the arrangements she had made with James and the Stirlings.

"That's great news, Rosa; you've done really well." her dad said.

Rosa said, "I'm going to phone Matt later and tell him the news. The arrangements are all down to him, he helped me see the best way forward. We have a good deal; I owe him a lot."

"Yes dear, he's always been there for you. Did Eva like her present?" her mum asked.

"Eva loved every present she got. She is going to write thank you cards to everyone. Our present went down well, especially with her grandad buying her the pony."

"What did we get her, Em? And what did you buy her, Rosa?" her dad asked.

The Other Side of the Fence

Rosa answered, "We both gave her money, Dad. She is going to need it now to kit out the pony. We also went half each and got her a play set of four stables with four different coloured horses and riders, plus lots of accessories like water buckets, little blankets, brushes, saddles and loads of other things; she had a wonderful birthday."

Two weeks later, because it was raining, Rosa, Gemma and Katie decided to have their lunch break in the office.

"Gemma, are you ever going to eat your lunch? You have been at the window for half an hour." asked Rosa.

"Just checking the weather, I think it's finally stopped raining, I'm pleased to say." She moved from the window to the door, opened it and stepped outside.

Rosa could hear her talking to someone; she looked at Katie with a puzzled expression and stood up. She saw a horsebox outside the office and two men standing at the tailgate.

"What on earth is going on out there?" she said walking to the door.

When she got outside, one of the men, reading off a yellow ticket, asked, "Rosa Maddox?" She nodded. "Four Horseshoes Riding School?" he said in an Irish accent. She nodded again. "Well, this is for you; sign here please, Miss Maddox."

Rosa looked totally confused; she looked at the delivery men for an explanation.

Gemma said, "Rosa, I know what it is, just sign it."

"We have a letter addressed to you, Miss." one of the men said, as he unbolted the tailgate. He then went inside and backed out a black stallion from the horsebox.

The Other Side of the Fence

"Is that Penric?" Rosa said in disbelief, looking at Gemma.

"Yes, read the letter; I know all about it. Mr. Stirling asked me when we went to buy Archie on Eva's Birthday; I said you would love him."

"Bye, all!" one of the men shouted from the passenger seat, "Enjoy your horse, Miss." the other man said as he got into the driver's seat. They then drove out the main gate and were gone.

Rosa opened the letter; it read:

Dear Rosa,

I hope I have done the right thing in buying Penric for you. I did check with Gemma that you would like him and that your stables had room for another horse. I wanted to do something special for you, to let you know how sorry I am about how I misjudged you, the first time we met. Please accept my apologies for treating you badly regarding Eva Marie; as you know, I thought I was protecting her from you.

Rosa, you are a very brave and special lady; I hope we will always remain friends.

Edward Stirling.

Rosa went up to Penric, who immediately nuzzled her.

"Can you believe this, Gemma; how generous." she said.

"I know, Edward Stirling admires you so much. When we first arrived in Ireland, for Eva's birthday, he told me then, that he wanted to do something nice for you. I didn't know how much he wanted to spend so I didn't know what to say. That's why, after what happened at the stables with Penric, he asked me to go with him to buy Archie; that's when he asked me if you would like Penric. I said of course you would. I did do the right thing, didn't I, Rosa? You do like him, don't you?"

"Of course I do;" replied Rosa, "he looks so much like my Star. I'm a bit stunned at the moment and in shock at such a generous gift. I admire Edward Stirling; he's quite a remarkable man. You certainly did right, Gemma; I could see how unhappy Penric was and I was upset that I couldn't buy him. I knew he would be too expensive for me when the groom said Penric's dad had won the Irish Grand National."

"You're right, Rosa, he was expensive. Well, he was till Mr. Stirling got involved; he was brilliant; they didn't even argue with him. You could see they thought he might walk away. He told them straight that he was buying two horses, one of which he was going to be paying them for permanent stabling, the other, transport costs to England. Plus, he would be paying for Eva's riding lessons. The people at the stables were pleased when he said that he had bought the horse especially for you; they said it was the first time Penric had reacted to anyone. Mr. Stirling told them about our 'top-class' riding school in England, so they knew he would be going to a good home; I just kept nodding. In the end, Mr. Stirling paid good money for Penric and they reduced the price for Archie."

Turning her attention to Penric, Rosa kissed him and said, "My lovely Penric the Second, this was meant to be; Fate has bought us together. You are going to be one happy horse here and from now on, I'm going to give you all the love and attention you have been missing all this time." She turned to Gemma and said, "Can you lock up please, Gemma?" then, patting Penric, she said, "Come on Penric, let's go and meet all your new friends." as she walked him towards the stables.

"Don't you mean Rosa's got a new best friend?" Gemma said, smiling.

Rosa looked back at Gemma; she pulled Penric's head closer to hers and said, "Happy day, Gemma. Happy Day."

61

A couple of months later, the plans for the extension at River Road Farm had been passed. It would now be full steam ahead to get it done as soon as possible.

Billy said, "It would be nice if we can get the inside work all sorted and cleaned up in time for Christmas. Then at least when Eva comes and stays, in the New Year, she can have her own bedroom."

Rosa said, "It's good that she is dancing in the school Christmas show this year, at least we won't be worrying who she is spending Christmas with. Anyway, don't worry, Dad, Eva's quite happy staying at Gemma's with Sarah, when she comes to England. And she's a proper little worker down at the stables; I sometimes wonder whether it's us or the horses she comes to see."

Her mum said, "You can see Eva's yours, Rosa; she's your double, only blonde."

"I won't be in for tea tonight, Mum;" Rosa said, "I'm going to Matt's; he wants to tell me something about this girl he's been seeing for a few months." Rosa tutted at her mum, "Don't say a word."

Her mum put her fingers across her mouth, as if to zip it shut.

"Very funny, Mother." Rosa said, smiling.

Gemma dropped Rosa off at Matt's front door. Matt came out and opened the car door for Rosa, thanked Gemma for driving Rosa and they both waved as Gemma drove off. Matt and Rosa walked into his house and Matt took her to the kitchen, where he had been cooking tea.

"It's Chicken in a wine sauce, with new potatoes and salad." he said.

"Mmm, smells nice." she said.

"It will be a while yet though. Let's sit and have a drink; I can tell you what's been happening with me."

They sat at the table, which was all nicely set for their meal.

"OK, start talking." said Rosa.

"Well, it's like this, Rosa. As you know I have been seeing this woman for a few months; she's the very nice, pretty, blonde customer of mine, who owns a grocery shop. She comes here every week for her fruit and vegetables. She's separated from her husband and has ten-year-old twin boys."

"So, what's wrong?" Rosa asked.

"Well, first, she's not like you; you make me laugh and we can talk for hours; you talk, I talk; but with her, I don't talk at all; we have nothing in common, only fruit and vegetables. All she does is talk about the price of fruit and veg, and her husband; I know more about him than I do about her." Rosa tried not to laugh. "Lately, when we are together, I can't wait for her to say that she'd better go to pick the boys up from their dad's. She then tells me how her poor husband is probably tired, because he's been hard at work all day. Then she kisses me, says bye, tells me that she'll see me the next day she's free and I say OK. I'm just not happy, Rosa; it's not what I want." he said, looking sad.

"Oh, Matt." said Rosa, getting up from her chair and going over to him. She stood behind his chair and put her arms round him, crossing them across his chest, and kissed him on the top of his head. "How can I help? I want my Matt to be happy again."

Just then, a timer went off. Rosa stepped back as Matt stood up, not answering her question.

"Sit down and make yourself comfortable, Rosa. I'll go and get the dinners; won't be long." he said, going through to the kitchen.

Rosa was puzzled at Matt's strange behaviour and sat down again.

In no time, he was back. He put a bottle of champagne and two champagne glasses on the table, lit the two candles that were already there, then left again and returned with two dinners.

Putting one plate down in front of Rosa, he said, "Enjoy, my Lady."

"Matt." Rosa demanded, "Champagne? What's going on?"

"Oh, sorry, Rosa; it's to celebrate. You said you wanted to help me; well, you can." he said, opening the bottle of champagne.

The Other Side of the Fence

"Yes, so how can I help?" she asked, curiously.

Pouring the champagne, Matt said, "First, I need to fill our glasses, so we can make a toast." he said lifting his glass, for her to chink it.

"Matt whatever are you on about; a toast to what?"

"To celebrate me being the happiest, dumped person ever." he said with the biggest of grins and chinked her glass. "Rosa, I can't tell you how happy I am. She rang last night, said that she was sorry, but it was all over between us. She's gone back to her husband and hoped I wasn't too upset. She then apologised, saying that she will have to buy her goods from someone else."

Rosa burst out laughing.

"That's great news, Matt; I'm so pleased for you. That's definitely worth a toast." she said, raising her glass and taking a mouthful of champagne, "Matt, I'm sorry that I'm laughing, but your build-up to get to the point of you getting dumped, was the weirdest and funniest I've ever heard. Don't laugh, but when you lit the candles, I thought you were going to ask me to marry you."

"Sorry, Rosa; I love you, but no more women for me for a while; I've just suffered months of misery. Eat up, before it gets cold." he said, quite casually.

-

At the beginning of January, DS Parker came to see Rosa. "I've got some good news for you, there isn't going to be a trial. The evidence against Davenport is so overwhelming; girls are still coming forward, from years before you went to the college. We cannot understand how he got away with it all those years. He's pleaded guilty, so no trial. When he goes for sentencing, our lawyers are expecting him to get nine to ten years, hopefully even longer; plus, he will be on the sex offenders register for life. We've still got plenty of paperwork to do and witnesses to interview, but when we've finished, he will go to court and be sentenced." Before he left, he said, "I'd like to thank you, Rosa, for all your cooperation; it must have been very hard for you. If you want to, you will be allowed to go into court to watch the sentencing; I will keep you informed."

62

Rosa was disturbed, once again, from her reminiscing.

"Rosa, Hun, are you alright? You've been down here for ages; I was getting quite worried. You'd better get back to bed; you've got a busy morning, in a few hours, with that big delivery coming really early."

Rosa stood up, dropping a few things from her memory box onto the floor.

"Just leave them," she said, "I will pick them up later. I'm sorry; I wasn't tired, so I got the box out while I drank my hot milk. There's a lot of memories in there; some good, some bad. I drank the milk, then completely lost track of time. I'm glad you came down though; I can't be late in the morning, I know what Gemma and Katie are like, bless them; they will take it all in and sort it before I get there. Then, when I walk in, they will be sitting there, relaxed, drinking tea and making me feel guilty. I will go up, but before you come back to bed can you set me a timer for three hours please?"

The Other Side of the Fence

"OK, don't worry about us. When you get up, just look after yourself. Make sure you have breakfast before you leave in the morning, Hun. Don't forget, your mum will be coming before I leave and will stay till you get back; and have you remembered that me and your dad have a meeting about Riverside Road, after work? I shouldn't be too late though."

"Yes, I did, thanks. If Mum's here all day, that will be tea sorted." she smiled to herself, "See you tonight." she said and blew a kiss as she went upstairs. "I'm tired now, so it won't be long before I fall asleep."

She laid down, smiled and thought, "He's so lovely, so caring." She pulled the covers over her, closed her eyes and fell fast asleep.

Arriving home, after a long, hard day at the riding school, Rosa was pleased when she walked through the door and saw her mum.

"Hello mum, everything OK? We've been so busy, I've had to bring some paperwork home with me; but first," she said, bending down, picking up her little boy, "lots of love and big cuddles for his majesty, the best boy ever; and a nice cup of tea."

Her mum said, "Hello Dear; you're in luck, I've just made a fresh pot. Sit and relax; I'll bring you a cup over."

While Rosa was playing with her son, her mum brought her cup of tea and said, "Look what HM found." as she put two £10 casino chips from her pocket onto the table, "He looked all pleased with himself, but I was worried he would choke on them. So, I said, 'Let's give them to Mummy as a present.' and he gave them to me. I said aren't you a good boy, gave him a cuddle and asked him where he got them. They were on the floor near your chair; I think he thought they were biscuits."

"Yes, you're right Mum; they could have been dangerous; they must have fallen on the floor when I got out the chair last night. I thought I'd picked everything up this morning when I came down. It does make me laugh how you call him HM."

"Bless him;" her mum said, laughing, "he has us at his beck and call; I'm always saying 'Yes, Your Majesty.'"

Rosa looked at the pile of paperwork she had put on the table and said, "You know, Mum; now that the shop's all sorted and Sydney and Jess are fully qualified instructors; Me, Gemma and Katie can have any days off we want, because we only need one in the shop with a helper and three instructors at the riding school, each with a helper from the college. It's all going to plan."

"I'm glad, Dear; you've all worked very hard. Do you want your dinner now, or wait for the others? They shouldn't be too long now."

"I'll wait. Have I got time for a nice hot bath?" Rosa asked.

"Of course, Dear; that's what I'm here for. Everything will be ready when you come down."

Rosa laid in the bath, thinking how she got the £10 chips. She thought, "Of course, how could I forget that night at the Casino. The girls, my surprise Thirtieth birthday; they are what I had left. It's all coming back to me."

It was just before closing time at the riding school. Rosa, Gemma and Katie were in the office, doing rotas for riding lessons for the five of them. Sydney and Jess had become fulltime members of staff and the equestrian college was sending them two girls to do work experience, each Holiday. Some of the girls enjoyed it so much, they stayed on after their work experience had finished and worked weekends, because if there was a break in the time schedule, they got a chance to ride the horses.

Gemma looked up and said, "Right Rosa, it's your birthday next week and the girls want to know what you have got planned?"

Rosa replied, "Nothing; I haven't even thought about it. Do they want to go somewhere special?"

"Of course they do; anything for a party. You are going to be thirty you know. Do you want us to surprise you and book a place for a meal of our choice?"

"Yes, do that; but make sure it's not my birthday weekend, because James is bringing Eva over for my actual birthday day. Lily is coming as well and bringing their little boy; he's lovely, Eva adores him. James says that Eva's a proper little mother to him."

"OK; are you sure you're going to be happy with us planning your party?"

"Yes, of course I will. Just tell me how I've got to dress on the night." Rosa answered.

On the night of the party, looking out of the window, Billy called. "Rosa, the limo is here; it seems to have lots of giggling girls hanging out the windows."

Rosa came through to say cheerio.

"Oh, you do look nice, Dear." her mum said.

"Thanks, I needed that, Mum." Rosa smiled.

She was wearing a red, short sleeved cross over top, that tied at the waist, black trousers and high heels. She wore tiny red button earrings and carried a small black bag.

The Other Side of the Fence

"Yes, you do look nice, Princess;" her dad said, "It's about time you dressed up. Who knows, you might meet Mr. Right. Where are you going?"

"I have no Idea; I was told to dress up and a limousine would pick me up at eight o' clock tonight. The girls have organised everything. Bye:" she said, kissing each of them on the cheek, "love you both; don't wait up for me." and a happy excited Rosa disappeared down the hall and out the front door.

She got into the limousine and was greeted with balloons, poppers, hooters and champagne.

"Where are we going?" asked Rosa.

"Relax and drink your champagne." said Gemma, "You will soon find out."

Twenty-five minutes later, the car stopped. Rosa got out and looked up to the roof of the building they were about to enter, to see a large, illuminated sign, which read, 'Blue River Casino And Restaurant'.

Gemma said, "We have booked a meal in the balcony restaurant; it overlooks the river on one side and the casino floor on the other. Then, after the meal, you can just sit and either watch the river or watch people play on the roulette wheels, card tables and fruit machines. But you won't be watching, Rosa, because we have already got you some chips, so you can play in the casino."

Rosa was trying to take it all in. "Oh, my goodness," she said, in amazement, "I said this years ago, but what a sheltered life I've led. Oh well, here we go again; another first for me, from you lot." She then led the way into the casino, with all the other girls following her.

After the meal and several drinks, Rosa said, "Thank you girls, that meal was delicious."

The Other Side of the Fence

The waiters had just finished clearing the tables, when 'Happy Birthday' music started playing and a rather large birthday cake appeared with blazing candles; the girls all burst into song.

"Hurry up; blow the candles out and make a wish before the candles melt all over the cake." said Jess.

Rosa managed to blow all the candles out in one go and the girls immediately started cheering with cries of, 'Speech, speech.'

An embarrassed Rosa finally stood up, tapped on her empty glass and said, "What can I say. Thank you all for coming and wanting to celebrate my birthday with me. This has been lovely and a really nice surprise. The meal and the cake were excellent and I hope the rest of the evening is as good. I do want to thank you all for your help and support over the last few years. As you all know, I'm a quiet, shy person." she said, glancing round, pretending to frown when she heard lots of giggles; then smiling, she said, "And although you do keep leading me astray, I still adore you all. Just one thing has really upset me though." she paused and they all looked at her puzzled; then, she laughed, "My glass has been empty for ages."

A big round of applause and cheering brought a smile to Rosa's face, as she sat down and Gemma filled her glass.

Sydney and Jess had been standing, leaning on the balcony rail, during Rosa's speech.

"Rosa, you just said that you hope the rest of the evening is as good as the meal. Well, I think we can all guess what you wished for, because it has just arrived." said Sydney, nudging Jess to look down to the casino floor.

"Don't be daft; how do you know what I wished for." said Rosa.

The Other Side of the Fence

Jess and Sydney huddled together, giggling and pointed to the casino floor, "Gemma, come and look." said Jess.

Gemma looked over the balcony and said, "Oh I can't believe it. Well, if you want an extra birthday present Rosa, you'd better take a look; the girls may be right."

"What ever are you all on about." said Rosa, as she looked over the balcony to the casino floor.

"Look over to the group of men that have just walked in, you will see your wish has been granted." said Gemma.

Rosa tutted but looked to where Gemma was pointing.

"Ha ha, Rosa, you have gone all red." laughed Jess.

In the Casino, Rosa had just seen, looking as gorgeous as ever, Detective Sergeant Parker.

63

All the girls, except Rosa, ended up looking over the balcony to see what was happening below.

Gemma said, "I know several of the men with the detective; they are policemen; three of them came and dug up Rosa's clothes in my dad's garden."

"Gemma, the one in the grey top has just seen you; he's telling the detective; quick, wave." said Katie.

DS Parker looked up, waved and gestured 'would you like a drink?' Gemma signalled back, no thanks.

By now, Rosa was feeling embarrassed and went back to their table. She sat with her back towards the staircase and quickly poured herself a large glass of wine. Drinking most of it in one go, she said to herself, "For goodness' sake, Rosa, take deep breaths and stay calm."

Sydney said, "Prepare yourself, Rosa, the detective's coming up"

The Other Side of the Fence

"Well, hello there, ladies, long time no see; how are you all?" DS Parker asked.

"We're fine thanks, DS Parker." replied Gemma.

"Girls, girls, please; it's Vince when you see me off duty." he said, "It's only DS Parker when I'm at work."

"Hello girls." said his friend, who had also come upstairs, "We have met." he said, looking at Gemma.

"This is Joe." said Vince, "He took the photos in your garden, Gemma. I'm sorry girls, he's not available; it's his stag night; he's getting married next Saturday, poor chap." he said, laughing out loud, "But there's plenty to choose from downstairs, if you're looking for that special someone."

"Take no notice of him, he's had a drink." said Joe, "Talk to someone who's nice and friendly, like me. Are you girls celebrating something?"

"Yes, it's Rosa's birthday, she's over there, where we just had a meal. There's plenty of birthday cake left if any of you are hungry?" Gemma said.

"We might take you up on that later." Vince replied.

Sydney said, "It's the first time any of us have been to a casino. We've all got chips, but don't really know what to do, so we were just watching from here."

Joe said, "We'd better go back to the others now, but when you girls are ready, come and find us; we can show you what to do; it's easy."

"Joe, I'll be down in a few minutes; I'm just going to see Rosa and wish her happy birthday." said Vince and walked over to where Rosa was still sitting, with her back to everyone.

"Hello Rosa, I hear it's your birthday." Rosa heard Vince say from behind her.

Rosa turned and said, "Yes, it is. I left it to the girls to organise something for me and this is where they brought me. So far, everything's been lovely."

"Ah, so far. Now I'm here, you must be thinking that the evening's just got perfect. Is it OK to give the birthday girl a birthday kiss?" he said, leaning forward ready to kiss her.

"It certainly is." she answered, offering him her cheek.

"Oh, no lips?" he said, looking sad, "It is your birthday, and you look really nice. Come to think of it, it's the first time I have seen you not wearing riding gear."

"Feel free." she said, smiling; then thinking, "I can't believe I just said that!"

"Close your eyes then." he said. He put his fingers under her chin, lifted her face up to his and kissed her tenderly on the lips, "Happy Birthday, Rosa; I hope all is good with you?" he whispered.

She smiled and nodded.

Before he left, he touched his lips with his finger, gently put it to her lips and said, "See you when you come downstairs."

Rosa sat there, looking stunned. "What just happened?" she said to Gemma, who had come over to see her, "I can't believe what I just let happen. I've got to stop looking into those gorgeous brown eyes of his. What with them and his smiles; I just melt."

The Other Side of the Fence

"You loved every minute of it; he is so confident and a definite charmer." said Gemma.

"Yes, I did, I really did. I am going to be so embarrassed though, next time I see him."

"He's just told us his name is Vince; he's here on a stag night"

"Vince Parker; sounds strong; I bet he's married. I don't want to know though. Are you all going down to the casino?"

"Yes, but first, I'm going to get this cake sorted. The waiter said they'll box it up and leave it downstairs in the cloakroom. We will enjoy it tomorrow, on our morning break."

The next hour was great fun; the stag party were hilarious. Some of the girls were still watching from the balcony and laughing at the stupid antics going on below. Two of the girls had already paired up with two of the men and were happily joining in.

"My poor Jack; if he had to put up with all this on his stag night, I bet he hated it." said Gemma, "I definitely think our hen party in Ibiza and Katie's in Ireland were far better."

"My goodness, Gemma, do you realise that Eva's nearly nine. Where's the time gone? That was over nine years ago! What a lot has happened in those nine years. Anyway, enough of years ago; this is now. Come on you lot, let's go downstairs and let the games begin."

"Yeah, about time! Come on girls," someone shouted then started singing, "Hi Ho, Hi Ho, it's off to party we go."

"Shush, not in here." said Katie, "Save it for the next time we go to Ibiza." That made them all laugh.

Vince showed Rosa how to put bets on the roulette table. One minute, she was all excited because of how much she had won; the next, it was nearly all gone.

"This is a stupid game." she declared.

"Come on, you have a little left; I will show you how to play another game, it's called blackjack; you have to beat the dealer by getting higher cards than him."

Rosa liked that game; in fact, she actually won. She then played the machines and ended the night with exactly £20; two £10 chips. Vince said he would cash them in for her.

"I would rather keep them as a reminder of tonight." she said.

Katie came up to Rosa and said, "Drink up, Rosa, the limo is here. I'm telling everyone to meet at the main entrance in five minutes."

Vince said, "When you have finished your drink, I'll walk with you to the door."

"Thanks, I don't think I will be walking very straight though." she giggled.

As he walked her to the door, Vince put his arm round her and asked, "Have you enjoyed your birthday, Rosa?"

"Yes, I have; it has been one of the best." she said.

When they reached the main door, she said, or rather slurred, "Oh look, two of my party are exchanging phone numbers with two of your party; how sweet."

As Rosa was about to leave, Vince said goodbye and put his hand out to shake Rosa's. She laughed and shook his hand, but as she turned to leave, he didn't let go of her hand, instead, he pulled her back and kissed her. Laughing, she went to leave again, but he pulled her back and kissed her again.

The doorman, who had been holding the door open for Rosa and the girls to leave, said, "Come on, Detective, this door's heavy; either arrest her, or let her go."

"Just one more." Vince said. He kissed her and then let her go. Everyone burst out laughing.

As she went out the door, she looked back, smiled and said, "Goodnight, Vince, I've loved every minute."

As she passed the doorman, who was smiling, she apologised, then she thanked the limo driver for waiting.

She sat down in the back of the car and looking round at the girls, said, "Thank you so much, I've just had the best time. I loved it." Then, with a contented smile, she leant back, closed her eyes. Suddenly, she opened one eye, to focus and asked, "Where's Gemma?" Then seeing her, she smiled and pointed at her, "There she is. Good you've got the cake." and closed her eye again.

They all nodded and laughed when Katie said, "I think we can safely say, Rosa's one very tipsy, happy, thirty-year-old birthday girl."

64

Rosa had spent so long reminiscing in the bath; the water had started to go cold. She quickly dried herself, got dressed and went downstairs. When she walked into the dining room, she saw that everyone had already started eating.

"Oh, sorry I've been so long." she said.

"Hope you don't mind, Rosa; they were hungry when they came in and it was ready, so I said you wouldn't mind if they started. I've put yours in the oven, Dear." her mum said.

"Of course, I don't mind. I didn't mean to be so long. Hi, all." Rosa said, walking past them to get her meal, "Hope the meeting went well?"

"Yes, everything has been sorted, thanks to your man here;" her dad said, "he's a brilliant negotiator."

"Of course he is; that's why you took him. You know me; only the best." she said, smiling as she put her meal down on the table and sat down.

"I feel a lot better after that lovely bath." Rosa said, "It was nice and relaxing; I ended up thinking about my thirtieth birthday surprise at the casino that the girls did for me. It's funny, it was really good, yet in all these years since, we have never been back there."

"That's where those two casino chips that Alfie found, came from, Mum."

"I'm pleased that mystery has been solved." her mum answered.

Finishing their meals, Rosa's mum said, "It's getting late Billy; we had better be going, unless you want me to help with the clearing up Rosa?"

"No, that's fine, Mum; you have done enough for me today, thanks. See you tomorrow about twelve, if that's OK."

Just as Rosa's parents were leaving, the phone rang. Rosa answered, and stopped her mum and dad from going out the door.

"Who is it? What's wrong?" asked Billy.

"Well, by the look on Rosa's face, I would say it's Eva." Emily answered.

"It's Eva, Dad;" Rosa said, "She wants to come over for two weeks, in a couple of weeks-time. She wants to know if you can put her up in my old rooms, if they're available? She's bringing her boyfriend, Chris, for us to meet, who she's been dating for six months. Is that OK?"

"Yes, definitely; we will look forward to seeing them both." he answered.

The Other Side of the Fence

Rosa continued talking to Eva on the phone, "Yes, that's fine Eva; all sorted…. Yes, I can hear it; don't worry, I understand…. OK, see you in two weeks. Bye, my lovely."

Putting the phone down, Rosa said, "Eva was sorry that she couldn't talk; the lines all crackly."

When Rosa's mum and dad had left, Rosa went back into the dining room to find that the table had already been cleared and she could hear the sound of dishes being washed; she went into the kitchen.

"Thanks for doing all the dishes, Hun. I would help but you look as if you've nearly finished." she said, laughing. She opened the fridge and said, "I think a nice cool lager for the man of the moment and a nice glass of wine for his lovely lady." She then stood directly behind him and with both arms outstretched, she held the can of lager in one hand and the bottle of wine in the other. "Only after he's finished his chores though." she said, laughing again.

He did an about turn, put his wet hands round her and said, "All finished, My Lady; the man of the moment now wants his payment of a kiss and a cuddle." He pulled her to him, kissed her on the lips and said, "Thank you Ma'am that was nice."

"You're welcome, young Sir. Seriously though, thank you so much. I bet you're as tired as I am. Let's take these upstairs, watch TV and have an early night."

"Yes," he said, "sounds like a good idea. I'll get some glasses and another can. Bet we fall asleep in the middle of the film, like we usually do." he laughed.

"You go up; I will make sure we're all locked in and that Alfie is settled. I will bring some of those cheese straws and a couple of the cake's mum made earlier."

The Other Side of the Fence

They put on a DVD and put as many pillows as they could find behind them.

"Mmm, this is nice." he said, "Are you comfy my love?"

"Yes, I'm loving it." she said and laid her head on his shoulder.

A short while into the film, Rosa said, "I think the schoolteacher did it, don't you?" When she got no reply, she said, "I think it's the teacher." and lifted her head off his shoulder to look at him. She smiled; he was fast asleep. She made him comfortable, covered him up and turned the film off. While she was up, she put her robe on and feeling the two chips in the pocket, she put them in a small draw at the side of the bed.

She still had quite a bit of wine left in her glass, so she made herself comfortable, sitting upright on the bed, sipping her wine and thought, "So, my little girl is courting, is she? Eva and Chris; yes, that sounds nice." She smiled to herself, "I've just had a brilliant idea, the Casino. We can take them out for a meal and a night out at the Blue River Casino. Yes, good thinking, Rosa. I'll book it when they get here and see who else wants to go."

Rosa didn't feel at all tired. "So much for an early night." she thought, as she poured herself a drop more wine and laid back. "I wonder if Eva's boyfriend looks like a film star? I remember Eva saying that the first time she met Vince. My goodness, that was a long time ago."

Rosa had seen Vince a few times during the investigation and trial, but only as Detective Sergeant Parker, as he was on duty. They had always got on and she was comfortable in his company, so it was nice to see him, off duty, at the casino. Then, one day when Eva was in England on holiday, they happened to see him, off duty again, in town. Vince was helping a girl of about sixteen into his car, when he saw them. He said something to the young girl, closed the car door and went over to speak to Rosa.

"Hello, Rosa, long time no see; how are you? Still happy now that Davenport's locked up?" Turning to Eva, he said, "Hello, and who is this? She's very pretty; looks like you, so she's got to be your daughter."

"Yes, this is my daughter, Eva." Then pointing over to his car, Rosa asked, "Is that your daughter?"

"Definitely not. No, too much worry for me. She's my niece; I've just picked her up from the dentist for my sister. Rosa, I've been wanting to ask you, but never had the opportunity, with it being inappropriate when on duty. Would you like to go out for a few drinks and a meal; just us two? I don't get many nights off, but it just so happens that I'm free tomorrow." He looked back at his car and said, "I've got to go, as my niece has to get home. Pick you up at eight, OK?" he said, walking back to his car.

Rosa just stood there; she didn't even get a chance to answer.

As he drove past them, he pipped and smiled.

"He's very handsome, Mum; he should be a film star." said Eva.

"That's really funny, Eva, that's exactly what I said when I first saw him. He's a detective sergeant in the police force; he helped Mummy catch a very bad man and put him in prison. I will tell you the story, one day, when you're older."

"I hope you are going out with him tomorrow, Mum. I would, he is very handsome." said Eva.

The Other Side of the Fence

"Eva! I can't believe you just said that; you sound like Gemma." said a shocked Rosa, laughing out loud, "Yes, I'm going, but I must tell Gemma first. When we have finished shopping, we'll go to the riding school, so that I can tell Gemma. How does that sound?"

"I'm ready if you are Mum. Can I ride Penric please?"

Rosa laughed, "People say that you're a smaller version of me. That's exactly what I would have said at your age. But first, let's go and buy some fresh cream cakes to take; we'll be very popular." said Rosa, taking Eva's hand and hurried as fast as she could, towards the cake shop.

65

The next night, at seven-thirty, Rosa, still in her dressing gown, sat on the bed, surrounded by clothes.

Rosa's mum knocked on the bedroom door, entered and said, "Oh dear, I can see by the pile of clothes on the bed that things aren't good."

"I don't know what to wear. I wish I had bought something new; he's seen me in everything I've got."

"Right," said her mum, "you've only got twenty minutes left; so, let's put everything away you definitely don't want to wear and see what's left."

Five minutes later, after a lot of sorting, her mum said, "There you go; now you only have a choice of three things. It's a nice evening, so you don't want anything that's going to make you hot, so put that jumper away. Two left; which one are you most comfortable in?"

"The cream blouse." replied Rosa.

"With your black trousers; very classy. Now put it on, calm yourself and be ready."

"Thank you, Mum; I have waited so long for him to ask me out; I think I had a bit of a panic on. I'm fine now." she said, just as Eva entered the bedroom.

"I had to see you before you go, Mum; I hope you have a lovely time tonight." said Eva.

"Thank you, Eva, that's a lovely thing to say." said Rosa, checking herself in the mirror.

Vince pulled up at Rosa's front door at eight o' clock sharp.

"This is all new." he said, "Your own personal driveway and front door; very posh."

"Yes, it's the new extension; it makes it feel more like a house, with me in a semi-detached bungalow. We are still connected inside though." she said, as she got in his car.

Looking at her sitting next to him, he smiled, nodded and said, "Very nice."

"Thank you; it's been a long time since anyone has said that." she said, blushing slightly.

"Is it OK if we go out into the country? My mate told me about a country pub that serves good meals."

"That's fine, Vince. Let's go; I can see my mum and Eva straining to see you from the upstairs window." she replied, laughing.

They drove down very dark roads, through a village she didn't know and soon arrived at the pub.

As they drove onto the car park, Rosa said, "Isn't it pretty?" It had hanging baskets full of different coloured flowers all round, with a few tables and chairs outside. She could see through the windows as they approached the arched doorway; the tables all had little oil lamps on them.

"It's so quaint; I'm impressed." said Rosa, as they were taken to a table in a little alcove hideaway.

"What would you like to drink?" Vince asked.

"White wine, please." she answered.

"White wine and a non-alcoholic lager, please." he told the waiter.

Looking at the menu, Rosa ordered chicken breast in mushroom sauce, while Vince ordered a steak.

Sipping her wine, Rosa said, "Vince, you know all about me; I know nothing about you."

"Right, give me your hand." he said. Then, holding it across the table, he said, "OK, ask away; what do you want to know?"

"Are you married?"

"That's a definite no"

She smiled, "How old are you and have you got any brothers or sisters?"

"I'm 38; my birthday's in October. I have one brother, not married but courting and one sister who's divorced; she's got three children; the girl you saw, who's seventeen, and two boys, five and two. They are good kids and I help when I can."

"Do you live on your own?"

"No, I live in a flat with two other detectives, who are confirmed bachelors; now that they're both divorced. It makes it hard on any relationships because they are always

The Other Side of the Fence

about. Oh! here comes our meal." he said, letting go of her hand.

By the time they had finished the meal and sat talking over drinks and coffee, it was nearly eleven o' clock. Vince drove Rosa home.

When he stopped the car outside her front door, he asked, "Everything OK?"

"Yes, very OK; it was really nice. You can thank your friend and tell him he was right."

"Rosa, I really enjoyed tonight and I'd love to do it again, but I need to tell you something first."

"Here we go." thought Rosa, "He is married. I knew it; it's been too good to be true."

"It's my job." he said, "You know I'm a detective sergeant; well, that makes me on-call practically twenty-four hours a day. When there's an incident; if it's big enough, they will call me; that's why you didn't see me have a drink tonight; I have to be able to drive if I'm wanted. If you can put up with me being out with you and it happens, or cancelling a date at the last minute, I would like to take this further. What do you think?"

Rosa was listening, looking straight ahead. Vince gently touched her cheek and turned her head towards him. She looked into his eyes and said, "Yes, Vince. If that's how we can be together, then I'm willing to accept what you've said. I've been on my own for so long, I'm sure I will be OK when you have to work."

He leaned over and kissed her. She didn't move; she stayed close, hoping for another kiss, which he did. The kisses were gentle; with each one, Rosa melted more and more.

"That's wonderful, Rosa, we are going to have a great time. I often have to go away for days at a time, staying overnight in hotels all over the country. When I have to go on my own, you can come with me, if you want. Then, when I've finished work, the rest of the time, we can be together. I will leave what rooms I book at the hotel to you; either two single rooms or one double." he said, then hesitated before saying, "You know, I really felt for you when we first met and you had to tell us your story; you looked so sad and vulnerable, I wanted to hug you and make it all go away. Since we met, I have had to stop myself asking you out several times; especially that time in Gemma's garden, but we are not allowed to mix with witnesses; I would have lost my job, but it's OK now that the case is closed."

They kissed some more before Rosa said reluctantly, "I'd better go, I've got to get up early tomorrow."

Rosa got out the car and bent down to say goodnight. Vince smiled at her and said, "Goodnight, Rosa. I'll phone you in the morning to check that you still want me."

As she unlocked her door, she said to herself, "What a night. Will I still want you in the morning, Vince Parker? You can bet money on it. Tomorrow morning and every morning." She turned, waved and went inside.

66

The next morning, Rosa walked into the office to be greeted by the four girls sitting on chairs, all in a line, with one empty chair facing them.

"What?" Rosa said, smiling.

Gemma replied, "Sit down. Kettle's nearly boiled, so tea or coffee won't be long."

"I just love you lot; you're so funny. I've just had all this from my mum and Eva." laughed Rosa.

"Now it's our turn." said Gemma, "Start from when he picked you up last night."

"And be prepared to answer questions." added Katie.

Rosa told them everything, from start to finish; even about going away with him.

"So, did he try to get fresh?" asked Katie.

"No, just two very gentle kisses." she answered.

They all looked at each other.

"He's too good to be true." said Jess.

"I'm sure everyone will agree;" said Katie, "that when ever you want to go away with him, we will cover for you." The girls looked at each other and nodded, then Katie added, "As long as you keep us up to date with what's happening between you two. It's the only bit of excitement we have at the moment."

"OK, thank you." said a happy Rosa, "I will write down every detail and report back to you."

"Will you really?" asked Jess.

"No! definitely not." said Rosa, laughing, then added, "Well, maybe just bits."

Over the next few weeks, Rosa only saw Vince three times a week. Sometimes, it would be for a couple of hours before he had to leave; other times, it would be the same routine, dark country roads leading to a small, out of the way pub, have a meal and drinks, then drive back home, with a few clumsy fumbles and kisses in the car; though, admittedly, they were getting a lot more passionate. When Rosa got back indoors, she sat quietly, thinking that it wasn't a bit like she thought it was going to be.

"I like him so much; if I want him, this is how he said it would be." she said to herself.

Just then the phone rang; it was Vince; he said, "I'm glad you're still up; I had to tell you that I've just been told to go to London for an overnight stay in a couple of days' time. If you would like to come, should I book one room or two?"

"Oh Vince, how wonderful; I can't wait. Book a double, so we can be together."

Vince had to start work in London at ten o' clock, so, Rosa was up, ready and eagerly waiting for Vince to pick her up at five-thirty in the morning. She felt excited at what the day would bring.

"You can't have a long-time relationship in a parked car and a pub." she thought, "If this all goes well; when we get back, I'll ask Mum and Dad how they feel, if I sometimes let him stay overnight."

"He's here, Mum." called Rosa, seeing Vince pull into the drive.

Coming through to Rosa's, her mum said, "Have a lovely time, Dear. I will lock up for you; see you tomorrow."

"It will probably be quite late." Rosa said, then kissed her mum, grabbed her bag and went out to meet Vince.

Vince had booked an early check-in at the hotel and they were in their room by nine-thirty.

Standing at the big window in the room, overlooking the river, Rosa said, "Vince, this is so beautiful and I've got you all to myself; even if I do have to wait till two o' clock."

Vince went over and stood next to her.

"Sorry, Rosa, I need to leave now, so I can get everything done that I came here to do. Why don't you relax here for a while, then go down for breakfast and put it on my account; they serve till eleven. If you leave the hotel at about one-thirty and turn left onto South Bank, then stay on the South side of the river and walk for about fifteen minutes; you will see a restaurant that has a big balcony overlooking the river; you can't miss it. I will meet you there at two o' clock; make sure you have your phone with you."

"OK, I've got all that. I've never seen this part of London before; I think I will order room service and sit at the window, watching the river, till it's time to leave." She then walked with him to the door.

"OK. I've got a lot planned, so enjoy the rest." He kissed her and said, "Be careful, I will see you later. Don't forget your phone."

After a restful few hours, Rosa got ready to leave. As she left the hotel, she said to herself, "OK, Rosa, out you go into the big city; turn left and start walking."

She enjoyed the walk and kept stopping to watch the entertainment happening on the embankment. Before she knew it, she was at the restaurant. She was too shy to go in on her own, so she walked to the river wall and stood watching all the activity on the river.

"Good afternoon, Miss, do you want a guide for the rest of the day?" a voice said behind her.

She turned round to see Vince laughing.

"It's all so lovely." she said, "Yes, I do; do you know one?"

"Indeed, I do. He has booked a table at this restaurant for a light lunch, then a slow walk along the Embankment to do a bit of shopping and people watching. He's booked a ride on the London eye, for six o' clock, so we can see all over London; then, it's over Westminster Bridge to see all the great buildings and up the Mall to Buckingham Palace. A taxi to Leister Square for a meal; then, when we are ready, a taxi back to our hotel. How's that sound?"

The Other Side of the Fence

"Very tiring, but great. So many famous places to see and a ride on the big wheel; I can't wait."

After a long, tiring day, they were both ready for an early night. Rosa had had a shower and put on the pretty, lilac satin nighty she had bought, it had two thin straps and was, for her, very expensive. The room was dark, except for the one small lamp on the dressing table, where Rosa was sitting, looking through the brochures of all the places they had visited. The bathroom door opened, which made Rosa look up. In the mirror, she could see Vince standing behind her, with just a towel round his waist. He smiled as he walked towards her. Looking at her in the mirror, he moved her long hair to one side, then, he very gently ran two of his fingers up and down her spine; it made Rosa tingle. He leant over and kissed her neck, while he gently removed the straps of her nightie, one at a time, pulling them down over her breasts; his hands were warm, as he gently caressed her breasts. She surrendered and leant back, so he could kiss her on the lips. Crouching down, he turned her on the stool to face him; then, leaning forward, he took both her hands and pulled her towards him, to kiss her. Still kissing, they stood up; she was loving what he was doing and was not embarrassed when her nighty fell to the floor. He smelled fresh from the shower and his body was warm against hers. As they edged closer and closer to the bed, their kissing became more and more passionate. He picked her up and laid her on the bed; then, laying on the bed next to her, he turned to face her. Rosa was happy at last; Vince was going to make love to her. Unlike James, who was a tender and caring lover, Vince had more passion. She wasn't complaining; she was OK with both ways; she was just surprised how different two lovers could be. Vince laid at the side of her, looking exhausted; she had waited weeks for him to make love to her and now it was over.

Rosa leaned over and kissed his chest; she smiled as she said, "Detective Sergeant Parker, that's not the first time you've done that."

67

Rosa's romantic trip to London with Vince, was soon over. Back home, Rosa mentioned to her parents about having Vince stay over. Her parents laughed, saying that she was over thirty and they hardly thought she needed their permission.

Rosa told Gemma how lovely the whole time in London was. She told her all about the places Vince had taken her and how attentive he was. Gemma smiled and started singing 'Love is in the air' as she made them both a cup of tea before their first lessons of the day.

Drinking her tea, Rosa thought to herself, "Why do I feel guilty. Is it because I thought of James while Vince made love to me? I don't understand why I wasn't completely lost in the moment, after waiting for so long."

For the rest of the year, Rosa got used to fitting in with Vince and his crazy working hours. She loved the days when they went away together; they had wonderful times visiting Cambridge, Brighton, Southampton and several times to London. Vince had also got on well with her mum and dad; sometimes he would call and have a cup of tea with them when Rosa was out at work. It was lovely and relaxed when he did stay at hers overnight, although his terrible shift pattern meant that he sometimes left at two in the morning or arrived at six in the morning and left again at nine.

Christmas was getting closer and things were working out well for them to be able to spend their first Christmas together. Her Mum and Dad had been invited to spend Christmas with Billy's brother and family; Rosa was also invited but declined, so she could spend it with Vince. Eva was at the Stirlings' this Year and Matt was going to see his son. Vince said that he could get most of Christmas Day off, so it was all working out OK.

Christmas Day arrived and there was so much activity, with everyone visiting and exchanging presents. Rosa was happy listening to Christmas songs, while cooking Christmas dinner with all the trimmings. Vince asked if she could cook for about six o' clock; that way, they could have the evening together. At three o' clock she put the boned turkey in the oven and shut the door, just as the phone rang; Rosa went cold.

"So sorry, Rosa; I can't get away. I'm the only DS available and there was a big disturbance last night. A big fight broke out in one of the nightclubs, causing a lot of damage and some people ending up in hospital. I can probably get away around midnight, when the other DS comes on duty."

"Don't you dare come here at that time; I will be in bed!" shouted Rosa and slammed the phone down; she then burst into tears. "Why am I putting myself through this." she cried out loud.

The Other Side of the Fence

Rosa tried to calm herself and thought, "I must love him, to put up with his stupid job. The hours he works, poor baby, I bet he's not very happy either, having to work on Christmas day. He did say at the beginning that this would happen and I agreed, so how can I complain."

Rosa continued to prepare the dinner, thinking, "So, Rosa, if its Christmas dinner for one, so be it. He'd better not turn up here at midnight because I won't be very sociable." she said wiping away the tears.

Rosa sat reading, waiting for the dinner to finish cooking when the phone rang. Rosa answered it, ready to slam it down again.

"Hello, my lovely." a voice said, "I hope I haven't disturbed you, but I can't let the day pass without wishing my favourite girl a Merry Christmas. I'm back early, I felt like a gooseberry, sitting there with my ex and her boyfriend, so I left. Paul's coming for a week, next week, so I will see him then. Hello, hello, Rosa, are you there? It's Matt."

Rosa, realising it was Matt and not Vince, quickly tried to compose herself and said, "Hi Matt, how lovely to hear your voice; have you had Christmas dinner yet?"

"Yes, sort of. I hated it; I felt too uncomfortable, so I didn't eat much; but I'm fine."

"Matt, I'm on my own and I've got lots of food, if you want another dinner?"

"Where's Vince?" he asked.

"Don't ask. Are you coming?"

"You bet; I'll be there in a few minutes. I'll come on my bike and bring a bottle of wine; it sounds like we both need a drink." he said.

When Matt arrived, before he had had a chance to knock, Rosa opened the front door. He had hardly got through the door, and put his bag down, before a crying Rosa's arms were round him.

"Let it all out, my lovely, I'm here; tell me what's happened." said a sympathetic Matt, hugging her.

Through the tears, Rosa told Matt what had happened.

Finally, she calmed down and said, "Thank you Matt, you're wonderful. I feel much better now that I've got it all off my chest. I know he will be here in the morning, all apologetic. He will give me that smile and I will forgive him; like I always do. Anyway, enough of that; come on, the dinners all ready. You open the wine and let's enjoy what's left of Christmas Day. I'm really hungry and ready for my dinner; what else have you got in the bag?"

"I've brought us a film to watch, 'It's A Wonderful Life'; I hear it's a real weepy. I thought we could get drunk and have a good cry; brilliant for a couple of sad ones like us."

While eating their dinner, they pulled all twelve crackers, put on the hats, one on top of the other, laughed at all the stupid jokes and pulled all the party poppers over each other. They were both happy and relaxed, when the phone rang. Rosa answered, still laughing at their antics; it was Vince.

"I'm sorry;" he said, "I tried to get away. I love you so much, I wanted to be with you."

The words took her aback; she looked at Matt and mouthed the words, 'Its Vince.'" Matt heard her say, "OK, but not too early…. Bye, see you in the morning."

Rosa filled their glasses from the already open bottle of wine and sat down next to Matt; he was sitting on the floor, staring into the fire; he still had his silly hats on and was covered in streamers; he started pulling them off and said, "Do you want me to go?"

"Are you crazy!" she answered, "There's nearly a full bottle of wine to drink and another waiting to be opened. We'll save the films for another time; Vince has just told me that he loves me, so I don't feel like crying just now." she said, ruffling his hair, so that the hats and streamers fell off, "You up for a game? I've got lots; Me and Eva are always playing them. First, I will challenge you to a game of Scrabble, then we can go from there. We have got lots of games, wine and food." she said, getting up to get the games, "Stay there, Matt, it's going to be a long night." she laughed.

It was well after midnight when Matt decided to leave; he said, "I'd better go, while I can still ride my bike. After sharing two bottles of wine, I think I can still ride it. Rosa Maddox, you're a bad influence on me."

They had laughed so much all evening, especially when Matt said, "Why do we always say, 'Oh dear' after we have laughed out loud?" and the more they laughed, the more they said it, which made them laugh even more.

Matt tried to walk properly to the front door; he turned to Rosa and said, "Night, my love, hope you're OK now? At least you know that he loves you; that should make you feel better. No one loves poor old Matt. Oh, I stand corrected; my dogs do." he laughed.

"Matt, are you OK? You can stay the night if you want; I can get some blankets and you can sleep on the couch."

"I'm fine, Rosa. I need to get home; I told my dogs I would only be an hour." He kissed her on the cheek, stood back, looked at her and said, "You know I love you too?"

As she turned him round to help him out the door, she said, "Yes, I know you do, Matt; I love you too. You take care and phone me when you get back, so I know that you're home safe."

68

Rosa had fallen asleep on the couch and was woken the next morning by someone knocking on her front door.

"I'm coming." she said and went to stand up, "Oh, my head." she said, as she held it, "I'm coming." she said again and went to open the door; it was Vince.

"Can't stop, but I'll be back later." he said, "I just came to bring your pre.." he stopped, as he saw the state of the table and floor; then said, "What ever has been going on in here? Well, it doesn't look as if you missed me much yesterday."

"Erm, the girls came round to cheer me up." she lied; even she was shocked at the state of the room. She looked at the mess all over the floor; it was covered in cushions, streamers, bits of pulled cracker, dirty plates and dishes; you name it, it was on the floor. There were four glasses, two on the floor, two on the table and two empty wine bottles, balanced, one on top of the other. The strangest, was a large vase with lots of scrabble pieces scattered all around it; she suddenly remembered, it was a game of who could get the most scrabble pieces in the vase. Rosa stood there like a naughty little girl.

"Tell you what, Rosa, you look terrible. I will come back on my next break, at around three this afternoon; it will give you time to sort yourself out. You want to tell those girls to come back and help you clean-up."

"Thanks, Vince;" she said, "I will sort it. Did you say you had bought my Christmas present; where is it?" she said, excitedly.

"I'll bring it back later." he said, then kissed her cheek and left.

The first thing Rosa did, was to phone Gemma and tell her what happened.

Gemma laughed out loud. "Now that's really funny." she said, "OK, we can say it was Sydney and Jess; as it happens, they spent yesterday with us, as they were on their own."

"Thanks Gem, you're a star. See you tomorrow."

Rosa then rang Matt; a very tired voice answered, "Hi, Rosa, I should have stayed on your couch last night, I only just managed to get as far as mine. I've only just woken up."

Rosa told Matt about Vince coming round and seeing the state of the room. Worst of all, she told him about the lie she had told Vince; then she said, "Anyway, Matt, you couldn't have slept on my couch; that's where I woke up."

"Well, I ended up walking home. I tried to ride my bike but I kept weaving over to the other side of the road and falling into the bushes. Do you want me to come and help you clear up?"

The Other Side of the Fence

"No way." she answered, "I will get dressed, have some breakfast and then clear up."

"OK, just before you go; always remember that I'm here anytime you want to play who can get the most scrabble pieces in a vase. I think I won; it was great fun. Let's do it again next year." Then, he laughed.

"OK, but at yours; then you can clear up." she laughed, "Bye, love you." she said and put the phone down.

At about three o' clock that afternoon, she had just finished hoovering the last few bits up, when Vince walked through the door.

"Now that's better." he said, looking round, "And you, my love," he said, as he walked over and lightly kissed her, "look like you live on this planet again." then, flashed one of his 'melt her heart' smiles.

"Have you had dinner yet?" she asked, "I've got lots of food; Mum and Dad are coming through later, around six, for dinner, but there's plenty if you want some?"

"Could I just have a meat sandwich and a cup of tea please? I can't stay too long; I just popped out to give you your present and explain about yesterday." he said.

He stood in the kitchen while Rosa was making his sandwich and tea, and explained, "I volunteered to cover the Christmas holidays because all the other detectives are married with children; and, I think, parents should be with their kids on Christmas Day. To be honest, I felt really awful about letting you down; that was, until I walked in this morning. Then, I was pleased, but jealous, when I saw you had had such a good time."

As they sat down together on the couch, he pointed to a small table nearby, saying, "Anyway, there is your present."

The Other Side of the Fence

Excitedly, she said, "Wow! two pressies." She opened a small, pretty bag first.

"I hope you like it." he said, as she opened a small box; it was a bottle of Chanel NO 5.

"My word, I like number one present very much." she said and kissed him.

Finishing his sandwich, he said, "Quick, open the other one, before I have to go."

She opened a very posh envelope and pulled out a white card, edged with gold. Her eyes widened as she read out loud, "Luxury full spa day for two, with overnight, fully inclusive hotel accommodation, on a date of your choice. La Mer Hotel, Leicester, Leicestershire."

She put it down on the table, jumped on him and kissed him all over his face, saying "I love it, thank you, thank you, I love it." As she got off him, she picked up the card again and just stared at it, reading it again.

"Hmm, I take it that you liked that present as well then." he said, laughing. She nodded, still reading it.

"When can we go?" she asked.

"It's valid for a year, so I'm thinking more in the warmer months, if that's OK. I'm sorry Rosa, I really must go. I'll call you when I'm next off duty; it might be a couple of days, so don't worry." he said, as he got up to leave.

Rosa went with him to the door and kissed him, saying, "Thank you for my presents; you sure know how to please a woman."

When Vince had gone, Rosa took her presents through to her bedroom. She stuck the spa invitation in the edge of the mirror and putting the perfume on the dressing table, she noticed a small, long box, wrapped in Christmas paper.

"Oh No!" she said out loud, "I didn't give him my present."

Then, going back to the lounge, she sat on the couch and thought, "Well, that's it, Rosa, now you'll have to wait for the next time the police will let you have him for a few precious hours."

69

After his brief visit on Boxing Day, Rosa only saw Vince once in the next five days.

"I hate his job." Rosa told Gemma, "Can you picture being married to him; you've got to be a really strong person. One minute you're on a high, the next, you're upset because he's cancelled arrangements that you've made. You know, I've seen Matt more than him over Christmas."

"You must really love him to put up with it." said Gemma, "Anyway, I can help you with a definite date; eight o' clock, till whenever, New Year's Eve; I'm having a party; everyone will be there. Invite him, surely they can spare him for a while?"

"OK, I will. I know what he will say though, 'I will try and just hope there are no incidences.'"

"At least you won't be sitting alone at midnight. You are coming, aren't you?"

"Yes, I will; if he comes, he comes; if he doesn't, he doesn't." Rosa answered defiantly, "Do you know, this is the first New Year's Eve party I've been to in years? The one I missed and regret the most, was all the celebrations of the millennium. I was in a bad place; that whole period was one big blur."

"Oh, Babe, I'm so sorry; hope you enjoy this one, it's at the village hall, so should be good. We have put a lot of effort into it; we've even hired a DJ."

On New Year's Eve, Rosa made a special effort getting ready for Gemma's party. Vince said he would try to make it, but if he did, it would be after twelve; so, Rosa was quite relaxed.

When she walked in, she didn't feel awkward because she knew everyone. The one person she didn't know, who really stood out, was a pretty blonde, wearing the shortest skirt Rosa had ever seen; she turned out to be Katie's younger sister. As midnight approached, Rosa was happy; she was mixing with everyone and had had a dance with Matt, who had said how nice she looked, which pleased her. He was wearing a black shirt and trousers; and she loved his hair, which she always teased him about in the summer when it got bleached by the sun, by saying that he had had it bleached at the hairdressers; but now it had turned really dark and it was quite long. He said he hadn't had time to get it cut, but she liked it this length, it had just started to kink at the ends; she thought he looked quite rugged.

Rosa was talking to Sydney, who was making her laugh, telling her about what had happened at the stables that day, when she happened to look over at the bar and saw Matt standing there. He nodded and smiled when he saw her and she smiled back. At that moment, Katie's sister walked up to him, put her arms round his neck and

The Other Side of the Fence

appeared to be flirting with him. She then pulled away slightly, laughing, then leant forward and kissed him.

"Oh, my word, Sydney, did you see that?" Rosa said.

"Yes;" Sydney replied, "why, what has she done wrong?"

"She just kissed him. Who does she think she is, coming in here, flirting with our men?"

"Oh, sorry, are you going out with him?" Sydney asked, looking surprised.

"No, I'm with Vince."

"Well, I don't understand what she's done wrong then; he can't wait forever for you."

Rosa was taken aback. "What are you saying, Sydney?"

"I'm saying, Matt, who has loved you for years, can't spend the rest of his life waiting for you to decide that you love him; anyway, you're with that Vince chap, who we all think is making you very unhappy."

"Sydney, your wrong, Matt's my friend,"

"Yeah, take note the next time he looks at you."

"I am with Vince and I do get upset when I don't see him; that's all. We are good together; I've just got to get used to his job and hours."

"It's nearly twelve;" said Sydney, "best I go and find my boyfriend; bet he's at the buffet."

They started the countdown to midnight; Rosa was sitting at a table and looked up, hopefully, when the entry door opened; but no Vince.

The Other Side of the Fence

"Up you get, my lovely; time for 'Auld Lang Syne'." she heard Matt say. She turned to see Matt offering her his hand.

At the stroke of twelve, he held her close and kissed her, just that fraction longer than usual.

"Happy New Year, my lovely, I wish you all the happiness in the world." he said and gave her another, shorter, kiss

Everyone stood and sang, 'Auld Lang Syne' while lots of balloons appeared, with several of them being burst; then, there was dancing to the usual party songs. Matt was dancing with Rosa to Abba's 'Waterloo', when the music suddenly changed to a song from 'Phantom of the Opera'; everyone laughed when Matt shouted, "About time, now everyone can get their breath back." The song was 'All I Ask of You'; several couples got up to dance, so Matt and Rosa stayed on the floor. Matt, being tall and muscular, made Rosa look tiny in his arms. They were dancing very close, hardly moving; Matt held her, one hand round her waist, the other, wrapped around her hand, holding it close to his chest. She filled up when the words, 'I'm here, nothing can harm you,' were sung and he lifted her hand, kissed it and held her that extra bit tighter. She always felt safe with him, especially in his arms. When the words, 'Say you love me,' were sung, she thought, for a second, that he held her even closer, but dismissed it, thinking it was because of what Sydney had said.

They were dancing, lost in the song and the moment, when suddenly there was a tap on her shoulder, "Sorry to interrupt this lovely moment, Rosa." said Gemma's husband, Jack, "I've just come to tell you that Vince is in the car park. He said that he can't come in, as he's on duty."

The Other Side of the Fence

"Oh, thanks, Jack." Rosa replied taking her hand out of Matt's, "Sorry, Matt. Love you, but I've got to go." She quickly got her bag and coat, shouted goodbye and Happy New Year to everyone, then headed for the door and the car park.

Jack looked at a bewildered Matt and said jokingly, "Poor Matt, that was a bit like Cinderella. Shall I see if she's left a shoe outside?" Then, seeing that Matt was not amused, he quietly said, "Sorry, Matt." and hurried away, back to Gemma.

Rosa got in the car. Vince leaned over, kissed her and said, "Happy New Year, Babe. Sorry you had to leave the party, but I'm off till six, so couldn't resist coming to get you; I thought we could have a nice few hours on our own, hopefully back at your place?"

She snuggled up to him and said, "Sounds like the start of a good year to me, Officer."

70

Two weeks after Gemma's New Year's Party, Rosa was out riding Penric. As she passed one of Matt's fields, she saw him checking his fences. She hadn't seen him since the party because the riding school was very busy, due to the school holidays; plus, she had been putting in a lot of extra hours, so that she could visit Eva during her half-term; and, if she got the chance, go away with Vince.

She got as close as she could to Matt and called him. When he saw her, he went over.

"Where have you been? I haven't seen you for ages." she said, "I wanted to tell you what a lovely time I had at Gemma's party and to tell you how sorry I am about how I left you so quickly."

"Well, to be honest, Rosa, I have been to see you a couple of times but turned back because Vince's car has been there. You seem happy enough, so I've presumed that you're OK and have left you alone. You know where I am if you ever need me. I'd better carry on; I've got a lot of fences to check before it gets dark. You take care now."

As Matt walked away, she said, "And you."

Rosa was quite upset at Matt's attitude and the atmosphere. She patted Penric's neck and said, "That didn't sound very good, did it, Penric."

Rosa was very busy and the next few weeks flew by, but she did get to spend a few days in Ireland during Eva's half-term. During her visit, Rosa saw for herself the vast improvement in Eva's riding; even her teachers at her riding school said that Eva was their star pupil. When ever Rosa and Eva were together, whether in Ireland or England, the two of them spent many hours horse riding together. Although Rosa was always in pain with her legs the day after riding, it never stopped her, or the enjoyment she got from riding with Eva.

Rosa had finally settled down and accepted the strange hours that Vince worked. Because of the cold winter, they didn't go out much. They spent most of their time together at Rosa's, so she tried to make those visits romantic with candles and flowers. Sometimes, Vince cooked a meal, or he bought in different take-away meals and they would watch a movie. Sometimes, he would stay the night but always left before six the next morning. So he could relax, Vince had bought a few new casual clothes to leave at hers, so he could change into them from his work suits.

Soon it was to be Valentine's day and Rosa couldn't wait to see what surprise Vince had bought for her. Surprise was right; the surprise, was there was going to be a surprise, but not on that day; Vince had to work. He had got the day before off though and had booked a table at the restaurant he had first taken her to; it was the first time that they had been out since Christmas. He picked her up

The Other Side of the Fence

at eight o' clock and drove straight to the restaurant. Vince never drank alcohol in case he was called into work in an emergency, so he always drove. The restaurant looked as lovely and cosy as Rosa remembered and Vince had asked for the same table they had had. It was really cold outside, so it was nice that the table was near a cosy log fire.

Vince ordered the drinks and meals; then, while they were waiting, he suddenly said, "Happy Valentine's Day, for tomorrow, Rosa." and pushed a beautifully wrapped gift across the table.

"Oh, Vince, what is it?" she asked.

"I think opening it to see is always a good idea." he said, smiling.

She unwrapped a box and opened it.

"Oh, Vince, it's beautiful." she said, "Put it on me please."

Round her wrist he put a thin gold chain; it had a gold heart bearing a small diamond and had two kisses engraved on it.

She looked at him, touched the heart and said, "This is the loveliest thing anyone has ever given me."

He held her hand across the table and said, "That's because no one has loved you like I do."

On the drive home, Vince said, "It's your birthday in May, isn't it? Do you mind if we wait that long to use the Christmas gift of the spar break? If I book the time off now, before anyone else does, we can have a nice couple of relaxing days away. What do you think?"

"That's fine by me, the weather will be warmer by then as well." she answered.

The Other Side of the Fence

"Good, the whole break sounds fabulous, I will book it off as soon as I get to work tomorrow. I'm looking forward to it already; I can't wait. May will be here in no time." he said.

Life carried on and May came round in no time. The overnight stay and the Spa was the most relaxed Rosa had felt in years; from the moment they arrived until they left, she loved every moment. Vince was so attentive, she felt, at last, that he was all hers. When they arrived, he had already had flowers and champagne put in their room and after a full day of the spa's facilities, that night, a special meal with all the trimmings, plus a birthday cake, was delivered to their room; it was the happiest of birthdays for Rosa.

They had a lovely summer and Rosa had become used to the erratic hours that Vince worked.

The nights away had all but stopped; they just had the few hours that Vince had off, out and about around Suffolk. The last overnight stay they had was in August, to Southend. The place was nice but it rained most of the time, so they were either in his car or in their room, so Rosa was glad to get home. When she next saw Vince, she told him not to worry and that they could do something really special on October the nineteenth, his fortieth birthday. She shrugged it off when his response was less than enthusiastic.

October arrived and each time they met, Vince seemed subdued; Rosa was getting anxious.

On a visit to town with Gemma, while sitting in Maisie's café, Rosa said, "Something's wrong with Vince, he seems really low and it's making me paranoid. It's his fortieth birthday in a couple of weeks. I've got plans for it but I need to know what's wrong. Do you think he's going to finish with me? And, I hardly ever see Matt these days; I'm quite upset."

"Don't talk daft, Vince is not going to finish with you." said Gemma, "He's a detective, they have always got things on their mind, and Matt is just jealous because you seem serious about Vince; he's always had you to himself for years; even James wasn't a threat. He feels he has lost you."

"Oh bless, poor Matt; he will always have me, he's my friend; we go back a long way. I was going to ask Vince if he would like to move in with me because he shares a flat with two other policemen."

"Well, you'd better ask him what's wrong then; the sooner the better." Gemma said.

The following week, Vince arrived at Rosa's.

"Hi Babe." Vince said, as he came through the lounge door, "Didn't have time to ask you; my car was parked outside the fish and chip shop and they smelt lovely, so I thought that it would make a nice change. Hope that's OK?"

"Sounds great, I'm really hungry." replied Rosa.

They sat and ate them.

"Delicious." said Vince.

Rosa cleared away the dishes, then sat down opposite Vince and said, "Vince, give me your hands."

He looked puzzled but did as she had asked. She held them across the table, looked into his eyes and said, "What's wrong? Please tell me what it is?"

He looked at her for a while, then looked down at the table and said, "I can't see you for three weeks. I've got to go to Scotland for an inspector's training course. I can't take you because it's in a sort of college and you have to stay on site for the whole three weeks, which will include my birthday. I'm upset about it but it will be good for my career."

71

Although Rosa was disappointed at what Vince had just told her, he seemed quite happy that it was going to improve his career; so, she took a deep breath, put on a brave face and said, "That's fine, it actually works out well for me; I can now go to Ireland to help Eva; it's her half-term break and she's got a big show jumping competition coming up. She asked if I could get time off and help her prepare. So, don't worry about me; three weeks will go by quickly and you will be back, proud that you got a promotion; we can celebrate then."

He stood up, smiled, kissed her, and said, "I'd better be going back to work, Babe; I'll see you in three weeks after this weekend."

Rosa was at the airport, ready for her trip to Ireland. She had stopped at the newsagents in the departure lounge and bought a couple of magazines and a bag of sweets for the journey. As she walked out of the exit, she noticed a family coming towards her. She quickly darted back inside and hid behind one of the tall display units near the shop doorway. Her heart was pounding; the family she had just seen consisted of a girl of about nineteen, pushing a young baby in a pram, two young boys about four and seven, a rather attractive blonde lady pulling a suitcase and holding the four-year-old's hand, and a rather handsome man pushing a luggage trolley laden with suitcases; the handsome man was none other than Vince Parker and the girl pushing the pram, she recognised as the girl Vince said was his niece.

Just as they were about to pass the newsagents, the young girl said, "Hold the pram please, Mum, I'm just going to get some magazines for the journey." As she entered the shop, she added, "Do you want anything, Mum?"

"No thanks, Janie;" her mum replied, "we will go on ahead and gets some seats."

As the girl passed Rosa, to look at the magazines, Rosa quickly bent down and pretended to look for something on the bottom shelf. She could feel the blood draining from her face.

"Don't faint, don't faint." she said to herself.

Then, the oldest boy came into the shop and said, "Janie, Mum said can you get her some mints."

"OK," Janie replied, "stay there and don't move; I don't want to lose you."

Janie went to buy the mints and pay for the magazines. The boy started to walk round the stand Rosa was hiding behind; when he saw her, he said, "Hello, have you lost something? Are you going on holiday?"

Rosa nearly choked, as she answered, "Yes, are you?"

"Yeah, we're going to Majorca for nearly three weeks. It's my dad's fortieth birthday next week. My sister's buying us some sweets; she said I've got to wait here for her."

"Are you going with your mum and dad?" Rosa asked him.

"Yes, and my brother and sister and her baby." Hearing his sister calling him, he said, "That's my sister. Bye Lady, hope you find what you've lost."

"Bye, hope you have a lovely holiday." she said, smiling at him.

After a few minutes, Rosa left the shop; she was shaking and felt sick. Thankfully, the Ireland departures were in the opposite direction to the Majorca flights. Rosa walked to her departure gate like a zombie. She managed to get on the plane and as she sat there in her seat, she felt like she had been kicked in the stomach. Trying to piece things together, her mind was in a whirl.

"All those lies and promises, how could he keep that pretence up for two years. He couldn't, of course he couldn't." she thought, "There has got to be a simple explanation; was it even Vince I saw pushing the luggage trolley, or just someone who looked like him; yes, that's it." Then she got angry, "Rosa you're not stupid, it was him and he's not only married and a father of three, he's a granddad." Now she was arguing with herself, "Rosa, stop it!" she blurted out loud. She looked around embarrassed, but no one seemed to take any notice. "Just hurry up and land this plane, so I can see my Eva." she said to herself.

The whole trip to Ireland and the journey to the Stirlings' house was a blur. Rosa cheered up when she saw Eva and decided that this was Eva's time, so she tried to put what had happened at the airport to the back of her mind until she was back in England and could deal with it.

Eva couldn't wait to show her mum how good she was getting with her horse riding. She was all smiles, when her mum arrived, and they walked through the Stirlings' main door to see all the Rosettes and cups Eva had won, beautifully displayed in a glass display cabinet in the entrance hall.

Rosa turned to Eva, with tears in her eyes, and said, "I'm so proud of you Eva."

The competition was the next afternoon, so Rosa and Eva were up early and out practising. Rosa thought it was a really hard course, but Eva was fearless. The whole Stirling Family came to watch Eva win two of her events and come third in another. Then, it came to the final event, the main one that all the riders wanted to win, the time trial.

There had been two clear rounds before Eva's turn.

"That's OK." Eva said, "I've just got to do it faster."

Eva was doing brilliantly, then came a loud, 'Oh no!' from everyone, as she knocked a pole down, but they all clapped as loud as they could when she got her third-place rosette.

Rosa went to see Eva to console her, knowing how upsetting it was from her own competition days. She had expected Eva to be crying when she got there, but was impressed by Eva's positive attitude, for someone so young.

"I'm fine Mum. Sorry you came all this way and I was rubbish; I will do better next time and win it."

"That's a bit of Edward Stirling talking." Rosa thought. She gave her a big cuddle and said, "You're my girl; I came to see you to tell you how much I love you and to let you know how proud I am of you."

James nodded, he was standing next to his dad, and said, "Rosa, I know it's a little early yet, but we were wondering if you are thinking of having Eva for Christmas this year. If so, me, Lily, Mum and Dad can plan a few days away, skiing, if that's OK with you? I'm just checking because we'll need to book it."

Rosa looked at Eva, who was smiling and nodding vigorously.

"I think that's a yes, James." Rosa laughed, "You tell me what days you want and I'll come and get her." she said, putting her arm around Eva, and kissing her head.

"That's lovely. When we get back, I'm sure one or the other of us will be coming to England for a few days on business, so we can pick her up. Then we will book a nice family holiday with you, Eva, over the Easter holidays. Your mum can come too if she wants. How does that sound?" James said.

Eva smiled and nodded. She kissed her mum and then hugged and kissed her dad.

Rosa was upset to leave Eva but was pleased she was going back to England to sort things out. Her normal plan would have been to go and see Matt and talk it through with him, but she realised that she had treated him horribly at the end of Gemma's party.

"After all he's done for me, all I thought of, was me, me, me." she berated herself.

72

Rosa fell asleep on the plane back to England; her mind was exhausted, worrying about what was going to happen when she got back to England and confronted Vince; what could he possibly say? In fact, the thought of seeing him made her feel sick.

"I've only been away three days and already I need my Matt; he always makes things better." she thought, then got angry with herself, "Serves you right, you were a pig to Matt at Gemma's party; no wonder he's distancing himself from you; you humiliated him when you just left him in the middle of the dance floor and ran out to be with Vince. You didn't even bother to go and see Matt the next day to apologise. No, you were too busy seeing Mr. lying, Vince Parker! She recalled Vince's excuse, 'So sorry, Rosa, I've got to go to Scotland to become a better person.' Liar; no, you haven't, you're off on holiday with your wife and children." She wiped the tears from her eyes, then said to herself, "Don't you dare cry over him, he's not thinking of you; he's lying on the beach with his wife!"

The Other Side of the Fence

The plane landed.

"Thank goodness Dad's going to meet me, I'm too upset to drive." she thought.

Walking out of the airport doors, she shivered; although it was only October, it was really cold. She looked for her dad's car in the pick-up zone, but, to her surprise, she saw, smiling and waving frantically, her Matt. Smiling and crying at the same time, she rushed across the road to get to him.

"Rosa! look out for the cars!" he shouted, as she crossed the road without looking.

When she got to him, she dropped the handle of her little suitcase, which fell on the floor, flung her arms around his neck and kissed him.

"My goodness," he said, "are we in a film?" and pretending to look round for a camera, added, "Rosa, I'm confused; are you happy or sad."

"Both," she said, "tell you later. I'm so happy you met me, you're the one person I needed to see."

"Your dad asked if I would pick you up. I said of course I would; I haven't seen you for ages because you've been so busy. Now, do you want me to drive you home, or do you want to come to mine; we can get a takeaway and you can tell me what's wrong."

"Yours please, Matt." she answered.

Sitting in the front seat of his car, tears streaming down her face, she reached over and squeezed his hand, in thanks. She then lent back and closed her eyes. She felt safe; her Matt would sort it out for her.

The Other Side of the Fence

When they walked into Matt's lounge, it was lovely and warm, thanks to the log burner that Matt had lit earlier. Rosa already felt happy and relaxed.

Rosa was staring out of the window when Matt came in carrying the meals and plates.

"You OK, Rosa?" he asked.

"Yes, I'm fine." she answered, "I was just standing here thinking how much I love what you've done to this room; it's always warm and cosy in the winter; then, nice and cool in the summer when you open those two big doors onto the garden. It's all so lovely; you're very clever to have done all this."

After they had eaten their meals, Matt sat quiet and listened to her story.

"What do you think?" she asked.

"Well, I know you love him, I've heard you say it enough times, so you must give him a chance to explain. He doesn't know what you know yet; it could all be quite innocent. He did tell you, ages ago, that the young girl you saw him with was his niece, and you said that the boy said she was his sister. Listen to what he has to say; then, only you can decide what to do next."

Rosa looked across at him and smiled, saying, "I feel much better now, thank you for being so understanding."

Rosa was indoors and could hear fireworks going off outside when Vince was due to return. She was getting ready to go to the giant bonfire and firework display being held in one of the nearby farmer's fields; she was going with Gemma, Katie, their husbands and children. The place was full and although there were long queues at all the food stalls, they had just managed to get a hot dog each before the fireworks began. They all stood looking upwards at the exploding, colourful, rockets going off, one after another.

Rosa had just put the last piece of her hot dog in her mouth when she heard a voice behind her say, "Hi Babe, I've just got back; your mum told me where to find you."

Surprised and nearly choking on her hotdog, Rosa turned to see Vince. Still standing behind her, he put his arms around her and held onto her hands. Rosa had her nice warm winter coat on and was wearing a large blue scarf round her neck.

Vince snuggled into her neck and whispered in her ear, "I've missed you, Babe, and laying next to you. How long are these fireworks on for?"

"About another ten minutes." she said and thought, "And I'm not rushing out like last time; you can wait for me, until it's finished."

He said, "I'm off until two; I can't wait to be with you." He then pulled her scarf away from her neck and kissed it; then whispered, "In bed."

This made Rosa giggle. She turned and looked at him; he just stood there grinning and mouthed a kiss.

"You're so naughty." she said, "Watch the fireworks, they are nearly finished."

Rosa didn't hurry saying goodnight to everyone; she knew it was annoying Vince, but she didn't care; it was giving her a chance to think of what to say when they got back to hers.

"About time." Vince said, as they got in the car, "I did say I've only got till two."

When they arrived at Rosa's, she unlocked the front door, but before she could put the light on, Vince was holding her arm and pulling her towards him.

He kissed her passionately, then, started to undo her coat, saying, "Oh, how I've missed you, Babe."

Pulling away, she said forcefully, "Vince, stop it!" She then walked away and put the light on.

"I'm sorry, what's the matter, what have I done?" he said, shocked at her outburst.

"Sit down please, I've been waiting for you to come back; I need to tell you something important."

He sat down like a little boy that had been naughty and looked at her, puzzled. Rosa told him exactly what she had seen at the airport and about the conversation with the young boy. When she had finished, she just sat, looking at him, waiting for his explanation.

He slid his hands across the table and gestured for Rosa to hold them; she hesitated but held them.

"OK," he said, "The woman is my sister, the girl is her daughter; I told you that she is my niece, Janie. The baby girl is hers; the baby's father is not around. The two boys are my nephews; the youngest is Jamie and the one you spoke to, that's Robbie; he's always called me dad, since his dad left. He used to get upset at school because all the kids had a dad and he didn't, so he started calling me dad and we left it. I told you that I do what I can for them, as her husband left her and she was all alone. When he said that we were going on holiday for dad's fortieth birthday; his mum had probably mentioned that it was my fortieth and he thought that's why they were going. I took them to the airport and to their departure gate; that's when you saw me. I was in departures because I was flying to Scotland two hours later. I dropped them off, then went to find the rest of my group at the Scottish departure gate."

"And the suntan?" she said, still trying to catch him out.

"The college was in the mountains, running team building exercises. It's not a suntan, it's a snow tan; I got it when we went up in a cable car and then carried on by foot to the top. It had been snowing for days and we were told that we could carry on in the snow, as long as we kept to the paths. It was tiring but worth it; the views were breath-taking."

73

Whatever Vince told Rosa, she accepted; she believed everything he said; why would he lie? How he explained what happened at the airport all fitted and made sense. She accepted that it was her being paranoid and that her mind had overreacted. He just had this way with him; he would look at her in a certain way and smile, then she would go weak and crumble, and her fears would all disappear.

Rosa thought Matt was right, when he said that she was the only one who could decide what her future would be. Well, she was convinced that all was well and felt happy and relaxed with his explanation; so happy, in fact, that it was her who led Vince to the bedroom, where they spent a few passionate hours; when Vince, did indeed, show her how much he had missed her.

Before she knew it, it was time for Vince to go back to work and he was once again kissing her goodbye at the front door. Rosa had put on her over large towelling robe and pulled it tight round her naked body, so she could walk with Vince to his car.

The Other Side of the Fence

"One last kiss." he said, putting both hands inside her gown and pulling her close to kiss her.

Pushing him away, she said, "Vincent Parker, that's enough, its cold. Get in the car and go to work."

Grinning, in his usual way, he said, "I can't help it, you're so lovely, especially dressed like that. I will try to see you tomorrow; if not, definitely in a couple of days time." he said, as he got in his car and drove off."

In the office, picking up their rotas for the day, Jess said to Sydney, "Can you hear her?"

Gemma said, "She hasn't stopped singing since she got here; he must be back."

Rosa came through to the large office, carrying some riding helmets.

"What?" she said, looking at the three of them, standing there, sheepishly.

"We presume you're very happy today." Jess said.

"Extremely happy." Rosa answered.

"We're pleased for you; we get upset when you're upset. We like you happy, but could you please stop singing?"

"Well, I haven't got any lessons for another hour, so I'm off to ride Penric; at least he listens to my singing." she laughed and off she went, still singing.

They all followed her to the door.

Jess shouted after her, "Poor Penric!" and they all burst out laughing.

Half an hour later, Matt came into the office to bring the girls their weekly orders of fruit and vegetables.

"Rosa not in today?" he asked Gemma, who was on office duty.

"You mean the girl who hasn't stopped singing since she got here? She's gone for a ride on her horse."

"What's he back?" Matt asked, looking hurt.

"Yes, I wonder how long this happy spell will last, till she's hurt again?"

"Yes, you're right, Gemma; but she has got to find out for herself. He's not good for her; one minute she's over happy, then the next, she is all depressed. It's been over two years of highs and lows for her; we've got to be here for her if and when it all goes wrong and she realizes. But for now, at least, she's happy."

Vince was back two days later and, as usual, they stayed in, with Vince bringing a take-away.

When they had eaten, Vince asked Rosa, "How would you like to go to London, a couple of days before Christmas. We can stay overnight, do some Christmas shopping and see the lights. I thought if we left really early on the first day, I can report for work at the station first thing, while you go shopping. Then, we can go for a meal followed by a visit to the 'Winter Wonderland', I hear it's well worth going. Then, the next day, before we come home, we can do some more shopping; it will be tiring but fun."

Rosa answered excitedly, "Oh, that sounds lovely. When you get the exact date, I will phone Angela Stirling and see if she and her sister are in London then; it would be nice to see them. If it's that near to Christmas, they might even have bought Eva over, before they bring her to me for Christmas. I feel quite excited."

The Other Side of the Fence

When Rosa rang Angela, it turned out, as Rosa hoped, that she would be in London at the same time and yes, she was bringing Eva for a few days to London, before she bought her to Rosa's for Christmas. They arranged to meet up, have lunch and take Eva shopping for something pretty to wear on Christmas day.

All too soon, Christmas was only two days away. Everything and everywhere was hectic but the girls said that they would be fine at the school, while Rosa went to London. It was holiday time at the college and lots of girls wanted to come and work at the school for the experience.

London turned out to be tiring but Rosa loved it. Although she didn't do much shopping for herself, she did buy a special Christmas present for Eva and bought her the dress for Christmas Day, so she was happy,

The next morning, they were having breakfast at the hotel when Vince got a phone call to say he was needed back at the station as soon as possible, so they were packed and on the road back home before ten o' clock.

"Well, that's the quickest overnight stay we have ever had." Rosa said, "But I did and saw what I wanted to, and at least we did get to the 'Winter Wonderland', which was quite spectacular and worth the trip. As for shopping in London, it's too hectic. I will enjoy shopping in good old Norwich better."

Before Vince dropped her off at home, he said, "Sorry about this, Rosa, but that's a policeman's life for you. By the way, do you still want that spa break for your Christmas present?"

"Oh, yes please, it was the best. Make sure we can book it at any time; I loved it on my birthday."

Rosa was totally relaxed; Vince had phoned her and said that he was on duty over Christmas Day and Boxing

Day, but he would try to find a couple of hours on one of them, to see her. Rosa had told him no, she would see him after Christmas, when he had actually got some time off. She had told him he couldn't sleep over anyway, until Eva had gone back to Ireland. She had thought, after she had put the phone down, that, come to think of it, that's all they did; eat, go to bed and then he's gone; or drive out in the country, eat, come back and go to bed, then he's gone. Rosa was determined to enjoy Christmas and not spend it worrying about when, or if, Vince would turn up.

Christmas was great fun. Matt had come to dinner and when Rosa handed out the crackers, she looked at him, grinned and said, "Only one cracker per person." Rosa loved watching Eva in her pretty party dress, enjoying herself. Gemma had come round after Christmas dinner with her two girls. It was lovely hearing laughter, as they ran in and out Rosa's rooms, and later playing the games they got for Christmas. Matt dressed up as Father Christmas, knocked on Rosa's front door and handed out gifts to everyone. Then he ran round to her mum's front door and walked through to Rosa's as Matt. The youngsters looked puzzled but didn't work it out. Her flat was alive with people and she loved it.

On Boxing Day, the girls were entered in the Christmas Gymkhana. Eva was immaculately dressed for the Concourse competition and won first prize in her section, while Gemma's eldest went as Minnie mouse and won first prize in the fancy dress competition. Anyone who didn't win a rosette still got a prize, so all the children were happy. They went back to Gemma's for tea. Matt was invited, as he had worked hard getting the horses in and out the horse boxes and to the Gymkhana and back. Everyone enjoyed the Christmas buffet Gemma had laid out and agreed that a happy Christmas had been had by all.

74

A week later, Rosa was woken by her phone buzzing away.

"Hello?" she said, half asleep.

"Morning, Sleepy Head, remember me, Vince Parker? Are you ever going to phone me to say you miss me and can't spend another day without seeing me? Seriously, Rosa, when can I come to see you?"

"Hello, Vince. I'm a bit slow, you woke me up. Vince, you know why you haven't seen me, I've got Eva staying with me; anyway, I said to you, phone me when you have actually got time off."

"Well lucky you; because I worked over Christmas, I've got half a day owed to me; I can have it off when I want, I've just got to let them have twelve hours' notice, so they can get someone to cover for me. How does that suit you? Is that enough time for you to let me come and see you?" he said, with a hint of sarcasm in his voice.

Sitting up in bed, she said, "How about tomorrow? I've got to work in the morning, then I'm free. Mum's taking Eva to Norwich for the day to visit cousins. Dad's taking them to the train station at twelve; Eva's never been on a train before; she's so excited. Dad's going to pick them up again later in evening. How's that all sound, perhaps we could go out somewhere special?"

"Oh, Rosa, can't we stay in, have a nice cooked meal, watch a DVD and have a few cuddles?"

"Of course, whatever you want.", she answered. This time it was her voice that had the hint of sarcasm.

The following day, Vince knocked on her door at exactly twelve thirty.

"Hiya, Babe." he said, as he came in, took his coat off, gave her a quick kiss and went straight to the couch and sat down in front of the fire; he even took his shoes off. "Come on," he said, patting the cushion next to him, "Come to Vincent and tell him what you have been doing, while I've been hard at work."

"OK." she said, walking over to lock the front door and draw the curtains; she knew what was going to happen next.

"I needed that, my lovely Rosa." he said, squeezing her tighter, as they lay in each other's arms on the couch, "I do love you, you know. If anything happens in the future, always remember that I loved you."

"That's a strange thing to say." she said, "Why did you say it?"

"Probably because of the work I've been doing lately; it's been quite dangerous."

The Other Side of the Fence

"Oh, my poor baby." she said, kissing his bare chest. He quickly responded by turning to her and kissing her passionately.

"Oh no you don't," she said, "I've got things cooking in the oven; a timer will go off any second and I don't want them to burn."

As she started to get up, he said, "Oh, don't go, just five more minutes." and pulled her back down.

As they lay in each other's arms, Vince asked, "Did you have a good Christmas? Did you miss me?"

"We had a brilliant Christmas; very busy, with lots of happy people." she answered, then added, "Don't let me lay here too long, or you won't get any dinner, only a burnt offering."

"OK, I give up." he said, letting her go and collecting all his clothes to get dressed.

They enjoyed the meal Rosa had cooked and watched a very good movie, then they exchanged gifts; he got her the spar overnight break, she asked for, and she got him a game for the PlayStation he got for his fortieth birthday. He had said the other policemen who share his flat enjoyed playing on it as well, but they needed more games.

All too soon, it was time for Vince to go and Rosa asked, "Vince, before you go, can I take a photo of us two together? I got a really nice photo frame for Christmas; I can put it at the side of my bed, so I can kiss you goodnight. You would like that, wouldn't you?"

"Yes, I would." he said and gave one of his irresistible smiles.

"I Wish he wouldn't do that," she thought, "it makes me go all weak."

"OK, Rosa, I'm ready; but do not show it to anyone outside of the family; don't forget, I'm a detective and they don't like my photo put about, because of my undercover work."

"Oh, OK, I promise I won't show it to anyone. You do make it all sound exciting; sort of 'James Bond' like."

Vince laughed out loud and said, "I don't think I would go that far, but thanks for the complement."

Just as he was leaving, Vince held Rosa close and said, "It's good news for New Year's Eve this year; I've got the two hours off before twelve and the two hours off after, so we can make arrangements to be together."

"Oh, Vince, I won't be here," she answered, disappointed, "I will be in Ireland. I'm taking Eva back at the weekend and staying for a few days. I can't really say I'm sorry, you've never had time off for the New Year before, so how was I supposed to know. It's all booked now and can't be changed."

Vince left in a huff, leaving Rosa feeling bad because after a lovely afternoon, she had upset him. She felt the atmosphere between them as he left.

"Now I've got another worry." she thought. She shut the door and started to tidy up, then said to herself, "Oh, leave it, Rosa, you can't worry about it now; do it all later. No! Just do it; it will be one less worry." She then started to laugh, because she was worrying about worrying.

She did the washing up and tidied everything, ready for Eva's return. She changed into her robe, made a cup of tea, sat down and found something to watch on the TV.

An hour later, a very excited Eva came through the door from Rosa's parent's house.

Rosa looked up and said, "Hello my lovely, have you had a good day?"

"Yes, I have." Eva answered, putting a couple of department store bags down, "It's been a really lovely day, I met lots of relations that I hadn't met before." she said leaning over the chair to kiss her mum. Then, doing a twizzle in front of her mum and sitting down next to her, she held her hand and said, "Mum, I'm the luckiest girl in the world; I live in two very different worlds and I love them both."

"Oh, Eva, what a lovely thing to say." a proud Rosa said, with tears in her eyes.

"It's true Mum; and I get spoilt in both places." she said, opening one of the bags, "This is what Nanny Em bought me, for when we go on holiday." She showed Rosa a dress in lavender blue.

Rosa, taken aback, asked, "Who chose that?"

"I did, don't you like it?"

"I love it, and the colour. I wore a dress similar to that on my first date with your dad, only mine had two thin straps; in fact, it was nothing like that, except it was the exact same colour."

"Really, Mum, you little hussy." They looked at each other and burst out laughing.

-

New Year's Eve in Ireland was like nothing Rosa had ever seen. Eva was right, she did live in two different worlds. The Stirlings spent their New Year's Eve at home. All the family and extended family were there; they held it in the large communal lounge, still brilliantly decorated from Christmas. When Rosa walked in, she had to stop herself from shouting 'Wow!' As well as the biggest, beautifully decorated Christmas tree, she could see hundreds of balloons, up at the ceiling, ready for midnight. The antique table was filled with a buffet, laid out and covered for later; there were coloured lights everywhere and they had even hired a DJ.

Rosa had a lovely evening talking to all the different sections of the family; they all made her feel very welcome. Rosa could see how happy Eva was; they sang, danced, and played games all evening. Come midnight, the balloons fell and a 'Happy New Year' was had by all.

75

When Rosa got back to England and saw Vince, he was fine. He suggested that they go on the spa day as soon as possible; obviously, Rosa agreed; it was so lovely the last time, she couldn't wait to do it again.

Trying to arrange it was more difficult than they thought; one or the other was too busy to go, or the weather was bad, or the roads were too icy.

It was the middle of March when Vince finally told Rosa, "I've booked us in for next week, I hope that's OK with you? You did say anytime."

"That's fine," she replied, "I can't wait to get away."

Once again, they had a nice time. They enjoyed the quiet, the relaxation and just being together.

Everything about the spa was special; except, it was over too soon; then, it was back to reality.

The Other Side of the Fence

It was Rosa's birthday. Vince had said that he would get the day off and they would go out for the day. He couldn't promise, but told her to pack an overnight bag, just in case he could get someone to cover for him. He said that he wouldn't tell her where they were going, as he wanted it to be a surprise for her; he told her that he would pick her up at ten o'clock sharp. She was ready at exactly ten and was standing at the window. After half an hour, he still hadn't turned up. Two hours later, she was still sitting on the chair next to the window, when she heard the adjoining door to her parents' open.

"Oh, Rosa, you startled me." her mum said, "Why are you still here? I thought you had left hours ago. I'm going into town and thought that I'd better come through before I go, and check that everything was locked up."

"Yes, still here." Rosa said, sounding downcast, "Obviously, something's gone wrong; I can't understand why he hasn't rung to tell me though. I'll ring him if he's not here in half an hour. You know what his job is like, he can be called on at any time."

"Yes, I agree; he should have called you and said why he's late. Shall I make us a cup of tea and sit with you for a while; then when he comes, you can go and I will lock up?" Rosa nodded, still looking out the window.

Rosa's mum made the tea, which they drank and chatted.

Putting her cup down, Rosa said, "Thanks, Mum, I needed that, it was hours ago when I last had a drink."

At one o' clock, Rosa rang Vince's phone. Hanging up and looking confused, she said to her mum, "That's strange, it says it's not the right number."

"Try again, perhaps you dialled it wrong?" her mum suggested.

The Other Side of the Fence

This time, as she dialled, Rosa's hand started to shake; she put the phone to her ear, hung up and said, "The voice said this number is no longer available. I reckon he's switched it off, so the station can't get him. I must have the time wrong, ten sounds awfully like two. I was excited when he told me; yes, that must be it. I will give him till two o' clock. You go, Mum, I will probably be gone by the time you get back."

Rosa had been back and forth to look out the window so many times, she eventually rang the police station and asked to speak to Detective Sergeant Parker, but was told that he wasn't on duty that day, or for the following seven days. When they asked if she wanted to leave a message she said 'No' and quickly hung up. By eight o' clock, she finally realised that Vince was not coming.

Rosa sat on the floor, wearing her fluffy onesie, in the dark, with a large glass of wine in her hand. She had put seven lighted candles round the fireplace and every cushion she could find had been put on the floor in front of the couch. A rather large bottle of wine was open on the table and her case was still at the front door where she had left it.

There was a knock on the adjoining door to her parents' house, then she heard her dad say, "Hello, Princess, is it OK to come in?"

"Yes, Daddy." she answered.

"Just checking you're OK?"

"I'm fine Daddy." she answered, "I'm not sad, I'm more angry; I can't understand why he hasn't called to say what's gone wrong."

"Matt's in the other room, he just gave me a lift home from his; I've been giving him a hand. Your mum told him that you're still here; he said he won't come through, as you will probably want to be alone." He turned to walk back through to his house, then stopped and said, "You know where we are if you need anything."

He had nearly closed the door when Rosa called, "Daddy, ask Matt to come through, he can help me drink this wine."

Matt went through to Rosa carrying a plate.

"Hi, Hun," he said, "you look nice and comfortable; stay there, I'll come and sit with you."

"What have you got there?" she asked.

"Your mum's sent some sandwiches; she said that you haven't eaten all day, so I've got to make sure you eat some of them."

"Bless her; that's my caring mother for you." she said, taking the plate from him and putting it on a nearby coffee table, "Pour yourself a glass of wine. You'd better bring the bottle with you, it could be a long night but I promise, no tears." she said, smiling at him.

"I like this," Matt said, sitting down on the floor, next to Rosa, "it's nice and cosy."

They sat eating sandwiches and drinking. Matt's glass was mostly lemonade; he said that he wouldn't drink because he was driving and may have to make a quick getaway if Vince suddenly turned up.

Rosa explained what had happened. "Wouldn't you think he could have called me."

Matt said, "Knowing him, he will explain why he hasn't turned up and you will forgive him, like you always do."

"I know what you're saying, Matt; I hate myself every time he gets away with it; he just says it's his job and I've found it's easier to give in. Anyway," she said, putting a cushion on his lap, lying down and putting her head on it, "don't let's talk about him, tell me something to take my mind off him."

"Well, you know my mare, Dulcie May, is pregnant; the vet checked her over today and said that everything's fine and thinks that she will foal in late September or early October."

"Oh, bless her; that's lovely. More like that please?"

"Right, close your eyes." he said, stroking her hair away from her face, "Cast your mind back and remember when we met. We certainly made up for the years we missed; we spent hours and hours sitting on that fence just talking; sometimes laughing so much, we nearly fell off. Then I built the bench so we could sit comfortably, you always sat on your side of the fence and me, on my side; we even had flasks and drank endless cups of tea. We've had so many good times together, Rosa, and are great friends."

She lifted her glass up to Matt's and as they chinked glasses, she said, "Well, it's not quite been the birthday I was expecting, but here's to us and our friendship."

"That's it." Matt said, "I will finish this drink then I'm off, before I say something I'll regret."

"What? Matt, what ever do you mean?" Rosa asked, looking up at him.

Matt got up from the floor and sat on the couch.

"I'm sorry, Rosa, I know that you're putting on a brave face about all this. I get angry seeing how he treats you. It's upsetting, seeing you so sad all the time and now he's ruined your birthday. If he turned up now, I would probably hit him; so, it's best I go."

The Other Side of the Fence

Rosa was shocked at Matt's outburst. Matt then stood up and said, "I'm sorry, Rosa, you didn't need to hear that, especially on your birthday; I'll see you tomorrow." As he reached the front door, he turned, blew her a kiss and left.

76

After a really bad night's sleep, Rosa dragged herself out of bed and got ready for work; all the time thinking about Matt's angry outburst.

"Bless him, he does like to protect me." she thought.

At the riding school, Katie had just picked up a new horse for the school. She had unloaded it from the horsebox and parked the truck at the side of the office, while her and Rosa took the horse to the stable.

Gemma was on duty in the office; she was in the back office making herself a drink when she heard the reception office door open. Walking into the Reception area, she saw a rather attractive woman standing there, she had one hand on a push chair, with a child of about one asleep in it, and in the other hand, she was holding a large bouquet of flowers.

"Can I help you?" Gemma asked.

The Other Side of the Fence

"I would like to speak to the woman who works here who goes by the name of Rosa." she answered, politely.

"You have just missed her; she will be back soon though, if you would like to wait?" Gemma said, pointing to a row of chairs.

"Thank you; yes, I will wait." she said and sat down.

Gemma asked, "I have just made myself a coffee; would you like a drink?"

The woman smiled but shook her head.

About ten minutes later, Gemma told the woman, "I have phoned her, she's on her way."

Within minutes, Rosa came through the door; the woman immediately stood up.

"Oh, hello." Rosa said, recognising the woman as Vince's sister. Rosa's mind went into overdrive, she had noticed the lovely bouquet and thought that his sister had come to let her know what had happened yesterday.

"Rosa?" the woman asked; Rosa nodded and the woman continued, "My name is Olivia Parker."

"Yes, I've seen you before; you're Vince's sister."

"Sorry to upset you, Rosa; I'm not his sister, I'm his wife; that's the story he tells all his women. He also tells them that our eldest daughter is his niece."

Rosa, who had gone behind the desk, sat down; Gemma went back into the small office and closed the door, but stayed near, so she could listen.

Olivia Parker carried on, "Rosa, we have been married over twenty years; we met at school. We have a grown-up daughter; this lovely little girl is his granddaughter, and we have two sons, four and seven."

Rosa sat there, open mouthed; she couldn't even speak, what could she say?

"Rosa, I'm really sorry for you, you're not the first this has happened to, and I'm sorry to say that you won't be the last. I see you're wearing the 'Vince Parker bracelet'; the same as the other three were wearing when I had to tell them. Rosa, I told him that I loved him, always had and always will, but if he wanted to leave me to be with you, I wouldn't stand in his way. I've said that he can still see the children. I love him but I don't want to stay with someone who doesn't want to be with me and the children. He is so full of remorse and wants to stay; he says he's sorry and doesn't want to lose me and the children, he says that he's weak and can't help himself. A good friend of ours saw you two in a restaurant and told me. He told lie after lie trying to say it wasn't true, then, yesterday morning, he said he had to go on a course for the day and might have to stay overnight. It all came out, when I saw the flowers in the boot of his car, after I'd walked with him to the car and opened the boot to put his bag in. Well, there you have it, Rosa. These are the flowers he bought for your birthday. He's a good father and detective," she said, shaking her head in disgust, "but a lousy husband. I am so sorry, Rosa; he's just weak, but I love him." She put the flowers down on the desk and said, "There is no way he will face you, but he wrote the card."

A stunned Rosa managed to control herself enough to ask, "Before you go, can I ask you something?"

"Of course," Olivia Parker replied, "What is it?"

"Where did Vince spend his fortieth birthday?"

The Other Side of the Fence

"We all went on holiday to Majorca for three weeks. We had a great time, a real family holiday. Why?"

"I Just needed to know the extent of his lies." Rosa said, "It sounds as if I've had a lucky escape, as they say."

"Believe me, you have, Rosa. Goodbye, I doubt you will ever see me again." Olivia Parker said, opening the office door and pushing the pram outside.

77

With tears streaming down her face, Gemma came out the back office, she walked straight up to Rosa, who by now had stood up and gone to the window, and put her arms round her.

"Rosa, I don't know what to say; I'm totally shocked by what just happened." said Gemma.

"Don't worry, I'm fine." Rosa replied and squeezed Gemma's hand, grateful for her concern.

Rosa walked back to the desk, picked up the flowers, read the card and said, "Huh!"

"What does it say?" asked Gemma.

"I'm truly sorry and two kisses." Rosa said, pulling the card off and ripping it up. She looked at Gemma and said, "Can you get rid of them for me please? If no one wants them, bin them; and can you see if someone can do my lessons please? I've only got two today."

"Of course; why, where are you going?"

"I'm going for a ride on Penric, he's outside; I was on him when you called me. Don't worry, he is all saddled up. I'm taking the small horsebox, so I can go somewhere different. I need to get right away for a bit and get my head round what just happened."

"Promise me you won't do anything stupid, will you?" a concerned Gemma said, looking at Rosa.

"Over that excuse for a man? No way! Gemma, what just happened has answered so many questions for me. I'm so angry, I've just wasted two years of my life, being lied to, because I was a stupid, love struck, idiot. It's embarrassing; I must go, I need fresh air. Love you." Rosa said and left.

After Rosa had left, Gemma phone Matt, then called Katie.

"What's up?" Katie asked.

Gemma told her as quickly as she could, giving her the basic facts, then asked, "Could any of you take Rosa's two lessons and could one of you come to the office as soon as possible please; I have phoned Matt, he is sorting things out at his and will be here in about ten minutes. He said that he's got a good idea of where she has gone and he's coming here to get me. We are taking my car, so that when we find her, he can drive the horsebox back."

"Yes, of course yes, I will sort it; just go with Matt and do what you have to do to find her. Sydney's just finishing her lesson and will be there by the time Matt gets to you."

When Matt arrived, they jumped into Gemma's car, with Matt in the driver's seat. They drove along the coast road to a long stretch of beach. They were on the top road, looking down.

The Other Side of the Fence

"There she is," Matt said, "sitting on those rocks."

They made their way down the slope to the beach and along to where Rosa was sitting, just staring into space.

Gemma, taking Penric's reins off of her, said, "I will walk him for you." indicating to Matt that she would take him up to the horsebox.

Matt sat down next to Rosa and said, "Well, here we are again, my lovely. If it's not me, it's you."

Holding Matt's hand, Rosa said, "Matt, honestly, I'm fine." She turned towards him and holding his other hand, continued, "Today has answered so many questions. All this time, rather than find out the reason why, I put them to the back of my mind, but it's all so clear now; why he always worked every Christmas, why he had to work New Year's Eve and why we never had an actual Valentine's Day; it's been two years of one lie after another. The worst was when he said he was on a course for three weeks, when he was actually in Majorca with his family. How stupid am I? I even saw him with his family at the airport! I'm so angry, Matt, I could kick myself."

Matt put a comforting arm round her and said, "I'm here, we will get through this together."

-

For how upset Rosa had been, she actually had a lovely summer. She spent three weeks in Ireland with Eva, spending days out and about with her and the Stirlings, including going to several show jumping competitions. Eva was very good. Eva now had her new, bigger horse; they were getting very close and becoming a perfect team. In her section, she was always in the top two places.

Then it was back to England with Eva, who was having the best time ever. She helped at the riding school and

The Other Side of the Fence

could ride the horses anytime she wanted. Most of the girls who worked at the Four Horseshoes, including Rosa and Eva had started to go to Matt's farm about three times a week, after they had finished work, to help him with all the fruit picking and vegetable collecting that had to be done. They had lots of laughs and were given free fruit and vegetables; but best of all, weather permitting, was when they had finished, Matt always had the biggest and best BBQ waiting for them; then, they would all sit round, chatting and having a great time. But, before they knew it, it was September; they had had a great summer and now it was all over.

78

At six in the morning, forty-two-year-old Rosa was woken up, when her son, Alfie, jumped on her.

"Oh no, Alfie;" she said, "it's too early, I've only just got to sleep." She lifted the duvet and said, "Come on, get in and snuggle up next to me."

She tried to go back to sleep but he kept trying to tickle her.

"It's no good, I'll have to get up." she said.

In a tired voice next to her, Alfie's dad said, "Shall I get up?"

"No," she said, yawning, "I will, you've got at least another hour before you need to get up. I'll take him down to the stables and let the horses out; then, I'll start on the breakfast when I get back."

When there was no answer, she smiled and whispered, "There's no arguing with that." Then, holding out her hand, she said quietly, "Come on you, let Daddy sleep; it's a good job you're so cute. Let's get dressed and go and see the horses."

Rosa prepared all the breakfast things and left them covered, so they would be ready to start cooking as soon as she got back from the stables. Rosa took some carrots for the horses, then walked with Alfie to where the horses were stabled, opened the stable doors and let the horses out into the paddock.

They went and stood by the fence and Rosa held Alfie up so that he could hold out the carrots for the horses. The two horses, Dulcie Mae and Gemini Girl, came trotting over to them immediately and ate the carrots.

"Alfie, stand still." Rosa said, "Let mummy take a photo, on her phone, of you with the horses and then one of you giving them a carrot. That's lovely" she said, picking him up and giving him a kiss on his cheek, "Alfie, my lovely boy, we both owe a lot to these two horses."

She was about to say something else when she heard her mum calling 'Alfie!' Alfie looked and saw his nan bending down with her arms outstretched; he ran up to her. She grabbed him and swung him round, saying, "How's my little Alfie boy today?" giving him a kiss and a cuddle. Rosa's mum looked after Alfie while Rosa went to work. She loved looking after him, she called him HM or His Majesty, because she loved her grandson and he could make her do anything.

Walking back to the house, her mum said, "I'm quite a bit earlier today, I thought I could help out a bit before you go to work."

With breakfast over and the washing up all done, it was getting quite late.

"Wherever has the time gone?" said Rosa, "I'd better go and get showered and ready for work."

In the end, Rosa was actually early for work; she made herself a cup of tea and sat quietly in the office, waiting for everyone to arrive. While waiting, she got out her phone and looked at the photos she had taken of Alfie with the horses. She stopped at the photo she had taken of the mare called Dulcie Mae. Thinking back, she thought, "You don't know this Dulcie but I owe you so much. It was you giving birth to Gemini that led to me having Alfie and the love and happiness I have today."

She sipped her tea and thought back to that particular night.

It was late summer, Rosa was all ready for bed; she was lying on the top of it, reading her book, when the phone rang.

"Hello?" Rosa said, cautiously.

"Hi, it's me, Matt. Sorry to phone you so late."

"Oh hello, what's the matter?" she asked, sitting up.

"It's my pregnant mare, Dulcie Mae. When I checked on her a short while ago, she was in the stables and had just started labour. I have just been back to check on her again and she wasn't there. I have found her in the field, the one where we sit and talk; I can't get her to move and she seems really stressed. I rang the vet but he's out on an emergency call. My friend, Andrew, is coming but can't get here for over an hour; I don't know what to do. I know you have delivered foals before; can you come and help her please."

"Of course, I'll be there as quick as I can." she said.

The Other Side of the Fence

As quick as she could, Rosa put her clothes and boots on. She put a few things in her medical bag, grabbed the first coat she could find and was just going out the front door, when she stopped and thought, "I don't know how long I will be, I'd better write a note to tell Dad where I am." She shoved the note under the door, separating her side of the house from her parents'.

"Yes," she said to herself, "if I'm not back and one of them comes through, they will see it."

She turned all the lights off and left. Outside, she decided to go on her bike, so she could get closer to where she needed to be. As she cycled, she felt a spot of rain in the air. She got to the riding school and cycled up as far as she could, then pushed her bike round the side of the fenced off building. It was pitch dark when she turned the bike's lights off, but thankfully, she found a torch in her bag. She left the bike, climbed over the first fence and got to the place where her and Matt always talked.

As she climbed over the fence, she thought, "Wow, all these years of us talking over this fence, this is the first time I have been over it." When she was on the other side, she looked across the field and saw Matt in the distance with the mare, who was lying on her side. "Oh, I'd better hurry," she thought, "the foal must be close."

As she got near, she heard Matt shout, "Rosa, thank God you're here!"

As soon as she arrived, she quickly wrapped the mare's tail out of the way and could see the foal's legs were already showing. As the nose appeared, she cleared it, so the foal could breathe easily. Rosa knelt down by the mare and started stroking her and talked quietly to her, calming her down.

The Other Side of the Fence

Looking up at Matt, she smiled and said, "Won't be long now."

As Rosa spoke the rain started and a short time later the rest of the foal appeared.

"It's a filly." Rosa said, with a tear in her eye.

It was now raining harder but Rosa was oblivious to it; she was attending to Dulcie Mae and her foal with such care and attention, she had to practically lay, fully outstretched on the grass, to make sure that Dulcie Mae and the foal were clear of each other. Matt could see by the light of the torches just how wet Rosa was; her jeans were muddy and soaking wet.

He could hear Rosa soothing Dulcie Mae, saying, "Good girl Dulcie, it's all over now; she's arrived safely and she is one strong filly." She could see that the foal, after a bit of slipping and sliding, was already up and walking about.

When Rosa looked up at Matt; he could see that even her hair was matted with mud.

She said, "Now that the foal's on her feet, her mum just needs a short rest, then she will get up and look after her. That's all I can do; the rest is up to her mother now. They do need to be in the stables as soon as possible though."

Matt bent down and put his fingers to her cheek to wipe away some mud, but he left them there and moved his thumb tenderly across her mouth.

"Rosa, you're wonderful." he said, holding his hand out to help her up. He saw her shiver, took his coat off and put it round her shoulders, pulling it together.

The Other Side of the Fence

He looked at her and said, with such tenderness in his voice, "Rosa, I have never loved you more than I do at this moment." Still holding the two ends of the coat together, he kissed her, not like the friendly kisses they usually exchanged; this kiss was different, it was tender, full of love and affection.

They both just stood there in the rain, a look of surprise and confusion on Rosa's face. Then, in a sudden moment of realisation, she went on tip toes, reached up and kissed him back.

Two bright torch beams shone on them.

"Hello there." a voice said, "Are those kisses of love, or congratulations on the birth?" It was Matt's two friends, Andrew and Fred; they had all been friends since school. Andrew was Matt's best friend and manager of his crops business, and Fred had one of the small holdings opposite Rosa's parents' farm; they both were dressed in the proper wet weather gear. Andrew continued, "Sorry I'm so late, Matt, I picked Fred up on the way; thought we might need his help. You two are soaking wet, better go and get dry, especially you, Rosa. We can see that you've done all the messy, hard work, before we got here. We can take over now and get them both safely back to the stables. I will report to you in the morning, Matt"

"That's great, Andy, thanks; I'll see you then." a grateful Matt said.

As they went to leave, Matt called out, "Thank you both for coming, its much appreciated. She's a lovely strong looking filly, I'm going to call her Gemini Girl, after my favourite girl here; she's a Gemini." Matt said, looking at Rosa who smiled back, lovingly.

The Other Side of the Fence

Matt linked arms with Rosa, so they could steady themselves in the mud, as they had decided that the quickest way back to Matt's house, was across the fields.

79

It was still raining hard and the ground was like a skating rink. Matt, now dressed only in trousers and shirt, was helping Rosa over the fences. The last fence was quite high and Rosa, who couldn't stop giggling at their situation, was balancing on the top rail. There was a ditch, now full of water on the other side; Matt had tried to jump it but landed in the water.

"Hold on, I will come back and fetch you." he said, stepping back into the water to help her; it was deep and the water went over his boots. "Yuk, that feels horrible."

He reached Rosa and gave her a fireman's lift off the fence to the other side of the ditch. Hanging over his shoulder, his coat was slipping off, over her head, but she managed to grab most of it before it fell into the water. Matt reached the higher ground and tried to put her down gently, but he slipped and she fell backwards onto the muddy grass.

"I'm so sorry." he said, as he sat down beside her, "Look at us, whatever do we look like, both soaking wet and covered in mud. How's the coat?"

"It's fine, just one corner got wet." she answered, then she laughed, "Not that the rest of the coat is any drier."

Every time they tried to stand up, one or the other slipped over; they ended up laughing uncontrollably.

"This is getting ridiculous, if anyone's filming us, they must think we need rescuing and have probably phoned the helicopter rescue team by now. Come on, Rosa, this time I've got it sussed." Matt said.

In what seemed like hours, they were at last in reach of Matt's house. He stopped and smiled at her in his big coat.

"We did it." he said. As Rosa looked up at him and nodded in agreement, she felt the cold rain spots on her face that made her close her eyes. Matt saw how lovely her face looked wrapped in his big coat and couldn't resist his next move; this time, he held her face with both hands and gently kissed her on the lips. His lips were cold from the night air but felt good on hers; never had she been kissed in such a tender, loving way before.

"Matt," she said, quietly, "what's happening to us; I hope I'm not going to wake up and find this is all a dream."

"I Love you so much, Rosa, but this is definitely not the way I was ever going to tell you."

"But I love it. What we have been through tonight, we will never forget. Tonight, was the perfect time to tell me you loved me. What you said and how you did it will always be special; no one will ever take that memory away, or ever take away how you made me feel the way you just did."

The Other Side of the Fence

As they reached the front door, he said, "Have you noticed something, Rosa? It's stopped raining."

"Quick, open the door then and let's get inside and get warm." she said.

Matt poured them each a large brandy.

"These will warm us up." he said, taking one over to Rosa, who by now had burst out laughing, hearing the squelching in his boots as he walked towards her. "Best I go and take them off." he said, grinning.

When he returned, he said, "Right, I've put the heating on. Now, we must get out of these wet clothes and get cleaned up. I'll go and find something to put on, then, you can have a nice hot shower."

"That will be great, Matt, thanks; I can't stop shivering."

Rosa was sipping her brandy, when, from the doorway behind her, she heard Matt say, "Right, let's get you cleaned up."

As she turned, she did a double take and butterflies fluttered in her stomach; Matt was standing there, wearing, low on his hips, a pair of black, knee length jogging shorts; his tanned chest, bare and a definite six pack showing; it was all she could do to stop herself from saying out loud, 'Wow, what a body!' She thought, "I know the kind caring Matt, but who is this Matt in front of me now? This Matt's sexy and exciting."

Matt led Rosa to the en-suite bathroom in his bedroom; Rosa, following, couldn't take her eyes off of him. When Rosa entered the bathroom, she was amazed at the luxurious décor; it had a double bath and a large, walk-in shower.

The Other Side of the Fence

"It's like it's out of a movie." she said.

"I don't use this one; it's just for show." he grinned, "I usually use the small one down the hall."

"Matt, I am so impressed; it's beautiful." she said.

Matt turned on the shower for her and said, "Leave it running when you have finished and I will follow you in. Here's a couple of towels; I'll sort out something for you to wear and leave it on the bed. Call me when you're done; I will be somewhere near."

After showering, Rosa dried off, wrapped one towel around her head and wrapped a larger towel around her body, tucking it in under her arms. She then called Matt.

They met in his bedroom and as he passed her, he said, "Stunning, absolutely stunning."

While Matt was showering, Rosa looked at the assortment of clothes Matt had laid out for her and decided to put on a large England T-shirt; it was extra-large, coming down just past her hips. She heard the shower stop running, so opened the bathroom door and went in to hang the towels up. Through the opaque panels of the shower, she saw the image of Matt; he had his back to her, drying his hair.

She stood there and thought, "All these years and there he is, the man who knows absolutely everything about me, and he loves me; could I ever love anyone more than how I feel about him right now. Since I saw him standing in the doorway, I can't stop looking at him; how can you see a person so differently in such a short space of time?" Still looking at him, she said to herself, "I want him. I want him so bad right now, I feel like what happened to me in Ibiza, when Rosa Marie Maddox took over from the normal, shy, Rosa; only last time, James was picked to seduce her; this

The Other Side of the Fence

time though, Rosa Marie Maddox wanted to be the seducer."

Even Rosa couldn't believe what she did next; it must have been the brandy, she thought later.

She found herself opening the shower door and going inside. Matt was drying himself with his back towards her; he had just put a towel round his waist when she put her two hands lightly on his shoulders and gently massaged them. Then, very gently, she moved her fingers back and forth across his back, followed by very soft kisses. Then, with both hands, she went under his arms to his chest and down to his waist until her fingers reached the towel, where she mischievously loosened it so it fell. Turning, he lifted her chin so he could look at her and sounding quite emotional, he said, "My beautiful, Rosa, I've waited such a long time for this to happen; are you sure?"

Leaning back on the shower wall, she looked up at him and said, "Yes, I know exactly what I'm doing; it's what I want. Kiss me again, like you did earlier."

Matt was now relaxed; he knew that what was happening to them, was what they both wanted. He took the towel from her hair and let her hair fall. He kissed the tip of his finger, put it to her mouth and very gently moved it along her lips. Rosa opened her mouth slightly in response and he let his finger stroke along the inside of her bottom lip; Rosa kissed it. Matt held her face again with both hands and kissed her as lovingly and gently as he did in the field; he then took her hand and led her out of the shower.

He picked her up and carried her over to the bed, gently laid her on it and laying next to her, he turned towards her and pulled the large, turned down duvet over them. They were quite happy, kissing and caressing each other; discovering each other's bodies. Matt kissed around her neck and tenderly touched Rosa's body all over, even down to her toes; she was lost in the loveliest, intimate feelings she had ever experienced.

After a while, Rosa uncovered herself from the duvet

"Phew, you're one hot lover, Mr. Johnson." she said, smiling, and before Matt could uncover himself, she quickly straddled him on top of the duvet. She smiled at him seductively and thought, "OK, Rosa, this is your moment. Matt says that he's waited a long time for this; so, let's make it worth the wait."

Kneeling astride him, she held the bottom of her T-shirt and slowly, tormenting him, took it off as seductively as she could; sometimes, nearly showing him her breasts, then quickly covering them, before finally taking the T-shirt off. She let his hands caress her breasts, while she put her hands on his chest, and with the tips of her fingers, she slowly pulled the duvet down, bringing her fingers together at his waist, then continued down with both hands, to just above Matt's manhood."

"That's it." Matt said, laughing, "Rosa Maddox, you're nothing but a temptress." He sat up, rolled her over onto her back, pulled the duvet to one side, and this time, he sat astride her, leaning forward with his two arms either side of her head. Looking down at her, their eyes met; they smiled and knew that what was going to happen next, would change their lives forever.

Being the true gentleman, he paused to make sure she was happy. He spoke softly, "I love you so much, Rosa. Are you sure; because there's no going back if we continue?"

She smiled, putting her hands up into his wet tussled hair and said, "I've never been so sure of anything in my life."

The Other Side of the Fence

It seemed that fate had led Rosa, that night, to her true love and soulmate, who had just been on the other side of the fence, all those years.

Two people didn't have sex that night; two people made love, and it was wonderful.

80

Gemma was fast asleep when her mobile phone started ringing.

"Who ever is ringing you at this early hour, its barely light?" her husband said.

Her eyes still closed, Gemma felt for her phone and answered, "Hello?" There was no answer; she thought she heard crying. She opened her eyes to see whose name was in the display; it was Rosa's.

"Go back to sleep." she told her husband; I will go downstairs. Then, to Rosa, she said, "Wait, I'm going downstairs."

Sitting down in the lounge, Gemma said, "Right, Rosa, what ever is the matter? Why are you crying?"

There was a long pause before Rosa answered, "They are tears of happiness, Gemma; in my whole life, I have never been as happy as I am at this moment."

"That's lovely, but do you know what the time is? I was sound asleep and you ring me and wake up everyone, just to tell me that your happy?"

"Oh, I'm so sorry, Gemma, is it too early? I didn't realise, I haven't slept and I wanted you to be the first to know."

Yawning, Gemma asked, "To know what?"

Rosa wiped her eyes and took a deep breath, "Are you sitting down?" she asked.

"Yes, go on."

"Matt kissed me."

"Is that it? He's always kissing you." Gemma said, testily.

"No, I mean he 'Kissed' me; really kissed me. He held my face with his two hands, kissed me and told me that he loved me. He said that he has always loved me."

"Oh, my word; what did you do?" Gemma asked, suddenly full of interest and wide awake.

"When he kissed me, I felt strange, like I have never felt before; I just wanted to kiss him back, so I did; it was wonderful. I can't believe what happened in those few minutes; my life won't ever be the same again."

"Oh, my goodness, I don't know what to say. Well, I do really; I can't believe how wonderful it all sounds. When did all this happen?"

"Just after ten o' clock last night; he rang me because the vet couldn't get there to help his Mare deliver her foal. She was getting stressed and I got there just in time to help her deliver her filly. I was still down on the grass in all the birth fluids, when it started to rain really hard. When Matt bent down to help me up, he put his fingers tenderly on my cheek; I thought he was going to wipe some mud off, but they stayed there, and his thumb came down and gently went across my lips and back again, then he looked at me like I have never seen him look at me before, with such love and caring. He said 'Rosa, you are wonderful; I have never loved you more than I do at this minute.' Then Andrew, his crop manager, arrived to take the horses back to the stables. I was soaking wet, covered in birth fluids and mud, so I went back to his to clean up; that's when he told me again how he felt."

"That was hours ago, what have you been doing since?"

"Well, for two of the hours, I was in bed with him."

"What!" Gemma exclaimed.

"That's what I have been trying to tell you, Matt just made love to me; well, actually, I ended up seducing Matt and it was the best ever. I have never felt or had anything happen to me that was anywhere as wonderful, tender or loving; I'm so happy. That was worth me waking you up for, wasn't it?"

"I'm gobsmacked, Rosa. Did you say that you seduced him?"

"Well, I had to. Thinking back, I can't believe what I did; I blush every time I think about it, but I thought if I don't do it now, it's never going to happen. He's so lovely and caring, but I know him, and if I hadn't let him know that it was what I wanted, he wouldn't have gone any further and we would have missed the moment."

"I love it, it's like something from a novel." Gemma said.

The Other Side of the Fence

"Trouble is, I'm starting to panic now. What if I've put him off me by what I did? It was as if someone else took me over; I saw him standing there and it wasn't the Matt I knew, it was if I had seen him for the first time and I wanted him."

"For goodness' sake, Rosa, he probably loved it. We can cover the office and your lessons till about twelve, when we have our break. Just get some sleep and come in then. And stop worrying."

Rosa pulled up at the office just before twelve. Entering the office, she was met by all the girls standing there, grinning and holding a large sign saying 'ROSA Loves MATT' inside a big red heart.

Smiling, Rosa said, "Very funny." and looked at Gemma, who just grinned and shrugged her shoulders.

Just then, they heard a knock on the office door. Katie opened it, and the other girls heard a voice ask, "Rosa Maddox?"

Katie stood back and showed the caller where Rosa was standing; it was a florist, who handed Rosa twenty-four red roses.

All the girls, except Rosa and Gemma, left the office; as they went out the door, Rosa could hear them happily talking about her and Matt.

"Whoever could they be from?" Gemma asked, grinning; then added, "Oh, what does the card say?"

Rosa turning an embarrassed red, smiled and said, "It says, 'My Love Always' and two kisses."

"There you go; worry over."

The Other Side of the Fence

Later, when Rosa had got back from work, Rosa's mum came through from next door and seeing the mess on the table, asked, "What ever are you doing?"

"I'm shredding a fantasy, a make believe, a never was, out of my life."

"What are you talking about?" her mum asked, "Aren't they the souvenirs you bought back, with Vince?"

"Yes, and I want him out of my life. I wasted over two years of my life on him, and it was all a lie. It was never going to go anywhere; he loved his wife more than he loved me. I don't ever want to see him again; and I won't, unless I get arrested. Mum, see those beautiful roses; well, sit down and I will tell you what happened to me last night; I know you will be pleased because it's something you have always wanted; they are from Matt."

Her mum sat down slowly, looking at the roses and then at her daughter, expectantly.

Rosa sat and told her very happy, but surprised, mum, the story of the night before; well a bit of it.

"I knew it, I always knew it." her mum said, "Everyone knew you two were right for each other; except you, Rosa"

"So, who would you rather me be with, Mum; someone who has always been there for me, who has loved me for years and wants to be with me always, or someone who could only lie and cheat to be with me; loved me a few hours a week, or anytime he could get away from his wife and children?"

"Come on, Rosa, I will help you shred?" her mum said, smiling, knowing, finally, that her daughter was truly happy.

The Other Side of the Fence

After they had finished, Rosa's mum said, "Well, Rosa, I'm pleased I came through; have you spoken to Matt since last night?"

"Yes, he rang me just after I finished work. I thanked him for the flowers and he asked me if I still felt the same as I did last night. I said, 'Yes, yes, yes.' We are going for a meal and a drink at the Riverside Restaurant and talk about what we want for the future."

Her mum got up to leave and said, "Well, have I got a lot to tell your dad when he gets home."

A smiling Rosa called, as her mum was about to close the door, "Don't worry if I'm not here in the morning, Mum, you know where I'll be."

81

Matt and Rosa had what can only be described as their first romantic meal together. It was different from any of the hundreds of meals they had sat down to before; every glance was meaningful; every touch was romantic. Rosa had returned to her usual shy self; while she was eating, if she looked up and caught Matt's eye, he would smile at her and she would go all girly. During their talk, they were so compatible, they agreed on everything about their future together; they even discussed about having a baby and agreed that if one came along, they would be thrilled. Matt was holding Rosa's hands across the table; she told him that she had always loved him, but since the night before, her love had changed; it was different, it was better, so much better.

He lifted their joined hands, kissed hers and said, "Back to mine?"

She smiled and nodded.

The Other Side of the Fence

They spent the next year not going anywhere; they were happy just being in each other's company. Christmas came and went, and a very happy time it was.

In January, as Rosa was spending more and more time at Matt's, he asked her to move in with him. Rosa was overjoyed. Matt said that as they would be living there together, they should redecorate, so that the house felt more like theirs, rather than Matt's; so, each evening after their own work, they would put music on while they worked. Rosa loved Matt's house and would be content painting rooms, while Matt did DIY work somewhere. They always finished about nine thirty, after one or the other had left off a bit earlier to get a meal ready. Everyone could see how happy they both were and said they were like two young lovebirds.

Another Christmas came and went and before they knew it, it was nearly Easter.

Matt asked, "What do you think about us going to Ireland? We can hire a car over there for a week and go exploring. If Eva's not at college, she can come with us or we can have some days horse riding with her and some days exploring?"

"Yes, I'd love it." Rosa replied, "There is some beautiful places to visit."

When Rosa rang James, to say they were coming, he insisted that they made the guest house their base.

Their trip to Ireland was simply the best ever; the weather was lovely and warm for the time of year. They loved the days they went out sightseeing; some days, Eva and her friend went with them, others, they went alone. Sometimes they stayed overnight in hotels and others they managed to get back to the Stirlings, who made them very

The Other Side of the Fence

welcome, inviting them to join them for their evening meal and spend the rest of the evening with them.

On their last day, they went off alone; they took a picnic and found a large car park, which had paths that they could take down to the beach and sea, or to a grass picnic area on the cliffs, which overlooked the beach and sea; this is where they laid their blanket and sat down in the sunshine. Matt was busy getting everything laid out and was pouring tea from a very large flask, when he looked up to see Rosa staring out to sea.

"Penny for your thoughts, my lovely?" he asked.

"I was thinking about the night you told me you loved me." she said, "How it was all fated; if the vet hadn't had an emergency, you wouldn't have called me. I can't get over, after all these years living next to each other, I had never been on the other side of the fence before; it was all meant to be."

Matt put the teas down on the little fold up stool they were using as a table, sat down next to her and put his arms round her; she snuggled into his chest.

"Mmmm, I'm so happy, Matt; I love you so much, I always feel warm and safe when you hold me in your arms like this. I remember at Gemma's new year's party, dancing with you to 'All I Ask of You'; you held me so close, I closed my eyes because I felt safe in your arms and I was lost in the moment. Now, I often wondered where that would have led, if a certain person, who I won't name, hadn't turned up and spoiled it." She snuggled even closer to him, "So many wasted years." she said.

"I know, but as you said, fate. They weren't wasted years; we have always been there for each other. I've had a great time, Rosa; let's make sure we come back again, after

The Other Side of the Fence

the summer, before Eva goes back to college; and we can possibly stay a bit longer next time?"

"That's a date, Mr. Johnson." she said, reaching up and giving him a quick kiss, "Now, where's the tea and sandwiches?"

Back in England, the weeks flew by. One day, while having breakfast together, Matt said, "Who's a birthday girl next week? Is there anything you would like to do, in particular? a big party, small party, family tea, or a meal just the two of us?"

"OK; if Eva's here with her friend, just family and a few friends for a buffet in the private room at Riverside; if she's not coming, tea and cake early with Mum and Dad, then just you and me at Riverside for a meal. How's that?"

Matt gave a thumbs up.

The day of her thirty-seventh Birthday arrived; Rosa had lots of cards and presents, and because Eva and her friend had come over, Matt had organised a buffet in the private room at the Riverside Restaurant. Eva and her friend stayed at Rosa's old flat, which had become more of a holiday home for family and close friends; Eva's nan and granddad loved having them stay and spoiled them rotten.

Everyone had finished eating at the buffet, when the lights were switched off and on.

"Can I have everyone's attention please." said the Manager; the room went quiet, "It's time for the arrival of the cake and singing 'Happy Birthday'." he continued, "But first, can I ask Rosa to stand up and close her eyes, while we get the cake ready in front of her."

Rosa hesitated but stood up, looking around the room as if to say to everyone, 'What's going on?'. She closed her eyes.

The Other Side of the Fence

"Keep them closed;" the manager said, "you can open them when I say open." Rosa could hear some shuffling, then, the manager said, "OK, Rosa, you can open them."

In front of her was Matt, on one knee, holding out a beautiful diamond and sapphire ring.

"Rosa Maddox, I love you; will you marry me?" he said.

There was an intake of breath all round; then, a round of applause when they saw Rosa standing there, smiling, tears in her eyes, saying "Yes, yes, yes!"

Matt stood up, put the ring on her finger and kissed her. Everyone started singing 'Congratulations'. Gemma and Katie were the first to give them a hug and wish them all the best for the future.

"By the way, Matt, loving the ring." Gemma said, "Don't forget, Rosa; we have your bridesmaids and page boys already made for you." she added laughing.

"Can't wait to see you at work tomorrow and start planning." said Katie and they went away giggling.

Rosa's mum and dad had just reached her, when the cake appeared and everyone started singing, 'Happy Birthday'.

"Are you OK, Princess?" her dad asked.

"To be honest, I'm still in a bit of a shock. Didn't he do it lovely though? I'm so lucky he waited for me. I must go and find him." She gave her parents a hug and went to find Matt.

She saw Matt talking to several friends; she went up behind him and whispered, "Love you."

He turned round, pulled her forward and holding her close, he said, "Have you all met Rosa, my future wife?"

82

After the excitement of the engagement in May, it was a very busy summer for both of them; plus, there was the excitement of planning a wedding for June next year. Rosa and the other girls had a night out, once a month, to put all their wedding ideas forward.

Matt was pleased that the girls all helped out again this year, picking and packing his crops for him, in the evenings after work. His BBQs afterwards, were still a great success.

Their planned trip to Ireland soon arrived, which had been booked for early October; the earliest they could get away. They knew that Eva would be at college, studying to be a lawyer, so she could join her grandfather's firm; but as she had a show jumping competition the weekend her mum and Matt were due to arrive in Ireland, they coincided the start of their holiday with the day of the competition. They planned to arrive in time to watch it, then move on to the nearest hotel, on their planned route.

The Other Side of the Fence

Everything went smoothly; Rosa stood watching Eva be her usual, brilliant self. They watched her receive her trophies, then, after lots of kisses, hugs, and a quick chat to a proud grandfather, Edward Stirling, it was time to leave.

Over the next six days, they were busy, touring around the beautiful scenic island of Ireland. They grew closer than ever; it was all so romantic; whether they were holding hands as they walked through the well-maintained parks, having picnics at the attractions they visited, or romantic candle lit meals at their hotels. Their nights were quiet and relaxing, with early nights ready for early morning starts. Everything was perfect; the only problem, it was over far too soon.

Before they knew it, they were back in England and both back at work. All anyone was talking about was, it will soon be Christmas, then it would be full steam ahead to the June wedding.

Matt, but mainly Rosa, had decided on a smallish wedding. They would get married at the village church, then have the reception at the village hall; basically, a copy of Gemma's successful wedding, only smaller. No horse and carriage, only Eva, Gemma, her youngest daughter and Katie's little girl to be bridesmaids. Then, at last, Matt's first trip abroad to Majorca, for their honeymoon.

Rosa, Eva, Gemma and Katie, were planning a girly day out, in London, around March to look for wedding and bridesmaids' dresses. All the wedding plans were sorted; or so they thought!

"Can you believe another Christmas has come and gone, and it's the middle of January already?" Gemma said to Rosa, one day while they were sitting in Masie's café, both looking out the window at the snow, "Why didn't it snow like this at Christmas, my kids would have loved it."

The Other Side of the Fence

"I suppose we'd better start thinking of getting back soon. Now that it's starting to lay, do you think we ought to check if the girls are OK?" said Rosa.

They decided to get some cakes for the girls and go back to the stables to see if they needed any help getting the horses inside and their rugs on.

"Which fresh cream cake do you want today?" asked Gemma.

"I don't want one thanks, just the thought of it makes me feel sick. In fact, I was sick yesterday and told Matt that I thought I must have caught a bug from something I ate. Also, I've been so tired lately, I can hardly keep awake, especially when I finish work; I just want to get into bed and curl up. To be honest, I was pleased when I woke up this morning and saw it was snowing, so I could have a rest."

"Right, you drink that water, while I go and get the cakes and pay."

"Oh, why, what's up?" she said looking at Gemma.

"Sometimes you're so thick, Rosa. Don't you remember this same conversation once before?"

Frowning, while she thought, she suddenly said out loud, "You mean I'm pregnant!" The other people in the café, turned, looked and smiled.

Yes, come on; you know where we are going next." said Gemma.

Rosa bought a pregnancy test and said to Gemma, "I will do it when I get home, so that Matt will be the first to know."

They walked to the car through the snow; Gemma kept making Rosa laugh, by saying, "Excuse us please, pregnant woman coming through." every time they needed to get past someone.

When they got in the car, Gemma said, "What is it with you and weddings, that you have to get pregnant?"

"Very funny." Rosa laughed, "We don't know for sure yet, but we will be very happy if you're right."

Arriving at Rosa's, before she drove away, Gemma wound the window down and said, "Be careful, mind you don't slip and make sure you ring me as soon as you know."

Matt came through the front door, banging the snow off his boots and leaving them in the front porch. Hanging his coat up, he walked in to find Rosa.

"Hello, my lovely." he said and gave her a kiss, "It's snowing really hard out there now and the wind's started. If it keeps this up, there'll be snow drifts by morning; so, it could be an early start for me, to clear us, then your parents' and then help anyone in trouble."

Rosa had the pregnancy test box in her sweatshirt pocket and smiled, excited to tell him her news.

Matt was standing in front of the fire, "That's better, he said, "I can feel my body warming up. I've got a bit of good news for you and the girls; you know that barn on the right, halfway up the drive to the riding school?" She nodded and looked puzzled, as he continued, "Well, we have just emptied it, which is why I'm a bit late. Anyway, we moved all the equipment out of there, and into the barns nearer the crop fields, so that now, all the equipment we use is together. Well, I thought you girls would like it to use as a storeroom, for now; then, perhaps in the future, get planning permission to do it up and use it as an equestrian equipment centre. It's ideal, the main door faces the road, so you can make a driveway to it, off of your drive that runs up to the riding school. You're always telling me that people ask you if you sell horse riding gear." Rosa sat down and Matt, looking concerned, sat down beside her, said, "What's the matter, have I said something wrong?"

"No, no, Matt; what you just said sounds really lovely; I know the girls will be thrilled, but I have been waiting for ages to tell you my news and I can't wait any longer because I really need to go to the toilet."

"Sorry, my love, I have been talking nonstop since I came in. Off you go",

"I can't, this is what I've been waiting to show you since you came in." She showed him the pregnancy test box.

He grabbed her hands and said, looking at her with such adoration, "Oh, Rosa, are you?"

"I don't know yet, I've been waiting to go and check since you came in." she said, getting up and heading towards the downstairs toilet. She looked back, smiled at him and said, "Fingers crossed."

She was soon back and said, "We've got to wait a short while; if a blue line shows, then I am."

They sat close together, nervously looking at the test stick.

"There's a blue line!" Matt yelled, excitedly.

"Yes, that's a definite blue line." Rosa agreed. They kissed and sat, holding hands, just looking at each other, then stood and cuddled.

Matt scooped her up and twirled her round and then stopped, "Oh, sorry." he said, putting her down gently.

Rosa told Matt that it was Gemma who made her buy the test.

"I've got to tell her, because she's sat at the end of her phone right now, waiting to hear from me. I will tell her not to say anything until I've been to the doctors tomorrow to confirm, and after we've told our families. Is that OK?" she asked, as Matt was looking distant.

"Yes, yes." he answered, "Whatever you say; I was just reliving how happy I was when that blue line came up."

When they went to bed that night, they stopped at the bedroom next to theirs and opened the door, to a room all clean, with the paint work painted white, just waiting to have the walls done, and finished off.

Matt looked at Rosa and said, "Now that's fate; the last room to be decorated and its next to ours." He cuddled her and asked, "What colour do you reckon the nursery is going to be, blue or pink?"

"As long as the baby's OK, I'm easy with either; but we'd better leave it till we know." she answered, as she snuggled under Matt's arm, "This is so exciting. Love you."

"Love you too." he answered.

The results from the doctor confirmed that Rosa was three months pregnant; the baby was due on the twenty-first of June.

83

On the morning of the twenty-first of June 2014, at nine o' clock, both Rosa's and Matt's families received a text message, saying,

'Matt and Rosa are pleased to announce the arrival of their son, Alfie Henry Johnson, (Henry is after Matt's dad). Alfie arrived at 4am, weighing in at seven pounds six ounces, Mum and Baby are well. Expect to see many photos of Alfie shortly. Love from his extremely happy mum and dad, xxx'

Over the next few days, many decisions were made. Rosa's legs had been painful but had stood up to this pregnancy pretty well. Rosa would have six months off work to be with Alfie. Rosa's mum would help her with the baby for a couple of weeks; then, when Rosa felt happy to return to work, her mum would look after the baby. Going back to work would be gradual; a few hours at a time, at first, then, adding more hours and perhaps another day, as and when she felt able. The cancelled wedding would now take place on Rosa's fortieth birthday, and instead of a honeymoon for two, it would now be a family holiday in Majorca, with Gemma, her husband and their two youngest; they did think of Ibiza but decided they were a bit too old for Ibiza and foam parties.

Since Alfie was born, Eva had come over from Ireland most weekends; she stayed in Rosa's old flat, or overnight with Matt and Rosa. Eva loved being with Alfie; she and her nan would take him out while Rosa visited the girls for a catch-up chat at the stables, or while she went out for a ride on Penric. Although Matt was busy, he was also a very good, hands-on, dad, and loved any time when it was just the three of them. Rosa liked how everyone was so helpful; she said that it definitely hastened her recovery. She often sat and thought, with tears in her eyes, how different things were when Eva was born, then, she would smile when she remembered how good Matt was, even then.

When Alfie was five months old, they even managed a few days in Ireland. James had phoned and suggested that, if they wanted to get away for a few days, they were welcome to stay in the guest house.

Rosa said, "I bet that's come from Eva, so she can show everyone her brother."

Matt said, "I'm happy to go, if you are? Ring him back; a few days away would be great before I have to start thinking about work again."

Alfie was no trouble on the plane journeys. Matt and Rosa felt totally relaxed for the few days they were there; they didn't need to go far, there was plenty to do locally. The Stirlings were their usual, helpful selves; in fact, one or the other of them offered to take Alfie for walks, or just sat with him, while Matt and Rosa went swimming, or Rosa and Eva went horse riding.

The Other Side of the Fence

Just as they were leaving, James was talking to Matt; he said, "Eva always loves it when her mum comes to stay, and now with her brother here as well, it is lovely to see her so happy. Any time you can get away and want to come over, if the guest house is vacant, you will be welcome to stay."

"That's really kind of you, James." Matt answered, "I know Rosa loves it here, and it's so easy for us to get here. So, we might take you up on that offer; though, I'm afraid it won't be until after the summer; Christmas through to October is when we are at our busiest. So, if you are able to keep the guest house vacant for early October, we would love to come." he said smiling. He then thanked James and shook his hand.

Never had the time passed so quickly, as it did over the next few months. Rosa was back at work, the riding school was busier than ever, Alfie was now walking and needed to be watched every minute; and they were rushing to get Matt's crops in and sorted, so that they could get away to Ireland in early October, before the weather got too cold.

Once again, when they arrived in Ireland, they felt welcome and relaxed. One day, Angela arranged to take Lily, Eva, and Rosa out for a meal and a visit to see the famous 'Kildare Village Luxury Shopping Destination', where Angela and her Sister-in-law owned one of the hundred designer boutiques; it was just along the road, near the village.

At first, Rosa was apprehensive about leaving Alfie, who was upset about his mum going without him. Matt put his arm around her shoulder and walked her out to the car, saying, "You go and relax; it's not far away and you might find something nice to buy. We'll phone you if we need you."

Once in the shopping centre, after browsing some of the shops, they stopped for lunch. They chatted away while eating, until Angela said, "Ready girls? We've only got one hour left on the car park."

Leaving the restaurant, they passed a shop opposite, with a display of wedding dresses in the window; Rosa stopped.

"That's it!" she said, excitedly, "That's the dress I want for my wedding. We've got an hour; I'm going in to try it on." Excited, to say the least, they all followed Rosa into the shop.

When Rosa came out of the dressing room, there was a sharp intake of breath. Rosa had piled half of her hair on top of her head and the assistant had placed a pretty pearl and diamante tiara into the front of it. The sleeveless ivory satin dress had a very delicate layer of white lace over the top and the V neckline was edged with scalloped lace, as was the hem of the lace at the bottom of the A line skirt. Around the waist, a small, ruched belt made from ivory satin, finished with a diamante and pearl clasp, set the whole dress off. Poking out from the hem of the dress, you could just see the ivory, three-inch heeled shoes that belonged to the shop, that Rosa had borrowed.

The assistant asked, "Do you mind if I just add one thing; well, two actually, that I think would really set the dress off to perfection?"

"Please do." Rosa replied.

The assistant disappeared and came back with a short, delicate, lace veil, that she clipped into the back of Rosa's hair, and a stiff, net petticoat, that she put on under the dress; she then stood back; Rosa looked amazing.

"Mum, I love it, you look wonderful." said Eva.

The Other Side of the Fence

"Wow, what a difference that makes; it's breathtaking." said Lily.

"I've never seen anything so lovely." said Angela.

The assistant said, "I don't have to say this, but that's the loveliest I have seen anyone in a wedding dress, since I've worked here; it's so simple but absolutely perfect."

Rosa swayed in front of the large shop mirrors; she felt more than happy that this was the right dress for her.

"Shall I buy it? she asked the girls.

'Yes, yes, yes!' they all answered.

"And let me buy you the diamante tiara; its perfect." Eva added, "Then I can wear it when I get married."

"I'm sorry," the assistant said, "but putting my salesperson's hat back on; as you can see, we have the perfect shoes to go with the dress."

They all laughed, and a pair of ivory three-inch heeled shoes were purchased. There was still seven months to go before the wedding, so it was decided that Eva would keep the tiara, dress and petticoat, in her wardrobe; then, deliver them in the new year, when she visited England.

As they left the shop, Angela handed Rosa a little bag with the shop's logo on it and said, "You will need this; plus, it will remind you of our lovely day out." It was a white lace garter, with a small blue bow on it.

"Thank you, Angela, that's a lovely thought." Rosa said, kissing her on the cheek, "I'm not taking the dress home yet, but I could be tempted to put it on, while I walk up and down, learning to walk in the shoes." she laughed.

Christmas, for Rosa and Matt, was lovely but hard work. Alfie was fascinated with the tree; he wanted to touch the baubles all the time, so he had to be watched anytime he was near the tree, in case he pulled it over. Family and friends joined them for the day on Christmas Day. After a late dinner, there were lots of fun and games, until nearly midnight. Then, after they had all gone, Matt and Rosa sat quietly and started to watch their favourite Christmas film, but only got halfway through, because they were so tired, they couldn't keep awake.

From then on, nearly every other day, they were attending a Christmas party at someone's house, through till the last one on New Year's Eve; then, it was back to work.

Eva brought Rosa her wedding dress in early January and the preparations started for the wedding.

May 2016, a forty-year-old Rosa woke up in her old bed, at her parent's; no seeing the bride before the wedding, her mum had insisted. Rosa smiled when she opened the curtains and saw that the sun was shining; she gave herself a pinch, just in case she had dreamt that this was her wedding day.

"Ouch! that hurt." she laughed, out loud.

Her wedding dress was hanging on the wardrobe door.

"Yes, it's happening and it's today. They say life begins at forty; well, Rosa Marie Maddox, let life begin." she said out loud.

84

Eva, Gemma, her youngest daughter, little Alfie and Katie's three-year-old daughter, Millie, were waiting for the bride in a small room at the back of the village church. Gemma stood looking through a crack in the closed wooden doors.

"I can only see Matt's side of the family from here." she said to Eva, "I can see Matt and his best man Andrew; they look handsome in their wedding outfits; they are talking to Matt's mother and Paul."

There was a tap on the door.

"The bride's arrived." a voice said and the doors opened.

When Eva saw her mother, she said, "Mum, you look stunning." Then handed Rosa her bouquet of ivory roses.

Looking at Eva and Gemma, Rosa said, "So do you and Gemma; your dresses look very classy."

The Other Side of the Fence

The bridesmaids wore dresses in a lovely champagne colour and carried posies of cream roses, blue cornflowers, and white gypsophilia. Alfie, in his suit and blue bow tie, stood next to Millie; hopefully they would walk down the aisle together. Millie looked very pretty in her white dress with a blue satin sash, blue and white flowers in her hair, and carrying a posy.

The organ started to play and Alfie looked tearfully at his mum.

"Oh, bless him, it scared him." said Rosa, bending down to reassure him that everything was OK, "You hold Millie's hand and walk in front of Mummy and granddad, and we'll go and find Nanny."

After a nod from her dad, that they were ready, the organist started playing 'Here Comes The Bride'.

Rosa turned to Eva and Gemma and said, "Ready girls?"

They nodded and Rosa holding the arm of her father, was on her way to marry the man she loved; the man who showed her what true love was.

Rosa had the broadest of smiles as she walked down the aisle, acknowledging all the Stirlings, the girls from the riding school and their families, aunts, uncles, cousins, both sets of friends and her Mum, already wiping tears from her eyes; and finally, to Matt.

"Love you, you look beautiful." he said, quietly, as they took their places.

The Reverend John Miles started the marriage ceremony; their eyes never left each other's as they said their vows and exchanged rings.

The Other Side of the Fence

Finally, the Reverend John Miles said, "You may now kiss the bride." When they kissed, everyone applauded.

While signing the register and marriage certificate, the reverends wife, Louise, played the hymn, 'Love Divine', then it was time for 'Mendelssohn's Wedding March' and the church bells started ringing.

Outside the church, there was the photo shoot and confetti throwing, followed by a loud rendition of 'Happy Birthday'

As they stood there, Matt asked, "Are you happy, Mrs. Johnson?"

Rosa held his hand and replied, "So happy, Mr. Johnson; so very, very happy."

Everything throughout this magical day was perfect, from the reception at the village hall, to how beautiful it had been decorated, to the food, the dancing and the great all round party atmosphere.

At the end of the speeches, Matt stood up again and said, "Now, I would like to say a few special words to my lovely wife, Mrs. Johnson." Then, looking at her, he continued, "Rosa, I just want to tell you how much I Love you." He paused, picked up a gift box and said, "I love you today, I loved you yesterday, I will love you tomorrow, I will love you always." He then kissed her and handed her a musical jewellery box. He nodded for her to open it, which she did; it played the music to the song, 'Always'. The words, 'I'll be loving you, always, with a love that's true, always.' were written on the inside of the lid.

Everyone stood up and a big round of applause filled the room, with cries of, 'Speech, speech.'

The Other Side of the Fence

Rosa, tears streaming down her face, shook her head, pointed to the box, her heart, then to Matt; she was speechless and filled with emotion.

The tables were cleared, ready for dancing. Matt and Rosa stood up for their dance; they had chosen, 'All I Ask Of You.', the song that they danced to on the night of Gemma's New Year's Eve party. Rosa took her shoes off; she wanted to dance in Matt's arms, snuggled into his chest, which she now called her happy place.

The next day, tired but happy, it was all go, as they were off to Majorca that very afternoon. Alfie sat on the plane as if he was on a ride at the fair ground, while Matt, sitting next to the window, was the one who was the most excited.

The hotel they had chosen was brilliant; no sooner had they arrived, than the children were invited to join the hotel's children's club and were whisked away, while their parents unpacked and got ready for the evening meal and the night's entertainment.

The next day, the men were playing with the children in the pool and the girls were lying on sunbeds, relaxing.

"This is what it's all about." said Gemma, "Just lying here, only moving to go for food, then getting all dressed up for the evening meal, a drink and the night's entertainment."

"I love it." said Rosa, "And I know Matt's having the best time; I have never seen him so relaxed."

"And I love the children's club; the children are happy and I am happy." laughed Gemma.

This was their routine for the next six days and in no time, sad that they had to leave, but happy for the best holiday ever; they were on the plane back home; ready and happy to book the same holiday again, for next year.

85

With the honeymoon over, life at the riding school returned to normal.

Soon after, Rosa arrived at the office early. She arranged the office chairs into a circle, ready for a team meeting, because today was the day that they would decide whether to expand the business, by turning the Barn, Matt gave them, into an equestrian clothes and equipment shop. They were financially sound, but it would need a bank loan to pay for the new drive to the shop, plus they would need to pay at least three or four more skilled staff, who were able to work both the shop and the school.

They talked and discussed it for two hours and then took a vote; It was overwhelmingly passed by all five of them. Depending on how successful the shop was, they would start with one of them always in the shop with one of the new staff; the other new staff would work between the shop and the school, hopefully needing more staff as the business grew. All five of them were excited and decided to start straight away, because everything would take a long time to get passed and built.

Before they left the office, they stood in a circle, arms round each other's shoulders, and Rosa said, "Watch out world, the 'Four Horseshoes Equestrian Centre' is coming to town. Open the champagne, Gemma. Sorry girls, we've only got paper cups."

After nearly two years, the equestrian centre was ready to open. Matt and Rosa went to the airport to meet Eva; she had come to stay for two weeks, as she wanted to be there for the grand opening. Rosa was shocked when she saw Eva come out through the arrivals door; they hardly recognised her; Eva's long blonde hair had been cut to about three inches, plus they were expecting her to be on her own, but she was walking towards them, arm in arm, with not the smartest of young men.

"Mum, this is Chris; we met at University, nearly six months ago. I phoned Nan and she said it was OK for us to stay at the flat."

Chris held out his hand to shake Matt's and Rosa's.

"Pleased to meet you both." he said.

Sitting together in the back of the car for the drive back to the farm, Rosa asked, "What's happened to your hair Eva, didn't you like it?"

Running her fingers through it, Eva replied, "We think it looks cool, and now, it's the same as Chris'."

"I'm a bit shocked, Eva." Rosa said.

Eva grabbed her mum's hand and said, "I love it, you'll get used to it. I have given up horse riding as well; Chris doesn't like horses."

Chris shouted from the front seat of the car, "They stink and they made her stink!"

Rosa frowned, and thought, "And already I don't like you, Mr. Who Do You Think You Are!"

On the opening day of the equestrian centre, all the girls were there, and were kept busy, very surprised at the number of people who had turned up to buy things; even the bales of hay that Matt had put outside the shop for people to sit on, were selling well. Rosa and Katie, walking past, took note.

"Better write that down; we can start selling hay and all sorts of horse food." said Rosa.

They were still giggling when they went inside to tell the others that The Four Horseshoes Equestrian Centre needed to expand already.

Chris suddenly had to cut short his stay and go back to Ireland. Rosa said it was because he didn't like the farm and she wasn't sorry to see him go. He practically insisted that Eva went with him, but Rosa was pleased that Eva defied him and stayed. Now they could spend some alone time together and that's what they were doing that evening.

Eva was showing her mum photos of her university friends.

"Isn't he the one you bought here a while ago?" Rosa asked, pointing to a young man in a group photo.

"Yes, he was so boring; we finished soon after we got back to Ireland."

"He look's nice." Rosa said, pointing to a young man with dark hair.

The Other Side of the Fence

"That's Greg; he and the one next to him, Ben, are my friends; they are really nice. Greg reminds me of Matt, always doing things for me and my friend, Emma, who I share a room with at Uni. That's Emma." Eva said, pointing to a pretty redheaded girl, "The four of us want to be lawyers. The boys used to come to our room to study, but Chris didn't like it, so we stopped it. I tried to tell him that he was my boyfriend and that they are our friends; if we have any problems, we help each other. But that didn't help."

"Chris doesn't like much, does he Eva?" Rosa said, "All I hear, is Chris doesn't like this, Chris doesn't like that; are you sure he likes you Eva, my lovely girl? I've learnt a lot about relationships over the years; I'm just saying that if you have any doubts whatsoever, just take a step back and think to yourself, 'Am I truly happy.'"

"Don't be silly, Mum; of course we are happy."

"Yes, as long as you do what he wants." Rosa said under her breath.

"Chris is lovely; he gets jealous sometimes and thinks I work too hard. He wants me to take a break from Uni and go travelling with him and his friends to Australia and Thailand; but I said I can't do that; I promised my dad and granddad that my priority was to get my diploma and graduate; I want to be a lawyer and work with granddad. He said that he is expanding, opening offices all over Europe, where his lawyers will spend so long at each office. He is going to take me, Emma, Greg and Ben on as trainees and says that if we are all good enough, after the two-year training period, we could all work for him. It sounds exciting; I can already speak good French and will probably learn Spanish next."

That same evening, Eva was looking through Rosa's photograph albums with Rosa. They sat with a glass of wine and Rosa was telling Eva who was who in the photographs.

When they got to the last page of one of the albums, Eva asked, "Why are the six photos on this last page numbered one to six?"

"Because throughout my life, those six men have had the biggest influence on me." Rosa answered and pointed to the first one.

"Number one, Billy Maddox, your granddad Billy. He taught me, when I was very young, that if you have been trusted to do something and you don't do it properly, no matter how severe the consequences, you must accept them."

Rosa then pointed to the next one, it was a photo from a newspaper clipping.

"Number two, Charles Davenport. You know what that man did to me when I was fifteen. For years, he went on to stalk and terrify me. He taught me that I could hate and hate with a vengeance; only revenge was ever going to satisfy me. I did get my revenge, when it was my evidence that was crucial in proving him guilty." Rosa punched the air and clapped her hands in celebration, "Yes!" she exclaimed, then looked at a shocked Eva. "Oh, sorry, I do get excited thinking about what he put me through and how I finally got him."

Rosa pointed at a photo of James.

"Number three, James Stirling, your dad. Your dad is one of the loveliest people I know. His tenderness taught me that for all that Davenport had done to me, I wasn't emotionally damaged. He gave me the confidence to believe in myself and to be a strong woman. And, of course," Rosa said, smiling at Eva, "he gave me my beautiful daughter."

Rosa pointed at the next photograph.

"Number four, Edward Stirling, your granddad Edward. He taught me that no one in this world is too big or powerful to say sorry, or admit they were wrong. That's what your granddad had to do to me, and I admired him for it. As it turned out, the Stirlings were the best family I could have entrusted my baby daughter to; they have loved you and brought you up to be one special lady to be proud of." she said, giving Eva a loving hug.

"Then came number five, Vince Parker." Rosa said pointing to the next photograph, "Huh, how best to describe Detective Sergeant Vince Parker. I was like a lovesick schoolgirl; I was definitely smitten by him. Thinking about it, all these years later, I don't know if I was in love with him, his looks, or the excitement of his job. Our two-year relationship was all make believe, built on his very clever lies. He certainly taught me that there is such a thing as tainted love; our romance was never going to go anywhere. It ended when I found out that he was married and he loved his wife more than he loved me, which I suppose was good for his poor wife because they had children. Did he ever really love me, or did he love me in his own selfish way? I will never know."

Finally, Rosa pointed to the last photograph.

"Number six, Matt Johnson. Matt showed me that there is a special love that goes far deeper than any other love; it's called true love. I found it the night fate took my life in its hands; the night Matt phoned and said he couldn't get a vet for his horse, Dulcie May, who was in trouble giving birth, so could I help. It was raining hard and I was on the floor, soaked and covered in mud, having just helped deliver her foal. Matt helped me up and told me how proud he was of me. Then, he kissed me, like he had never done before, and told me that he loved me, that he had always loved me. What happened later that night changed our lives. I say fate took over; it was very strange, that night was the first time I had ever been over that old fence and that's where I found Matt, my true love and soul mate; where he had been all those years; THE OTHER SIDE OF THE FENCE."

ABOUT THE AUTHOR

Pearl Allard has lived most of her life in the picturesque county of Norfolk, England. For many years, she has written poetry, winning a number of competitions. 'The Other Side of the Fence' is her first novel.

Printed in Great Britain
by Amazon